THE ACCUSED
- - - - -
THE SNATCH
- - - - -
Harold R. Daniels
Introduction by Nicholas Litchfield

Stark House Press • Eureka California

THE ACCUSED / THE SNATCH

Published by Stark House Press
1315 H Street
Eureka, CA 95501
griffinskye3@sbcglobal.net
www.starkhousepress.com

THE ACCUSED
Copyright © 1958 by Harold R. Daniels and
published by Dell Books, New York.

THE SNATCH
Copyright © 1958 by Harold R. Daniels and
published by Dell Books, New York.

All rights reserved under International and
Pan-American Copyright Conventions.

"The Solidly Considerable Talent of Harold R. Daniels"
copyright © 2023 by Nicholas Litchfield.

ISBN: 979-8-88601-048-0

Cover design by Jeff Vorzimmer, ¡caliente!design, Austin, Texas
Cover art by Harry Schaare
Text design by Mark Shepard, shepgraphics.com

PUBLISHER'S NOTE:
This is a work of fiction. Names, characters, places and incidents are either the products of the author's imagination or used fictionally, and any resemblance to actual persons, living or dead, events or locales, is entirely coincidental. Without limiting the rights under copyright reserved above, no part of this publication may be reproduced, stored, or introduced into a retrieval system or transmitted in any form or by any means (electronic, mechanical, photocopying, recording or otherwise) without the prior written permission of both the copyright owner and the above publisher of the book.

First Stark House Press Edition: October 2023

THE ACCUSED

Alvin Morlock isn't looking for a wife, but after a wild weekend away from his duties teaching English to a bunch of unresponsive college students, meeting Louise is a nice surprise. She seems so demure, quiet and sensitive. But after their hasty marriage, Morlock finds out that Louise is anything but demure.

It starts with her not paying the household bills, several hundred dollars' worth. Then she starts staying out, coming back drunk and argumentative—or not coming back at all. All Morlock wants is a bit of peace and quiet. All he wants is to be left to his memories of better days... Now he finds himself on trial for murder, with every witness testifying against him.

THE SNATCH

There are three of them now, but the plan started with two—Howard Mollison and Lou Morgan. Mollison is a used car salesman who got in too deep with a financial scam, and now has to come up with several thousand dollars in a hurry. Morgan tried to keep up his social position and borrowed more than he could afford, and is just as desperate to get his hands on some quick cash. So the two of them decide to kidnap the money-lender Anacosta's young grandson.

Mollison doesn't trust Morgan to do the job right, so he brings in simple-minded Patsy to guard the kid at the old textile mill. He knows he can get Patsy to do what's necessary when the job is done. But he was right not to trust Morgan. Because Morgan begins to develop a conscience. Keeping the boy alive is more challenging than the snatch itself because Morgan has to outwit his own partner to do so.

Harold R. Daniels Bibliography
(1919-1980)

Novels:
In His Blood (Dell, 1955)
The Girl in 304 (Dell, 1956)
The Accused (Dell, 1958)
The Snatch (Dell, 1958)
For the Asking (Fawcett, 1962)
The House on Greenapple Road (Random House, 1966; Dell, 1969)

Stories (alphabetical listing):
The Brill Case (*Alfred Hitchcock's Mystery Magazine*, Nov 1957)
Deception Day (*Ellery Queen's Mystery Magazine*, Jan 1967)
The Haunted Woodshed (*Ellery Queen's Mystery Magazine*, Aug 1961)
Inquest on a Dead Tiger (*Ellery Queen's Mystery Magazine*, Sept 1962)
The Master Stroke (*Ellery Queen's Mystery Magazine*, Oct 1960)
Point of View (*Ellery Queen's Mystery Magazine*, May 1961)
Road Hog (*Ellery Queen's Mystery Magazine*, Sept 1959)
Search the Crying Woman (*Alfred Hitchcock's Mystery Magazine*, March 1958)
Tee Vee Murder (*Manhunt*, Dec 1960)
Three Ways to Rob a Bank (*Ellery Queen's Mystery Magazine*, March 1972)

7
The Solidly Considerable Talent of Harold R. Daniels
by Nicholas Litchfield

15
The Accused
By Harold R. Daniels

147
The Snatch
By Harold R. Daniels

The Solidly Considerable Talent of Harold R. Daniels

by Nicholas Litchfield

Highly successful and prolific in the crime and detective fiction markets, novelist Harold Robert Daniels [1919-1987] was another of those 1950s paperback writers who rose to prominence in lightning-fast time and then departed the literary scene while at the height of his fame. Exactly what drew him away from his typewriter remains something of a mystery.

Born on November 4, 1919, in Winchendon, Massachusetts, Daniels managed to sustain a fruitful writing sideline while working a variety of jobs, often doing freelance work. After serving in World War II as an artillery officer, he was assigned to write portions of the history of the Ninth Air Force (Daniels, 1966). Like his father, who made a career working as an Associate Press editor, Daniels forged a career as a senior associate editor of the Boston-based *Metalworking Magazine*, writing articles and addressing technical societies across the country (*Hartford Courant*, 1963; Daniels, 1966).

The emergence of his "astonishingly effective" (O'Hara, 1956) debut, *In His Blood*, in 1955, brought him instant acclaim, earning rosy reviews and good press coverage. Famed *New York Times* critic Anthony Boucher considered this "striking" (Boucher, 1958) mystery the year's "best strict detective novel" (Boucher, 1955). Buoyed by the credibility of Daniels' likable lead and the deft focus on psychology and police procedure, he deemed it "unusually convincing" (Boucher, 1955). It was subsequently shortlisted for an Edgar Award in 1956—the first Dell paperback to be honored by the Mystery Writers of America (Boucher, 1956a)—becoming the runner-up in the Best First Novel category. Daniels followed it with the "unusually exciting" (Boucher, 1956b) *The Girl in 304*, the "powerful" (Alexander, 1959) *The Accused*, and the "much better than average" (Rabb, 1958) *The Snatch*, all before the end of 1958.

That same year, Anthony Boucher opined that, of all the paperback original writers, Daniels probably possessed "the most solidly considerable talent" (Boucher, 1958). Bestselling author John D. MacDonald also sang Daniels' praises, and "Road Hog," one of the short stories Daniels placed with *Ellery Queen's Mystery Magazine*, was adapted twice for television, in 1959 and 1986, becoming two episodes in the *Alfred Hitchcock Presents* series.

Interestingly, the director of the first adaptation, which aired in December 1959, was Stuart Rosenberg, who would go on to direct the Oscar-winning *Cool Hand Luke*, and famed mystery writer Bill S. Ballinger, who wrote seven *Alfred Hitchcock Presents* teleplays for seasons five and six, was credited with co-writing the script. (More on the life and works of Bill S. Ballinger can be found in the Stark House Press collections *Portrait in Smoke / The Longest Second* and *The Tooth and the Nail / The Wife of the Red-Haired Man*.)

During the late '50s and early '60s, Daniels was equally hard at work at his typewriter, churning out stories for major publications like *Alfred Hitchcock's Mystery Magazine*, *Ellery Queen's Mystery Magazine*, and *Manhunt*. By day, he produced textbooks and composed technical papers for the metallurgic industry, but he found time in the evenings to complete two further novels during the early half of the '60s. "I would hear him banging away at night on his manual Royal typewriter, and now and again, a new box of books would appear," his son, Brian, recalled. "Sadly, his family obligations didn't allow him more time for fiction." (Brian Daniels, 2010)

This collection features two of Daniels' novels from 1958, both originally released by Dell. The opener, *The Accused*, released in the April of that year, is a psychological suspense story about a married couple's disastrous, deadly relationship. The accused, Alvin Morlock, a pathetic, insecure, poorly paid English Literature instructor at a small-town college in Massachusetts, faces a first-degree murder rap. Financial and marital struggles seemingly push him to despair. His wife, Louise, the victim, far from the respectable marriage partner he longed for her to be, becomes a wasteful, slovenly housewife who resents spending time with him. A gambler, a lust, and a slattern, she devotes her energies to spending her husband's money on the pursuits that bring her happiness and which, in turn, cause him embarrassment. It is a marriage destined to end badly, and apparently, it ends in the worst possible way, but until the dénouement, the reader remains unclear about precisely what happened and about Alvin Morlock's guilt or innocence.

Alternating between a murder trial and the events that led to this wretched scenario, Daniels holds the reader's attention through succinct courtroom scenes and prolonged flashbacks that recount how they met, their arguments and indiscretions, and glimpses of their teenage years. As the various secondary characters take to the stand, disclosing opinions and revelations about the victim and the accused, the author gives us a broader picture of the married couple, explaining their traits and motivations and their foibles and vices. Far from straightforward, it is an unpredictable tale, with the author masking key details and dark secrets while presenting a grim exposé of a loveless union and the conceits and deceptions that drive spouses apart.

Grim, seedy, and somewhat frustrating, opinions are divided on the robustness of the story. Frank Ernest Pardoe, the chair of the Crime Writers Association, wasn't overly impressed, commenting, "Only a slight air of naïve enthusiasm saves the book from utter insignificance." (Pardoe, 1961) *The Sacramento Bee* criticized its "trite, hackneyed story" but enjoyed the constant time reversals, calling Daniels "a good writer with a rather novel approach to flashback technique" (The Sacramento Bee, 1958), and Edgar Award-winning author Jon L. Breen was critical of the believability of the story's trial. Among his scrutiny of 421 novels containing trials, he singled out the book as having a horribly inaccurate trial procedure (Papke, 1999).

Contrastingly, the UK's *Evening Chronicle* considered it a "story that grips from the beginning to end" (Gillespie, 1961) and *The Spectator* called it "an extremely skillful double-narrative" with "tremendous grip" (Ray, 1961). Reviewer George Kelley appreciated the interpolated flashbacks, recommending it as "a fine crime story made finer by the courtroom trial" (Kelley, 2010). In spite of mixed reviews, the novel won top honors in the Mystery category at the 1958 Maggie Awards (The Daily Sentinel, 1958).

My verdict is that Daniels was exceptionally shrewd in his approach to defining his central characters and giving credibility to their actions. This one plays like a true crime tale, full of darkness and despair and unsavory types, and the fleeting courtroom scenes prove a necessary gimmick to maintaining suspense and adding layers of depth to Alvin and Louise. Powerful, insightful writing compels the reader to stay to hear the testimonies and the resolution.

As for the next story, *The Snatch*, which hit bookstores in November of '58, this was a novel that John D. MacDonald believed "belongs among the modern classics of crime and punishment." Capturing the reader's interest from the outset, it is an absorbing yet shocking crime drama about the kidnapping of an eight-year-old boy. The story covers the planning, execution, and aftermath of the heinous crime orchestrated by Howard Mollison, a longtime swindler. Mollison has bounced from city to city for years to escape punishment for his long list of misdemeanors. Ironically, while working in New England, he falls prey to a blackmailer, and his ensuing scams to pay the ransom lands him in a tight situation at work. Desperate for cash and looking to exact retribution on the shady moneylender who denied him financial help, he plans to snatch the shylock's beloved grandson and extort money from him for the boy's safe return.

He is assisted by the outwardly respectable Louis Morgan, a bank teller with financial troubles who owes a debt to the same moneylender, and Patty Galuk, a dim-witted handyman who idolizes the charismatic Mollison. Both are committed to Mollison's cold-hearted plan, despite misgivings, and it's a plan that certainly leaves a lot to chance. Mollison's shrewd calculations and bold tactics work to his advantage, but what he doesn't take into consideration is the loyalty and morality of his two accomplices and his own lack of self-control.

Truth be told, *The Snatch* is difficult to enjoy. While the author's capacity to instill suffering and sensitivity in his unwholesome central characters adds heft to the tale, scenes of child cruelty are heartbreaking and unacceptable and highlight villainy at its worst. Nevertheless, this remains a deeply affecting and suspenseful crime novel, and Daniels' slick pacing and provocative setup make this one of those harsh, edgy tales that pull the reader into its grim surroundings and hold them there until the fierce, final moments.

Four years after *The Snatch*, Daniels produced another solid effort—*For the Asking*. For some, the author had been "too long absent from the paperwork novel racks" and this, with its "unusually good, detailed detection" proved a welcome return (Boucher, 1962a).

It took another four years before his next novel appeared in book racks. *House On Greenapple Road*, his sixth work, released in hardcover by Random House in 1966 and as a Dell paperback in 1969, was an immediate triumph and became his most revered novel. Few had any complaints about the strong psychology of its female character and the disarming ending. Prominent critics praised it as "really excellent" (Offord, 1966), "shrewd, biting and ingenious" (Matthesen, 1966), "expertly told" (Cromie, 1966), and "as convincing as a true crime study" (Kirsch, 1966). *The Kansas City Star* considered it "definitely the best and most intelligent police procedural of the year" (Grella, 1966).

Purportedly, Warner Brothers purchased the film rights (Germain, 1966). Daniels' story was subsequently adapted into a television movie and aired in January 1970, elevated by Oscar-nominated actresses Janet Leigh and Julie Harris and the likable TV actor Tim O'Connor (most memorable as Dr. Elias Huer on *Buck Rogers in the 25th Century*).

Bestselling author Bill Pronzini, appreciative of both versions of the story, regarded the film as "faithful to the novel and just as suspenseful as a result" and the novel as a "taut and baffling thriller, told in a semi-documentary, ex post facto style that makes excellent use of flashbacks" (Pronzini, 2022). As with *The Accused*, Daniels' strong characterizations, masterfully executed flashback technique, and enlightening final disclosures lifted the material.

Concerning the movie version, executive producer Quinn got a heck of a lot of mileage out of Daniels' book. His TV show *Dan August*, which aired on ABC from September 23, 1970, to April 8, 1971, was based on the *House On Greenapple Road* movie, with Quinn Martin managing to persuade Burt Reynolds to play the title character. The series was not renewed, but episodes spawned five more TV movies (Marill, 1987).

Sadly, *House On Greenapple Road* turned out to be the end of the road for Daniels the novelist, and despite his notably "strong" (Boucher, 1962b) shorter efforts featured in Ellery Queen anthologies, his fiction petered out in the early part of the 1970s. His final story, "Three Ways to Rob a Bank," appeared in *Ellery Queen's Mystery Magazine* in 1972. Included in *Ellery Queen's Crookbook*, published by Random House in 1974, it was widely considered one of the standouts. *Associated Press* Books Editor Phil Thomas relished the plot (Thomas, 1974), UK reviewer Bill Stewart of the *Evening Chronicle* picked it out as one of his favorites (Stewart, 1977), and the Canadian daily *Star-Phoenix* thought it "predictable but charming" (J.R.N., 1974).

Whether Daniels produced fiction after 1972, I am unable to tell. Creative and productive for more than a dozen years, successfully producing popular stories despite a full-time job, it strikes me as odd that he didn't seek to capitalize on the success of his sixth novel. It may be that there's an undiscovered cache of unpublished material, or it might simply be the case that his enthusiasm waned. Some may say that *The Los Angeles Times* Book Editor, Robert R. Kirsch, jinxed things with his flattering analysis of *House on Greenapple Road*. After explaining how the author achieves complete credibility from the first paragraph, he goes on to discuss the authentic procedural elements, the believable ending, and Daniels' artistic merits. "There is, also, a solid and unhurried narrative style, an eye for detail, an intuition of character, and an ear for the spoken word which gives the reader the sense of old-fashioned witness," he marveled. "Daniels is for me a real discovery. This is the first detective story by him I have read, and I am quick to say I can hardly wait for the next one." (Kirsch, 1966)

For whatever reason, Daniels exited the crime fiction scene at the top of his game, departing with an array of literary prizes, film and television credits, and well-deserved plaudits. He left behind a tidy stack of crime fiction that warrants attention, and for that, we must be truly grateful.

—June 2023
Rochester, NY

....

Nicholas Litchfield is the founder of the literary magazine *Lowestoft Chronicle*, author of the suspense novel *Swampjack Virus*, and editor of ten literary anthologies. His stories, essays, and book reviews appear in many magazines and newspapers, including *BULL: Men's Fiction*, *Shotgun Honey*, *Daily Press*, and *The Virginian-Pilot*. He has also contributed introductions to numerous books, including sixteen Stark House Press reprints of long-forgotten noir and mystery novels. Formerly a book critic for the *Lancashire Post*, syndicated to twenty-five newspapers across the U.K., he now writes for *Publishers Weekly* and regularly contributes to Colorado State University's literary journal *Colorado Review*. Born in England, he has lived in various cities around the world and now resides in Western New York. You can find him online at nicholaslitchfield.com.

Works Cited

Alexander, Charles. "Book Briefs and Best Sellers." *Albany Democrat-Herald*, 10 Jan 1959, p. 10.

Boucher, Anthony. "Criminals at Large." *The New York Times*, 11 Dec 1955, p. 340.

Boucher, Anthony. "Criminals at Large." *The New York Times*, 6 May 1956, p. 303.

Boucher, Anthony. "Criminals At Large." *The New York Times*, 16 Sep 1956, p. BR24.

Boucher, Anthony. "Criminals at Large." *The New York Times*, 25 May 1958, p. BR21.

Boucher, Anthony. "Roundup of Criminals at Large." *The New York Times*, 12 Aug 1962, p. BR13.

Boucher, Anthony. "Criminals at Large." *The New York Times*, 7 Oct 1962, p. BR17.

Cromie, Alice. "Mysteries for purely selfish enjoyment." *Chicago Tribune*, 4 Dec 1966, p. 651.

Daniels, Brian. *Comment on* "The Crime Novels of HAROLD R. DANIELS, by George Kelley." *Mystery*File*, 11 Dec 2010, 3:07 p.m., mysteryfile.com/blog/?p=971.

Daniels, Harold R. *House on Greenapple Road*, New York: Random House, 1966.

Germaine, C.A. "Lots of Light Reading Available For Pleasant Summer Afternoons." *The Post-Crescent*, 7 Aug 1966, p. 66.

Gillespie, R.M. "The Accused." *Evening Chronicle*, 24 Jun 1961, p. 4.

Grella, George. "Still Seeking the Grail—the Best Detective." *The Kansas City Star*, 11 Dec 1966, p. 122.

Hartford Courant. "Tool and Die Assn. To Hear Boston Editor." *Hartford Courant*, 10 Nov 1963, p. 79.

J.R.N. "A feast of detective stories." *Star-Phoenix*, 28 Jun 1974, p. 61.

Kelley, George. "The Crime Novels of Harold R. Daniels." *The Mystery Fancier* (Vol. 3 No. 4), 2010, p. 14.

Kirsch, Robert R. "Book Report: Best Bets From Crime File." *The Los Angeles Times*, 4 Apr 1966, p. 81.

Marill, Alvin H. *Movies Made for Television: The Telefeature and the Mini-Series, 1964-1986*. New York Zoetrope, 1987.

Matthesen, Frankie. "The Courant Coroner." *Hartford Courant*, 19 Jun 1966, p. 143.

O'Hara, Scott. "Newsstand Jungle." *Tampa Bay Times*, 1 Jan 1956, p. 88.

Offord, Lenore Glen. "The Gory Road." *The San Francisco Examiner*, 12 Jun 1966, p. 196.

Papke, David Ray. *Conventional Wisdom: The Courtroom Trial in American Popular Culture*, 82 Marq. L. Rev. 471 (1999). Available at: scholarship.law.marquette.edu/mulr/vol82/iss3/1

Pardoe, F.E. "Crime Choice." *The Birmingham Post & Birmingham Gazette*, 6 Jun 1961, p. 3.

Pronzini, Bill. "A 1001 Midnights Review: HAROLD R. DANIELS – House on Greenapple Road." *Mystery*File*, 19 Apr 2022, mysteryfile.com/blog/?p=79268.

Rabb, Stanley E. "A grim story of crime." *The Galveston Daily News*, 30 Nov 1958, p. 17.

Ray, Cyril. "The Accused. By Harold R. Daniels (Book Review)." *The Spectator*, 19 Mar 1961, vol. 206, no. 6934, p. 728.

Stewart, Bill. "The New Books: Dark doings." *Evening Chronicle*, 26 Mar 1977, p. 9.

The Daily Sentinel. "Winners Named In Paperback Book Contests." *The Daily Sentinel*, 9 Oct 1958, p. 5.

The Sacramento Bee. "Books In Brief." *The Sacramento Bee*, 31 May 1958, p. 76.

Thomas, Paul. "Crookbook Has Tasty Morsel." *The Childless Index*, 25 Jul 1974, p. 7.

THE ACCUSED
Harold R. Daniels

Dedication:
"For my three sons — Mike, Dean and Brian"

Chapter 1

Ladies and gentlemen of the jury, the accused, Alvin Morlock, is charged with the ultimate crime, the crime of murder. It is the intention of the State to demonstrate, in the course of this trial, that he is guilty and that the degree of his guilt, which it will be your function to fix, demands the ultimate punishment by law. In other words, we charge him with murder in the first degree. Murder calculated. Murder premeditated. Murder ruthlessly and heartlessly committed on the person who had every reason to expect nothing but a cherishing affection from the accused.

The defense will undoubtedly attempt to arouse your sympathy by attacking the character of the victim of his homicide, Morlock's dead wife. They will tell you that she was extravagant, that she was a slattern and worse. But we will show you that Morlock himself was at least partly responsible for his wife's actions, and I would impress on you that whatever his motives for murder, they in no sense mitigate his guilt. It is not the dead Louise Morlock who is on trial here. It is her husband, and the charge against him is the taking of a human life.

The Commonwealth of Massachusetts vs. Alvin Morlock.
Opening remarks of Prosecution Attorney Gurney.

Morlock's tenement was the second floor rear of an old sandstone mansion. Once it had been a stately house, handsome in the dignity of spotless windows and immaculate grounds. On an April afternoon he hurried toward its shelter, head bent against the wind that buffeted his slender body. On other days he had felt almost sorry for the house, humiliated now by pigeon droppings and candy wrappers, by discarded cigarette packages and empty bottles that had once held cheap wine and now gleamed dully in the barren hedge. Today he was concerned only with his personal humiliation.

He hurried up the warped stairs to the tenement and let himself in. The door opened from the hall directly into the kitchen, a shabby room with a chromium dinette set looking out of place against oak wainscoting. There was a scattering of dirty dishes on the table. A plate of margarine had half melted into a greasy yellow pool and the bitter smell of reboiled coffee was in the air.

Morlock called, "Lolly?" There was no answer. Lolly — the name which had once denoted affection — now choked in his throat. She was probably downstairs, he decided, and walked into the living room. There was a desk in the room that he used for his own work. She used a drawer in a cheap end table for her correspondence. Morlock opened the drawer and took out an untidy stack of envelopes.

She had made no effort to conceal the mess she had made of their finances. The letters were all there. A slim pile from a department store. *Will you please remit?* A thicker pile from the appliance store that Morlock had just left. He read through them swiftly. Polite, at first, then insistent. Some of them quite clever in the manner in which they expressed dismay that a trusted customer could so badly disillusion them. From the gas and electric companies there were past-due notices but no letters. They hardly had to dun, Morlock reflected ruefully.

He sat wearily at his own desk after he had gone through the correspondence. In the last hour, the thought that he owed almost eight hundred dollars which he had promised to pay by morning had recurred to him a half dozen times, but with no lessening of its impact. He was stunned, overwhelmed by the personal disaster that had had its beginning only this morning when the hall monitor brought him a note from Dean Gorham requesting that he come to the Dean's office immediately.

Morlock had been discussing the minor British poets for the benefit of a bored and listless class in English III when the summons came. After he read it, he had felt no particular alarm although the summons was out of the ordinary. He was not a good instructor; he knew that. He also knew that he was good enough for Ludlow College. He stood up and called to William Cory to monitor the class.

In a class of louts Cory was the most loutish. In an undergraduate body seemingly more callow and less purposeful than any Morlock had ever instructed, Cory was the most callow. He was not the least purposeful, though, for Cory was apparently dedicated with fanatic zeal and boundless patience to bullying his instructors to the point of mute and hopeless exasperation. Those he could not bully he attacked with seemingly inane questions that had viciously calculated double meanings, with false naivete, and with brutal behind-the-back pantomime.

Cory was older and bigger than most of his classmates. He was attending Ludlow under the provisions of the GI Bill and this was his protection. The college's financial structure was shaky; the students attending under the Bill were the difference between bankruptcy and a threadbare solvency. There was an awareness of this among the instructors and consequently the Corys were tolerated. Morlock, in turning the class over to Cory in his absence, tried to convince himself that he was adopting the policies of the history instructor, Dodson.

"Give the bad ones responsibility," Dodson contended when the instructors were talking shop. "Maybe it will teach them some common sense. If it doesn't it will keep them out of your hair for a while anyway."

Morlock, watching Cory shamble up the aisle, knew that his purpose in picking Cory for monitor had not been the hope of instilling common sense but was based instead on an admission that he feared Cory, and that Cory could embarrass him if he chose, because of that fear.

Cory loomed up beside the desk, a hulking, square-faced man of twenty-three with a lingering rash of acne on his cheekbones. His eyes were green and small, his teeth already in poor condition. He affected a varsity sweater and denim jeans. The cuffs of the sweater were shiny with dirt and grease. Morlock turned his head aside to avoid the smell of perspiration and of underwear not often enough changed.

"Alla right, teach'—I got it," Cory said in a ridiculous imitation of an Italian immigrant. As he spoke, he looked toward the class expectantly. Looking for his laugh, Morlock supposed. Getting it, too. The watching faces grinned or smirked dutifully.

Once, in the hall, Morlock moved more hurriedly. He was a gray man — gray suit, gray eyes, light brown hair already starting to retreat from his high forehead. A worried man now that he had time to consider the possible implications of Dean Gorham's note.

Dean Gorham had a receptionist, a part-time student worker, young and pretty in a plaid skirt and cardigan sweater. She motioned Morlock into the inner office when he entered the Dean's suite, and he glanced down at her to see if he could read anything in her expression that might give him a clue to the nature of the crisis that had pulled him away from his class. If there was anything at all in her expression, it was the sort of contempt that Morlock was accustomed to seeing on the faces of the student body, and it probably had no relationship to the present circumstance. He hurried past her and into Dean Gorham's office.

Morlock had some respect for Gorham as a scholar. Gorham,

however, was a big, imposing figure of a man with a Roman profile. His statesmanlike stature had led to his being pushed into administrative assignments where he would be available for public display almost from the time he qualified as a teacher; so that his scholarship had drowned in a tide of paper, leaving him harried and unhappy. He looked up uneasily as Morlock came into the room.

"You, Alvin," he said fussily. "Close the door, won't you, and take a chair."

Morlock, not speaking, pulled up a leather covered chair from against the wall and sat down.

Gorham stood up and walked toward the window, where he stood looking out toward the meager campus with his hands clasped behind his back. He coughed once, started to speak and stopped, and finally turned back toward Morlock.

"This is very embarrassing," he began again. "I don't like to meddle in my teachers' affairs. I don't think I ever have with you, have I?"

Morlock — he had a growing and horrible suspicion now about the reason for Gorham's summons — said, "No, sir."

Gorham beat one fist lightly into the open palm of his other hand. "Maybe it would be easier if you read this," he said. He picked up a letter from his desk and handed it to Morlock.

Morlock said, "Excuse me," before he began reading. The letter was addressed to Gorham in his official capacity as Dean.

Sir, it read.

This is to call your attention to a situation which we feel you will wish to deal with personally in order to avoid undesirable publicity. A teacher at Ludlow, Mr. Alvin Morlock, is very much in arrears in his payments on several appliances purchased by him from us on our time contract plan. Repeated letters to Mr. Morlock have gone unanswered. Before taking legal action we are taking this means of attempting to reach an agreement as to prompt payment by Mr. Morlock. We shall appreciate hearing from you on this matter without delay.

The letter bore the heading of a local appliance store. When he had finished it, Morlock's reaction was shameful embarrassment. He wished for a moment that he were dead — anything rather than be in this room with Gorham and his own humiliation. He mumbled, "I didn't know, Dean Gorham. There must be some mistake."

Gorham snatched at the straw eagerly. "Of course. Of course," he agreed. "Those things do happen." While Morlock listened dumbly, he began to relate some anecdote about a bank deposit he had himself made which had been credited to the wrong account. There had been no mistake. He knew it and he was certain that Gorham knew it. The Dean was, in his way, trying to restore his dignity, as if his own self-respect had dwindled because he had been forced to shatter Morlock's.

Gorham, from a sense of duty, continued, "Of course, being teachers we are very vulnerable, Alvin. Caesar's wife, you know," he added with heavy-handed good humor. The Dean sat down behind his desk. "You've been married three months or so, isn't it?"

Morlock nodded.

Gorham said, "I thought so. Of course, there are expenses involved in setting up a household and sometimes it is difficult. At the same time, we must be very careful to avoid things like this, particularly since the college's own situation — " He continued hastily, "Of course, in this case it is a mistake. Clerical error probably. You'll take care of it then?"

Morlock rose. "This afternoon," he said. He turned and would have left the room but Gorham called to him.

"Alvin. I don't have much but if I can help — "

The unexpected kindness shook Morlock more deeply than his shame had. He tried to speak and could not. Instead he shook his head and rushed from the room, past the receptionist and down the hall to his own classroom. He paused to regain his poise before he entered the room; when he did enter, Cory was talking to the class, telling some dirty story. Morlock said, "That will do, Cory. You can return to your seat."

Cory stood up indolently. "Alla right, teach'," he said in the same moronic affectation of an accent. Morlock, infuriated, shouted, "Oh, for God's sake, Cory, stop being a jackass."

His glance was turned toward the class when he called out to Cory. He was surprised to see among the sly, anticipatory smirks a few smiles of congratulation, admiration, perhaps. He assigned a chapter for study and forgot the incident in planning what he would say, to Louise — or Lolly, as she called herself. It was not in him to rail at her or to demand any explanations; he accepted this at the same time that he admitted there was no other way to reach her short of physical violence. He had tried sarcasm and it had withered in the face of her stupendous lack of sensitivity. And Morlock was disarmed by his own sense of guilt. He had known — or at least he should have known, he reflected in the drowsy classroom — that she was incapable of handling money or any responsibility. But in the first days of marriage he had tried to see her irresponsibility as a rather charming naivete. When he could no longer maintain the absurdity that she was naive, he had still hesitated to destroy the illusion, and with it his marriage that he had counted on so heavily. He had once thought, a little desperately, that she would gain a sort of assurance through his trust in her. And now with that hope gone, he could not bring himself to ask her why she had not paid the bills, why she had not told him of the dunning letters. She would react in one of two ways. She would become sly and sullen, probing to find out how much he knew. Or — and this was much worse — she would become kittenish. *Daddy is mad at mother for spending his money?*

Morlock remembered quite clearly the circumstances surrounding her assumption of the family funds. Three days after they were married he had handed her a check — it amounted to seventy dollars — and asked her to cash it for him on the following morning. When he came home from the college on the next day she handed him some bills.

"I paid another week on the rent," she said brightly. "And I have to do some grocery shopping tomorrow. Do you want to give me the money now?"

The marriage was new enough so that this seemed a kind of sharing and a bond. He had meant to give her a few dollars for housekeeping expenses but he kept only a few dollars for himself and handed the rest back to her. "You might as well pay all the bills," he said. It was this demonstration of faith that he hated to take back in spite of a growing distrust.

Dismissing his thoughts of Lolly, Morlock decided that he would have to stop at the appliance store and find out exactly how much he owed — which brought up another problem. Somehow he would have to get money. From a bank, perhaps, although he did not have the slightest idea of how money was borrowed from banks. Or from one of those companies that advertised in the papers interminably: *Pay your bills. The money you need in one hour.* Morlock resolved to stop at the appliance store and then at the bank. But he would not tell Lolly. He felt a moment's panic at the thought that there were probably other creditors besides the utility companies. The grocer. The butcher. He reassured himself that she would have kept those paid, otherwise they would have no service, but he did not make a convincing case of it.

Prosecution Attorney Gurney: You have given your name as George Gorham and your occupation as being Dean of Ludlow College. What relationship did you have with the accused?

Gorham: As an instructor in English Literature he was under my administration.

Gurney: He wasn't a professor?

Gorham: Mr. Morlock did not have enough academic credits to qualify for the title.

Gurney: I see. Did you consider him competent?

Gorham: I considered him competent, yes.

Gurney: Competent for Ludlow College, you mean?

Gorham: I fail to see —

Gurney: Isn't it a fact that Ludlow College barely meets the minimum standards for recognition by the National Board of Regents?

Defense Counsel Liebman: Objection, Your Honor. The status of Ludlow College is irrelevant.

Presiding Justice Cameron: Sustained.

Gurney: Let it go. This backwater college, then —

Cameron: That will be enough, Mr. Gurney.

Gurney: Mr. Gorham, as Dean of the college did you ever receive requests from Morlock's creditors asking you to make him pay his bills?

Gorham: I did receive such letters.

Gurney: Did he pay his bills?

Gorham: I assume that he did.

Gurney: The letters stopped coming?

Gorham: Yes.

Gurney: Then you had the right to assume that he had paid them. Do you know where he got the money?

Liebman: Objection.

Cameron: On what grounds, Mr. Liebman? I would think the subject pertinent.

Gurney: I will be glad to rephrase the question, Your Honor. Mr. Gorham — should I refer to you as Dean Gorham, by the way?

Gorham: The title is an academic courtesy only.

Gurney: Dean Gorham, then. Is it a fact that Ludlow College carries a family life insurance policy on each of its instructors?

Gorham: It is not. The firm that carries the college's large policies makes available a small policy at low rates to faculty members. The college shares the cost with the individual faculty members.

Gurney: Did Alvin Morlock have such a policy on his life and that of his wife?
Gorham: He did.
Gurney: What was the face value of the policy?
Gorham: One thousand dollars.
Gurney: Do you know how much money Morlock owed at the time of his wife's death?
Gorham: Certainly not.
Gurney: But you do know that he was heavily in debt and that he was being hounded by his creditors.
> *The Commonwealth of Massachusetts vs. Alvin Morlock.*
> *Direct testimony of George Gorham.*

It was only half-past two when Morlock stopped in front of the immaculately gleaming facade of the appliance store. Embarrassment and shame waited for him in the building, and he hesitated before he entered. He had been here once before when Lolly had picked out a television set and a refrigerator and a stove. In that order, he remembered wryly. And the largest television set, the smallest refrigerator and stove.

He shook his head silently at the clerk who came to meet him and walked toward the back of the store where a green neon script sign marked the credit department. A fat woman with a sour expression came to her side of the waist-high counter. When he gave his name she said, "Just a moment, please," and went into a tiny cubicle of an office. She did not come out again. Instead, a tall, very thin man came out and walked to the counter.

The thin man said disapprovingly, "I'm the credit manager, Mr. Morlock. I've been waiting for you to come in about your account."

Morlock knew instinctively that this man would not make or permit any face-saving pretenses. He was holding a manila folder with the word *Delinquent* stamped on it in red ink, holding it in such a manner that the letters leaped flamboyantly to the eye. Morlock had half planned some evasive explanation, but he said instead, "I'm here. How much do I owe you, please?"

The credit man had expected the evasion, the lie. There was a routine to affairs such as this, Morlock supposed. The deliberate display of the red brand on the folder. The calculated air of disapproval. Next would come hinted threats. The credit man frowned at the folder.

"You realize, of course, that since you are delinquent the entire balance is due. We are prepared to forgo immediate payment of the whole amount if you bring your payments up to date, Mr. Morlock."

What dignity Morlock could now salvage depended on liquidating the entire bill. He plunged ahead obstinately. "The total, please."

The credit man opened the folder. "Two months delinquent," he said. "The balance due as of today, with interest, amounts to seven hundred and sixty dollars."

Lolly had made no payments whatsoever, then. Morlock, with no head for figures, remembered vaguely that the original total had been something over eight hundred dollars of which he had paid ten per cent at the time of the purchase. He had been appalled at the amount then; he was overwhelmed now by the prospect of the immediate payment of such a large amount of money. There had been, in his youth, no money for luxuries. The salary he received from Ludlow College had seemed like a great deal of money after the long years of privation when macaroni and cheese had been a dinner and hamburger a banquet. He had even been able to save a little before his marriage. What, in God's name, had she done with it?

"I'll be back in the morning," he said to the thin man, and left the store.

He had walked home after convincing himself that it was too late to stop at the bank, and found that Lolly was not home.

At four o'clock she had still not returned and Morlock went into the bathroom to shower and shave, finding a kind of peace in the rituals of habit. She had still not returned when he finished dressing and he wandered into the living room, picking up a book. It did not hold his interest, and he heard her footsteps in the hall before she slammed the kitchen door behind her.

Lolly came to the door of the living room and stood silently looking at him. He had had enough practice in the last few weeks to enable him to gauge her condition with a nice precision. Her face was slightly flushed but placid enough at first glance. On closer inspection, there was a strained tightness to the muscles of her jaw and chin and the pupils of her brown eyes were contracted. He didn't overlook the slight swaying of her body.

"Hello, Daddy," she said archly. There was a bright fleck of saliva at the corner of her mouth.

"Hello, Louise," Morlock said. He decided against bringing up the matter of the unpaid bills now. Her present mood was as unstable as it was unpredictable. She might interpret the most innocent phrase, the most meaningless gesture, as a slight. When that happened she was capable of flying into a murderous fury, beating him down with obscenities. Lately he had begun to wonder if the violences were genuine, but whatever they were, he had no stomach for them.

She walked carefully into the room. "I was downstairs with Anna," she said lightly. "Does Daddy want his supper now?"

He shook his head. "I'm not very hungry," he said. "I'll get something for myself by and by."

She said, "Oh." And, after a moment, "I think I'll go back down and see Anna then. Maybe we'll go to a show."

After she had left, Morlock went to the kitchen. He heated water in the kettle and rinsed the sink with part of it. He poured the remainder into a dishpan, adding soap powder and cold water from the tap. He then cleared the messy table and began washing the dishes, remembering how it had been in the days before Louise. He had had two rooms then and he had kept them immaculate. There had even been a sort of lonesome pleasure in coming home to the two rooms, in cooking his own meals. When the kitchen was clean he set a place for himself at the table and cooked eggs and toast and made coffee, welcoming the quiet of the tenement.

He cleaned up the few dishes he had dirtied and went back to the living room. He had been able to put aside reminders of his debts briefly. Now the stupefying thought that he must raise almost eight hundred dollars in the morning overwhelmed him again. There was the bank, of course, but banks wanted collateral, security. And they would want to make inquiries at the college which would take time.

Morlock remembered the newspaper which the newsboy left in the hall. He opened the pages to the classified section, looking for the half noted and remembered advertisements of the finance companies. There were a dozen or more of them, reading, as he remembered, *The Money You Need in One Hour.* Or, more enticingly, *No Co-Makers, No Embarrassing Questions. Your Employer Doesn't Have to Know.* He took a small notebook from his pocket and wrote down the addresses and telephone numbers of a few of the more promising companies. One of them promised to loan, with no security, up to fifteen hundred dollars for any worthwhile purpose. There was a chart below the advertisement showing the amount of monthly payments that would liquidate various sized loans in specific times. He decided that he would try to borrow eight hundred dollars. The payments per month, after the friendly overtures in the text of the ad, were of frightening proportions. Morlock, who during his life had lived by the simple philosophy of buying only what he could afford, decided that he could meet the payments provided the strictest economy was practiced in running the house. And he, of course, would have to assume the handling of the family finances. He did not decide how he would tell these things to Louise.

There remained in the back of his mind a small but potent doubt. What if they would not let him have the money, in spite of the glowing promises? There was his friend Paul Martin who taught chemistry at Ludlow. Paul always managed to give the impression of having money, although Morlock could not quite recall any specific indication. The thought of borrowing from Paul was repugnant, not in the sense that it was trespassing on their friendship, but in the embarrassment that would shame them both if Paul didn't have the money and had to refuse him. He decided that he would go to Paul only as a last resort.

Louise had not returned at eleven; Morlock was relieved rather than anxious. For some time now he had looked forward to bed with Louise with an emotion that approached revulsion — particularly when she had been downstairs with Anna.

He did not know what time she came in. When he came from the bedroom into the living room in the morning she was asleep on the couch, her coat thrown over her. Her mouth was open with her harsh breathing and there was a smell of staleness in the room. He walked softly past her and into the kitchen.

While he drank his coffee Morlock planned the morning. He would have to call the college and tell them that he would not be in. Louise, he would say, was ill. He would go to the bank as soon as it opened and apply for a loan. If there was to be a delay he would tell them to forget the application and visit one of the companies whose addresses he had copied down in his notebook. If he was refused, there remained Paul Martin, his best friend.

He dressed carefully, estimating the effect that even his choice of a necktie might have on the bank official and selecting the most conservative lest the official think him frivolous. Morlock — a most conservative man — did not perceive the absurdity of this.

Because he dressed carefully and because he had to call the college from a pay station he was five minutes later than he had planned in getting to the bank, and there was already a line of people ahead of him. The man immediately in front of him carried a paper sack and when he reached the cashier dumped the sack on the counter. There were literally thousands of dollars in the bag, and Morlock felt encouraged. The cashier had not seemed in the smallest manner startled. Surely, if money was so casually treated in this place, they would be inclined to be liberal. They might well say, "Why certainly, Mr. Morlock. We'll be glad to let you have the money you need." He daydreamed thus while the cashier finished with the man with the paper sack. When it was his turn he said as confidently as he could, "I'd like to arrange a loan," trying to create the impression that he was accustomed to making loans from banks, as if such an impression would influence them in his favor. The cashier looked at him disinterestedly and destroyed his illusion of confidence with three words.

"Commercial or personal?"

Morlock said hastily, "Personal," associating the word with the adjectives used in the finance company advertisements and hoping that it was the right one.

"Over there," the cashier said, nodding in the direction of a series of desks behind a low partition. "See Mr. Kaufman."

Morlock thanked him effusively and turned away.

Mr. Kaufman was a bland man of forty. He was polite with Morlock, and Morlock felt hope rise within him when Kaufman started filling in an application blank. They surely wouldn't go to the trouble of filling in an application blank, he decided, if they weren't favorably impressed. When Kaufman had his name and address and place of employment he asked, "How much money did you wish to borrow, Mr. Morlock?"

Morlock said, "Eight hundred dollars," saw Kaufman's small frown and added quickly, "I might be able to manage with less. Perhaps five hundred," thinking that Paul Martin would certainly be able to lend him three hundred.

Kaufman's questions became more direct. "And what do you wish to use this money for, Mr. Morlock?"

Morlock, watching Kaufman anxiously, explained. Before he was halfway through with the explanation, Kaufman began to shake his head from side to side absently. When Morlock had stumbled through a half-truth of his financial dilemma — he implied that an illness had prevented his keeping his credit good with the appliance company without actually identifying anyone as having been ill — Kaufman pushed the application form aside.

"I'm sorry, Mr. Morlock," he said. His regret sounded genuine. "You should have come to a bank when you bought your furniture." His voice registered a mild reproach for Morlock and all people who failed to realize that a bank was the one, the only proper place to borrow money.

Morlock got up and almost ran out of the bank.

And so he had not said the right things, made the right impression. There remained the finance companies. The first one he tried looked like a bank; it studiedly gave the impression of being a bank and the brisk young man who waited on him looked — he carefully rehearsed the mannerisms — like a promising young teller. Except that the young man did not carry on the pretense with the application blank as long as Kaufman at the bank had done. Morlock had rephrased his answer for the inevitable, "What do you plan to do with the money if your loan is approved, Mr. Morlock?" He did not have the chance to use it. The brisk young man's eyes became bored before he had gone beyond, "Own your own home?" Morlock's answer to that one had been effusive. They certainly planned to own a home someday. Meantime they had a good rent at so reasonable a figure that it would almost be foolish to give it up just now. When the question became, "What bank do you have an account in?" Morlock was already defeated by the disinterested eyes and he merely shook his head dumbly.

"I'm sorry, Mr. Morlock."

And at The Money You Need in One Hour, "Sorry, Mr. Morlock."

He became desperate and out of his desperation he reduced the amount of his request to three hundred dollars. That would be enough to bring the appliance store account up to date and leave enough for the other past-due bills. The restoration of his pride by paying off the whole amount became a luxury that would have to wait.

At *Your Employer Doesn't Have to Know,* "Sorry, Mr. Morlock." And because he was asking for so much less and they still refused to honor their advertised claims, Morlock became a little mutinous. He said stubbornly, "I have a good job. It doesn't pay very much money but it's regular. I don't see why you can't make a loan to me."

And the name of another company was murmured to him where he just might be able to meet the necessary requirements. This company made no pretense of being a bank. The front part of the building was a pawnshop; the windows littered with the ransom of a thousand hungers, mingled with the glitter of cheap-jack cameras and binoculars, knives, and jewelry. Morlock was told to go into a back room.

There was one man in the room. He sat behind a pine table reading a newspaper and he did not glance up when Morlock came in. He did speak. "How much you want?" he asked. His voice was thick with phlegm.

Morlock told him. He tried to make his own voice sound bright and alert; wanted to make this man see in him a shiny-honest young man who just happened to need a few dollars. He volunteered, "My name is Alvin Morlock. I am an English teacher at Ludlow College." And all the time he had the sickening feeling that it was wasted in this place. This man did not care beyond wanting enough information so that the borrower could not cheat him. On that basis he made his loans.

The man put down his newspaper. "And you owe seven hundred bucks to Starkweather's Appliance Company," he said. "You average seventy bucks a week." Morlock stared at him in astonishment before he reasoned that the man who had steered him to this place had undoubtedly telephoned ahead.

The man said wearily, "You guys . . ." and reached for a piece of paper.

There were more questions and when it was done with, the man opened a drawer in the table and took out a handful of currency. He shoved the paper at Morlock and said, "Sign there," and began to count the money. He counted out two hundred and eighty dollars.

Morlock protested. "I signed for three hundred dollars," he said, wanting to point out the man's mistake to him without angering him.

The man looked up quickly. "First month's interest and service charge," he said. "You don't want it?"

Morlock said weakly, "I didn't understand," and reached for the money.

The man reached for his newspaper. "See you the first of the month," he said.

Morlock hurried into the street.

Heavily in debt and hounded by his creditors.

Chapter 2

Gurney: Mr. Dodson, when you took the stand yesterday you testified that you visited Morlock's home several times after his marriage. As a matter of fact you knew Morlock's wife before that marriage, didn't you?

Dodson: I did.

Gurney: Mr. Dodson — you aren't a full professor either, are you, by the way?

Dodson: No.

Gurney: Not enough academic credits?

Liebman: Objection.

Gurney: I'll withdraw the question. Mr. Dodson, while you were on the stand you made a big issue of the fact that Louise Morlock was a sloven as a housewife; that she made no effort to become a respectable marriage partner for Morlock. You made quite a martyr of Morlock. Isn't it a fact, Mr. Dodson, that Morlock had no reason to expect anything else? Isn't it a fact that you and Morlock met the then Louise Palaggi in the course of a sordid outing during the Christmas' holidays?

Liebman: Objection.

Cameron: Sustained, Mr. Gurney, I think you can establish your point without this sort of language.

Gurney: I'll try, Your Honor. Now, Mr. Dodson, did you go to Providence, Rhode Island, with Morlock about two weeks before he was married?

Dodson: Yes. No. I should say he came with me. That would be more accurate. It was my idea.

Gurney: Had you been on any trips with Morlock prior to that time?

Dodson: No.

Gurney: What was the purpose of this . . . trip?

Dodson: It was a place to go. I didn't have anywhere else to go over the holidays and Morlock didn't either, as it turned out. I asked him to go with me.

Gurney: Where did you stay in Providence?

Dodson: At the Compton Hotel.

Gurney: Also your idea, I suppose.

Dodson: My idea.

Gurney: Did you have any definite plans for your . . . holiday?
Dodson: None in particular.
Gurney: No dates?
Dodson: No.
Gurney: You planned on a quiet holiday by yourselves?
Dodson: Not exactly.
Gurney: Actually you intended to pick up female companions, didn't you?
Dodson: We hoped to meet some women, yes.
Gurney: Well, how did you do? Did you make any pick-ups the first night?
Dodson: No.
Gurney: No? What about an Audrey and Lucy Zonfrillo?
Dodson: There were two girls named Audrey and Lucy in a place we went to. We bought them drinks but we didn't pick them up.
Gurney: You didn't pick up Louise Palaggi that first night?
Dodson: No.
Gurney: It was later that you picked her up, then?
Liebman: I ask the Court to direct counsel to refrain from harping on the expression "pick up."
Cameron: I suggest, Mr. Gurney, that you use another term.
The Commonwealth of Massachusetts vs. Alvin Morlock.
Cross-examination of Thomas Dodson.

Morlock had no particular liking for Dodson. Dodson was older, in his early forties, Morlock supposed, and had long ago given up any idealism in his approach to being a teacher. Dodson was an out-and-out time server. He hated his subject and he actively detested his students. They returned the sentiment enthusiastically. Dodson was stocky and he affected suits with vests, the pockets of which he filled with all manner of pens and pencils in neat rows. His hair was thinning and he wore it parted on one side. The hair was also coarse and it matted together in strands so that the yellowish pink scalp appeared more naked than if he had been completely bald. He gave an impression of being a hearty good fellow, but Morlock suspected that it was more than partly a pose which he put away each evening along with the vest and pencils.

He had approached Morlock in the teachers' rest-room the day before the school was to close for the Christmas holidays. Morlock was washing his hands. Dodson ran water in the adjoining basin and began to splash noisily.

"One more day," he said between splashes. "Then we can forget this dump for ten days. Where are you going, Al?"

Morlock had made no plans. He had assumed that he would spend a part of the holiday with Paul Martin and had only that morning learned — and been a little hurt by the knowledge — that Martin was spending the entire vacation with his married sister in Baltimore. He said uncertainly, "Nowhere, I guess." He added out of politeness rather than interest, "What are your plans, Dodson?"

Dodson dug his elbow into Morlock's ribs and chuckled. "I'm not going to hang around here," he said. "I'm going to get a room in a hotel I know in Providence. Been there before," he added with another nudge and a leer. "Did you ever go up on Federal Hill?"

Morlock shook his head.

Dodson winked suggestively. "There's places there — " He stopped abruptly. "By God, Al, you got to come with me!"

Morlock, faced with the prospect of a dull and lonesome ten days, was tempted to the point of wondering if even Dodson's company wasn't preferable to solitude. Seeing his indecision, Dodson pounced. "I tell you, Al, I'm the man that can show you around. They've got all these little clubs, you know, and stuff! My God, they hang around waiting to be picked up. Take a couple of guys like us — educated, professional men — we're big shots to them. And we can get rooms and split the cost."

Morlock said doubtfully, "I'd have to think about it."

Dodson said scornfully, "Think, hell! We'll just get in my car and go tomorrow night. We can be there by seven. You go in these places and order beer," he said. "A dime. That's all you have to spend while you look 'em over. They've always got a juke box or a small band on weekends. I don't mean bags when I say there's stuff there just waiting to be picked up. Young stuff, I tell you. Nineteen and twenty. And some of them Eyetalian and Polack girls will knock your eye out. Knockers on 'em like movie stars and they jump around wiggling their little butts . . ." Dodson paused, his eyes bright. "Treat you like a king."

And Morlock, even as he despised Dodson, agreed to go along.

Half a dozen times in the next morning he was tempted to tell Dodson that he had changed his mind, but the recollected words, "young stuff," held him back. Morlock convinced himself that he would find a decent girl among Dodson's more promiscuous Circes. He told himself that he would content himself with a mild affair with such a girl, let Dodson go to whatever extremes he wished. Morlock had made such plans before. More often than not they had ended sordidly enough; nevertheless he still hoped one day to fall in love. He did not belabor the obvious fallacy that such emotion was hardly likely to be found in the companionship or the haunts of Dodson, History II.

Later, he took some pleasure in telling Paul Martin of his plans. Martin, a chemistry instructor, had the sort of aloof dignity that Morlock would like to have. He had more than once sheepishly realized that he was involuntarily imitating Martin's mannerisms of speech. He admired Martin and he openly sought his friendship.

Martin asked, "Are you actually going to stay at a hotel with that — lump? You could have come to Baltimore with me, you know, if you had given me time to make arrangements."

Morlock had the distinct impression that Martin had added the final phrase as a hasty hedge against the possibility that Morlock might be willing to change his plans.

"Why not?" he demanded. "Dodson is a good chap."

Martin would have said "chap" instead of "fellow" or a simple "guy" and Morlock used the word self-consciously as a sort of defiance. He was as sophisticated as Martin, he felt.

Martin, acting as if he resented the whole business, walked away without further discussion.

Dodson drove to Morlock's rooming house to pick him up. His car was an old LaSalle convertible. Rakish once, weary now. Like Dodson himself, Morlock thought; regretting again, now that the time had come, that he had agreed to the Providence adventure.

In the car Morlock worried aloud. "Suppose it got back to the college," he said. "I don't think Dean Gorham would stand for it."

Dodson's somewhat pathetic bad-boyishness was increasing in direct ratio to their distance from Ludlow. "Stand for what?" he snorted. "We're just going to take a room in a hotel and go out for a good time. Even a teacher is entitled to a vacation."

Morlock said uncertainly, "It isn't just that. I mean if we got into any trouble. With the hotel, for instance."

Dodson whooped delightedly and slapped Morlock's thigh. "Hell," he laughed, "We're not staying at the Biltmore. The hotel we're going to doesn't care if you bring women up to your room. By God, if you haven't got one of your own they'll get one for you!"

Providence was twelve miles over the state line from Ludlow. Dodson drove the distance, not without skill, in less than half an hour and parked the old car in a public garage. "We'll leave it," he said, winking at Morlock. "I don't want to be able to drive tonight. We'll use, cabs."

The hotel to which he led Morlock was on a side street, a red brick building with bars on either side. The lobby smelled of antiseptic. It was, Morlock admitted, clean enough. Dodson said as they entered, "Wait here, Al. I'll register for both of us. What will we get — two adjoining singles?"

Morlock agreed and watched Dodson head for the desk, extending his hand in greeting to the desk clerk like an old and valued customer. He failed to note any similar reaction on the part of the desk clerk who appeared more bored than enthusiastic. Dodson, he supposed, could not help — what was the expression? — making a production out of his simplest act. He wondered what whimsical destiny had made Dodson a teacher rather than a salesman, say, or a bartender.

Dodson returned, waving two keys triumphantly. "All set," he said happily. He glanced at Morlock's suitcase. "Want me to get a bellhop?"

Morlock had seen no attendant in the lobby. He declined, and the two men rode the elevator to the third floor.

They ate in a small Italian restaurant on Federal Hill. "You'll see what genuine Italian cooking is like," Dodson had shouted, managing to convey contempt for all other cuisines. Actually the restaurant was dirty and smelly; the spaghetti flaccid and overcooked, its shortcomings poorly disguised with red, garlic-heavy sauce. Dodson ordered a bottle of Chianti with the meal. He seemed to enjoy playing the host, the worldly gourmet. He ate hungrily. Morlock ate little. He was amused by Dodson's assumption of the role of host, which seemed a little ridiculous since they had carefully agreed in the hotel room to share all costs evenly. Still, Morlock was gradually awakening to the promise of the evening.

They sought a bar after Dodson had tried to order *cafe Espresso* from the waitress who had never heard of it and who looked at Dodson as if she thought he were a little crazy.

The bar they found was one of twenty in an area of a few blocks. It outdid its neighbors in the matter of neon and there was a canvas canopy leading from the sidewalk to what was designated a *Ladies Entrance*. Dodson said confidently, "In here, Al. I'll do the talking. You should have seen the chick I met here last time!"

Dodson, Morlock supposed, had a hundred expressions which could be defined as meaning women in various states of willingness and availability. "Chick," was no more irritating than "stuff" or "bag." All three made him uncomfortable, affecting him in much the same manner as the advertisements for soup and cake mix and soda pop that made a fetish out of leaving the a and d out of the conjunction *and* in the unshakable conviction that this indicated the unqualified approval of the children who were supposed to speak in such a manner. Butter' 'n eggs! Chicks 'n stuff! He laughed at the thought, told himself not to be a stuffy damn fool and followed Dodson into the bar entrance.

They stepped down into a low-ceilinged room with a stamped tin ceiling. The place featured low lights — the brightest glow in the room came from a pin ball machine that stood in a far corner. The bar itself *took* up half of one wall and was interrupted by a set of three stairs leading upward toward the dance floor which had its own bar.

Dodson led the way to the bar in the low room, asking generously, "What will you have, Al?" which was unnecessary. They had already agreed to drink draught beer. ("Until we get a chance to look around and see what's loose," Dodson had said.) Morlock, looking around him, saw half a dozen men seated on the high stools that lined the bar. They seemed friendly enough, as one or two nodded; but there was a withdrawal common to such occasions. The men at the bar were regulars or they had established their worth by having been in the place for an hour or more and having spent an appropriate amount of money. Morlock and Dodson were new and therefore strangers.

The bartender served their glasses. Dodson drank his quickly and noisily. Morlock could feel the Chianti warming his stomach. He told himself again not to be stuffy and drank his beer. They ordered more and Dodson, who was speaking louder, began a conversation with the man next to him. He dragged Morlock into the discussion. "This is a friend of mine," he said pompously. "A professor. Al, this is — what did you say your name was?"

The man said, "Snapper," and signaled for drinks. "Glad to know you, Professor."

Morlock could feel his own natural reserve melting, dissolving in a tide of beer. He protested — it was not more than a token protest — that he was not really a professor but managed to leave the implication that he could be if he wanted to. And he signaled for a round himself, knowing that he was on the verge of drunkenness. The man who called himself Snapper was of his own age, with thinning light hair and a scar running from his cheekbone to the point of his jaw. He fingered the scar continually.

"Got this in an accident a month ago," he explained. "We were going down to Attleboro at two o'clock in the morning drunk as a hoot owl. I just got my car back yesterday."

In the space of two hours Snapper became their friend. Dodson proclaimed this with great and solemn conviction. Morlock, in a golden haze himself, recognized that Dodson was quite drunk and forgave him for it in the same moment. A rare tolerance had come upon him, and he did not resent Dodson even when he loudly explained to Snapper that they were footloose and anxious for company.

Snapper — he was drinking whisky instead of beer by this time — nodded his head wisely. "You came to the right place," he congratulated them. "In half an hour or so when the band comes in there'll be so many in there you'll have to beat them off with a club."

They waited for the band to arrive. The waiting reminded Morlock of other days, high school dances, the few others he had been able to go to when the youths would hang around outside the auditorium waiting for the music to start and pretending to be tremendously bored with it all and all the time yearning for the pretty girls inside the building. When the music started in the next room he and Dodson hung back for another drink so that Snapper would not think them eager. Except that now it was no longer simply a matter of pretty girls. . . .

Prosecution Attorney Gurney: Your name is Gino Fangio?
Fangio: It is.
Gurney: You are known as Snapper, are you not?
Fangio: They call me that sometimes.
Gurney: When did you first meet the accused?
Fangio: Sometime before Christmas.
Gurney: I'll refresh your memory. It was December 22, Thursday, wasn't it?
Fangio: I guess so, if you say so.
Gurney: In a barroom?
Fangio: Yes.
Gurney: Was he drunk at the time?
Liebman: Objection.
Cameron: Sustained.

Gurney: Was he drinking at the time you met him?
Fangio: A few, I guess. He and that other guy were out for a good time. Nobody was going to get hurt.
Gurney: Were you with Morlock for the rest of the evening?
Fangio: Well, about that time, he and the other guy —
Gurney: Mr. Dodson.
Fangio: Yeah, Dodson. He and Morlock went into the dance hall. I stayed out at the bar.
Gurney: Did they state their purpose in going into the dance hall?
Fangio: They wanted women. Dodson was —
Liebman: Your Honor, that is speculative.
Cameron: The last statement will be stricken. Do you wish to take an exception, Mr. Gurney?
Gurney: No, Your Honor. Snapper — Mr. Fangio — you stated that you stayed at the bar. Isn't it true that if you wished to meet an unescorted woman you would have gone with them into the dance hall?
Fangio: Yes.
Gurney: Women frequented the place?
Fangio: A lot of them came there.
Gurney: Without escorts?
Fangio: A lot of them came stag.
Gurney: In other words, it was a good place for a man to meet a woman without the usual conventions. Did you tell the accused that it was such a place?
Fangio: Maybe I did. I guess I did.
Gurney: What were your words as you remember them?
Fangio: I said that they could probably get fixed up if they went in and looked around.
Gurney: And was it right after that that they went in?
Fangio: Yes.

> *The Commonwealth of Massachusetts vs. Alvin Morlock.*
> *Direct testimony of Gino Fangio.*

Morlock and Dodson walked in to the dance floor together, in pretended deep conversation, pointedly not looking around until they were seated at a small table. There were other men going back and forth. Most of these boldly looked around the room, making audible comments on what they saw, and returned to the main bar again.

They ordered drinks and kept up the conversation. "Look at those cheap characters," Dodson said contemptuously. "I've seen 'em before. They don't want to get stuck buying drinks so they wait until the girls order before they go over and start moving in."

Morlock agreed that this was so. He was less and less interested in Dodson's conversation now and more and more interested in the people — most of them women in twos and threes. In the dim light it was hard to distinguish features but there were two girls — in their early twenties, he guessed — in a near-by booth and both of them seemed attractive. One of them caught his glance and smiled tentatively.

Dodson dropped all pretense. "See anything good?" he asked anxiously.

"Over in the booth," Morlock said. "What do you think?"

Dodson peered eagerly in the direction of the booth. "They're looking over here," he whispered excitedly.

"They're not pigs either." Still looking toward the booth he suddenly swore. "Dammit. Look at those two punks!"

Morlock turned slightly so that he could see without being obvious. Two youths were approaching the booth. They were, both of them, tall. Both were dressed alike in dark suits that were conservative to the point of being ostentatious. Morlock felt a wholly unreasonable fury at the two intruders. He and Dodson had seen the girls first. The two youths spoke briefly to the girls who then stood up and came into their arms. They danced toward the table occupied by Dodson and Morlock.

Dodson began swearing in a monotone. Morlock, afraid that he might be overheard, attempted to quiet him. "Maybe they came together," he said.

Dodson muttered, "Like hell," and bent to his drink.

Morlock shrugged. "We'll have to be quicker next time," he said.

The two girls danced closer. Morlock was not comforted by the knowledge that he had been right. They were pretty. Both had heart-shaped faces framed with masses of dark hair. Both had good legs, slim and graceful. They looked like sisters, Morlock thought. One was slightly taller than the other. The shorter one — she was about Dodson's height — wore a white satin blouse. Underneath it she wore a brassiere — Morlock could see the straps of it when she turned — that lifted her small round breasts delightfully. Her skirt was tight. When she leaned forward against her partner her buttocks also looked small and round. Dodson watched avidly. "How would you like to pat that!" he demanded. He had recovered his good nature. "Didn't I tell you there was stuff here?"

The band stopped; the two couples returned to the booth — and the youths left. Morlock stood up. "I want the small one," he said.

Their names, it developed, were Audrey and Lucy — Audrey being the shorter of the two — and they were sisters. Also they drank whisky sours although there had been only beer bottles on the table when Morlock, with a boldness that surprised himself and impressed Dodson, had walked confidently to their table and asked, "Can we buy you a drink?" While he had moved toward their table, Dodson had remained in his seat, watching him eagerly but ready, Morlock was certain, to ridicule him if the girls rejected his offer. They did not and in his wonderful new cloak of confidence he had turned and beckoned casually to Dodson to come over.

As Dodson walked toward him, the new Morlock watched him with some feeling of superiority. Dodson, he thought, would have wagged his tail if he had had one.

Both of the girls worked in a jewelry shop. Both were in the office, they explained quickly. Morlock doubted it and this, too, increased the magnificent self-esteem that he now felt. They were lying to impress him — and Dodson too. Probably they were pearl dippers.

Dodson lost no time in explaining that they were members of the Ludlow faculty. Morlock faulted him for this. Dodson had, when it came right down to it, no faith in his own attractiveness or his own personality. He therefore attempted to reflect whatever light came from being a professional man. Had he not earlier referred to himself and Morlock as educated men? Morlock felt that he needed no crutch.

He was seated beside Audrey. The upper half of her white satin blouse flared sharply to her shoulders so that he could see the upper halves of her white breasts, and where yesterday he would have painfully avoided the appearance of glancing at them, he now openly stared — and felt his earlier resolution to find a decent girl and carry on a mild affair melt in a warm tide of desire. Audrey had, in a few sentences, exposed her own complete lack of mental or spiritual assets. She had, Morlock admitted, no need of them. Having admitted this, he devoted himself to appreciation of what she did hold for men — the appreciation being visual and verbal and in both cases completely acceptable to Audrey.

After an hour and many drinks, she began to press herself against him when they danced. The abstract Morlock noted that she had a magnificent awareness of her really beautiful body and an equal knowledge of the manner in which she might best activate it. He sighed for Dodson who seemed to be making no progress whatsoever with Lucy, and had sunk to the point where he was now trying to make her drink more than she could handle. Unfortunately, he had to order for himself as well as Lucy, the result being a shabby race between sobriety and sex with Dodson ahead, if at all, only slightly.

Morlock danced twice with Lucy. She remarked that the band was good for a small outfit. Audrey had made this comment. She noted that there was a good crowd tonight. Audrey had made this observation, too. Morlock, having no designs on Lucy, was bored.

Another hour and Dodson was making definite progress. When the two girls left for the powder room after an appropriately cute explanation, he watched them sway away from the table and said pridefully, "I told you we'd find something in here!"

Morlock generously did not remind Dodson that he had made all the overtures.

Dodson continued, "She's hot. I'll bet we won't have any trouble getting them out of here and up to the hotel." There was in the manner he said it, Morlock thought, something suggestive of whistling in a graveyard, and he wondered how many times Dodson had come this far with one of his conquests and seen it the unconsummated.

They came back to the table, and Lucy said, "It's getting late. We've got to work tomorrow."

They had planned this gambit in the powder room, Morlock was certain. Strangely he was not particularly surprised or disappointed. Dodson's thick neck reddened. "We'll take you home," he said hopefully.

Audrey glanced at her sister and then back toward Morlock. "We've got our own car," she said.

Dodson half stood, and for a terrible moment Morlock was afraid that he was going to remind the girls of the money that he had spent on them. He did not. He controlled himself while they swayed away again. When they were out of hearing he began to curse them, viciously and obscenely.

Snapper consoled them in the lower bar. "I could have told you," he said sadly. "Those two pull that stunt pretty regular. You know what they did after they left your table?"

Dodson said sourly, "I don't think they went home."

Snapper swallowed his drink. "Hell, no. They've got regular boy friends. They leave them off in here to have a good time while they shoot pool across the street. You should have picked up something a little older. Those kids are only after what they can get. How much did you blow?"

Dodson said glumly, "Fifteen dollars."

Snapper whistled softly. "Too bad." He offered to help them make another choice; closing time was still an hour away. Morlock shook his head. He was feeling an exhilaration that was beyond anything he had experienced. He had never before reached this stage of drunkenness — usually he became quite sick after drinking half what he had tonight. He easily convinced himself that he had had no great desire for Audrey, that he could have had her if he had really wanted to. The way she had glanced at her sister before saying that they had their own car — he had practically sent her away. He glowed with his own nobility.

Dodson was becoming increasingly maudlin and it was apparent that he would make no more conquests.

In the hour that remained before the bar closed, Morlock had several more drinks, trying to retain his mood. Strangely, his thoughts became clearer but the mood began to dissipate the moment they left the bar and walked through the streets to the hotel. He had some trouble with Dodson. By the time he undressed, the mood was entirely gone.

He had had for years a recurrent dream in which he was a boy. Awake, he could never remember the dream in its detail. He could only vaguely remember climbing green hills beside a lake where the mists rose slowly in the cool morning; and yet sometimes the dream was realer than reality — certainly it was happier than reality. In the dream he had a companion, usually a girl a year or two younger than himself. Morlock often courted the dream. He even made preparations for it, putting on fresh pajamas, fresh sheets on the bed. Like a bride preparing the wedding bed. He wooed the dream by returning in memory to his own childhood before falling asleep. He was not often successful and there was always the risk that the sweet pain of nostalgia would go unrewarded by the dream.

Tonight his memory was acute. Lying on the bed, he let it drift rapidly back, the quicker to escape the dreary hotel bedroom. As he usually did, he remembered best when he was twelve....

There was a green pasture littered with great out-croppings of the conglomerate rock they called puddingstone. Through the pasture a path made aimless progress into a cool glade where oak trees formed a park. Beyond the glade were low hills that dressed themselves in white and silver birch, in aspen and wild cherry, and in the spring the wild cherry sang with white blossom. Morlock remembered the way they looked and smelled. He could not have expressed the beauty of the trees in allegory at twelve as he could now but he was completely aware of that beauty. And there was the smell of grass and earth and leaves and the cows in the pasture and even their droppings; and these smells were picked up and blended by the west wind of spring so that the very smell was alive with promise. Beyond the low hills were the somewhat more somber pines and among the pines stood a colossal mass of that same puddingstone that dotted the pastures. It had been rolled up and left there like some toy by the glaciers, and it towered above the pines and hemlocks that soughed mournfully beneath it. There were ledges and faults in the mass and crevices and niches where arrowheads could be found and occasional shards of broken pottery. They called this Abram's Rock after the legendary Indian who had plunged from it after the death of his bride. Here Morlock, when there was time, played the wonderful games that could be played upon such a mighty site. Here, when he was twelve, came Marian, a grave child of ten with black hair that hung down her back to her waist after the manner of an old-fashioned illustration of *Alice in Wonderland*. Morlock was with some other boys of his own age; when they saw her standing quietly near them there was a rustle of whispering and snickering. "There she is," one boy said. "The Portagee kid."

Morlock remembered then that a Portuguese family from the Cape Verde islands had moved into a worn-out farm not far from Abram's Rock. There had been some loose and irresponsible indignation. "Ain't no difference between a nigger and a Portagee. One's as black as the other."

This was the first member of the family he had seen and she seemed to be just like any other girl or boy he knew. Her skin was no darker than his own would be at the end of the summer. Her eyes were blue and set wide apart in her oval face. Morlock had been born on the shabby-genteel side of absolute poverty; he knew hand-me-down and make-do as brothers and he could recognize the signals of poverty in the girl's clothing. She wore a simple dress of some gray material. It was clean but there was a patch in the skirt and it fitted her in the shapeless manner of a larger garment that had been taken in. He was too familiar with the device to miss it. She wore a worn pair of boy's shoes and her legs were bare. Morlock, out of the kinship of poverty, felt sorry for her.

One of the youngsters in the group called suddenly, "Hey, Portagee! Who said you could climb on our rock?"

And another boy, "Sure. Let's chase her on home."

She stood her ground bravely but Morlock could see that she was frightened. She said in a low voice, "My fa'der say I can play here."

None of the boys had actually been much interested up to this point. The Portagee girl looked much like any other girl and was probably as dull a playmate. Now the heavy accent identified her as an outsider and her soft obstinacy offered them the opportunity to defy authority, the authority of her father, without risk. They surrounded her and one boy mocked her accent.

"What right has your fodder to say you can play here? He doesn't own Abram's Rock!"

The girl — she was very thin, Morlock noticed — began to tremble. Tears formed in the outer corners of her eyes but she repeated stubbornly, "My fa'der say I can play here."

Morlock pushed two of the boys aside. "Let her alone," he said as fiercely as he could. "She isn't bothering anybody."

They had a certain respect for Morlock. He was not as big as some of the boys in the group but he actually worked after school and earned money. Not nickels for running errands but half dollars and dollars for cutting lawns and hoeing gardens which he gave to his mother. He could be identified with authority. More to the point, they were bored and maybe a little ashamed of the incident. They ran off shouting, leaving Morlock with the girl. That had been his first meeting with Marian — actually her name was Marianna — Cruz. . . .

Morlock, lying in the sagging hotel bed, remembered this as he had remembered it on a hundred nights, waiting for sleep to transport him back to a time when he had been happier than he had ever been since.

Chapter 3

Gurney: On the night of December 22—they call you Snapper, is it?

Fangio: I already told you that.

Gurney: You have testified that you met the accused on the night of December 22. When did you next see him?

Fangio: The next night. He and the other guy, Dodson, came around. We decided to go to the Balboa Club. They were having a dance.

Gurney: That was Morlock's idea, wasn't it?

Liebman: Objection.

Cameron: Sustained.

Gurney: Let that go, Snapper. Did Morlock meet a woman at the dance?

Fangio: Sure he did. That's what we went there for.

Gurney: Did you introduce them or did he pick her up?

Liebman: Your Honor —

Cameron: I have cautioned counsel against repetitious use of that phrase. Mr. Gurney, you will please refrain from using it.

Gurney: Snapper, you, Dodson, and the accused went out on that second occasion for the avowed purpose of finding women. From your own testimony and Dodson's, Morlock and Dodson had been unsuccessful in an earlier attempt to pick — to make the acquaintance of Lucy and Audrey Zonfrillo. Did he drop his standards? Wasn't he anxious to meet any woman at all by the time you went to the Balboa Club?

Liebman: Your Honor, I object to counsel's leading questions.

Cameron: Sustained.

Gurney: Snapper, who was the woman the accused met at the Balboa Club?

Fangio: Her name was Louise. Louise Palaggi.

Gurney: Did you know her prior to that time?

Fangio: I'd seen her around.

Gurney: Did you introduce her to him?

Fangio: No.

Gurney: What did you do after the dance?

Fangio: We went to another place.

Gurney: Just the three of you?
Fangio: We took them along.
Gurney: Them?
Fangio: The women we were sitting with at the dance.
Gurney: And where did you go then? To still another place?
Fangio: We went to Morlock and Dodson's Hotel.
Gurney: With the women?
Fangio: Yes.
Gurney: And who was the woman with the accused?
Fangio: Louise Palaggi.
The Commonwealth of Massachusetts vs. Alvin Morlock.
Redirect testimony of Gino Fangio.

When Morlock and Dodson met him in the bar on the following evening, Snapper had said, "If you want to pick something up you could do better than hang around here. They come in here, all right, lots of them, but they're too smart. You ought to go to a dance. There's one on tonight at the Balboa Club. That's a Dago joint on the Hill."

Morlock had spent an uneasy day. He had killed time at the public library as a hypocritical sop to his conscience. Dodson had slept through the afternoon and Morlock had fully intended to tell him, when he awoke, that he was going back to Ludlow. He was ashamed of the incident with Audrey and Lucy which, in daylight, seemed cheap and contemptible.

Dodson would not hear of it, taking the attitude that Morlock's departure would spoil his, Dodson's, vacation. After dinner Morlock felt the familiar, wistful night magic and agreed to stay on another day.

There would be no more barroom entanglements, Morlock promised himself. A movie, perhaps, and then a sandwich and coffee before he went back to the hotel. But that was before Snapper's suggestion.

Dodson was enthusiastic. They went to the dance in Snapper's car.

The hall was crowded when they arrived and bought tickets. The band was just coming back to the platform after an intermission. Morlock sensed a heady excitement as the musicians warmed up with little runs and trills; he remembered those high school dances. Pretty soon they would come in with that big solid opening beat.

Dodson had been looking around the room. "This is more like it," he said.

Morlock, analyzing his own mood, missed the elation that had been there the previous night. Anticipation there was — there were any number of pretty women in the room — but it was not a lustful anticipation. Further, there was a cynical facet to his character; he had long ago recognized it. If it controlled him this night he would find himself on the sidelines, not dancing, criticizing the dancers with a sardonic smile on his face. The cynicism, he supposed, was a form of sour grapes.

Snapper became expansive. "I told you there'd be plenty of women here," he said. "Most of them will be looking for rides home when this is over. Thing to do is move in early. Let's go downstairs to the bar and get a drink."

Morlock had promised himself to drink very little. He had had too much the previous night and for once it had not made him sick. Miracles were seldom repeated. But Snapper bought a round and Dodson and then it was his turn.

The glow came and he danced, starting with the younger girls in the crowd. Dodson, he noticed, avoided the younger and prettier women and selected the older, less attractive ones — who could be expected to be grateful, Morlock thought, and remembered wryly that it had been Ben Franklin who had originally advised such selection.

In between dances they drank. To do this they held, by right of first possession, a table in the bar. There was another table jammed against their own and he became aware of two women at the table. They smiled each time he returned to the table from the dance floor. After a third or a fourth smile they acquired, by force of repetition, a relationship of sorts which Dodson noticed. After several dances he said, "I think we've been missing something, Al. Let's ask them to dance." He sounded patronizing, Morlock thought. Dodson had been having a fine run of luck, not having been once rejected as a partner. As a result he had taken on a jaunty confidence and his offer to dance with the neighboring women was made with a princely condescension.

"Go ahead," Morlock agreed. "Ask one of them. I'll ask the one that's left."

Dodson, drunk with himself, rose and walked toward them. He held a brief conversation with the two women at the table. One of the two got up and linked her arm in Dodson's. When they moved away from the table Morlock covertly studied the second woman. She appeared to be in her early thirties and her face was quite attractive. Her figure, what he could see of it, was full blown with a disciplined firmness that suggested corseting.

He stood up, a shade uncertainly, and walked to her table.

"Hello," he said, "are you having a good time?"

She smiled. Her teeth were white and perfect. "Very," she said. "Won't you sit down?"

He was grateful; he had been alarmed over the loss of perfect control of his legs. "Let me buy you a drink," he said. "My name is Morlock."

She acknowledged the introduction with a nod and another smile. "Mine is Louise," she said. "Louise Palaggi."

"Hello, Louise," he said dashingly.

When Dodson came back to the table, towing the other woman whom he introduced as Rose but mentioned no last name, Morlock was already deep in conversation with Louise Palaggi. She seemed greatly interested in everything he had to say and demurely declined Dodson's offer to buy another round. When Snapper joined them with a woman of his own, she refused his offer of a drink too. Morlock didn't, and as he drank he recognized with wonderful discernment the difference between her and the other women who were loud, raucous, and superficial.

He told her of his job at Ludlow and let her guess that he very seldom came to places like this but that sometimes he got so fed up with ignorant students ...

He indicated the loneliness of a sensitive man.

He had never known a woman to listen to him with such perception and sympathy. He told her this too.

He was quite drunk.

Louise told him, for her part, that she was lonely too. She had devoted the best part of her life, she let him guess, to the care of her father and her brothers, keeping up a home for them. She let him know, wistfully, that she was ignorant herself — she had had to leave high school in her second year to make that home — but that it was wonderful to be in the company of an educated man and she regretted that she knew so little.

He told her gallantly that she was one of the most intelligent women he had ever met — in a sense he was quite right — and that he could hardly believe that she had so little schooling.

She told him that she read a great deal.

Snapper and his woman and Dodson with his Rosie became aware, after a while, of the detachment of the couple. Rose thought it was cute; she said so, shrilly referring to them as lovebirds. Morlock, who would have been sickened ordinarily, smiled sheepishly while Louise protested; becomingly, he thought.

When the band played the last number and they got up to leave, Snapper suggested that they go to an after hours club where he was known. Morlock was watching Dodson, who seemed to be afraid of a refusal from his Rosie. He saw Dodson's face light up with relief and joy when Rosie was loudly enthusiastic at the plan.

Louise said shyly, "Well, I shouldn't —" but protested no more when Morlock was masterfully insistent.

After the club closed in its turn, they drove back to the hotel, Morlock and Dodson sitting in the back seat with Rosie and Louise. Dodson and Rosie were making love, openly and grotesquely. Morlock was embarrassed. Louise Palaggi, with what he thought a charming and ladylike reticence, ignored them completely.

They would, it was agreed, go up to Dodson's room for a final drink.

She was diffident about it but she went with them. In the elevator Morlock began to regret that he could not go to bed. He'd had, for him, a tremendous amount of liquor. The surging lift of the elevator made him aware of it.

When Dodson had fumbled open the door of his room, he went at once to the bed with Rosie, falling on the mattress in animal abandon. Snapper and his woman found a chair. Morlock said unsteadily, "Let's go next door to my room."

He was physically and mentally aroused by her presence, by the woman smell and softness of her. In his room he fell on the bed and reached for her, pawing at her breasts and trying to pull her down beside him.

"No," she said, and pulled away from him. She didn't seem angry. "No, Alvin."

And then he was sick.

Chapter 4

Gurney: You have given your name as Attilio Palaggi. You are the father of the deceased woman?

Palaggi: Louise . . .

Gurney: Louise Palaggi was your daughter, wasn't she? —

Palaggi: She was my daughter, Louise. A good Catholic girl. She went to convent school for four years. She was a good girl, Louise.

Gurney: Mr. Palaggi, did the accused visit your home prior to his marriage to your daughter?

Palaggi: A good girl . . .

Liebman: Your Honor, there seems to be no point to this badgering of a decent old man. The defense will agree that Alvin Morlock visited the Palaggi home several times before his marriage to Louise Palaggi.

Cameron: Will Mr. Gurney inform the Court as to the purpose of this line of questioning?

Gurney: The prosecution only wishes to show that Morlock had every opportunity to observe the woman he met at the Balboa Club, to see that she was his inferior in education and upbringing, and that his marriage to her was not the result of any romantic attachment.

Cameron: You may continue, Mr. Gurney. Please be as considerate of the witness as possible.

Gurney: Very well, Your Honor. Mr. Palaggi, how many times did Morlock visit your home?

Palaggi: I don't know. I think, many times.

Gurney: During these visits he was frequently alone with your daughter, was he not?

Cameron: I will ask you once again, Mr. Gurney, what is the purpose of your line of questioning? What are you trying to establish now?

Gurney: The sordid nature of Morlock's relationship with Louise Palaggi prior to their marriage.

Liebman: Oh, objection!

Cameron: I'm not going to rule on your objection at this moment, Mr. Liebman. Mr. Gurney, can you amplify your last comment? The Court realizes that by admonishing you to show consideration for your witness we may perhaps have disarmed you. I am going to let you have some latitude in establishing your point.

Gurney: It has already been established by competent testimony that, the accused met the deceased, Louise Palaggi, at a dance without the usual formality of an introduction and at a time when he was deliberately seeking a woman. It has been shown that on the very night he met her, he took her to his hotel room and that thereafter he visited her home on several occasions. It is not stretching credulity to assume that he used the humble awe she felt for his position as a means to seduce her on that very first occasion, and that thereafter he pursued her with all the purposeful directness of a rutting boar —
Cameron: Order! I will have order in this courtroom!
The Commonwealth of Massachusetts vs. Alvin Morlock. Direct testimony of Attilio Palaggi.

Louise Palaggi had attended convent school until she was twelve years old. By the time she was fifteen — her mother had died while Louise was an infant — she was attending a city high school. She had put the teachings of the nuns far behind her and had already acquired the beginnings of notoriety on Federal Hill.

Her puberty had coincided with the era of the big name bands: the Dorsey Brothers and Glenn Miller, Benny Goodman, and Artie Shaw. When they played New England they usually played a stop at a road house fifteen miles from Providence. Louise was in her second year of high school when one of the big bands was booked in for a playing date that happened to fall on the last day of school. She was already considered wild by the women of her neighborhood, who clucked about it and wondered why Attilio — he had money enough from his contracting business — didn't marry again to provide her with a mother. She was pretty, they agreed, too pretty for her own good. And she picked out her own clothes and why couldn't Attilio see that she got them too tight over her bust and her behind?

She had already had dates with boys in the neighborhood. The dates thus far had included movies and school dances, canned beer, drunk warm and daringly in the back seat of an automobile, and lovemaking carried on in the same place. The love-making had been mild at first; lately there had been panting efforts to touch her fine breasts and to put hot hands on her slim bare legs. She had not, thus far, permitted it to go beyond that point although she had been aware of a growing desire of her own. Fear of her father and her four brothers stopped her. They adored her, the single woman in their house, and they would have killed the boy involved if she got into trouble. Beyond that, some faint vestiges of the chastity urged by the nuns at the convent school remained with her.

One day she had stopped after school for a magazine. On her way out of the drugstore she nearly bumped into a man not much taller than she.

He caught at her arm to steady her and said, "Sorry, Miss — " and then paused to stare at her. She was accustomed to such a reaction by this time and knew that he would now make a pass. She had two reactions of her own for these occasions. She would adopt an air of cold contempt, or she would smile.

"Let me buy you a cup of coffee," he said.

She had meant to use contempt. He was small and she liked taller boys. But he was older than the boys of her own crowd and very well dressed. Clothes-conscious herself, she liked that. She said, "All right."

It developed that his name was Eddie Mason and that he was at the track, an expression that puzzled her briefly until she realized that he meant the race track which operated just outside Providence.

"I've got three mounts tomorrow," he said. "How would you like to come out to the track and watch?"

Not for the world would she have admitted that she had to go to school. "Sure," she said.

It further developed that he had a new car and that he liked to dance. Before they separated she agreed to meet him later in the evening on the corner of the street where she lived. They would go to the roadhouse where Tommy Dorsey was playing a one-night stand.

She had never been to a roadhouse; she knew that her father would refuse to let her go if she asked. At supper she said that she was going to the movies with Frances Adiano, a rather plain girl who worshiped her and whom she treated with a casual contempt.

It was not only the day of the big name bands, it was a day of big songs. "I'll Never Smile Again," and "String of Pearls." Louise Palaggi was fascinated by the music and the surroundings. She had discovered a new world that she never proposed to leave.

Later, in Eddie Mason's car, she learned the price of living in such a world. She paid it, if not cheerfully, at least without more than token protest.

Her father would be waiting up, so Eddie left her a block from the house. While she walked that block she rehearsed the attitude she would use when she walked in. She was completely aware of the strength of her position in the Palaggi home; she had developed a naivete to center the attentions of her father and her four brothers on herself and away from any infractions of the few family rules that applied to her. But it was almost two o'clock in the morning, and she knew she would have to use a different tactic.

Attilio and her brother Dominick were waiting for her in the kitchen. The old man had drawn his trousers on over the heavy winter underwear that he wore to bed. His white hair was rumpled and his eyes were reddened with weariness and worry. Dominick, Louise's oldest brother, sat at the table, his arms folded across his chest. His eyes were hot and sullen. She was more frightened of him than of her father although, queerly, she sensed that he loved her more than her other brothers.

He stood up and pushed his father back when the old man would have risen. "Where have you been all night?" he demanded. "And don't lie about being at the Adianos'. We talked with Frances."

She was thankful that she had not tried the old approach, the innocent smile. Dominick, she thought, would have slapped her if she had.

Her one defense was attack. "You're not my father," she said. "If pa wants to know where I was, he'll ask me."

Attilio looked up at her. "I ask," he said tiredly. "Where you been, Louise, till such a time?"

She said contritely, "I'm sorry I'm so late, Pa. Some of the other kids got up a crowd to go dancing. I didn't think we'd be so late."

Dominick was watching her closely, looking at her clothes. He asked more quietly, "You all right, Louise? Nothing happened?"

She said angrily, "You see, Pa? He acts as if I was a whore or something just because I stayed out a little with the kids. He's got no right!"

She had, as she had planned, made the issue not her lateness but Dominick's criticism of it. Attilio turned to stare at Dominick.

"Such words I hope never to hear my daughter use," he said, "But she is right. Dominick, never say again to me that Louise is a bad girl."

Dominick and his brothers still treated the head of the family with Old Country deference. Dominick, who had said nothing of the sort, stood up angrily. "All right, Pa," he said bitterly. "If it was my say I'd give her a licking."

The old man said, "Is not your say. I am the head of this house."

Later, in her bedroom, Louise felt a little sorry for Dominick. He would be mad for a couple of days. Then he would bring her a present and make up. She thought, before she went to sleep, of the fun she would have at the race track with Eddie Mason. Thinking of Mason, she felt the last small twinge of conscience about what they had done in the back seat of his automobile. She could have stopped him if she really had wanted to. She hadn't wanted to and now that it was over it didn't seem such a terrible and mysterious thing. Forgetting the pain.

Eddie picked her up at noon, by prearrangement.

She had started from the house as if to go to school and spent the morning in the library. He had another man with him, a stocky man in his thirties with a loud voice and shrewd, piggish eyes.

"This is my agent," Mason said. "Herb Clark."

Herb would stay with her, it developed, during the races. When Mason had seated her in a box seat he gave her two fifty-dollar bills. "Have a ball, kid," he said. "But don't bet on any of the pigs I'm riding."

Herb said, when Mason was gone, "You better let me bet that money for you if you decide you like something, kid. The mutuel clerk might ask you how old you are. How old are you, anyway?"

"Eighteen," she said. She didn't like Herb. He was too patronizing. "And I've bet for myself before."

She hadn't. She had never been to the track before, but she knew about betting from hearing her brothers talking about it. In the first race she bet five dollars on a favorite. The horse ran second. She told Herb that she had bet ten and shrewdly put five in her purse. In the second race she bet a horse that he picked, betting ten dollars this time. The horse won, paying her more than a hundred dollars, and she changed her mind about Herb. When he offered to buy her a drink, she accepted. They drank cold beer at the mezzanine bar where the crowd was thick and the bartender had little chance to pay attention to her apparent age.

When Eddie joined them after the sixth race — he had no more mounts for the day — she was more than two hundred dollars ahead and was becoming shrilly drunk.

Herb, winking at Eddie, said, "We ought to get on out of here before the last race."

The ride toward Providence with the windows of the car open sobered her to the point where she realized the danger in facing her family — particularly the suspicious Dominick — with the smell of beer on her. They would, all of them, be working until dark on one of her father's construction jobs. She got into the house before they returned and went to her room, closing and locking the door. When, one by one, they came to knock softly on the door and inquire was she all right, she reassured them that she just didn't feel very well and that she would be up after a while. Turning away, they nodded wisely to each other. Louise, they told each other, was growing up. Probably this was her time of the month.

She saw Eddie Mason almost daily after that but she never again made the mistake of coming in after midnight, which had been established as her curfew. On the third date he asked her if she had a friend that she could get for Herb Clark so that they could double date. Louise had never completely outworn her original dislike for Clark and she was still a little frightened by him. Her first impulse was to say no, she didn't know any girl who would go out with the agent. She rejected the impulse lest Eddie think it odd that she knew no girls. "Sure," she said. "For tomorrow night."

Eddie nodded. "Just don't bring no rube," he said. "Herb — well, you know him."

In the morning she went to the Adiano house. Frances was in the kitchen, washing dishes. She was almost seventeen, a coarse-haired, dark-skinned girl. She did have a good figure. She was too happy to see Louise to be surprised at the visit. Usually she had to seek Louise out.

Louise had made up a careful little lie about Clark and Mason. "You'll like them," she explained. "They're not like the boys around here."

Frances was doubtful. Her family was deeply religious; she doubted that they would let her go out with strangers.

Louise ridiculed her. "You don't have to tell them," she mocked.

In the face of her ridicule, Frances agreed to meet her later in the evening. They would go, it had been agreed, to a drive-in movie.

Herb and Eddie picked Louise up first. Herb was curious about Frances, wanting to know not what she looked like but, "If she knew the score."

If she admitted that Frances was a quiet, religious girl with practically no experience with men, Herb would be furious. Eddie would also resent Louise's selection of Frances. In full knowledge of what Herb meant by asking if Frances knew the score, Louise said, "Sure she does, even if she don't act like it."

She watched Herb closely when they met Frances. He did not seem to be disappointed at her lack of prettiness. When they were parked in the far reaches of the drive-in — there were no individual loud-speakers then, only one great one that drowned out all conversation — she could feel the vibration of a struggle in the back seat over and above the disturbance she and Eddie were making. She heard too the muffled protests and the low cursing of Herb. After a time she heard a cry of pain and a wail from the back seat. Eddie sat up and said, "What the hell?"

Sobbing, Frances broke away from Herb and flung open the door to the back seat. Before she could get away Herb grabbed her and drew her back. "Get going!" he snapped to Eddie. When they were clear of the range of the loud-speaker Frances' sobbing quieted some. She moaned to Louise, "He did it to me. He did it to me, Louise!"

The two men let them out a block away from Frances' house. When they stopped the car, Herb looked curiously at Louise. "You bitch," he said, and then they drove off.

Frances had by this time stopped her moaning. Louise, out of a new fear, said, "You better not tell, Frances. It would only make things worse."

She had to argue the point for several minutes before she convinced Frances; even then she had little hope that the other girl would not run immediately to her parents.

She lived in fear for the next two days but there was no word from Frances' parents. Going to market in the morning, she saw Frances herself, white-faced, but they did not speak. On the following afternoon, when she was beginning to hope that nothing would come of the incident at the drive-in, Louise came home to find her brother Dominick sitting at the kitchen table staring moodily into space.

"You're home early, Dom," she said brightly. "Sick?"

He stood up. "Frances Adiano went to confession this morning," he said flatly. "The priest told her she better tell her folks what happened to her the night she was out with you."

Louise backed against the kitchen sink. "It wasn't my fault," she whimpered.

Dominick said something obscene in Italian. "They are going to send her away," he said. "You know something, you little bitch? They are going to send her to Boston to her uncle's house. I'll tell you something else. Her mother is wearing black for her." He took two steps toward her and slapped her with his callused hand, knocking her to the floor where she crouched, afraid to cry out. Dominick bent over her, his face contorted. "What am I supposed to say when I see her brother or her father? You tell me that, you hear?" He straightened and wheeled away only to turn back. "The Adianos won't tell Pa. They've got shame for Frances. If he finds out, I think I'll kill you."

Louise was sufficiently frightened by the incident to keep to the house for the next week or so. After that she called Eddie at his hotel and arranged to meet him again. By the time the horses moved on to another circuit, taking him with them, she was known in a half a hundred cafes and night clubs on the Hill. She became a pet of the small-time mobsters who congregated in such places. She had money when she needed it. The gamblers in the places she frequented would make small bets for her for luck when they phoned in their own bets. She became skillful at shuffleboard. There was a table in almost every bar and she could challenge the best players on even terms. She did so only when she had to. It was easier to find some half-drunk player who didn't know her or of her and she did not hesitate to cheat on the scoring when it was possible to do so, confident that her patrons would protect her against any accusations if she was caught. She never went back to school.

Dominick seldom spoke to her. The old man, Attilio, seemed to age overnight and to shrink inward like a winter apple. The other brothers, in their turn, tried to reason with her and they became enraged at her defiance and came to follow Dominick's example. It was not a happy house.

About a year later, when her reputation was completely shattered, old Attilio fired a drunken laborer. The laborer, frantic with rage, cursed at the old man. When he could not find enough bitter things to say about the old man himself, he screamed, "You think you so much, you! That girl of yours, she is no better than a whore anybody on the Hill can sleep with."

Dominick had driven a sand truck up in time to catch part of it. He leaped down from the cab without stopping to switch off the motor and was on the man, beating him to the ground in a shuddering huddle before he could say more. The old man turned away without speaking. He went home and never again came on a job. He would sit by the hour in the kitchen, not speaking. He treated Louise, whenever he saw her, as a little girl. When she would come in stupidly drunk, he never seemed to notice.

More and more often she began to stay away from home. For a month at a time she would have a room in a hotel. She made the winter tour of Florida with the race track crowd. When she came back after being gone three months, Attilio greeted her as if she were a child again and had just come home from school. A pattern was established that lasted until she was in her thirties.

Several weeks before she met Alvin Morlock for the first time, an icy fact was brought home to Louise. She was getting old. She had been sitting in a bar listening to two youths boldly discussing the women in the place. They had started with two girls at the far end of the bar and had worked their way back and she had complacently waited until they came to her. "There's something," they would say. "She could put her shoes under my bed any time." She had waited while they had discussed the woman next to her. Then one of the youths had said, "She was a real doll once. My brother used to go out with her." He was obviously referring to her, Louise Palaggi, and she could scarcely believe what she was hearing. She ordered another drink; while she drank it she remembered the spans of three and four days without a date that were becoming common now, and which she had put down as chance or coincidence. That night she studied her face and body carefully. The faint haze of black hair on her upper lip was becoming increasingly more difficult to hide. There were wrinkles at the corners of her eyes and mouth and the skin of her throat had become papery. There was a definite thickening of her hips and lower body and the breasts that had been so firm were softening. She was familiar with the dramatically sudden aging of Italian women; she had seen it a hundred times. Almost overnight a red-lipped provocative bride could become a shapeless, sexless old woman.

She could fight it but it would be at best a delaying action. Frightened, she began a deliberate search for security. She had sense enough to know that she would not find it in the sphere in which she then moved. She began a careful preparation by renewing certain old friendships. This was not easily done. The girls — women, now — of her youth had to be carefully approached. She had openly and contemptuously violated the standards by which they lived, and it took every trace of a charm that had been considerable to overcome their wary distrust. But it had to be done. They had their clubs and their dances. To the dances came the retired mail carriers and the widowed grocers, the eager greenhorn *paisans* from the old country, and the substantial middle-aged men newly loosened by death from the silver cord that was so strong in Italian people.

She had felt that she could be, with ease, the belle of the local dances and she was frightened again when she was little more than a wallflower at her first discreet appearance. She studied the younger women, tight-breasted and slim-waisted, who competed for the available men and shrewdly concluded that she was overmatched. This first sortie took place at a dance sponsored by a parish womens' club. She conceded that she would have to lower her standards. Her visit to the Balboa Club on the night that she met Alvin Morlock for the first time was the result of that concession. On that night old Attilio had said to her, "You my good girl, Louise. You don't be out too late."

Chapter 5

Gurney: Since counsel for the defense is obviously going to persist in obstructing any efforts to get the testimony of the father of the deceased woman into the record, we ask that Attilio Palaggi be dismissed and that Thomas Dodson be recalled to the stand.

Cameron: Mr. Palaggi may stand down. Thomas Dodson will be recalled. The bailiff will caution witness that he is still under oath.

Gurney: Mr. Dodson, getting back to the little excursion you and the accused made to Providence in search of women —

Liebman: Your Honor, this is a travesty of proper cross-examination.

Cameron: The Court agrees. Mr. Gurney, you have been repeatedly warned. Please save any further inferences for your summation.

Gurney: Very well. Mr. Dodson, how long did you and Morlock stay at the Hotel Compton?

Dodson: A little over a week. Through New Year's Eve. Then we had to get back for our classes.

Gurney: Did Morlock see Louise Palaggi frequently during that period?

Dodson: I suppose he did. He didn't spend much time with me.

Gurney: He spoke to you of her?

Dodson: Yes.

Gurney: Did you go out in their company at any time during that week?

Dodson: No. I didn't see her again . . .

Gurney: Never mind. You didn't go out with them. How did he speak of her?

Dodson: I don't know what you mean.
Gurney: As a conquest? Was he in love with her?
Liebman: Objection. Any answer would have to be speculative.
Cameron: Sustained.
Gurney: But he did see her every night during the time you stayed at the Hotel Compton?
Dodson: Yes.
Gurney: Getting back to that first night you took the women to your rooms, were you intimate with your companion on that occasion?
Liebman: Will the court instruct the witness that he doesn't have to answer incriminating questions? He is not on trial here.
Cameron: You understand that you don't have to answer, Mr. Dodson?
Dodson: I understand. Under the circumstances I'd rather not answer.
Gurney: Your privilege, Mr. Dodson. You wouldn't know, of course, if the accused was intimate with his companion? When they went to his room, I suppose they could have been playing gin rummy or discussing poetry.
Liebman: You can't attack the character of the accused by innuendo, Gurney.
Gurney: What character? You think they *were* playing gin rummy? Morlock knew what he was getting into and I'm proving it.
Cameron: We will have no more of this bickering. Counsel will address his remarks to the Court.

> *The Commonwealth of Massachusetts vs. Alvin Morlock.*
> *Re-cross-examination of Thomas Dodson.*

Louise Palaggi had rejected Morlock on the night of their first meeting only after careful consideration of the effect of such a rejection, and not out of any particular repugnance at his drunkenness. Within ten minutes of his approach to her table, she had decided that he was adequate for her purposes. He was personally presentable, which was a plus. He had a secure job with a reasonable income — she supposed that professors made reasonable incomes. More than that, she became aware of an odd liking for him, a tenderness aroused by his false boldness in striking up an acquaintance. The kind of boldness she was accustomed to was by no means false. She would have to be careful, though. He was sensitive. Quiet, studious. He would be studious, being a professor, according to the fat one, Dodson. Dodson was trouble, though. She would have to wean Morlock away from Dodson; who was noisy and a drunkard but who would certainly not be fooled by Louise Palaggi; he would never stand quietly by while Morlock married her.

While Morlock was still coherent she had invited him to Christmas dinner, a gamble that was partly forced on her. If they went to any dance or night club on Federal Hill she would be greeted with a familiarity that would undoubtedly alarm Morlock. The gamble had its advantages. Morlock was cultured, educated. She was neither but she could surround herself with the trappings of both and let him draw his own conclusions while she kept quiet and let him speak.

The next day she cleaned house, with her father happily puttering after her. There were very few books in the house, and books, to her, were the very symbol of education. Dominick had a library card; he used it to borrow Westerns occasionally. She used the card to draw half a dozen books from the library, making her selection from a catalogue on the library bulletin board listing the great classics of the century and adding a book of collected poems. All the books except the poetry volume she left in the living room; that one she took to her bedroom.

Music, too, was culture, and here she had weapons of her own. She had been brought up in a home where arias were sung before breakfast; she had absorbed Verdi and Rossini with the air she breathed when this had been a happy house. Old Attilio had records of a great many of the operas, and Dominick had bought the old man a good record player.

There remained the matter of dinner. She solved it by buying steaks and a packaged salad. They would have wine, of course; there was plenty of it in the house.

The final problem was her father. Dominick was out of town and the other brothers were married and living in homes of their own. She could send the old man to spend the night with any of them or she could let him stay, which would be more in keeping with the impression of chasteness that she wished to create. She studied him objectively. He was withered and old, but with his immaculate white mustache and his silky white hair he was not undistinguished looking. Nothing to be ashamed of. And he could be an asset in conversation if the talk turned — and she would see that it did — to music. Early enough she could send him off to bed.

On Christmas day she bathed and dressed carefully. She put on a new girdle that bound her thickening hips and stomach — and after some thought took it off again. In case it became necessary to use her ultimate weapon, she wanted her body to seem soft and desirable. She put on a black dress that accented her white skin and complemented her thick black hair.

She had an alert mind and a retentive memory when she chose to use them. When she was dressed she picked up the volume of poems and riffled the pages until she found one that appeared to be shorter than most of the others. She lit a cigarette and began reading the poem half aloud. When she had finished it, she read it again, glancing away from the page from time to time. At the end of an hour she could recite it verbatim from memory.

She memorized the name of the poet and looked in the table of contents for additional poems by him; the names of these she also memorized. She looked at the clock on her dresser. It was six o'clock. She was thoroughly bored with the poem but she could relax. She did not delude herself that she could carry on the deception for long. She did not intend that it should take long. She had already decided that she would marry Morlock, and she had dedicated herself to the project with all the skill she had.

Morlock threaded his way along sidewalks still crowded with displays of Christmas trees and greenery. A light snow was falling and carols echoed from loudspeakers in a dozen cafes. He had started out to keep his appointment with Louise Palaggi primarily from a sense of obligation — she had been very understanding — secondarily from a desire to escape Dodson who had, in his own words, scored with the woman he had picked up at the dance, and who was at this moment happily getting ready to go out with Snapper and try to duplicate the feat. Morlock could barely remember what Louise looked like. Now, with the old familiar nostalgia of the carols in his ears, he was rather happy that he actually had a date; that he would spend an evening with a woman who apparently liked him and who was obviously not cheap. Hadn't she refused him her body? Still, he felt a faint embarrassment at the prospect of facing her after the episode in the hotel room.

The Palaggi house was high and square and homely with its icing of fretwork — a three-decker, they called such houses on Federal Hill. There was a lamp in the window with a red silk shade. It made a warm glow in the darkness. Morlock rang the bell and Louise Palaggi opened the door.

"You're just on time," she said.

Morlock stamped his feet to rid them of loose snow and followed her into the house, making some inane comment about the weather.

Louise took his coat and introduced him to her father, trying at the same time to put him at ease. She asked the old man if he wouldn't play some records, knowing that he would play some of his operas. Culture. She excused herself to bring wine and again to start dinner so that Morlock's impression was that she was a domestic woman making a fuss over him.

He was naive, but not a fool. Looking about the room he saw the books, recognized the second-hand look of library property and glanced at the library form in the back of several of the books which showed that they had been withdrawn that same day. A score or a hundred students had tried variations of the same strategy. Morlock, recognizing the transparent little scheme, found it touching and pathetic rather than sneaking and hypocritical, and he was rather nattered that she had gone to such lengths to make a good impression on him. (He was to wonder, much later, if she had actually anticipated this reaction, if she had plotted such a double trap.)

She wasted little time, when dinner was over, in sending the old man off to bed. She had managed, by this time, to augment the impression planted the night she met Morlock that she had spent most of her youth caring for her father. Old Attilio, dazed with happiness at the sudden warmth in this cold and empty house, left them willingly enough.

When they were alone in the living room, she came over to sit beside him on the lumpy old couch. The lamp with the red shade was at her left shoulder. It softened the lines of her face and flattered her; she was conscious of this. Morlock, watching her as she crossed the room, was aware of the womanliness of her body. He was by now full of a sense of well-being and he felt sorry for Dodson who was undoubtedly drunk by this time.

"About the other night," he said. "I hope you weren't offended."

She was surprised again by her own tenderness for Morlock. "Don't feel bad about it," she said. "You had a lot to drink. I suppose I asked for it, going up to your room with you like that. You must have thought I was pretty easy."

He protested that he hadn't thought anything of the kind.

Louise would have liked to keep the conversation revolving about what had happened that night because of the relationship it established; but she realized he actually meant it, that he was genuinely ashamed of his actions, and she shifted the subject adroitly.

"I'm sorry I couldn't have invited your friend tonight," she apologized. She added, after a swift analysis of Morlock's shame balanced against the certain factor that Dodson would not have been ashamed at all, "You don't seem at all like him." She left it hanging. If Morlock wanted to make something of it, it was there.

She was growing more confident. What little self-conscious awe she had felt over the fact that he was a college graduate and a professional man had dissolved completely.

Morlock, caught between a vague sense of loyalty to Dodson and a human desire to accept the implied compliment, wavered. "We're not very great friends," he explained. "We both happened to have no plans for the holidays so we came in to Providence together." He felt somewhat a Judas, until he reflected that Dodson was probably quite happy with whatever he was doing at the moment.

After Dodson had been dismissed, Morlock found himself enjoying his date with Louise Palaggi immensely. She had spent her adult life catering to men; tougher men, more sophisticated men than Morlock whom she found very easy to please. When, after quite a lot of wine, he awkwardly put his arms around her she yielded briefly before she pulled away.

"It isn't that I don't want to, Al," she said. "We're both grown up. But I'm not cheap and I don't want you to think that I am."

Morlock was — later — more pleased than displeased by the refusal. Going back to the hotel when the evening was over, with his footstep ringing in the cold air, he reflected that for all the pretense with the library books she was really very intelligent, very good company. And she had had to take care of the old man all these years. She, like himself, had missed something out of life.

In the days that followed he saw her almost constantly. He met her brother Dominick and had the impression that Dominick was being put on parade for his inspection. He liked Dominick, who had a reserve that matched his own. When the thought came to him that his company was being taken for granted, he was rather grateful for the sense of belonging.

They did not go out with Dodson and Rosie again. Morlock was embarrassed about this but Dodson was unconcerned. "If you've got something lined up," he said, "good luck." He stopped laughing and said seriously, "Don't get in over your head, Al. Rosie's told me things about that Palaggi woman."

They spent most of their evenings in the living room. Dominick was seldom home and they had the crowded old room to themselves after the old man was sent off to bed. Morlock came to look forward to the long evenings, feeling pride in being eagerly welcomed, basking in the attention she paid him when he read to her.

Outside of the one poem which she had recited for him (she introduced it by saying, "This is my favorite, Al, by the author of . . ." just like a movie credit), she had nothing to contribute except her attention, but she made the most of this. She had a trick of resting her chin on her infolded hands and watching his face while he read or talked of what he had read. This, after the long years of bored and indifferent student audiences, was hardly short of intoxicating to Morlock, even while he guessed that her interest was at least partially a pose.

It even occurred to him from time to time that her objective almost had to be marriage. He did not run from the thought. It was almost enough to be wanted that much — on any terms.

Louise, after several evenings of this, was bored with Morlock's company in spite of her fondness for him. On New Year's Eve she sent him away early, letting him guess that she was sick. (He was shyly pleased with the delicate intimacy of the hinted revelation and the close relationship the very revelation itself implied.) He left, feeling quite gallant. When he was safely gone, she changed her dress and called a cab. Far enough from Federal Hill she allowed herself to be picked up in a cafe and thereafter surrendered herself to drinking and to her companion with complete abandon. It was the last time, she promised herself. Afterward she would be faithful to Morlock. After they were married. It did not occur to her that he might not ask her.

Gurney: That will be all for now, Mr. Dodson.
Cameron: Does the defense wish to question witness further?
Liebman: Not at this time.
Gurney: We would now like to introduce two documents which I will ask the Court to admit in evidence as exhibits A and B. I show them to counsel for the defense.
Liebman: I don't need to see them. I've already examined them.
Gurney: The documents, Your Honor, are a true copy of a marriage certificate issued in East Providence, Rhode Island, on January 9 of this year and signed by valid witnesses including Thomas Dodson, and a copy of an insurance —
Liebman: Now wait a minute — they haven't been admitted as evidence yet. You can't read them out.

Cameron: Let me have them, Mr. Gurney. . . . Do you have any objection to their admission as evidence, Mr. Liebman?
Liebman: No. I just didn't like the way counsel tried to get them in.
Cameron: They will be marked as requested and admitted as evidence.
Gurney: I show them to the jury. They are a marriage certificate dated January 9 of this year and an application to the Dempster Insurance Company for a policy on the life of Louise Palaggi — Louise Morlock, that is — dated January 10. He didn't waste any time, did he?
Cameron: That comment will be stricken. Mr. Gurney, I will not tolerate another such aside.

The Commonwealth of Massachusetts vs. Alvin Morlock.
Introduction of documentary evidence by Prosecution
Attorney Gurney.

Morlock and Dodson drove back to Warfield, the small town in which Ludlow College was located, on New Year's Day. Morlock had made a tentative agreement with Louise to come to Providence on the following week-end. Dodson was glum and taciturn as he faced the prospect of four more months in the classroom. Classes began two days later.

Morlock was lonesome for the first few days after his return. His room seemed emptier, his evenings longer than they had been before meeting Louise Palaggi. Soon enough the loneliness slipped away and he was guiltily conscious that he had perhaps missed the solitude as much as the companionship. At the end of three days he had already begun to consider various excuses to prevent his going back to Providence on the weekend.

That night, his landlady met him as he came in the door. "You've got a visitor," she said. "I invited her to wait in your room." The landlady — she knew romance when she saw it — wore a conspiratorial smile.

Morlock muttered, "Thank you," and hurried to the stairs, uncertain as to whether he was happy or annoyed. The visitor, he was certain, could only be Louise.

She was waiting inside the room. When Morlock entered, she ran to him and threw herself against him. "I got lonesome for you, Al," she said. "Are you glad I came?"

He remembered to put his arms around her. He was very glad, he told her; he told himself.

Louise had half expected that Morlock would call her during the early part of the week; when he did not she knew that she had overestimated the pull of her sex and that Morlock would probably cancel their date for the week-end. She had been, she decided, a shade too hard to get, and there remained only one thing to do. She would remind Morlock that she was a woman and that he was a man.

Morlock had planned to spend the evening correcting term papers. Now he hastily changed his plans. He called Dodson and arranged to borrow his car. He took Louise to dinner and a movie and drove her back to Providence. When they got out of Dodson's old car, she took his hand and said, "Come on in, Al."

When she had hung their coats in a closet she came and sat beside him on the couch. He was aware of the woman softness of her body, and he was convinced now that he had been glad to see her, convinced that he really had been lonely. When he reached for her she came into his arms with an eagerness that matched his own. The night dissolved in a warm bath of sex.

They were married five days later by a Justice of the Peace in East Providence. Dodson stood up for Morlock. Morlock would have liked to have asked the austere Paul Martin, whom he considered a closer friend than Dodson, but he had hesitated out of fear that Martin would not approve of Louise. Louise Palaggi stood alone. Morlock had supposed that there would be a rather elaborate wedding with a traditional Italian reception to follow. Louise explained that since she was marrying him, a non-Catholic, her family chose not to come. He was just as pleased, he told her, and half meant it.

Morlock approached the ceremony with a sort of tender determination. He did not love Louise. She had none of the qualities he had supposed he would look for in a wife. Still, she had an Old World approach to marriage. She would make a home for the two of them. If she was unlike him in intellect, she was like him in that she was alone and lonely. They would make an enduring marriage, he determined, and was a little embarrassed by his own feeling of nobility.

More than any other emotion, Louise felt a warm sense of security. She was a solid married woman with nothing to fear. She would be a good wife. She would cook Morlock's meals and keep his house clean. Even while she thought this, she had the feeling that they were children playing with dolls and that the whole thing was a game.

On the following day, Morlock, a tidy man in his personal and business habits, stopped at the Bursar's office to report his marriage. After the ritual flurry of congratulations by the girls working in the office, a heavy set man with a jovial face approached him.

"I'm Ed Hale," the man said. "I handle the insurance for the college. You'll want to increase your own insurance now, and we've got this little family policy that the college helps out with."

"I was going to take care of that later," Morlock said, wanting time to think about it.

"It won't take a minute," Hale said. He went on, bludgeoning Morlock, scenting a commission of a few dollars.

Morlock, already embarrassed by the very nature of his errand to the office, signed the application hurriedly and rushed away.

Chapter 6

Gurney: Your name is Anna Carofano?
Mrs. Carofano: That is my name.
Gurney: Are you married?
Mrs. Carofano: Not any more. My husband died three years ago.
Gurney: And you presently operate a rooming house in Warfield, Massachusetts. Is that correct?
Mrs. Carofano: More of the tenement than a rooming house. I've got three tenements in the building, not just rooms to rent.
Gurney: I see. Were you acquainted with the deceased?
Mrs. Carofano: You mean, did I know Louise Morlock? Sure, I knew her.
Liebman: If it please the Court, the defense will stipulate that the accused and his wife maintained a residence as man and wife in the tenement house belonging to Mrs. Carofano as of January 13 of this year.
Cameron: Mr. Gurney?
Gurney: We'll go along with the stipulation. Mrs. Carofano, would you say that they were happy while they were living in your house?
Liebman: Objection, Your Honor. The answer would be argumentative.
Cameron: I think in this case that the witness is reasonably qualified to express an opinion. I think we will let the question stand, Mr. Liebman. Do you wish an exception?
Liebman: No.

Mrs. Carofano: I don't know if he was happy or not. She wasn't.
Gurney: She told you that she wasn't?
Mrs. Carofano: Sure. A lot of times. He'd come home at night and read a book. She said he never talked to her unless they were having a fight.
Gurney: Did they quarrel frequently?
Mrs. Carofano: Sometimes it would be every night. Then, for a while they'd get along a little better. He was always criticizing her, the way she cooked, the way she kept house. And he never took her anywhere. She said he thought he was too good for her just because he was a teacher at the college.
Liebman: Your Honor, hasn't this gone far enough?
Cameron: I think the testimony is becoming irrelevant, Mr. Gurney.
Gurney: Yes, sir. Now, Mrs. Carofano, did the accused ever, to your knowledge, strike his wife?
Mrs. Carofano: I don't know if he did or not. I do know that more than once she was afraid to go home.
The Commonwealth of Massachusetts vs. Alvin Morlock.
Direct Testimony of Anna Carofano.

Morlock and his new wife moved into a hotel for the first few days of their marriage. It was agreed that Louise — Lolly, she liked him to call her — would find an apartment that they could afford. On the fourth night Morlock came home to the hotel to find her dressed and waiting.

"Al," she told him, "I've found a place. I paid a week's rent and there's some furniture in it already that we can have. Let's go and see it right away."

"Of course," he said. He was happy to see her excitement. Their marriage had thus far been prosaic. Morlock had fancied himself bringing home little gifts, finding her cooking his meals. This had been impossible in the greenhouse hotel existence. Now, with their own place, it would be different. He could bring Paul Martin home for dinner, a nice little affair with wine and after-dinner brandy. Morlock had never had an after-dinner brandy but he suspected that Paul Martin would be impressed by it.

Lolly seemed so happy at the prospect of moving that Morlock forced himself to hide his shock when they turned a corner and she said triumphantly, "There it is."

The tenement was ugly, sordid ugly. He had not expected a vine covered cottage; neither had he expected to live in a house that was flanked on one side by a grocery warehouse and on the other by a bar. When they were inside, he tried not to notice the cracked and stained linoleum, the leprous plaster. "It's nice, Lolly," he said. "We'll fix it up in no time at all." Later, when they left the house to go back to the hotel for the final night, he glanced around him and was struck by the thought that only this neighborhood in all of Warfield resembled Federal Hill in Providence; only this house and a few of its neighbors were architectural cousins to the three-deckers of Lolly's birthplace.

They bought appliances on credit. Morlock brought home paint and brushes and sandpaper and turpentine, with a little picture in his mind of a magazine cover picturing a young couple restoring an old tumbled down house. On the magazine covers the house had graceful lines — as did the people — and needed only a dash of paint to restore its beauty. The tenement that Lolly had picked for them needed more than paint.

There was a wooden wainscoting in the kitchen. It was about five feet high and covered with a Joseph's coat of a dozen layers of paint. Under all this paint, Morlock explained, there was undoubtedly fine walnut. (It was cypress.) This would be their first project. They would strip off the old paint and wax the fine wood. The boards in the wainscoting were eight inches wide.

There had been some excitement for Louise in the first few days of their marriage. When the excitement was burned out, there came the novelty of moving to the new tenement. Other women, she was aware, would have been content, happy, even, with the project of fixing up a home. She waited impatiently for the miracle to happen to her. The wooden boards of the wainscoting were symbolic. Starting with a section of two boards she began scraping and sanding. It was hard work and the turpentine raised welts on her hands. She stayed at it for most of a day, not quite knowing what would be revealed to her when she had stripped off the old paint. When Morlock came home he was delighted.

"It's beautiful, Lolly," he exclaimed. "Look at the grain of the wood."

Actually she had been disappointed. It was, as he had said, wood. She privately thought it had looked better with paint on it. On the following day she did two more boards and thereafter one at a time, sporadically. At the time Morlock went to trial for her murder, less than one wall was done.

For years, food had been to her something that you ate so that you would not be drinking on an empty stomach. But after they bought the stove and moved into the tenement, she made a real effort to plan and cook picture-book meals for Morlock. He came home one night to pot roast and mashed potatoes, broccoli and endive salad. The very next night he came home to cold pot roast and canned peas. The cooking phase lasted days less than the restoration phase.

There came a period when she became addicted to watching television, watching the day by day adventures of the heroines of the daytime serials. Other women, she knew, found them of absorbing interest. She convinced herself that she watched out of a sense of duty to Alvin. After just three weeks of marriage, she was having to fight hard to keep up any sort of pretense at being a happy housewife. One afternoon she walked toward the television set and stood staring down at the screen where a stereotyped heroine was weeping over her lover lost. Louise said out loud, "Bull—," and reached down and cut the set off. She was pleased with the word. She had carefully avoided swearing and vulgarisms except of the mildest kind since her marriage. She said it again. Then she took her coat from the bedroom closet and walked briskly from the tenement.

The bar and grill adjacent to their tenement was called Fagin's and the words, *Ladies Invited,* were stenciled on the front window. Louise walked in without hesitation. It was dim and smelled pungently of beer. A kaleidoscope of a juke box sang softly to itself in a corner of the room. She felt a long-missing contentment as she walked toward the bar and sat on a high stool. There was a sign behind the bar that had the words *Bartender on Duty* in red enamel over a small piece of slate. On the slate was chalked, *Jimmy.*

"I'll have a beer, Jimmy," she said pleasantly.

When it came, she sipped it slowly while she looked around the long room. There were half a dozen men drinking quietly at the bar. Four men were clustered about a shuffleboard table opposite the bar, noisily arguing about the game. There was one woman in the room and Louise automatically measured her. She was plain and quite fat; her face was raddled and her eyes vacuous. Louise discarded her.

When her beer was half gone the bartender brought a fresh glass and nodded toward the shuffleboard table. "On Billy Harrison, Miss," he said. She glanced swiftly along the bar. Jimmy, the bartender, had refilled all the glasses. Billy, whoever he was, had bought for the bar and was consequently not making a play for her. Nevertheless, she lifted the glass and turned and nodded in the direction of the shuffleboard players.

There had been a slight lessening of talk, of laughter, and a withdrawal when she walked in at the door and moved toward a stool. She had expected it and she had sensed it. When she had called the bartender by name, there had been a relaxation. Not complete but a relaxation when it became apparent that she was wife to no man in this place and was not here as a troublemaker. When she turned to salute the drink buyer, the noisy talk and laughter in the room returned to its former level. With the gesture she identified herself to these people as a fellow traveler if not a friend. A middle-aged man with a soft hat on at the far end of the bar took out a scratch sheet and began to study it. Now she was home. These were people she understood, friendly people who never read books and who cursed when they felt like it and used dirty words.

A young man took the stool beside her. He wore tight jeans and a gray sweatshirt. His hair was dark and curly and his eyes brown and beautifully clear. He smiled and nodded his head in the direction of the shuffleboard. "You play?" he asked.

"A little," she said, returning the smile and wishing that she had dressed more carefully.

"Want to challenge?" he asked.

"All right," she agreed. She was familiar with the Unwritten law that bar society had developed to keep traffic moving at the shuffleboard table. The winners of any game must accept any challenges or forfeit the table. The bar had a law of its own — not unwritten. The losing team must buy a round for the winners.

"My name's Eddie," he said. She remembered with a sharpness that other Eddie who had been a jockey.

"Call me Louise," she said happily.

"Okay, Louise. Try hard now. I'm on the tab already. You play on Billy Harrison's end. He's half stiff."

She felt vastly protective toward this handsome young man. She would save the game for them both. "Don't worry," she said confidently.

They played and won the first game, with Eddie shouting down encouragement from his end of the table. "Nice shot, Louise." And, "Way to go, Louise." She barely remembered in time not to show too much skill, not to beat Billy Harrison too badly. By the end of the game she was indelibly Louise to the other players and to all the patrons of the bar.

They were challenged and won again. Eddie was now openly

boasting of her, introducing her to every newcomer as his partner as proudly as if she were his wife. More proudly. They won beer and they bought beer and Louise glowed, happier than she had been since that afternoon when she heard the two young punks refer to her as having once been something to see. Well, she was something to see right now, wasn't she?

She planned shrewdly a means to protect these golden hours. If she were home at five there would be time to get Al's meal ready and straighten up the house a little. Then tomorrow afternoon — every afternoon — she could come to this place. As long as she left in time to get his supper ready. That left the mornings and the evenings. She could sleep late in the mornings. But she began already to begrudge Morlock the evenings, especially now at four o'clock on the afternoon of the day that she discovered Fagin's.

When they lost a game — "My fault, Louise," Eddie grimly admitted — they went back to the bar, taking stools beside the man with the scratch sheet. Louise had noted the men who came in and bought one or two drinks and talked briefly with this man, and she had placed him in his proper category. A bookmaker. She did not feel clever about her discovery. There would be one in a place such as this as a matter of course, and she accepted him as being the bookie as matter of factly as she accepted the bartender as being a bartender or the ladies' room as being a ladies' room.

More out of a desire to impress Eddie with her sophistication — she thought of it as knowing the score — than any urge to gamble, Louise asked the bookmaker, "Are they still broadcasting the fifth race at the Fairgrounds?"

He studied her briefly and then nodded. "If you want something, you'll have to put it in right away."

"Let me take your Armstrong," she asked. When he handed it to her, she glanced quickly at the entries with Eddie looking over her shoulder. She fumbled in her purse for money. "Five to win on War Command," she said casually.

Eddie asked Jimmy to turn the radio on. He said anxiously to Louise, "I don't know, partner. That favorite looks hard to beat."

"He can't carry that much weight," she reassured him.

War Command broke fast out of the starting gate. He was in front by three lengths down the back stretch, by five turning for home and by seven lengths under the wire. Eddie, throughout the race, moaned and pleaded, "Stay out there. Come on, baby, stay out there!" Louise watched him with a tolerant, almost maternal smile.

The man in the soft hat gave Louise twenty-eight dollars. She handed ten of it to Eddie. "We're partners," she said when he made a token protest. Then she bought a round of drinks for the bar. She felt confident, sure of herself, but she watched the clock. At fifteen minutes before five she got up to go.

Her friends mourned. Couldn't she stay for another one? How about one more game, Louise?

She walked toward the door, a woman of determination and dignity. Jimmy, the bartender, called anxiously, "We'll see you again, Louise?"

At the door, she turned and smiled. "Sure," she said. "See you tomorrow."

Except for the prospect of a long evening with Al, she was quite happy.

Louise hurried up the granite steps to their tenement. Mrs. Carofano, the landlady, was sweeping the front hall on the first floor. Louise smiled and started up the stairs. Mrs. Carofano called after her, "What's the rush? Stop and have a cup of coffee with me."

Louise smiled again and shook her head. "I have to get Al's supper," she said, feeling vaguely like a martyr.

In the kitchen she hastily set out a meal. She waited, in some apprehension, for Morlock to come in. She retained some of the Old World attitude toward marriage that was prevalent on Federal Hill. Women — wives — did not go out drinking in public cafes in the afternoon. She considered chewing gum or brushing her teeth to eliminate the odor of beer and decided against it. Let him find out. It would be interesting to see what he would do about it. She knew what her father or her brother, Dominick, would have done. What they would have done, Morlock didn't do. He came in and kissed her absently, not noticing the odor if any remained. Louise did not feel relieved but resentful.

Morlock had a habit of reading while he ate. He had given it up in the first days of their marriage but had lately resumed it. She watched him as he ate. After supper he would read the paper or correct student examinations, seldom speaking. He would probably stay up until long after she, in boredom, had gone to bed.

Morlock had tried, at first, to make conversation as he had made it in the parlor of Louise's home on Federal Hill, but it had been one-sided. Louise was inconceivably uninformed about the subjects in which Morlock was interested. When he tried, as he had planned earlier, to bring the arts to her, he found that she preferred to turn the television set on — with the volume turned up high enough to prevent conversation.

They had had their first serious quarrel several days before Louise's excursion to Fagin's Bar. She was, it had developed, an atrocious housekeeper. Morlock had gone to the bathroom to wash before eating. When he had wet the facecloth and brought it up to his forehead, he had been revolted by the sour odor of curdled soap. He had been angry enough to say, "For God's sake, Lolly, the least you could do is rinse a few things out once in a while."

She had promptly sailed into battle, almost happily it seemed to him, beating at him with words he would not have believed she knew. Out of his anger he had exploded with a list of her shortcomings. With every one that he mentioned she had responded with a torrent of vileness.

For two weeks after her first visit, Louise spent her afternoons in Fagin's Bar. It developed that Anna Carofano was also a regular at the place and Louise complained to her many times. "He don't give a damn," she said bitterly. "I cook his meals and keep his house clean and all he does is sit there with his damn books." The fact that she neither kept the house clean nor went to any pains to cook a decent meal, Louise considered beside the point. Nevertheless, during the two-week period she carefully left the bar in time to be home when Morlock arrived. She let it be known that she did this out of fear of her husband, getting satisfaction out of the stature this impression of her as an abused wife gave.

One day she didn't bother to leave in time to be home when Morlock arrived. She had been engrossed in a gin rummy game in which she had won heavily, and she had been drinking whisky rather than her usual beer.

She came in the house an hour after Morlock had arrived. Before she opened the door she armed herself with a defensive anger in case he chose to make something of her lateness.

Morlock was sitting at the kitchen table. Hearing her, not looking up, he said mildly, "Hello, Lolly. Been to a movie?"

She stood in the doorway, swaying slightly. After a moment she said something so obscene that Morlock was briefly stunned. When he did not immediately respond, she repeated the phrase. This time he rose from his chair, his face pale.

"You're drunk," he said.

"What if I am, professor?" she said, raising her voice. "You're too good to get drunk, I suppose. What about that night in Providence when you puked all over your bed?"

"Lolly," he said. "For God's sake."

She stared vaguely at him, remembering that she was furious but completely unable to recall what she was furious about or if there was anything to be furious about. She clutched at the first thing that came into her mind. "Books," she said. She made it sound as if she had spat. "You and your books. You want me to tell you what you can do with your damn books?"

Morlock, defenseless in the face of her irrational anger, said, "That's enough, Lolly. Let me help you to bed now and we'll talk about it in the morning."

She was slightly appeased now that she had his attention. She held up another grievance, selecting it like a candy from a box. "A movie," she said bitterly. "That's what we do around here for a big time. Why don't anyone ever come to see us? Your fat friend Dodson, he's the only one you bring home. Well — him."

"Lolly," he pleaded, "keep your voice down. Let me help you to bed. I'll make you some coffee and bring it to you."

Her mood suddenly changed. "All right," she said. She giggled. "You'll have to help me off with my clothes."

In the bedroom she lay deliberately limp on the bed while he tugged and hauled to undress her and to get her nightgown on. When he was finished, she pulled him to her and kissed him wetly. Morlock pulled away, and then, fearing that she would sense his revulsion and become furious again, looked for an excuse.

"I'll go make the coffee," he said. "We'll have a cup of coffee and a cigarette together first." He hated himself for the hypocrisy, but when he had gone to the kitchen he moved as deliberately as he could, hoping that she would fall asleep.

This was the second of their quarrels. Thereafter they were repeated almost weekly. On the occasion of a later quarrel Morlock became furious himself; a mistake he did not repeat. Her coarseness, the obscenity of the accusations she made, completely shattered him. He could not match her in either volume or vileness. After that quarrel they made no pretense of making up.

She began to go out in the evenings, usually pretending that she was going to a movie with Anna Carofano. Morlock was not fooled by the pretense, but he did not particularly care. After three months of marriage, he preferred solitude. As an escape from the sordid atmosphere of the tenement, he began to dwell more and more in the past. He became aware of a longing to return to the scenes of his boyhood.

After the humiliating time with the Dean and the appliance company and the loan agency, he decided to implement the longing. On the next Sunday he arose early. Lolly was still asleep; he dressed quietly and went out to have coffee in a restaurant. In the afternoon, after they had had dinner, he decided, he would try once more to talk with Lolly. Their marriage, on its present basis, was impossible. He considered divorce or separation only as remote extremes. He had not married Lolly for love. He could not exactly define now why he had married her. There had been the flattery of her attention on those long evenings in the three-decker house on the Hill. There had been the warmth, after the empty years, of being expected and wanted. There is some Pygmalion in every person. He had recognized her lack of culture and wanted the egotistic satisfaction of developing her mind. The cliché was repugnant but it was a part of the marriage. There had been sex, of course. And still another part of the marriage was — sympathy? Knowing these things and admitting them, he could not now divorce her or leave her when she seemed so badly in need of help.

He finished his coffee and left the restaurant to walk through streets, dozing in Sunday somnolence, to Dodson's rooming house. Dodson's bedraggled convertible was parked at the curb. He knocked at the door and entered. Inside the building he walked through the old-fashioned, high-ceilinged hall to Dodson's room.

Dodson was asleep. He woke him. "Tom," he said, "I'd like to borrow your car for a couple of hours."

Dodson said sleepily, "Go ahead. The keys are on the dresser." He asked more alertly, "Anything wrong, Al?"

"No. I just want to take a little drive and do some thinking."

Dodson turned over and went back to sleep. Morlock took the keys and went out to the old LaSalle. Dodson kept the engine in good running order and it started easily. Morlock headed out of Warfield on the road to South Danville, the town where he had been born, where he had been a boy, and where he had not returned in fifteen years although it was only a short ride from Warfield.

He had a half-formed idea of driving through the town and seeing how much of it he remembered. He did not intend to visit Abram's Rock until he stopped at a filling station for gas; then, remembering that it was only half a mile away, he had a tremendous urge to see it again.

The filling station attendant was helpful. "Sure," he said. "There's still a road leading right up close to the rock; but you'd better not try to make it in the car. The mud would be right up to the axles."

Could he, Morlock asked, park in back of the station and walk in? He could. He got out of the old LaSalle and started walking toward the great gray boulder. He felt an odd excitement as he entered the grove surrounding the rock. The air was warm and turbulent with the promise of spring. Abram's Rock seemed as awesomely solid, as overwhelmingly huge as it had in the vanished years. Morlock, slowly climbing its flank, remembered the solace he had found here as a child. Even now the rock had that power. Here he had played with Marianna Cruz. Here he had come when he was troubled. Here he had made plans and dreamed dreams. The plans had been fruitless and the dreams had been just dreams. But on Abram's Rock this seemed of little importance.

Chapter 7

Gurney: You have given your name as William Davis. Will you tell the jury your occupation, please?

Davis: I operate a filling station in South Danville.

Gurney: And that is near Warfield, isn't it?

Davis: Twenty miles, maybe.

Gurney: Did you ever see the accused before?

Davis: Yes.

Gurney: He was brought up in South Danville. Did you know that?

Davis: I heard about it since the trial began. I've only lived there six years or so myself. I didn't know him from the other time he lived there.

Gurney: Under what circumstances did you see the accused?

Davis: He drove up one day in a big old LaSalle convertible. You don't see many of them any more. I guess that's why I remembered him. He bought five gallons of gas and asked if the road to Abram's Rock was still open.

Gurney: Abram's Rock?

Davis: It's a big boulder, maybe two hundred feet high. There's a dirt road leading there from the back of the gas station but you can't drive a car over it in the spring. Too muddy.

Liebman; The witness is neither a geologist or a weather forecaster. Can't we get on with this trial? I'm sure the prosecution will have adequate descriptions of Abram's Rock for our benefit from more qualified witnesses.

Gurney: Your Honor, the prosecution intends to show premeditation in this crime. We are trying to develop that the accused, Morlock, knew every inch of Abram's Rock.

Cameron: We will bear with you.

Gurney: Mr. Davis, you have testified that Morlock asked you if the road to Abram's Rock was open. When did this take place?

Davis: About a month before he killed —

Liebman: Your Honor!

Cameron: The jury will ignore the interjection by the witness. Mr. Davis, you will confine yourself to answering the questions of counsel without volunteering conclusions.

Gurney: That would have been in the early part of April?

Davis: Yes.

Gurney: What did he do after you told him about the road being muddy?

Davis: He asked me if he could park his car in the back of the station. I told him he could and he did. He got out and started walking up the road toward Abram's Rock.

Gurney: Did anything in his manner at that time strike you as peculiar?

Davis: He seemed sort of . . . fuzzy.

Gurney: How long was he gone?

Davis: An hour and a half, maybe.

Gurney: Did you see him again on subsequent days?

Davis: Sure. After that he came every Sunday. He'd park the car and walk across the fields.

The Commonwealth of Massachusetts vs. Alvin Morlock.
Direct testimony of William Davis.

When he had made his way to the top of the rock, Morlock sought out a sunny spot protected from the wind and sat down, giving himself over to a sort of bitter nostalgia. The rock had called to him and he had come, drawn to it by all the powers of memory. Not all the memories were pleasant; he had come here when his father died, when he was twelve. He had never known his father well; he remembered him not as a parent but as a wasted, infinitely patient man who spent his days and his months and years in a ground-floor bedroom. Morlock did not see him often but he did remember his eyes, dulled with pain and shame. He had some illness that they did not speak of. Morlock's mother, each day of her life, performed some service for her husband from which she would return, closing the bedroom door softly behind her while she closed her eyes for a moment in weary repugnance. She never complained aloud.

Morlock had two older sisters; these two, with his mother, made all the preparations for the funeral, leaving him very much to himself. A few aunts and uncles came. Morlock saw that these were as poor as his own immediate family. He had no suit for the ceremony and there was no money — there never was — to buy one. His mother made over a gray flannel suit that had been given to one of his sisters during a period of service as a maid. He wore this to the church and to the cemetery.

It rained steadily during the actual burial. At twelve, just beginning to be conscious of his clothes, he stood in the rain, self-consciously aware of the ill-fitting suit and of the ragged haircut one of the uncles had given him at the last moment. To compensate for his clothes, he stood as straight as he could so that some of the sparse gathering patted him on the head and said, "There's a little man."

When it was over and they gathered in the living room of their house to make plans, Morlock hurried to his room and changed his clothes. Slipping out of the back door so that no one would see him and call to him to stay in the house, he made his way through the fields to Abram's Rock, the wet grass whipping his bare legs as he ran. Near the top of the rock was a great crevice that was bridged by a fallen tree, making a shelter of sorts. He climbed to the crevice and crawled beneath the tree so that he was partially protected from the rain. Then, only then, he began to cry, his head tucked against his drawn-up knees. He cried partly out of the aching, conventional sorrow of a boy at losing his father, but also out of pity for the man who had spent those years in that musty smelling bedroom and out of grief for the shame in that man's eyes.

When he was finished with crying he looked up, not having heard anyone approaching but sensing a presence, and saw at the level of his vision a pair of bare brown legs emerging from a skirt of some coarse material. He came out from beneath his shelter to see the Portagee kid — he so identified her in his quick, shamed anger at being found in tears — standing quite still and gravely watching him. He said petulantly, "What are you doing out in the rain, kid? Don't you have any sense?"

She said quietly, "You're out in it. Why were you crying?"

He bent his head and tried to steady his voice. "My father died," he said.

She skipped across the crevice and slid down beside him, sitting as still as he. "I'm sorry," she said. "My mother died when I was eight."

For perhaps several minutes neither of them spoke again. Morlock no longer resented her presence; she no longer intruded in his grief but rather shared it and made it lighter for him. After a time he said, "You shouldn't be out in this rain. You'll catch your death of cold." Unconsciously, speaking to this child younger than himself, he parroted the words his mother had used a hundred times.

She shrugged. "Where I used to live it rains all the time. Nobody minds it. Besides," she gestured in the direction of the farm where her people lived, "everybody is drunk back there. They always get drunk when they can't go out and work in the fields."

Morlock was shocked by the blunt explanation. Drunkenness was a disgrace and a shameful thing that people spoke about in whispers. He felt pity for this child who spoke of it so calmly without knowing what she was saying. He said uneasily, "I'm sorry."

She shrugged. "It doesn't matter. They hit each other and throw things. By and by they go to sleep. It doesn't matter." Morlock found her accent pretty and wished she would speak more. She stood up. "I guess they asleep now. I go get something to eat. You hungry, boy?"

Morlock shook his head.

"We can sneak into the kitchen and get something if you like," she said.

"I guess I'd better go home myself," he said. He started the descent to the ground. When he was halfway down he looked back. She was standing where he had left her. When she saw him looking back, she called, "I'm sorry about your father. You come here tomorrow?"

Because he was a boy he called back casually, "I guess so. Maybe." But on the way home he felt an odd anticipation at the thought of seeing her again.

His mother was alone in the kitchen when he came in the house; the uncles, the aunts and the sisters were in the parlor. She looked at him, wet and forlorn in the doorway. They were an undemonstrative family, but she made a rare gesture. She came toward him and dropped to her knees and hugged him wordlessly.

They were used to being poor, but hardly as poor as they were in the time directly after his father's death. There were periods when they were actually hungry. Morlock helped as much as a young boy could. He had his lawns to mow, his errands to run. He spent the entire afternoon of one bad day gathering empty bottles and making the rounds of the stores collecting the few cents' deposit on them. When he had collected enough money, he bought frankfurters and rolls and a small package of tea. These things he brought to his mother as another boy would have brought the first silvery pussywillows of the spring. When their financial pressures eased some and there was time for play, he spent all of that time at Abram's Rock with Marianna Cruz. Their games were solemn games played without the boisterous clamor that other children made. Morlock told her the legend of Abram's Rock. She was fascinated with it and they enacted it many times. Often she would bring food to the Rock. Later in the year, when the corn ripened in the neighboring fields, they would steal a few ears. These they would roast in hot ashes. They would play their sober games until the shadows of the hemlocks lay long across the mossy flanks of Abram's Rock. It was, for Morlock, a golden summer.

They were seldom bothered by the other children. Occasionally a crowd of them would come whooping to the Rock and join in whatever game the two were playing but the games never held them long. They would stay for a time and then, like a noisy flock of starlings, they would whirl away in a group. Once one of them shouted as if it were a shocking state of affairs that Marianna was Morlock's girl. The rest of them took it up, giggling and gossiping, hoping to shame Morlock and the girl. Morlock's reaction was more of surprise than resentment or shame. He seldom considered Marianna to be a girl. She was a comrade and a friend.

The summer waned and before they were aware of it it was time for school to begin.

Morlock asked her, "What grade will you be in?" He himself would be in the sixth.

She had been unusually quiet for several days. Morlock had supposed it was because of some family situation. Now she said in a troubled voice, "Woman was out to the house to see my fa'der. I will be in the first grade." She looked straight at him, holding his eyes with hers in a way she had. "I'm afraid to go there to that school," she continued.

Morlock, who liked school with its books and its crayons and its pencils, asked in astonishment, "Why should you be afraid? You'll like it!"

She began to cry very softly. "Way I talk," she said. "Way I dress. I got no good clothes. They will laugh at me."

Morlock said loyally, "There's nothing wrong with the way you talk." He felt a rage at the thought that they might laugh at her, and he continued fiercely, "They better not. You can walk to school with me if you want to. I won't let anyone laugh at you."

Her face brightened. "Then I won't be afraid," she said with complete faith.

Morlock, the following morning, half regretted that he had invited her to walk with him to school. They would laugh, certainly, at the way she talked and the way she dressed, and he could not defend her against the whole school. And they would laugh at him for walking with her. Yet he had promised and so he waited for her.

She came early, walking quite slowly, head down, until she saw Morlock waiting for her. Then she began to walk faster, hurrying toward him. When she was abreast of him she slowed again and they walked on together. As they came nearer to the school, the sidewalk began to blossom with the back-to-school dresses of little girls and she began to hang back. Morlock, out of a sudden pity, said, "Don't be afraid, Marianna."

Now there were small boys and big boys; at the fence that bounded the schoolyard a whole cluster of them. When they saw Morlock and the girl they began to jeer and catcall. "Hey, Alvin — where did you get the Portagee girl friend?" And, "Hey, Portagee! Bet those are the first shoes you had on all year!"

Morlock felt a furious flush of embarrassment. Then he felt Marianna's small hand creep into his own and he was ashamed of the embarrassment, ashamed of the regret that he had earlier felt at having offered to let her walk with him. This was his friend of the golden summer and to be ashamed of her was worse than being a traitor. He held his head high and said aloud, "Don't pay any attention to them, Marianna. I'll take you to your teacher." And he wished that he could kill them all.

There were yet a few weeks of summer. They met after school each day at Abram's Rock, which by now was almost like a home to them. It was their refuge, their sanctuary, and they knew every nook and cranny, every weathered scar on its great gray flanks.

Chapter 8

Gurney: Your name is Paul Martin and you are an instructor at Ludlow College, is that correct?

Martin: It is.

Gurney: What is your subject, Mr. Martin?

Martin: I hold a masters degree in chemistry.

Gurney: What is your relationship to the accused?

Martin: Morlock? He is a colleague. He is — was — an instructor at Ludlow.

Gurney: Not a friend?

Martin: Hardly. Morlock did make overtures. I would say that we were acquaintances.

Gurney: What form did the overtures take?

Martin: I don't know. It's hard to say exactly. He made a point of seeking me out, trying to cultivate me. He was rather a lonely man before his marriage. I felt sorry for him.

Gurney: Before that marriage did you ever spend an evening with him?

Martin: Several. We would have dinner and then perhaps go to a movie.

Gurney: I am certain that you made no excursions to Providence with Morlock.

Martin: Certainly not.

Gurney: What about after the marriage?

Martin: He asked me several times to take dinner at his home. When it would have become embarrassing to refuse again, I accepted.

Gurney: And when was that?

Martin: About a month before his wife's death. In April, it would have been.

Gurney: She was present at that dinner?

Martin: Yes.

Gurney: In what condition?

Liebman: Objection.

Cameron: Sustained.

Gurney: Put it this way — in the course of the evening did she consume any alcoholic beverages?

Martin: She did.

Gurney: To the extent that she was visibly affected?
Liebman: You're just putting the same question in different words.
Cameron: I'll have to agree with defense counsel. What are you trying to demonstrate with this line of questioning, Mr. Gurney?
Gurney: I'm trying to show a motive. I want to demonstrate that the accused found himself in an intolerable situation. He fancied himself quite a gentleman; too good for the deceased. He was especially anxious to impress Mr. Martin. With her around, he couldn't make the pretense.
Cameron: I think I will let you continue, Mr. Gurney. Please be more careful in the manner in which you elicit testimony.
Gurney: Thank you, Your Honor. Mr. Martin, what was the result of Louise Morlock's drinking?
Martin: Her conduct became embarrassing. I had been trying to carry on a conversation with her — out of politeness. She had very little to say. When I tried to draw her out, she became quieter — that was at first — and hardly spoke at all.
Gurney: Was the accused visibly affected by her conduct — this withdrawal, this refusal even to carry on a conversation?
Martin: Oh, yes. He seemed annoyed at first. The situation was awkward. I finally tried to steer the conversation around to something that would at least be of interest to Morlock and myself. He was, well — sullen would be the word for it. I supposed that he was embarrassed about his wife's behavior.

The Commonwealth of Massachusetts vs. Alvin Morlock.
Direct testimony of Paul Martin.

On the afternoon of the Sunday he first revisited Abram's Rock, Morlock returned Dodson's car and went home to find Louise up and dressed and making motions at straightening up the house, which she sometimes did following her nights out with Anna Carofano. "Lolly," he said, "I've got to have a talk with you." She glanced at him and returned to her dusting. "I'm here," she said. "I'd like you to sit down, Lolly. This is important."

"All right. Do you want a cup of coffee?"

"No, thanks." He sat down at the kitchen table. "The Dean had a letter from the appliance company last week, asking him to make me take care of our account."

She started to speak and Morlock shook his head.

"Don't lie about it, Lolly. I've already talked to them. There hasn't been any mistake. You haven't paid the bill. Do you have any of the money put away?"

"No."

Morlock continued quietly, "We can't go on the way we're going, Lolly. I've borrowed enough money to bring us up to date. I'd better handle the money from now on. Do you mind telling me what you did with it?" When she did not immediately answer he continued, "Let it go. We can't do anything about it now, anyway. I've been thinking, Lolly. Maybe part of all this is my fault. I do bring home a lot of work and we haven't had friends in."

She was quick to seize the initiative. "Because you think I'm not good enough for them. I know all about that."

"I'm going to ask Paul Martin to dinner," he said. "I've told you about him." He had several times mentioned to Martin that he would like to have him out for dinner some evening, being careful to make the remark indefinite enough not to suggest an immediate acceptance. Now, he decided, he would ask Martin to come — the following evening, in fact. If Martin was snooty about the tenement or Lolly that was just too bad.

He asked Martin the following morning. "Paul," he said when he met Martin in the hall, "Louise and I would like to have you come to dinner tonight if you aren't busy." He was both relieved and worried when Martin, even though somewhat condescendingly, accepted.

Morlock left the college as early as he could that afternoon. He hurried home in some anxiety, fearful that Lolly might not be all right. He had come to measure her by this standard — she was all right and had not been drinking, or she was not all right. Her all-right evenings were becoming increasingly rare. She had become more and more excited over the prospect of Martin's visit, rousing from the sulking mood that she had adopted when Morlock had taken the handling of family money from her.

She actually had the house cleaned up when Morlock arrived. She had scrubbed the kitchen, where they must necessarily eat, and borrowed curtains somewhere. She greeted him gaily. "You're home early, Al. How does it look?"

He answered enthusiastically, "Fine. Lovely," feeling that she was as eager as he to make something of this fresh start-, as willing as he to contribute more than a fair share toward its success.

They had decided upon veal cutlets for the main course. There would be wine with the meal. Morlock, when he went out to buy food for the dinner, also bought a bottle of brandy — the brandy intended to impress Martin.

Martin arrived a few minutes before seven. Morlock and Louise had been waiting for him for perhaps ten minutes. She had bathed and put on a black taffeta dress that became her very well. This, Morlock thought, is marriage. The couple you saw on the covers of the household magazines, dressed up and eagerly waiting to shower hospitality on their callers. Things would be better now and it certainly was his fault, the way Lolly had acted. Why hadn't he done this before?

Martin knocked at the door; Morlock had given him explicit instructions about how to reach the tenement — apartment, he had called it — and Morlock rushed forward to open it.

"Good evening," Martin said, shrugging out of his topcoat. He glanced about him as he did so, and Morlock watched him anxiously. He had intimated to Martin that the place was laughably Bohemian. "Third floor, you know, and a smell of cooking cabbage eternally in the halls." Now he fretted over whether Martin would keep up the pretense that the tenement was truly Bohemian and not just sordid. Martin was noncommittal. "Quite a place you have here," he continued. "So hard to find a decent rent," Morlock murmured.

"Lolly, this is Mr. Martin. He's the chemistry instructor at the college. Sit down, won't you, Paul, I'll mix a drink."

Lolly smiled and admitted that she had heard a great deal about Mr. Martin and that she was pleased and she would have one too, please, Al. Morlock went to the kitchen and mixed drinks, making Lolly's very weak. When he brought them in Martin was seated, talking to Lolly.

"I was surprised that Alvin married," he said. "I'd thought he was a confirmed bachelor like myself." His tone indicated that he was quite satisfied to remain single. "Did he struggle much?"

Fine, Morlock thought. They were going to get along. Paul wasn't going to be patronizing.

Morlock made a second round of drinks, leaving Lolly out, while she cooked the supper. When it was ready they sat at the kitchen table to eat, Morlock watching Martin anxiously to see if he liked the food. Apparently he did. He ate hungrily and had several glasses of red wine. Near the end of the meal he said, "I'm very fond of Italian cooking. You are Italian, aren't you, Mrs. Morlock?"

"My people were," she explained.

"From Providence," Morlock added. "They're in the construction field."

Martin nodded. "I see. What school did you go to, Mrs. Morlock?"

Martin was referring to college, using the casual "school" in the affected manner of an educational snob. Morlock knew this, and tried to guess if Martin was deliberately being sarcastic.

Completely misunderstanding, Lolly said, "Gordon High — but I never finished. I had to stay home and take care of my father." The explanation sounded ridiculously contrived — a line from *East Lynn* or *Over the Hill* — Morlock hurriedly suggested that they go into the living room for brandy, trying to create the impression that this was a nightly habit in this household. Lolly stayed in the kitchen to clear off the dishes. By the time she rejoined them, Martin had had two brandies and was becoming increasingly expansive. He rose when she came into the room.

"We were talking about your husband's favorite subject," he explained. "I've been telling him that the Bacon myth might not be as much a fantasy as he believes." Morlock had more than once suspected that Martin's own knowledge of literature was superficial, consisting of a few catchwords and stock phrases. He had accused himself uneasily, on those occasions, of being disloyal. Martin continued, "Are you a great reader, Mrs. Morlock?"

She had seated herself in the chair opposite the couch where the two men sat. Morlock brought her a drink — a small brandy. She apologized that she didn't really read very much.

Martin held out his empty glass to Morlock and expertly switched the conversation to hypnotism. "You've been reading about the reversion techniques, I suppose?"

She had not been following them too closely, she explained.

It became a nightmare. Morlock was at first grateful to Martin for trying to find a subject in which Lolly would feel at ease. After the third or fourth change of subject he realized that Martin was probing and exposing, deliberately humiliating her. She knew nothing of the ballet, of history, or of painting. She knew, it appeared, very little about anything.

Morlock could see what Martin was doing but he was helpless to prevent it. His immediate reaction was anger that Martin should so needlessly spoil his little party. His second reaction was one of pity for Louise who was by this time, numbly shaking her head to most of Martin's questions. He was embarrassed for her rather than ashamed of her, and he tried several times to rescue her. When Martin persisted in his probing, Morlock began to hate him for his cruelty, but before his emotions overcame his good manners Martin contemptuously discarded Louise. He began a discussion of college affairs with Morlock in which Louise could have no possible interest. After a while she excused herself and went out to the kitchen. Morlock, preoccupied with concern for Louise and thoroughly disliking Martin by this time, contributed very little to the conversation.

Liebman: You testified on direct examination that Louise Morlock's conduct became embarrassing on the night of your visit to Morlock's home.
Martin: I did.
Liebman: To digress a moment, Mr. Martin, are you a British citizen?
Martin: Certainly not.
Liebman: Educated in Britain?
Gurney: Your Honor, the nationality and educational background of the witness can have no possible bearing on this matter.
Liebman: I'd like to point out that counsel for the prosecution has made a point of establishing the educational background of previous witnesses as well as the accused. By the rules of evidence it becomes my prerogative —
Cameron: You need not continue, Mr. Liebman. Since the prosecution has elicited testimony as to educational background on direct examination, you have the privilege of rebuttal in kind.
Liebman: Thank you, Your Honor. Mr. Martin, you state that you are not a British citizen and that you were not educated in Great Britain. Yet I have detected a strong British flavor in your speech. Where did you get the accent, Mr. Martin — is it an affectation?
Gurney: Objection. The character of the witness cannot be assailed on such a flimsy basis.
Cameron: Sustained. Mr. Liebman's final remark will be stricken.
Liebman: Your Honor, I am questioning the credibility of the witness. It appears to me that any man contemptible enough to disclaim a friendship and cheap enough to affect an accent —
Cameron: That will do, Mr. Liebman.
Liebman: Mr. Martin, where did you actually go to college?
Martin: Canton, Ohio.
Liebman: Did you ever travel abroad?
Cameron: The witness will speak up.

Martin: No.

Liebman: On the night of your visit to Morlock's home did you drink any alcoholic beverages yourself?

Martin: Yes. Brandy. And wine with dinner.

Liebman: You don't suppose your own conduct might have been affected?

Gurney: Objection.

Cameron: Sustained.

Liebman: Mr. Martin, when the conduct of the deceased woman became embarrassing, what was the reaction of the accused?

Martin: Well, naturally I left early. Morlock walked down the stairs with me. He was bitterly angry.

> *The Commonwealth of Massachusetts vs. Alvin Morlock.*
> *Cross-examination of Paul Martin.*

Morlock paid little attention to Lolly's absence in the kitchen. She returned after a few moments only to go back to the kitchen again after listening to Martin's droning conversation. Martin himself had rather more than a moderate amount of Morlock's brandy. When Lolly returned for the second time, she sat in her chair in such a manner that her skirt was pulled above her knees. When she did not rearrange her clothing immediately, Morlock looked more closely at her face and saw the vacuous half smile that she usually wore when she had been out with the Carofano woman. When he went to the kitchen on a trumped-up excuse, he saw that she had been drinking from the bottle of whisky he had used to make their before-dinner highballs.

He hurried back into the living room to hear her say, "Do you like what you see, Mr. Martin? Would you like to see more?" With the words she pulled her skirt higher.

Morlock said, "Stop it, Louise," and wheeled to explain to Martin. Martin, when he turned, was laughing.

"Let her alone, Alvin," Martin said. "I want to see what she'll do next."

She turned suddenly sullen "Books," she said. "All you know about is books, either one of you." Her voice became more shrill. "You think I'm just an ignorant Dago from Federal Hill, don't you? I'm not as ignorant as you think."

Morlock stepped over to put his hand on her arm.

"Don't, Lolly," he pleaded. "Nobody thinks anything of the kind."

She flung his hand away. "What do you know about it?" she

snapped. "You're not so much. You're not even any good in bed." She laughed sharply. "You're a fairy, that's what I think. Both of you. A couple of fairies."

She began to cry. Martin stood up. "I think I'd better go, Morlock," he said coldly.

Morlock turned away from Lolly. "I think you'd better," he answered. "I'll get your coat." He got the coat from the closet and handed it to Martin, not holding it out for him to put on. When Martin was ready, Morlock opened the door to the hall and snapped the light switch. The dingy hall remained dark. "The bulb is probably burned out," he said. "I'll see you to the street." He turned back to glance at Lolly who was huddled in her chair, still crying. "I'll be right back," he called gently.

He preceded Martin to the street and walked a few paces from the door with him. "Martin," he said, "that was one of the crudest exhibitions I ever saw in my life. If I was half a man I would have thrown you out of my house when you started dissecting her."

Martin paused. "Oh, come, Morlock," he said. "She *is* an ignorant Dago from Federal Hill. And a drunkard. I didn't make her what she is."

"She was all right," Morlock said. "She was trying to be nice and entertain you because you were my friend. She really tried, you dirty bastard. Don't ever even say good morning to me again." He was annoyed with the childish sound of his ultimatum, and he wheeled away from Martin without saying more.

When he was a few steps from the tenement entrance he saw Lolly rush out of the door, and he called after her. When she did not turn, he ran after her. She entered a building that was gay with neon tubing and he followed after her so swiftly that he had to fling up his hand to keep the door from hitting him in the face. Fast as he was, she was already seated at the bar when he closed the door behind him. He walked to her side, feeling he had had enough scenes for this day. "Come on home, Lolly. I told him off. The whole thing was his fault."

The bartender brought her a drink, putting it down warily.

She turned to face Morlock. The tears had spoiled her careful make-up but she was no longer crying. She laughed and cried shrilly, "Get away from me, you damn fairy."

Pleading with her would accomplish nothing; Morlock was certain of that. In the face of the hostile, staring faces in the room he could only retreat as quietly as possible.

He waited until past two o'clock for her to come home, and finally fell asleep in a kitchen chair. She could probably never sustain the excitement of getting ready for a visitor over any period of time. Martin was probably right — she was a drunk and there was no chance for this marriage. He hated Martin for destroying what chance there had been — if there had been a chance — because it had not been Martin's right. He was certain that there would not be another chance.

Chapter 9

Gurney: I call Francis Macomber to the stand. For the record, now that you have been sworn, will you give your occupation?

Macomber: I am a second class patrolman on the Warfield Police Force.

Gurney: You have a regular tour of duty — a beat?

Macomber: Yes. It takes in Kosciusko Street north and south to Main and Chestnut.

Gurney: Do you know an Anna Carofano?

Macomber: I do. She owns a couple of tenements on my beat.

Gurney: Do you know the accused in this case?

Macomber: I do now.

Gurney: Did you ever see him prior to this trial?

Macomber: I did.

Gurney: Officially — in the line of duty?

Macomber: Yes. On the evening of April 17.

Gurney: What happened on that occasion?

Macomber: It was about six o'clock. I was making the rounds, checking doors and like that, when I saw a woman sitting on the steps of one of Mrs. Carofano's tenements. The accused was standing beside her. I was a block away. I couldn't hear anything and it didn't look like anything out of the ordinary at first. Then I saw him —

Gurney: Who?

Macomber; The accused. Morlock. I saw him lift his hand and slap her across the face. I ran up to where they were. She was crying. He hit her at least three more times before I could reach him and grab his arm.

Gurney: Were there any witnesses to this sorry business?

Macomber: You know how people are. If they see a cop move fast they figure something has happened and they swarm around. I guess maybe a dozen people were there.

Gurney: What happened then?

Macomber: I said to him, "Cut that out. I'm a police officer." The woman got up and ran up the steps and into the house. Morlock — the accused — just stood there and looked after her. Then I said, "I don't want any woman beaters on my beat, Mister. What's your name?" He gave me his name and I asked him if the woman was his wife. He said that she was. So I started to make out a report on the fight. I asked him if he lived in the tenement where the woman ran in, and where he worked. He told me he lived there and that he was a teacher at the college.

Gurney: Go on.

Macomber: We have sort of a rule about college people and professional men. People that publicity would hurt. I told Morlock to get in the house and that I didn't want to ever hear about him laying a finger on her again or I'd pinch him. He didn't say anything, just went tearing up the stairs after her. I hung around a few minutes but I didn't hear anything so I called in to the desk sergeant. He told me to write it off as quelling a domestic disturbance without using any names, and I did.

Gurney: And how many times did you say the accused struck his wife?

Macomber: At least four.

The Commonwealth of Massachusetts vs. Alvin Morlock. Direct testimony of Patrolman Francis Macomber.

On the day following Paul Martin's visit, Louise awoke with the sun streaming in the window. She glanced at the clock in some surprise; it was almost two o'clock. She had come in at four a.m. Her head throbbed and her throat burned. Her clothes were piled neatly on a chair beside the bed. Al must have undressed her when he got up to go to work. She swung her feet down and reached for a robe behind the bedroom door. In the bathroom, she splashed cold water on her face and scrubbed her teeth. The living room was orderly and neat. He must have picked up and emptied the ash trays and rinsed the glasses they had used. It wasn't going to buy him anything. The hell with him and with his fairy friend, she thought.

He had left the coffeepot ready. All she had to do was light the burner underneath it. While she waited for the water to percolate, she opened the cabinet above the stove where they kept what liquor they had in the house. The whisky and the brandy bottles were gone. He had hidden them but he had left a little red wine. She wasn't going to be bothered hunting around for wherever he had hid the stuff. She poured a little of the wine into a water tumbler and drank it. It seemed tasteless and insipidly sweet. She turned off the burner under the coffeepot. While she waited for the coffee to settle she was struck by a sudden and fearful thought. She hurried to the bedroom and snatched up her pocketbook.

There was a bulk of bills in it and she laughed in sudden relief as she counted the money. If he was going to cut her off from the family funds she would have to watch herself. More than once money had been stolen from her purse in one barroom or another but her more immediate fear had been that Morlock might have rifled the purse to keep her from going out. What he didn't know, the dirty Shylock, was that she could have a tab at Fagin's any time she wanted one.

There were eleven dollars in the purse. She snapped it shut and went back to the kitchen where she poured coffee and drank it swiftly, an urgency growing in her to be away from this place and seated at the shining bar in Fagin's place.

She put on the black dress she had worn to please Morlock and his friend. She would show him. She posed in front of the mirror, pulling in her stomach and throwing out her breasts. Not all done by a long way. Men still looked after her when she walked by, wanting her, thinking how it would be to sleep with her.

Fagin's was almost deserted; two or three regulars and Frank, the bookmaker, sat at the bar. Eddie, the good-looking boy with the dark hair and the clear brown eyes — he was now accepted as her regular shuffle-board partner — whistled when she came in.

"Some doll," he said admiringly. "Where you been, Louise — to a wedding?"

Jimmy, the bartender, brought her a drink. "On Fagin, Louise," he said. "Not to a wedding, not in black. Black is for wakes."

She relaxed, content with their admiration, soothed by the easygoing familiarity of these men. "I had this on last night," she said.

Jimmy nodded. "I heard you were in," he said, not mentioning Morlock.

She drank her drink quickly. "Let me have another," she said. "Give Eddie one, too. I feel like getting tight."

Jimmy and Eddie waited politely for an explanation. "I had a fight with my husband last night," she said. "He came in here after me and I told him to get away and leave me alone. To hell with him." Eddie said, "Sure, Louise. To hell with him. How about a game? Billy and Jimmy against you and me."

She shook her head. "Let's sit here and talk, Eddie. I don't feel like playing right now." She was feeling the warmth of the whisky already. Today the whisky didn't seem to make her gay as it usually did. Encouraged by the sympathy of Jimmy and Eddie, her real friends, she began to feel more and more sorry for herself and more and more bitter toward Morlock. She hadn't really meant it when she called him a fairy. He was not a fairy, she explained carefully to Eddie, but he acted like one with that fag, Paul Martin.

When she got down from the stool to look at the selections on the juke box, she stumbled and nearly fell. Impossible that she was half drunk this soon, she reasoned. She was thinking as clearly as if she had had nothing at all to drink.

There was a section on the juke box that listed old time tunes being revived. She read them carefully. How could she be drunk when she could read so easily? "Sunny Side of the Street."

"Blueberry Hill." That's when they had the good songs. "Dance with me, Eddie," she commanded.

Eddie got down from his stool. He was really a good-looking kid. He put his arms around her and she leaned against him. They began to sway back and forth. Eddie was pressing too hard, thrusting his lean belly against her. She knew what he was after all right. Trying to get her worked up. She giggled. What if he did? Who cared? She pushed him away suddenly. "I want another drink," she said.

Eddie said fuzzily, "Sure, Louise," and they walked arm in arm to the bar. Jimmy brought the drinks and she reached for money to pay him with. Funny where it went. Seven dollars left. She gave Jimmy a single and asked him to change the remaining dollar bill. The five she tucked in her compact, remembering vaguely that for some reason she had to be careful of her money. Oh, yes, that was it. Shylock Alvin was going to handle the money from now on — him. She had spent more in a single day out at the track than he made in six months. When Jimmy brought her change she bought two packages of cigarettes, Lucky Strikes for herself and a package of Pall Malls for Eddie. He was a good kid. When she gave him the cigarettes, he said, "Let's dance again, Louise."

It felt good to be wanted. She said, "Sure," and they moved away from the bar again and into each other's arms. "Chapel in the

Moonlight." That was nice. When had she danced to that song before? Oh, yes — it had been Tommy Dorsey's band, that first night — how long ago? — that she went out with the jockey, Eddie Mason. The other Eddie. But this Eddie — come to think of it, she couldn't even remember if he had ever told her his last name — pretty young to be playing an old timer like that except that it was slow and he could do — what he was doing now. Pushing hard against her. She giggled again and moved her own body against him. Fresh kid. If that's what he wanted she could give him lessons.

They broke apart reluctantly when the music ended and walked slowly back to the bar. While she ordered another round of drinks, she was aware of an animal desire to have Eddie possess her. After a moment she giggled again. It would be a good joke on Morlock. She had been unfaithful to him several times since their marriage — twice in Anna Carofano's bedroom and once in a parked car. Sexual fidelity meant so little to her that she hardly considered herself as having cheated Morlock. But to bring this kid to their home and in Morlock's own bed — this would pay him back for taking the money from her and for bringing Paul Martin to their home to insult her and call her a Dago from Federal Hill. She didn't remember that the words had been her own and not Martin's.

When she had finished her drink, she said, "This damn dress is too hot. I'm going over and change into something else." She looked sidelong at Eddie as she spoke.

He said huskily, "I'll go along and help you change," trying to keep his tone light so that he could pretend that he was joking if she acted offended. When she merely shrugged, he called to Jimmy the bartender. "Let me have a pint, will you, Jimmy?" he asked. "Make it Carstairs. You'll have to put it on my tab until Friday, all right?"

Jimmy said, "I guess," and got a bottle from beneath the bar. He put it in a paper bag and handed it to Eddie.

They left the bar and started toward the tenement. It was really funny, she thought, the way Eddie tried to look as if he weren't in a hurry. He sprang ahead to hold the door open for her. Ah, wasn't he being polite though! He wouldn't be so polite when he got in the bedroom. She still had it, for Eddie or any real man. Al? He could drop dead.

She held the door to the living room aside while Eddie stepped in and then closed it behind her, smiling at him. As the door closed, he reached for her with both arms, the bottle still held in one hand. With the free hand he pulled her closer. She pushed him back, laughing.

"Let's have a drink first," she said. "We've got lots of time."

He asked huskily, "What about your old man, your husband?"

She said, "I thought we already said to hell with him."

Eddie, said nervously, "Sure. But just the same we don't want him to come in and find us." He put the bottle down and moved toward her again, reaching for the front of her dress, trying to get his hand on her breast.

A little irritated, she pushed his hand away. "Don't tear my dress," she said sharply.

He moved away and she picked up the bottle. "You stay here," she said. "I'll make us a drink." She smiled, her anger forgotten, at his crestfallen expression.

When she returned, carrying the drink, she moved past him and toward the bedroom. When he followed her into the room, she pointed toward the bed and handed him his drink. "I'm going to take it off," she said. "I don't want you ripping it." She reached down and pulled her dress over her head. Standing in her slip she still teased him, lingering over her drink. She moved a step toward him, lurched and caught herself barely in time. "Go out in the kitchen and get the bottle," she said.

He left, hurrying. When he returned she was lying on the bed. He fell on top of her . . .

He was just a kid, she thought. No lover at all, all impatience and fumbling ineptness. Al, for all he was a Shylock and thought he was too good for her, was a better and more considerate lover. She pushed Eddie, half asleep now, aside and drank from the bottle he had placed beside the bed.

She had really had too much this time. The room was spinning, spinning. She relaxed, drowsing. Anyway, she was even now. Better wake up and get Eddie out before Al came home. He didn't have to know about this. She was satisfied, knowing what she had done herself, keeping the secret to laugh about. She would tell Anna Carofano, of course.

She awoke from a doze to see Eddie, his back to her, standing beside the dresser. She blinked, trying to get her eyes into focus, before she realized what she was seeing. The little sneak was going through her purse. She sprang naked from the bed and snatched at it. He dropped it and it fell to the floor in a clatter of metal. Her compact, her cigarette lighter. A few coins.

"You son-of-a-bitch," she screamed, "what do you think you're doing!"

He said, "Ah, don't get sore, Louise. I just wanted to borrow a couple of bucks."

She was almost insane with anger. Unable to find words she slapped him across the face with all her strength. He fell back against the dresser, hand against his cheek. He looked as if he couldn't believe what was happening. She took her eyes from him to reach for her purse. In that moment, he lashed back at her with his closed fist. She had stooped and the blow missed her face, catching her on the shoulder and knocking her to the floor. He stood over her, his eyes narrowed.

"You've got a hell of a nerve, you bitch," he said. "Give me the dough. You got what you wanted, didn't you? You think I cared anything about coming over here with an old bag like you?"

She got to her feet as he snatched up the compact and opened it, taking the money from it, holding her off with one hand as she clawed at him, unable to speak, unable even to scream. He pushed her away and ran from the room. She started after him, half crazed, and only remembered when she was halfway into the hall that she was naked. With silent, desperate fury she raced back to the bedroom and threw her robe over her naked body. She raced down the stairs, wanting only to catch Eddie and hit him and hit him; when she reached the front door he was not in sight. Reaction hit her then, swift and furious. Even a hot pants kid. She began to cry in racking sobs that shook her whole body. Morlock, coming home at that moment, found her sitting on the top step. He ran up the steps and bent to look at her. "Lolly," he said, "what is it? What happened?"

She continued to cry in shaking spasms that would not let her catch her breath. Recognizing hysteria, Morlock slapped her across the face, trying to hit her hard and unable to make himself do it. When the sobbing continued, he hit her again. It was at that moment that the policeman grabbed his arm. "Cut that out," he said. "I'm a police officer." The slaps or the words reached Louise. She scrambled to heir feet and rushed up the stairs. Morlock turned to explain, but the policeman was saying, "I don't want any woman beaters on my beat, Mister." There were people gathered around, staring, giggling. Morlock, humiliated, tried to explain but the policeman beat at him with questions. He answered them in monosyllables, wanting only to hide his head, to be away from the staring faces and to get to Louise.

When at last he was permitted to go to her, she was in the bedroom, lying on her stomach with her face buried in her arms. She would not answer any of his questions.

Chapter 10

Gurney: Mr. Murphy, when you were sworn you gave your name as James Murphy. What do they call you — Jimmy?
Murphy: Most people.
Gurney: And you work as a bartender in Fagin's Cafe, is that correct?
Murphy: Yes.
Gurney: Did you know the deceased, Louise Morlock?
Murphy: Well, I didn't know her last name. I'd heard it but it didn't mean anything to me until this thing happened. I called her Louise and let it go at that.
Gurney: Do you know the accused?
Murphy: I know him now.
Gurney: Did you ever meet him before this trial?
Murphy: I did. Somebody pointed him out to me some time ago as Louise's husband.
Gurney: He wasn't a customer of Fagin's, then?
Murphy: Him? No.
Gurney: What about Louise Morlock — was she a good customer?
Murphy: She was a regular.
Gurney: And what, precisely, does being a regular involve?
Murphy: Every bar, unless it's in a downtown location, has regulars. People that come in every day and spend some time. If you don't have maybe twenty regulars to count on, you might as well close up. Louise came in every day. There were other people that came in because they expected to find her there. Your regulars make the place like a club. She spent a little money and she was an attraction to the place.
Gurney: How long was she a regular?
Murphy: Almost from the time she moved into the neighborhood. That was a while after New Year's.
Gurney: Was she a heavy drinker?
Murphy: Not at first. Then, sometimes she'd get started early and have a little more than her share. I've seen lots worse. I never had to shut her off.

Gurney: You say that Morlock — the accused — was not a customer.
Murphy: That's right.
Gurney: Then how did you happen to meet him?
Murphy: I went looking for him. Louise owed me some money.
Gurney: A personal loan?
Murphy: No. A bar tab.
Gurney: Isn't it against the law for bars to give credit?
Murphy: Sure. But it wasn't Fagin's bar that gave her the credit. Take a bartender; if he wants to let a regular run up a little tab on his own responsibility — it's not his license. Fagin isn't involved. But if the tab isn't cleared up, the bartender that served the drinks is stuck for the money. Louise had me stuck. That's why I looked up her husband.
Gurney: How much did she have you stuck for?
Murphy: Forty-two dollars.
Gurney: Forty-two dollars! That seems like a lot of money for a bar bill.
Murphy: Well, that's how much it was.
Gurney: How long did it take her to run up this bill?
Murphy: A couple of weeks. I can tell you when I went looking for Morlock. It was Saturday, the 28th of April. The reason I know is that tabs are supposed to be cleared up Friday. I had so much money out that I wasn't going to get any of my own pay. So I gave her one day and then went looking for him.
Gurney: And you found him?
Murphy: Sure. I kept watching out the window for him to come down the street. I already told you I had somebody point him out to me. I walked out to him and I said, "Mr. Morlock?" He said, "Yes," like it was a question. So I told him about the money Louise owed me.
Gurney: What was his reaction?
Murphy: Well, he already looked worried, nervous. When I told him about the forty-two dollars, he flinched as if I'd hit him. Then he apologized for his wife and said he didn't have any money right then but that he'd take care of it just as soon as he could. Then he said, "She won't be around any more."
Gurney: What did you think he meant by that?
Liebman: Objection —

> *The Commonwealth of Massachusetts vs. Alvin Morlock.*
> *Direct testimony of James Murphy.*

Louise awoke on the morning following the incident with Eddie and heard Morlock moving about the kitchen. She lay still, looking around the room and planning the words of explanation she would use. Her purse had been picked up, together with its contents and placed on the dresser. She looked hastily around for the whisky bottle, hoping that it had been kicked under the bed and out of Morlock's sight. It wasn't, which meant that he had found it so that she would have to incorporate it in whatever lie she told.

She still had her robe on. Getting up, she went to the bathroom to rinse her face and walked out to the kitchen, a little frightened at the prospect of facing her husband. If she were married to someone like her brother Dominick, she would know what to expect. A smash in the face, a beating that would bruise her body — but a beating that was also a form of penance, a beating that was punishment but opened the way to forgiveness. But if she were married to an Old Country man like Dom it never would have happened. By reasoning thus, she transferred some of the blame to Morlock.

He turned as she came into the kitchen. "I've got coffee made," he said. "Sit down and I'll pour some for you."

Morlock, looking at her white face, felt an impersonal compassion for her. He had seen the whisky bottle on the bedroom floor. He had seen her underclothing scattered around the room and her body, naked under the robe, and he had drawn his own conclusions about what had happened. He had been able to perceive dimly that she had, in her way, been exacting a form of vengeance for Paul Martin and for his own detachment from her. Also, she was in her middle thirties. Becoming aware that her youth and good looks were disintegrating swiftly, and frightened because she had nothing to fall back on. He had failed her as a prop. Now she was trying alcohol and other men, and she would have to find out for herself what a miserable support they were.

He sat across from her at the kitchen table. "Do you want to tell me what happened?" he asked her.

"I laid down for a nap," she said. "I didn't feel very good after Monday night. I woke up when I heard a noise and I saw a man standing over the bed. He had a whisky bottle in one hand. I started to scream and he hit me and told me to be quiet or he'd kill me. Then he took my purse and started looking through it. I was afraid to yell out."

Morlock asked, "Do you remember what he looked like? Do you

want me to report it to the police?" Her story was a lie; he knew it and she knew that he knew it. His question was no more than a tacit acceptance of her transparent little story.

She shook her head. "It would only make trouble and they'd never get him." Then, wanting to hurt him, she said, "Al, you didn't ask me what happened then. He raped me."

Morlock knew she was taunting him with her guilty admission. He turned toward her with the rage of the cuckold rising swiftly in him, caught himself and only said woodenly, "You'd better see a doctor right away." Then he left the room.

She heard the hall door close behind him, not gently but not slammed either. She stared in the direction of the hall and then cried out to the closed door, "Go on, then! Get out! What do you care what happens to me?" She reasoned with childish logic that if he pretended to accept her story, he should then show the proper reaction. If he didn't accept it he should have hit her, kicked her. For a moment, when she said that she had been raped she had thought that he was going to smash her. Now, out of frustration and shame she called after him, "You queer, you. You don't even care about that."

Her rage quieted and she felt the need for a cigarette. She went into the bedroom for her purse; when she opened it she saw three dollar bills. There had been no money in the purse. Eddie had taken the last five-dollar bill. Al must have put it in there. It did not occur to her in her anger that he might have put the money in her purse out of consideration. She began craftily to guess what his motive had been. The amount was significant. Three dollars. Three bucks. Enough for cigarettes and a movie and two or three drinks. Or, if you skipped the movie, quite a few drinks.

She bathed and dressed and turned on the television set to kill time until after lunch. Fagin's was open in the morning hours but the chairs were still stacked on the tables and Jimmy would be busy cleaning up for the day's trade. Unable to accept her rejection by Morlock or the humiliation by Eddie, she waited until one o'clock to go out. When she did go she approached Fagin's with some hesitation. Eddie, she was nearly certain, would hardly dare to come back to the place after what he had done. She might have called the cops for all he knew — and she had had a perfect right to. Still, wondering what she was going to do about it, he might be hanging around or he might have talked to Jimmy on the telephone. She decided to be bold about it; she had either to be bold or not go in at all. She straightened her shoulders and walked in, smiling. "Hi, Jimmy," she greeted the bartender. It was hard not to look around to see if that bastard Eddie was in the place.

Everything was all right; she sensed immediately that Eddie had not come back. Jimmy said, "Hello, Louise. Drink?"

"Just beer," she said lightly.

The three or four men in the place looked up and nodded or spoke. Frank, the bookie, held out his Armstrong, not speaking. It was all right. And if Eddie did come around later, she would have her own version of what had happened — one that would make him look stupid.

She left Fagin's place in the afternoon in time to make Morlock's supper. There was food in the refrigerator; not much, but enough to make a passable meal. When he came in he was burdened with two paper sacks of groceries. Trying to show me up, she thought, showing me that he doesn't trust me even to go to the supermarket, letting everybody know what a lousy wife I am.

Morlock greeted Louise quietly. He did not kiss her — never again was to kiss her — and after silently eating his meal, he sat down in the living room and read the paper while she washed the dishes. They spent the evening in perfect decorum, speaking little. After she went bed, he walked into the bedroom. She had turned out the light but she could see his silhouette against the living room door and she felt a happy, eager anticipation. Maybe she was a drunk and a cheat but if he came to bed with her, it was forgiving her in a way and she would show him how nice she could be; make it up to him in the only way that she was any good.

Morlock bent over the bed and took the pillow from his side. He said, "Good night, Louise," and walked out of the room, closing the door behind him. She felt shame for just a moment. Then the shame turned inward, feeding on her, poisoning her. It was in that moment that she made her decision. Whatever happened to her, Morlock was going to be a part of it. She would drag him after her.

He slept on the couch in the living room. She made a point of getting up when she heard him stir and hurrying to the kitchen to start breakfast so that he would not have the satisfaction of acting the martyr. He ate the breakfast she put before him as he had eaten the supper, silently. When he started out for work she called after him — she would almost have preferred biting her own tongue but there was no alternative — "Al, I haven't got any money."

He turned to face her; "I left you some yesterday," he said. "Did you use it all?"

"I went to a movie."

He reached into his pocket and took out a handful of change. "I've only got about a dollar and a half," he said. "I'll give you half of it. There won't be any more until Friday." He put the money on the table and went out.

At Fagin's that afternoon, Louise played shuffleboard with much determination but with unbelievably bad luck. Needing to win, she could not.

"Jimmy," she said finally, "my old man doesn't get paid until a week from Friday. I guess you'll have to put me on the cuff."

Jimmy said easily, "Why sure, Louise. Anything you want."

She had put Morlock's payday a week ahead in case — it was then Thursday — he tried to buy her off with three dollars again. She had indicated to Jimmy when she would pay; she would not have to worry about money, outside of change for cigarettes, for more than a week.

Since she had credit she might as well use it. After a time she approached Frank, the bookmaker. "I'm short for a while, Frank. Can you cuff me?" she asked.

Frank glanced from her to Jimmy. Jimmy said, "She's all right, Frank. I'll be good for it," and the bookie nodded.

"Let me have the Armstrong," she demanded. In the race that would later be broadcast, she picked an overwhelming favorite. "Give me five to win on Blue Glitter," she said. Frank shrugged and wrote up the bet. Blue Glitter finished a poor third.

When Morlock came home on Friday, he made no mention of money. He was going in to the college on Saturday to conduct a make-up examination, he said.

When Louise arose on Saturday, he had already gone but he had left a ten-dollar bill on the kitchen table.

Since he was now buying the food, this money was obviously intended for her use as she saw fit. Just as obviously Morlock did not intend to give her any more.

She could, she knew, pay her tab as well as Frank the bookmaker's five dollars with the ten and have a dollar or two left. But since she had credit for a week, why should she? Also, her luck was bound to turn.

Saturday afternoon she lost ten more on favorites. In desperation she picked an eight to one shot on Monday and lost another ten. When on Tuesday she walked toward Frank, he silently shook his head, indicating that he would take no more bets until her bill was paid.

She was drinking less now and sticking to beer. On Thursday she asked Jimmy, keeping her expression light, "What's my tab, Jimmy? I've got to take care of you tomorrow."

He took a slip of paper from the cash register and studied it. "Forty-two bucks, Louise, counting what you owe Frank." He added anxiously, "Don't be late with it, Louise. I've got to square up with Fagin."

She had not the remotest chance of getting that much money from Morlock. He probably thought he was doing her a big favor by giving her ten dollars for a week. On Friday she did not go to Fagin's directly after lunch. Instead she dressed carefully in the black taffeta and caught a bus going toward the college.

She had been to the college once or twice with Morlock. Once when their marriage was new and they were pretending that it was something that it was not, she had met him on a Friday afternoon after going to a movie. They had gone into a stucco office building set aside from the campus. There were a dozen girls inside the place. Morlock had gone to the counter that crossed in front of the door and one of the girls had come up to meet him. She was an ugly thing with mousy hair and no more breasts than a mackerel. Morlock had said, "Hello, Grace. This is my wife. Louise, this is Grace. She's our best friend."

Grace had simpered and handed Morlock an envelope containing his pay check.

Louise was aware of the danger involved in what she was about to do. She carefully balanced that risk against Morlock's dislike of scenes and decided that the risk was slight — unless he had already called for his check. Actually, she decided, she had no choice. Against what might happen, what Morlock might do, was the certain knowledge of what Jimmy and Frank would do if they didn't get their money.

Walking with great dignity and no hesitation, she entered the little stucco building and felt a tremendous surge of relief when the same girl came to the counter. She smiled. "Hello, Grace," she said. "Remember me? Mrs. Morlock? I'm supposed to meet Alvin on the campus. He asked me to stop in and pick up his check."

And all the worrying had been for nothing. Grace smiled and

said, "Oh, sure, Mrs. Morlock. I'll get it for you."

With the check in her purse, Louise walked away from the office building. There was one more danger; she might run into Alvin. She didn't. Off the campus again she caught a downtown bus. She cashed the check at a drugstore with no difficulty: the druggist merely read the face of it and scarcely glanced at her own scrawled endorsement — in Morlock's name — on the reverse side. There was a bus station close to the drugstore. She walked in and bought a ticket for Providence. To hell with Morlock. To hell with Jimmy and Frank the bookmaker. While she waited for the bus, she went into a cocktail lounge and had two highballs.

Two hours after Louise left the office building, Morlock entered. He stood at the counter waiting for Grace, drumming with his fingers in nervous preoccupation, looking up at length to find Grace looking at him.

"Mr. Morlock," she said. "Your wife picked up your check right after lunch."

He could not believe it. He stammered, "What?" and even in his disbelief he sought wildly for some means of diverting this final shame.

Grace saved him. "She said she was supposed to meet you on the campus."

Morlock struck his own brow in mock dismay and grinned at Grace. "So she was," he said. "She'll make me take her to dinner for this." He strode away from the counter, as if in a hurry to keep his forgotten appointment, and headed for the campus in case Grace might still be watching. When he was out of sight of the office, he turned and hurried to catch a bus for Kosciusko Street.

She would not be there. He was certain of that; and yet he was dismayed when he found the tenement empty. He ransacked her closet. She had not taken her clothes. She could not, with seventy dollars, afford to replace them, and therefore she must have gone back to Federal Hill where she had dresses and other things. Morlock made a cup of coffee and sat back to think about it. He would be out of it cheaply if he never saw her again. He had no money. He would have to borrow from Dodson or someone else to keep going and he would have to stall the loan company and the other creditors. But little by little, given time, he would work his way out of debt.

On the following evening he was stopped in front of the tenement by a man who introduced himself as Jimmy.

"Jimmy Murphy, Mister Morlock. I'm the bartender at Fagin's there. I hate to mention this but your wife owes quite a bill. We've got to have the money."

"How much?"

"Forty-two bucks. I know it sounds like a lot but she was betting with the book on top of running a tab. We really got to have that money."

"I'm not able to pay you right now," Morlock said. "She took everything I had too, but I'll get it for you just as soon as I can. I can give you some of it next Friday." He started to say, "But don't ever let her have credit again," but remembered that she was gone now. More to himself in reassurance than to Jimmy, he said instead, "She won't be around any more."

Chapter 11

Gurney: You are a second grade detective on the Providence, Rhode Island, police force, Officer Jacobs. Did you have occasion to arrest the deceased, Louise Morlock, on the night of April 29th?

Jacobs: I did.

Gurney: On what grounds?

Jacobs: I could have run her in for any one of several things: making a disturbance, common drunk. I was as easy as I could be. I charged her with loitering.

Gurney: And you say that that was on Sunday, the 29th of April?

Jacobs: It was. I rechecked the blotter when this investigation was brought up.

Gurney: And what is the usual disposition in such cases?

Jacobs: It's up to the judge. Depending on circumstances, anything from ten to thirty days.

Gurney: Was Louise Morlock sentenced?

Jacobs: No. We let her go with her husband. We've known Louise for years — we were glad to get —

Liebman: Objection.

Cameron: Sustained. You know better than that, Detective Jacobs.

Jacobs: I'm sorry, Your Honor. We let her call her husband Monday morning. I wasn't around when she called, but I was there when he came in to get her. I took him aside and sort of warned him a little bit; told him we didn't want to see it happen again or we'd have to send her over the road.

Gurney: What was his reaction?

Jacobs: He was sore, of course. Most husbands are on a thing like that. Most of the time they choke all up and tell us what they are going to do when they get their old woman home; what will happen to her if it ever happens again.

Gurney: Did Morlock make any such threats?

Jacobs: No. He seemed more concerned about whether the arrest was going to be in the papers.

> *The Commonwealth of Massachusetts vs. Alvin Morlock.*
> *Direct testimony of Detective 2nd Grade Melvin Jacobs.*

Louise got off the bus at the downtown terminal and immediately caught a local bus for Federal Hill, again getting off in front of the old three-decker where her father lived.

She had decided to say that Alvin had gone to a teachers' convention for a week and that she was visiting only for that length of time. Once re-established in the house she could fall back into the old routine. She did not plan to return to Morlock, but she did have the assurance of a husband in reserve — and if he tried anything silly like divorcing her, she would make him pay.

Dominick and the old man were sitting at the kitchen table, eating supper, when she entered the room. She said lightly, "Hi. Got anything left to eat?"

The old man rose immediately, his face beaming. "Louise," he said, coming forward to hug her and kiss her. "My girl. Dominick, you get you up and get some thing for your sister. Go down the block and get steak, chicken, anything."

Dominick went on eating, his face bent toward his plate. She could, she knew, use her power over the old man to make an immediate issue of her return. Not wanting a scene so soon she said, "I'm not that hungry, Pa. Whatever you've got will do for me."

He bustled happily to the stove. "I fix you something nice. You sit down now, Louise. You see."

She said casually, "All right, Pa. I'm going to be here for a week. Al had to go to a convention and I didn't want to be left alone."

Dominick asked harshly, "Where is the convention?"

"New York," she answered him.

"Right in the middle of the term he goes off to a convention?"

She flared at him. "What do you know about teachers? Why don't you mind your own business?" He said nothing more until they had finished eating. He left the kitchen and she hoped that he had gone out.

She was not to do the dishes. The old man winked and nudged. "I guess you tired of cook and wash for your old man, eh? I clean up. You go play phonograph."

Dominick was sitting in the parlor, his big hands folded on his knees. He got up when she came into the room. "Where's your bags?" he demanded.

"What bags?"

"You came to spend a week, but you didn't bring no clothes. Sure, I believe this. You got clothes here. Why should you bother, eh?" He advanced until his body vas almost touching hers. His eyes were hot, his face twisted in the anger he could not express by raising his voice. "Listen to me, you whore, you. You left your husband, the poor bastard, and you think you can come back here to slut around and live off the old man and me. That's what you think. Now you listen to me. You don't stay even tonight. You get out. Get out and I'll tell the old man that you had to go back home. If I ever see you again in this house I get you away somewhere and beat you until you are nearly dead. And if I see you after that, I beat you until you *are* dead. Get out now, right now, before he comes in here."

"I haven't got any place to go, Dom," she pleaded, backing away from him.

"Go back to your husband."

"I can't," she wailed.

"Then go to hell." He pushed her toward the door. At his touch, she whirled and tried to run toward the kitchen. Dom's hand closed on her neck with such violence that his fingers nearly met at her throat. She could not scream, she could not breathe. He opened the door and pushed her so violently that she nearly fell down the steps. On the sidewalk she turned to scream at him but when he came toward her, she turned and hurried up the street.

Within a few minutes the initial shock of Dominick's violent expulsion wore off. She still had most of Morlock's paycheck, nearly seventy dollars. She would get a room, buy the few cosmetics she needed. She would think about it later. Meanwhile, she wanted a drink.

The bars and clubs were the same as they had always been. Only the people seemed different. She stopped in several, intending each time to stay only briefly and then to see about getting a room. And then she was given a warm welcome in one of the smaller bars. She had walked in to see a fat little man waving a handful of bills. She smiled and said, "Hello, Porky. You buying?" She remembered him from the old days.

He was half drunk, she saw. He turned and said, "Hey, Louise! Where have you been keeping yourself?"

"Here and there."

He rushed over to put his arm across her shoulders. "Give Louise a drink," he demanded, waving the bills. "Hey, Louise, what about a game of gin? Let me win back some of the dough you won off me."

The bartender — she remembered him too — said, "Watch out for him, Louise. He won forty bucks this afternoon. He can't lose."

"Come on, Louise," Porky insisted. "For a buck." She could make money from this little drunk, Louise thought. A mark. See that he kept drinking — and she would be careful about how much she drank herself. "You'll never get even with me playing for a buck," she said. "How about five?"

She began to play conservatively, getting down as soon as possible on each hand in order to avoid a schneider which would cost double. Porky was a nervous, noisy player: laughing happily when he went down for a good score and cursing when he lost points. Not a good player but tonight a lucky one. He won two games in which she barely got on the board and she became angry with herself. She would win, she was confident that she would win; but each game that he won meant just that much more ground that she would have to make up before she began making money from him.

Porky's luck, good to begin with, became fantastic. Twice he ginned before she even made a run in her and. He schneidered her on the third game and crowed happily.

"Hey — what I tell you! You want to get even, we play ten."

She finished her drink and said angrily, "All right. Ten."

She won the ten-dollar game and felt better. Now if she could schneider Porky she would begin to get into his money. As winner she bought drinks.

She did not win another game; she lost six consecutive times. Porky was quite drunk by now and she would have been able to cheat him — she did manage to cheat a little on the point count — but the game had attracted attention by this time and there were too many people standing near the table. One man, a wise guy, she thought, several times corrected her when she counted in her own favor.

She was in a bad jam. She had less than two dollars left. Until now they had put the money on the side of the table before each game. It was her deal as loser of the last game. Without putting her money up, hoping that Porky would not notice, she began to deal the cards.

The wise guy said, "What about getting the dough up, Louise?" He was staring at her coldly.

"Why don't you mind your own damn business? Come on, Porky. Discard."

Wise guy said, "You've got your money up, Porky. Where's hers."

Porky looked troubled. "You're supposed to put it up, Louise. You know that."

"I was going to," she said, "until this nosy bastard butted in. I got the money right here in my purse." She appealed to Porky's drunken sense of gallantry. "You want me to show you?"

Wise guy butted in again. "She hasn't got more than a couple of bucks in her purse, Porky. She's been trying to cheat you all night. Make her get the dough up or don't play with her."

Porky was unhappy. He had been playing and winning and having a fine time and now these people wanted to fight. "I know you got the money, Louise. Why don't you put it on the table and we'll play. You're due to win one."

There was nothing she could do now; nothing she could say. Wise guy had spoiled it. She did not consider what the consequences might have been if she had played and lost and been unable to pay. She had taken such chances before and relied on her sex and looks to get her out of it.

She got up defiantly. "If that's the way you feel, the hell with you," she said, and walked from the room with the laughter following her.

She no longer had enough money for a room. She entered a cafe and tried to call Rosie, the friend of that first date with Morlock. She was not home. Louise sat at the bar and ordered beer, trying to make herself think what she should do. It was much easier to drink beer and not think. She began a round of bars, insinuating herself between groups of men so that she was offered drinks often enough but received no more substantial bids.

Louise, who had allowed herself to be picked up on hundred occasions in the old days, had never solicited.

Her contempt for the slatterns who did was the more powerful because of her fear that she might some day sink to the same level —

though she never really admitted this fear to herself. At one-thirty in the morning, lurching a little, her stockings awry and her lipstick smeared; at one-thirty, half drunk and loose mouthed, Louise Morlock approached a tall man on a street corner. "Say, Jack," she began.

The man said, "Oh, oh. You'd better come with me, dear." He waved a hand and a car appeared. She got in the back seat and sank into the cushions only half aware that the car was a police car.

She was allowed to make a telephone call Monday morning. Sick and ashamed, she asked the operator to get Ludlow College in Warfield for her.

Morlock had spent most of Sunday at Abram's Rock. The great monolith was now a touchstone for him. He could sit on its ancient gray head and be transported out of his troubled world and back to the golden days when he had played here with Marianna Cruz. He went to his classes on Monday refreshed, as though he had taken strength from the rock. He was preparing a lecture in the teachers' lounge when Louise's call came. There were several other teachers in the room; because of their presence he kept the shock from his voice.

"Al," she said. "I'm in trouble. They've got me at the police station. Al, come and get me, will you?"

He asked in a low voice, "Where?"

"In Providence. Al — will you?"

"I've got classes this morning," he said. "I can't get out of them on such short notice. I'll get there as soon as I can."

Driving to Providence in the afternoon in Dodson's car he tried to think of a solution; when he walked into the police station he had not found one, other than to take her back with him. They would have to reach some sort of an understanding. In the meantime he would have to make it clear to her that he was a teacher; his job depended on his reputation and that of his wife. The fear came on him then that it might already be in the papers; might have gotten back to Warfield. When the detective who had arrested Louise took him aside, he blurted out, "Did it get in the papers?"

The detective seemed a little irritated at the interruption.

"No," he said. "Where married women are involved we keep it quiet as much as we can."

Chapter 12

Gurney: I call William Cory.
Cameron: The clerk will swear the witness.
Gurney: Mr. Cory, what is your occupation?
Cory: I am a student at Ludlow College.
Gurney: A veteran?
Cory: Yes. I was in the army two years.
Gurney: Were you a student in any of the accused's classes?
Cory: Mr. Morlock? Sure. I had English with him.
Gurney: Did you know Mrs. Morlock?
Cory: I met her, yes.
Gurney: Under what circumstances?
Cory: I went to his house one Sunday to see about my marks. They were bad. I wanted to see if I could take any special test or anything to improve them.
Gurney: On what date was this visit?
Corey: May 6th.
Gurney: Was Morlock home?
Cory: No.
Gurney: What happened then?
Cory: Well, I asked where he was and what time he'd be home. Then I left.
Gurney: I remind you that you are under oath, Cory. How long did you actually stay?
Cory: I don't know. Maybe half an hour.
Gurney: Half, an hour to ask two simple questions?
Cory: I already told you I don't know how long it was. Maybe it wasn't half an hour.
Gurney: Mr. Cory, wasn't it long enough for you to have intimate relations with her?
Liebman: I object, Your Honor! What is he trying to do — impeach his own witness?
Cameron: This is highly unusual, Mr. Gurney. Unless you can show a strong justification for this line of questioning I shall have to rule for the defense. Come to the bench, please.
Gurney: Your Honor, I have a reluctant witness here. I chose the method I used as the only means to an end. I can produce witnesses

numbering at least twelve who will state that Cory admitted — *bragged* is the word — to having intimate relations with Mrs. Morlock, the deceased. I submit that the accused was faced with the prospect of becoming a laughing stock for the whole school and that this is part of the substance of motive. I don't want to drag a bunch of students in here and sully them with this thing. If Mr. Liebman will go along with me I can establish what I want without doing that.

Cameron: I will let the question stand.

Gurney: I ask you again, Cory. Were you intimate with Mrs. Morlock? Don't be shy. I understand that you bragged about it to half the school.

Cory: I was.

The Commonwealth of Massachusetts vs. Alvin Morlock.
Direct testimony of William Cory.

Out of vast relief and a little shame Louise had been wildly penitent when she and Morlock left the police station to ride back to Warfield. Morlock had been white-faced and silent during the first half of the ride. He had then stopped the car at the side of the road and turned to face her.

"I want you to know," he said, "that I wouldn't have come after you if I had had a choice. I can't afford any more of your escapades, financially or otherwise. I married you and I'll see that there's a roof over your head because I think you'd wreck me if I didn't."

She reached for his hand and he drew it away. "Al," she promised, "it won't happen again. I've learned my lesson."

"Did you see your father while you were in Providence?"

"I know what you want," she answered. "You'd like me to go back there and live and you'd be rid of me. Al, I don't blame you. They wouldn't take me in. Please, Al . . ."

He was silent as he started up the car and drove the rest of the way home. They met Anna Carofano in the hall. Louise said, "Hello, Anna," but the other woman stared coldly at her without answering. Because of what had happened at Fagin's, Louise supposed. Louise wondered if Jimmy the bartender had come to Al for his money, but she could not find the nerve to ask about it.

The penitent mood began to fade on the next day. Bored with the tenement, afraid to go to Fagin's — she had no money anyway — she began to feel injured. She had, after all, told Al that she was sorry. She was willing to come more than half way toward a reconciliation but he treated her like something dirty. He hadn't even left her money for cigarettes. By the end of the week she was convinced that most of what had happened was Al's fault. She had, in that time, not left the tenement.

When she had asked him for money on Friday, "Enough for a movie and cigarettes, Al," he had said flatly, "I can't do it, Louise. It will take me months to pay off our bills now." She had screamed at him then, but he had merely stared briefly at her and gone out. On Sunday she did not dress. Al had left the Sunday paper and gone off somewhere, and she sat in her robe in the parlor halfheartedly looking at the racing results. When she heard the knock on the door she was startled. It had been a week since she had seen any face but Al's. Anna, probably, she thought, hoping that it was and that she was all through being mad and would tell her what had happened at Fagin's about the tab.

Cory, the professional ex-GI, had determined to force an understanding with Morlock. He couldn't figure it out. Morlock, one of the easiest to bully and bluff of the whole faculty, had in the last few weeks hardened. He had been ruthlessly failing Cory on paper after paper and Cory was now worried. Driving to Morlock's place — he had obtained the address from the Bursar's office — he had planned his approach. He would be open and honest, call Morlock "sir," admit his errors, and appeal to his sympathy. "I know I've been a pretty poor student, sir, but I'd like to ask you as man to man for one more chance." The advantage of this approach was that if it failed he could switch to bullying and if that didn't work either he could threaten to go to the Dean and complain that he was being discriminated against. The Dean wouldn't stand by and see a GI Bill student flunked. It would mean that the V.A. might come snooping around.

He was a little surprised at the sight of Morlock's home; he had supposed that teachers were able to afford something a little better. He walked up to the third floor, practicing his approach, looked in vain for a bell and finally knocked. He was further surprised when he saw Louise. If he had pictured Morlock's wife at all he would have expected some mousy little creature with a thin face and a scrawny shape. This woman standing in the doorway was big and strapping and — built. A little on the full-blown side maybe, but something nevertheless.

More than he would have thought Morlock could handle. He gave her the boyish smile. "Mrs. Morlock?" he asked.

Louise, happy to have the monotony broken, returned the smile. "Yes," she said. "Come in. My husband isn't home but I'll be glad to take a message."

He stepped inside and she closed the door.

"I'm at the college," he explained. "In one of your husband's classes. My name's Bill Cory."

"Sit down, Bill," she said. "Would you like a cup of coffee?"

He didn't particularly want the coffee but he was fascinated with the way she moved; the way the robe almost came open. So help him if he didn't think she didn't have anything on underneath it. "Sure," he said. "I'd like it."

Maybe, the way she was acting, he ought to change to another approach; the rough, surly one. He would delay his decision.

It didn't take her long to get the coffee. When she put it in front of him he could see right down the front of the robe and she *didn't* have anything on under it. He had heard of situations like this; first time he'd ever run into one. She sat down beside him, so close that he could feel the pressure of her thigh.

Louise had been aware of the way that Cory followed her with his eyes. "A hard up kid," she thought at first, finding some amusement in it. Studying him, when she brought in the coffee, she changed her mind about his being a kid. Where she had planned to give him something to think about, something to look at and then send him on his way, she suddenly saw in him a means of getting even with Morlock. She saw it with almost blinding clarity.

"It's too bad we haven't got something better than coffee," she said. "Al won't be home for hours." She was afraid for a minute that she had been too crude; that he might be scared off. He got quickly to his feet.

He was aroused by the sight of her breasts and the feel of her thigh. By God, he had *never* run into anything like this. "I can take care of that," he blustered. "You leave it to me, Mrs. Morlock."

"Lolly," she said, smiling. "Sure you can get it on a Sunday?"

"Sure," he said. "I know half a dozen places. Leave it to me."

He was gone for half an hour. In that time she bathed and put on fresh make-up. She did not dress but put on the robe again.

Liebman: Cory, how old are you?
Cory: Twenty-three.

Liebman: You say you spent two years in the army. Overseas?
Cory: No.
Liebman: No combat, then.
Cory: No.
Liebman: How long did you say you spent with Mrs. Morlock?
Cory: I already said I don't know. Maybe it was half an hour.
Liebman: But it could have been a lot more?
Cory: I guess it could.
Liebman: Did you make any plans to see her again?
Cory: She said I could come again on the next Sunday.
Liebman: And did you?
Cory: Yes.
Liebman: That would have been May 13. Were you intimate with her again on that occasion?
Cory: Yes.
Liebman: Weren't you afraid that her husband might discover you?
Cory: She said that he went off every Sunday . . . there wasn't anything to worry about.
Liebman: How many people did you tell about this affair?
Cory: Some of the guys. I don't know how many.

     The Commonwealth of Massachusetts vs. Alvin Morlock.
       Cross-examination of William Cory.

  Louise was waiting for Cory when he came back with the whisky. She had several drinks and then matched his eagerness with her own; hers the more satisfying because of the revenge she was getting on Morlock. On the second Sunday he brought the whisky with him. She planned that second tryst in spite of the danger that Morlock might not go out. She was by this time accustomed to his Sunday absences and she was gratified to see him leave early for wherever it was he went. That evening, when Morlock came in, she sat across from him at the supper table and studied him. Where had he been? Her curiosity began to grow.
  Cory, on the occasion of his first relations with Louise, kept the affair to himself. Cory, brute of the back seat, had been overwhelmed by a carnality that very nearly frightened him. After the second meeting with Louise, he could not hold the knowledge in. He rolled it over and over in his mind, trying to find some way of using it. It wasn't every day that a student shacked up with a professor's wife.
  Maybe, he thought, he could use it to blackmail Morlock into

giving him passing grades. He considered this and then rejected it. Then, because it was too obscene, too scandalous, and too heroic a thing to keep secret, he began bragging of it. "You guys think you've had a piece," he would say. "You ought to see what I've been getting . . . and from who." Then he would tell them.

Morlock, on both Sundays, came home to find Louise almost gay. He could smell whisky. If he gave any thought to it he supposed that Anna Carofano had been up to see Louise and had brought a bottle. Until the trial he never knew that she had betrayed him with Cory.

Chapter 13

Liebman: Cory, you have testified that you had several rendezvous with Mrs. Morlock in the weeks immediately preceding her death. You held these trysts only on Sundays, didn't you?

Cory: Any other day he was liable to be home.

Liebman: And you, in fact, were with her on the Sunday she died, weren't you?

Cory: Sure, yes, but it wasn't like the other times. She was getting sore about him, where he was going every Sunday. She wanted to know what he was doing. She followed him one time and saw him get in Mr. Dodson's car and drive off. So then she wanted me to come early the next Sunday and wait around the corner in my car; she wanted me to take her wherever it was he went. She thought he was seeing some other woman.

Liebman: The irony of this didn't strike you?

Cory: What?

Liebman: Let it go. Cory, did she ever discuss with you the advantages of doing away with the accused?

Gurney: Objection.

Cameron: Sustained. Do you want a ruling on that, Mr. Liebman?

Liebman: No. I take it, then, that on Sunday, May 20th, you generously agreed to help the suspicious Mrs. Morlock as she shadowed her husband?

Cory: The 20th?

Liebman: The 20th. The day she died.

Cory: Well, yes. I did. I didn't want to. All the time I was seeing her I was spending a lot of money on whisky and cigarettes and I was pretty near broke. I had to gas up my car — I didn't know how far he was going or anything like that. She never offered to help pay for it. And I was scared that he might see me with her.

Liebman: My heart goes out to you, Cory.

Cameron: We can do without the sarcasm, Mr. Liebman.

Liebman: I stand reprimanded, Your Honor. Cory — what time did the accused come out of the house?

Cory: I don't know. I was around the corner waiting for Lolly — for Mrs. Morlock. I got there about eight-thirty because he always left a little after that. I waited about ten minutes and then she came out and got in the car and told me which way to go.

Liebman: Was the accused familiar with your car?

Cory: I didn't think so but she said not to take any chances. I stayed a couple of blocks behind him — he was walking then — until he got in Mr. Dodson's car and started out of town. Then I stayed far enough behind so he couldn't see that he was being followed or who was in the car with me. He drove steady as far as South Danville, not in a hurry, and then he parked the car behind a filling station and got out.

Liebman: Did you stop at that time?

Cory: No. I slowed down a little but I drove on past and pulled off the road a little bit and stopped.

Liebman: How far past his car was that?

Cory: Maybe fifty yards. He didn't look back. Mrs. Morlock was the one that said to stop there. We sat in the car and watched him walking up a little dirt road. He was looking straight ahead.

Liebman: What was her attitude at that time?

Cory: She seemed pretty excited. She said, "Come on. Let's see where he goes." I told her that I didn't want any part of it and she got mad. She made me promise to wait for her and I said that I would unless her husband was with her when she came back. She hurried off the way he went — he was out of sight in the trees — and I stayed in the car and waited.

Liebman: You're sure you stayed in the car? You're sure you didn't go into the woods with her?

Cory: I'm sure. I never got out of the car.

Liebman: How long did you wait?

Cory: I guess it was about twenty minutes. Then I saw Mr. Morlock come running down the road. The road I told you about that the two of them walked up. You could tell just from the way he was running that something had happened and his face was bleeding.

I started up my car and got out of there.
Liebman: Thou faithful lover. That's all, Cory.
*The Commonwealth of Massachusetts vs. Alvin Morlock.
Cross-examination of William Cory.*

What had been hardly more than an idle curiosity about Morlock's absences each Sunday grew and festered in Louise's mind. He had a hell of a nerve, she thought, treating her like a prisoner, not letting her have any money, not speaking to her and all the time carrying on some affair of his own.

How else could he be spending all that time? She reasoned, more cunningly, that if she could catch him at it she would have the satisfaction of bringing him down to her own level — the level on which he placed her — and he could no longer humiliate her with her own shortcomings. But she would have to catch him in the act; right in the middle of the act so that he could have no possible defense. She had tried to follow him one Sunday, thinking that he would head for some cheap hotel room or walk-up flat.

She would, she thought, give him just time enough and then she would rush in. She practiced the things she would say to him, and to his woman. Or if she could catch him at something queer like with that fag, Martin . . . so much the better. She rehearsed the things she would say until even the accusations she rejected remained in her mind as referring to facts accomplished, actual things she had seen. There was no longer any possible doubt in her about what he was doing, and her spying took on the air of a crusade. When, on that first Sunday of her espionage, he got into Dodson's car and drove away she raged in her frustration and was more than ever convinced of his guilt. When Cory came, she asked him to drive for her so she could see where Morlock went. He was difficult but she had a sensual power over him that made him easy to control.

She watched Morlock throughout the week, impatient for Sunday to come, clutching her obsession to her like a mother clutching an infant. When Sunday did come and he did leave, she rushed to the appointed place to meet Cory, afraid that he might not be there. He was there and she got into the car, hardly aware of Cory at all.

Morlock, in the few weeks since he had rediscovered the sanctuary of Abram's Rock, had already worked out a routine for his visits. By arrangement with Dodson he had the use of the old LaSalle until evening on each Sunday; in return he filled the car's tank with gasoline at the filling station adjacent to the rock and thus repaid the filling station proprietor as well as Dodson.

He could park the car in back of the filling station and take the road to the rock without speaking to anyone, which was very important. He had reached a point where any conversation at all was an intrusion. Aware of the dangerous psychological ground on which he was treading, he rationalized. The rock was the only place where he could escape Louise, he told himself; the only place where he could be free of half a hundred reminders of the failure of his marriage.

He was aware of his own hypocrisy. In actual fact, he knew, he was visiting the rock less as a refuge than as a retreat from Ludlow, from being a second-class teacher and a failure. He spent hours each week on the rock, not in idle, harmless contemplation of what might have been but in an actual return to his youth. Here he and Marianna had played and daydreamed. Here he had been happy.

On Sunday, May 20th, he walked toward the rock in quiet anticipation. At the very summit there was a spot where the sun warmed the granite and where there was a fallen tree that he could sit on. Once he had crouched in tears at that very place, he remembered. And Marianna had come to him to ask, "Why are you crying?" That had been the day of his father's funeral.

Today he would remember more pleasant times. He had the faculty of selecting his memories as an orchestra leader might choose a single work from all the creations of a composer. Morlock was also aware of the danger in this power of selection. He was not, he decided, hurting anyone except possibly himself. If he preferred to spend his solitude in a return to what was past — that was his privilege.

This gray slope up which he struggled — how many times he had seen Marianna skip to the top, slim and bare-legged, as graceful as he was clumsy.

When he was at last at the summit he found his fallen tree and sat down, warm from the exercise. Beyond he could see hills and pastures, green with the new grass of spring and populated only with grazing cattle, brown and black and white and looking like playthings from this height. There were towering spruce and hemlocks below the sheer side of the cliff over which he looked, but their tops never reached the height of the rock. This was the place where Abram, the Indian of the legend, had leaped, it was said. He remembered when he had told Marianna the story. Her eyes had widened and filled with pity.

"Was he killed?" she wanted to know.

"Sure," he had told her with the contempt for death of boyhood. "It's almost a thousand feet down."

"He must have missed her very much," she said thoughtfully. "Had they been married very long? What made her die?"

"I don't know," he had answered. "I guess she just got sick or something. Indians didn't have doctors."

She had been quiet for a little while. Then she said, "She must have been very glad that he loved her enough to jump when she die."

At twelve he had been less interested in the legend than she. Nevertheless, when it was her turn to choose the game they would play, or the direction of their pretending, she often chose the legend of Abram as a focal point to set the stage. He never entered halfheartedly into the game because it was of her choosing or something that he might privately consider sissified; when she pretended that she could hear the dead Indian princess crying in the depths below them for Abram, he pretended that he could hear it too.

Once, when they played this game, she said gravely, "If they made me go away from here, I would wish that I could jump like Abram did, Alvin."

He asked, in astonishment, "Why?"

"Because I would be sad at leaving here and going away from you."

He was touched. "I guess I'd feel the same, Marianna."

And it occurred to them both simultaneously. They would make a pact, solemnly and with pomp. They were friends. If anything happened to the one, the other would do as Abram had done.

These things were the subject of Morlock's reminiscence when he heard the sound of someone approaching behind him. He had to recall himself to the present violently and with great conscious effort. He got to his feet and turned in the same motion; when he saw Louise climbing the last few feet to the top he could not believe what he saw. When he did believe it he said, "Louise — for God's sake, what are you doing here?"

She had followed him up the rutted road from the filling station, stumbling in her high heels and flogged by the outstretched whips of birch and alder that had invaded the road. She caught only a glimpse of him from time to time but she had kept on, realizing that he could hardly have turned off the road. After a few minutes she had begun to perspire from the effort of trying to keep him in sight. The perspiration had stung her where the branches had scratched her skin but she had been unconscious of any pain in her urge to confront

Morlock in all his guilt.

Even when he had started to climb the rock, she had not doubted for a moment that her obsession was based in reality; she only wondered at his choice of a trysting place. She had taken off her shoes to get a foothold on the smooth surface and started climbing the barely visible old trail to the top. She had come close enough to the summit to see him several seconds before he heard her and turned and she was profoundly disappointed when she saw that he was alone and that there could be no other person on the bare summit. Unable to believe this she glanced at every pebble, every crevice in the granite.

"I followed you," she said when she had caught her breath. "Al, I thought you were seeing someone, the way you've been gone every Sunday."

He was outraged at her intrusion. "How did you get here?" he demanded.

"I got someone to take me," she said. A quick suspicion returned to her, a saving hope. Probably she was just too early. Probably someone was coming right this minute, the someone he was seeing. She turned to look back down the trail.

Morlock, after his first anger, felt a despairing sense of loss. The rock would never be the same again. It could never again be a sanctuary. With her mere presence she had dirtied it. He saw her backward look and interpreted it correctly.

"Don't bother," he said. "There isn't anyone coming. You shouldn't have come here, Louise." He watched her move toward him, looking curiously about her, like a filthy alley cat in a shrine. "This is all I can stand, your coming here," he said. "You're going to have to get out. I don't care where you go or what you do. I'll help you with what money I can, but you've got to go away from me."

"What did I do?" she demanded. "You can't blame me for thinking you were up to something — seeing some woman probably. You haven't come near me — I know that much."

"This place had a meaning for me," he said. "I used to play here when I was a kid. This is where Marianna — " He caught himself and finished lamely, "And the other kids used to come."

She seized on the name instantly, picking it from all the other words he had used with instinctive awareness of its importance to him.

"Marianna," she said. "Sounds like a Dago like me. Who is she, Al?"

"She was a girl I used to know when we were kids," he said. He tried to divert her. "Come on, Louise. I'll take you down."

She had wandered close to the steep edge. She peered over and drew back quickly with a mock shudder. "Hell of a drop. What was she like, Al," she said, taunting him.

"She was just a girl."

"And you came up here to play with her?"

"Oh, damn it, yes. Now come on down."

She was not through. Glancing at her, he saw that she was smiling maliciously. Lowering her voice, she asked slyly, "What did you play, Al? Doctor?"

When he understood, he took a step toward her, his face contorted. In his fury he slapped her twice across the face. Louise, stepping back from the blow, brought her shoeless foot down on a sharp pebble. To transfer her weight from the injured foot she took still another step backward, this time into empty space.

Morlock, lunging to catch her, nearly went over the sheer edge himself. Staring down he could see her body twist and turn and hear her thin, terrified wail. She seemed to fall for an impossibly long time before the green boughs of the hemlocks reached up to receive her. In that moment he was aware of a great rushing tide of revelation. That was how it was to fall, the body turning, the lips screaming. That was how Marianna Cruz had died.

He had never let himself think about it before. Now it was thrust on him. He sobbed once, and began to run down the trail. There was heavy undergrowth around the base of the rock. It tore his flesh and his clothing as he forced his way through. When he came to her, Louise was lying face down on a mass of detritus from the rock.

Her clothing was hardly disheveled and there was nothing gruesome about her appearance. She might have been sleeping there except that her body was curiously flattened, out of proportion. Morlock turned her over and then, without feeling for her pulse, he began to force his way through the underbrush to the road that led to the filling station. And Cory, sitting in his car, saw Morlock running, head down, unaware of the blood streaming down from his face.

As he ran Morlock frantically made plans. Louise had already cost him too much, in dignity, in self-respect. He would not let her cost him his freedom — his life, perhaps. She was dead. He was certain that she was dead so that there was no person except himself who could say what had happened on top of the rock. She had fallen accidentally. It happened all the time. That was what he would tell them. He would have to assume a grief that he did not feel, but he could do it. He must do it. He had a driving obsession to get her body away from the rock and this he could do by pretending to refuse to believe that she was dead. He would get someone to help him to get her away from there and at the same time add color to his picture of bereavement. Alive or dead she desecrated Abram's Rock.

Chapter 14

Gurney: I will recall William Davis to the stand.
Cameron: Witness will remember that he is still under oath.
Gurney: Mr. Davis, getting back to Sunday, May 20th, I'd like to ask you if you saw the car driven by the last witness, Cory.
Davis: I didn't see any car. I didn't see her then, either.
Gurney: Her?
Davis: Mrs. Morlock. This Cory already said he pulled ahead of the filling station before he parked. I was pretty busy. I did see Morlock's car when he pulled in but I didn't pay much attention to him. I knew where he was going.
Gurney: Tell us what happened then.
Davis: Maybe half an hour after Morlock got out of his car and went toward the rock, I was sitting in the station making out bills. All of a sudden I heard footsteps coming like someone was running — I've got gravel around the gas pumps. You can't walk on it without making a racket. I got up to see what was going on and just then he came in the door. He was breathing hard and his hair was all mussed up. He had a couple of bad scratches on his face. He yelled, "She fell from the rock. Help me." I tried to steady him down so I could find out what happened. "Who did?" I asked him. He said, "My wife. Help me, please." I've got a stretcher that the Civil Defense issued me in the station. I knew that if she was hurt she'd have to be carried out to the road. I called the town constable — we don't have a police force — and I told him to come out to the station and to send an ambulance. Then I went with Morlock. I was carrying the stretcher and I had a hard time keeping up with him. I asked him how it had happened and he said —
Liebman: Your Honor, I don't think that would be admissible.
Gurney: It would be in the *Res Gestae*. I can give you any number of precedents.

Cameron: I'll have to agree with Mr. Gurney, Mr. Liebman.
Liebman: I'll withdraw the objection.
Cameron: Witness will continue.
Davis: He was pretty broken up. He said, "I don't know, I don't know." He kept after me to hurry. Well, pretty soon we came to where she was. I took one look at her and I told him that I was sorry for him but it wasn't any use and we might as well go back and let the ambulance men handle it but he insisted that she wasn't dead and we should get her to the hospital. So the two of us got her on the stretcher and started out of the woods. Halfway there we met Tom Harrison — he's the constable — and Doctor Sedge.
The Commonwealth of Massachusetts vs. Alvin Morlock.
Redirect testimony of William Davis.

Gurney: Doctor Sedge, the witness who preceded you has stated that you were present when the body of Louise Morlock was being carried from the woods surrounding Abram's Rock. Would you give the jury an account of what happened from that point?
Sedge: I am an intern at the County Hospital. I was on call on Sunday — the Sunday in question — and when Constable Harrison telephoned for an ambulance to meet him at Mr. Davis's filling station, my immediate thought was that there had been an auto accident. I got in the ambulance and told the driver where to go. When we got to the station, Constable Harrison was already there. The station was unlocked but there was no one in sight and we were puzzled for a moment until the driver looked up the road and saw two men with a stretcher. We hurried to meet them.
Gurney: "Them" being the accused and Mr. Davis?
Sedge: Yes. Constable Harrison took one end of the stretcher and the ambulance driver took the other. I told them not to stop and put her down but to keep right on going to the ambulance and I would examine her on the way to the hospital. It seemed to me that she was either dead or moribund —
Gurney: Moribund?
Sedge: Dying. I felt for a pulse while I walked along beside the stretcher but I could find none. She was probably dead then, although she might have been barely alive. In deep shock the pulse is often extremely difficult to detect. On the way to the hospital I was able to examine her more thoroughly. She was, by that time, unquestionably dead.

Gurney: From a fall?

Sedge: I would say from injuries resulting from a fall. I examined her at the hospital again. Among other injuries, she had a fractured skull and pelvis, several fractured vertebrae, one of which had pierced the pericardium, and fractures of the left femur and tibia. I assumed that the specific and immediate cause of death was hemorrhage due to the piercing of the pericardium. The medical examiner later conducted an autopsy and confirmed this.

Gurney: Were there any superficial injuries? Scratches or bruises such as those resulting from a blow?

Sedge: There were many such but these could also have been the result of her fall.

Gurney: Did the accused ride in the ambulance with you?

Sedge: He did. He had lacerations on his face. When I was certain that I could do nothing for the woman I offered to take care of him. He was in a state of shock; almost numb with grief, I thought. He hardly seemed to understand what I was saying. I cleansed his cuts and scratches when we arrived at the hospital. I told him that I had notified the medical examiner and that he could wait in the hospital reception room.

Gurney: What was his reaction?

Sedge: He seemed startled that it would be necessary to notify an official. He asked, "Do you have to do that? She fell from the rock. It was an accident."

Gurney: You spoke of lacerations on his face. Could they have been inflicted in a scuffle or fight?

Sedge: I would say so, yes. He claimed that he scratched his face while running to the spot where his wife fell.

Gurney: That will be all, and thank you, doctor.

Cameron: Does the defense wish to cross-examine?

Liebman: Not at this time. I reserve the right to cross-examination.

Gurney: I shall now call Police Chief Charles Stewart to the stand.

Cameron: I do not wish to press you, Mr. Gurney. In order that the Court may determine the future course of this trial, however, I should like to know how many more witnesses you intend to produce.

Gurney: This will be the final witness for the prosecution, Your Honor.

Cameron: Thank you. The witness will be sworn.

Gurney: Chief Stewart, you are the head of the Warfield Police

Department, are you not?

Stewart: I am.

Gurney: Did you personally arrest the accused?

Stewart: I did.

Gurney: On what date and on what charge?

Stewart: Tuesday, May 22. The charge was suspicion of homicide.

Gurney: What specifically led you to make the arrest after a lapse of two days?

Stewart: Well, first let me say this. In the event of the unnatural death of a married woman under circumstances that are at all suspicious, a police officer will automatically consider the possibility of homicide by the husband. This isn't my own conclusion. It is the sum of the experience of many police officials. More often than not it is a homicide.

Gurney: But you didn't arrest Morlock on just a possibility?

Stewart: The medical examiner doubted the story the accused sold him. He notified the district attorney who got in touch with me since Morlock lived in my jurisdiction. There was certainly insufficient evidence to justify an arrest at that time. We talked it over. The accused was a teacher at the college. If it got out that we were investigating him for the murder of his wife, he would have been ruined even if he was innocent. The district attorney asked me to make a confidential check and see if there were any indications that Morlock might have killed her: motive — that sort of thing. I found out most of the things that you have been hearing here during the trial. On the 21st — the day after the murder —

Liebman: Objection.

Stewart: I'm sorry. I should have said after the death of Morlock's wife.

Cameron: That much of the testimony as involves the word "murder" will be stricken. Please be more careful, Chief Stewart.

Stewart: On the evening of the 21st I visited Morlock in his home. I had already learned some facts about the financial trouble he was in. When I got there he was cleaning the woodwork in his kitchen. I immediately thought of bloodstains, but if there were any there he had probably removed them. He had enough turpentine and paint remover on the table to do a good job. I still didn't have enough evidence to arrest him. I talked to him for a little while and then left.

Gurney: And you arrested him the next day?

Stewart: I did. On the strength of an anonymous telephone call that

I received the following morning.

Liebman: Your Honor, I am going to anticipate counsel's next question. I'd like a ruling on the admissibility of the content of this telephone conversation before any portion of it is brought out to the prejudice of my client.

Cameron: The content of any such conversation would fall within the definition of hearsay and would not be admissible.

Liebman: Thank you.

Gurney: Your witness, Mr. Liebman.

Liebman: Chief Stewart, when you visited Alvin Morlock's home you found him cleaning woodwork in the kitchen and immediately thought of bloodstains. You knew then, beyond any possibility of doubt, that she had fallen to her death miles away. Then why the rigmarole about bloodstains?

Stewart: I did not know beyond any doubt that she had fallen to her death. As a matter of fact, when I left Morlock's home I called the medical examiner and asked if it was possible that she had been killed elsewhere and her body later thrown from the rock. I was told that it was not impossible. I thought — I still think — it possible that there had at least been a quarrel in the kitchen. I think that removing paint from woodwork is an unusual activity for a recently widowed man.

Liebman: And the next day you arrested the accused on the strength of an anonymous telephone call. Is this a practice of yours?

Stewart: The anonymous telephone call was one part of what was by then a large mass of circumstantial and other evidence against Morlock. As a matter of fact, the person who made the call is no longer anonymous. I have identified that person, to my own satisfaction, while sitting here in this court.

Liebman: Who was it?

Stewart: The student, Cory. The one who drove Mrs. Morlock to South Danville on the day she was killed. I recognized his voice as soon as he took the stand.

Liebman: You could be mistaken though, couldn't you?

Stewart: I could be, but I'm not.

Liebman: Well, we'll leave that for the jury to decide, Chief Stewart. I wonder, however, if you might clear up a little puzzle for me. You have heard Cory testify that he drove Mrs. Morlock to Abram's Rock. Yet earlier you suggested that the bloodstains on the woodwork in Morlock's apartment resulted from an assault by the accused on his wife, and that he then drove her to the rock and disposed of her body.

Stewart: I stick with what I said about the bloodstains. I still think there was a fight and the blood was Louise Morlock's. But now that you remind me about the boy's testimony, I think it might have happened this way —

Liebman: Never mind the speculation, Chief Stewart.

Gurney: Objection, Your Honor: Counsel asked the witness a question. Now he refuses to allow him to answer.

Cameron: The witness will be allowed to answer, Mr. Liebman. I'll rule on admissibility when he's finished.

Stewart: As I was saying, the deceased had Cory drive her out there after a quarrel in order to patch up things with her husband. The accused made no attempt, as far as we can learn, to make any secret of the visits he made to Abram's Rock. He knew that she would follow him up there, sooner or later, and that way he would avoid the self-incrimination involved in taking her there himself. He —

Liebman: Your Honor, I must protest the groundless insinuations...

The Commonwealth of Massachusetts vs. Alvin Morlock.
Direct testimony of Dr. Robert Sedge; cross-examination of
Chief of Police Charles Stewart.

Morlock made the return trip to Abram's Rock with the filling station owner trailing behind him, carrying a rolled up stretcher. The man kept asking foolishly, "What happened?" Morlock, needing to think, wished that the man would be quiet. He answered, "I don't know, I don't know," hoping that the man would interpret his answer as the sort of frenzied distraction that he would expect under the circumstances. He had already told the man, back at the filling station, that she had fallen from the rock. Now, he supposed, he wanted a morbid description of the details of the fall. Excitement for a Sunday morning. When they reached the spot where Louise had fallen, the man bent over the crumpled body and then straightened with a theatrically long face.

"It isn't any use, mister," he said. "The best thing we can do is leave her here and wait until the ambulance comes."

Morlock had to get her out of there. He said in grief-stricken disbelief, "Maybe she isn't dead. Please help me with her. We'll have to move her out to the road anyway."

The man bent to unroll the stretcher. "All right," he said, "give me a hand with her now and we'll roll her on face up."

The body was oddly flaccid. The filling station man said, "She must be all smashed inside."

Morlock bent to pick up one end of the stretcher — the front end. The other man moved to the back to spare Morlock the supposed agony of looking at his wife's body. With the heavy burden between them, they began to pick their way out of the woods toward the dirt road. The going was difficult and Morlock, not in the best physical condition, felt his heart begin to pound with the effort. Wanting to stop, he nevertheless kept on while the sweat broke out on his face and bile rose in his throat. Every ounce of his strength was being poured into the task of putting one foot down, ignoring the pull at his shoulders and arms, and then bringing the other foot forward in its turn. He hardly knew it when other hands took the stretcher from him.

When he could think again he was in the ambulance and another man — a doctor, he supposed — was looking at him curiously. "Are you all right?" the doctor asked.

The doctor's eyes were intelligent behind his glasses. Have to be careful now. Don't overact, Morlock told himself. He turned quickly to look at the stretcher. The doctor had drawn a sheet over Louise's face. Morlock put his hands up to cover his eyes. He did not want to meet the doctor's glance. The intelligent eyes would be filled with pity, sympathy for the bereaved husband, and Morlock could not face them. The doctor said sympathetically, "I'm sorry. I understand that she fell from Abram's Rock."

Morlock nodded, not speaking.

The doctor was looking at him intently. "Look here," he said. "You've got some nasty cuts on your face. We'd better have a look at them."

"They don't hurt," Morlock said. "I can wait until we get to the hospital. Are we almost there?"

In the hospital efficient hands wheeled the stretcher bearing Louise's body through one door and other hands ushered Morlock into the gleaming white emergency room. "Might as well clean those cuts up here," the doctor said busily. "I'm Doctor Sedge, by the way. Then when we've got you fixed up you can sit in the reception room and wait for the medical examiner."

Morlock repeated dully, "The medical examiner? Do we have to report this to him? It was an accident," wishing almost as he spoke that he had not acted so surprised. He hadn't thought about it, but he realized that there would be some sort of official inquiry. The question might have a guilty ring to Doctor Sedge.

If it had, the doctor did not show it. "A matter of routine," he said. "We have to notify him in the event of any accidental death."

The medical examiner came and there were questions; interminably there were questions before the official, a fat man with an overbearing manner, dismissed him. "That will be all, Mr. Morlock," he said pompously. "For now."

Morlock did not, of course, go in to the college on the day following Louise's death. He called Dean Gorham and was told that certainly, Alvin, we wouldn't think of your coming in for at least a week. Take as much time as you wish and if there is anything we can do. . . . Meanwhile, we are terribly sorry about your wife. . . .

Later he called the funeral parlor. Oh yes, Mr. Morlock. A tragic thing. Please accept our heartfelt and so on and of course we'll be glad to handle everything for you. Ah — is there insurance? We'll be glad to make financial arrangements, of course. . . .

Of all the people he knew, only Dodson, fat and slovenly and strangely decent, came to see him.

"Al," he said awkwardly, "I'm going to leave my car with you. You'll probably need to be getting around. Anything else? I've got a few bucks."

Morlock, deeply shamed, thanked him and saw him to the door. When Dodson was gone he puttered about the house absently. He was not at that time greatly frightened that he would be found out. Apparently Louise's death had been accepted as an accident. Well, in a way it was.

He had by this time almost convinced himself that he had not struck her hard enough to make her fall. In the kitchen closet he came upon the turpentine and paint remover that he had so hopefully brought home to Louise months ago.

For want of anything better to do — he planned to leave this house and its associations as soon as he could — he brought them out. There was one board in the wainscoting that Louise had started to strip, leaving it half finished. Might as well finish it, he thought. He was scraping the old paint when he heard a knock at the door. Not getting up he called, "Come in." When the door opened he turned to see blue serge and brass buttons, and then he was frightened.

"Good evening," the officer said. "I'm Chief Steward. I heard about your wife's accident. Thought I'd drop in and talk to you about it."

He was staring at the sandpaper and the paint remover, Morlock saw. It was silly to feel guilty about a thing of which he was innocent, but immediately the act of removing the paint took on a criminal meaning. He said fatuously, "Have a chair, Chief. I was just taking some paint off the woodwork. Something my wife started."

Stewart said, "No, thanks." He kept right on staring at the woodwork, Morlock noticed. Looking for bloodstains, he was certain — particularly after Stewart's next comment, "Did you and your wife quarrel a great deal, Mr. Morlock?"

Morlock answered, "I guess not any more than the average couple. We did have an occasional argument."

Stewart nodded. "I suppose," he said. "Probably about money. That's what most family quarrels start over. Was it money, Mr. Morlock?"

Morlock, faintly angry, began, "Look here — "

Stewart interrupted. "Don't be offended," he said. "I'll be frank with you, Mr. Morlock. Your wife died a violent death under circumstances that are a little suspicious. As part of my job I have been inquiring around — as much to protect you from publicity if there is nothing wrong as to find anything criminal in your wife's death. I'm sure you realize that we always investigate these things."

Morlock, who had not realized anything of the sort, said, "Certainly."

Stewart reached for the doorknob. "I'm not going to bother you tonight," he said. "Later in the week I may want you to come in and make a statement." And he was gone. Hurriedly, Morlock thought.

He went to bed but not to sleep. While the noise of the traffic, the rustle of humanity died about the old house, he lay with his arms folded under his head staring at nothing and seeing a body twisting down, down, down. Not Louise's body. Marianna's.

Cory could not sleep either, nor had he slept on Sunday night. When he had seen Morlock emerging from the woods with his face painted with blood, he had turned his old car and raced away from that place. Morlock's appearance, alone and bleeding, could only mean one thing.

He must have forced Louise to tell who had driven her out there, had helped her follow him. If she had told him that, he would have forced the rest of the story from her and now he must know all about him, Cory. God knew what he had done to Louise. Beaten her and left her lying there, probably, while he came looking for Cory.

Cory lived in a dormitory. Morlock, he knew, could find out where he lived and he would be coming for him. Ah, God. It wasn't fair. She had started the whole thing. Cory took an armful of his clothing and fled the dormitory. He started for Fall River. Morlock wouldn't think of looking for him there and he could hide in any one of a thousand rooming houses.

When he reached Fall River he felt the need of a drink. There would be plenty of time later to look for a rooming house. He parked the car and walked into a bar. There were people in this place, lots of them. Morlock could not touch him here.

After a time he decided that he might just as well stay here until dark, in case someone had seen the direction he had taken when he left Warfield and Morlock had found out. He was half again as heavy and strong as Morlock, but it did not occur to him that it bordered on the ridiculous for him to fear the smaller man.

Cory had long since recognized the physical cowardice within him and adjusted himself accordingly. He did not know the extreme of fear until he heard the news on the bar radio. Almost as an afterthought the announcer said, near the close of the program, "The wife of a Ludlow College instructor fell to her death this morning from Abram's Rock, a landmark in the South Danville vicinity. No further details were available at the time of this news broadcast."

When he heard the broadcast, Cory literally shook, and the bartender asked, "You all right, mister?"

Cory, certain that Morlock had killed his wife and equally certain that Morlock would kill him if he found him, said, "Sure. I'm okay." He spent the night sleeplessly in a rooming house. Morlock could not possibly know he was here, could not possibly find him, he told himself. But at each creak of the timbers of the old house, at each street noise, each footstep, he started.

The following morning he rushed from the place to buy a newspaper. He riffled through the pages, looking for a further report on Louise Morlock's death. When he found it, it told him nothing more than the news broadcast had. He was by this time near the edge of panic. He had very little money left; he could not stay here more than a day or so. He could not go back to Warfield, where Morlock was waiting.

He walked the streets until noon, seeking crowds to mingle with.

He then telephoned a friend at Ludlow, unable to stand the uncertainty.

"Johnny," he asked, "anything new? Anybody been looking for me?"

Johnny, recognizing Cory's voice, said, "Not that I know of. Where you been? You missed two classes."

Cory answered vaguely, "Oh — around. Hey, that was something about Morlock's wife, wasn't it? Was Morlock in his classes?"

"Are you crazy? Of course not. Say, what's on your mind? You didn't call up just to talk about Morlock's wife. With the record you've got you'd better get on in to class."

Cory hung up. It had been silly to ask if Morlock was at class. Certainly he would not be, but he had hoped for it against all common sense. If he knew where Morlock was for just a little while he could relax for that time at least. As it stood now, Morlock might be looking for him at this minute.

He spent Monday night in fear that became increasingly tinged with resentment. Here he was, broke and afraid, and Morlock remained free to find him and kill him as he had killed his wife. Why didn't the cops — ? Cory suddenly grinned as the solution struck him. Of course, he thought. Morlock had fooled them with some lie about an accident. Once they knew the truth — and he would see that they did — they would have to arrest Morlock.

In the morning he called the Warfield Police Station and asked cautiously to speak with the chief.

"You know about what happened to Mrs. Morlock, don't you? She lived on Kosciusko Street. It was in the newspapers."

Chief Stewart asked impatiently, "Of course we do. Who is this? What's your name?"

Cory said, "It doesn't make any difference what my name is. I just wanted to tell you that Morlock killed his wife. If she went off a cliff it was because he pushed her off." He hesitated, wanting to make a stronger case against Morlock but wishing at the same time to avoid possibly implicating himself.

"He found out that she was sleeping with some guy," he said finally, and hung up. He had only to wait until the noon news program now, and he could go back to Warfield. They would have to arrest Morlock now.

Chapter 15

Ladies and gentlemen of the jury, you have heard the evidence in this case and it now becomes your duty to weigh it, examine it, and determine if the accused is guilty, and, if he is guilty, in what degree. In the last two days the prosecution has brought before you witness after witness to testify against Alvin Morlock. Reviewing them briefly, we have proved that he was heavily in debt, largely as a result of his wife's extravagance. She gambled with his money and lost it. We know that he held an insurance policy on the life of his wife — a policy taken out only a handful of hours after his marriage. The sum of money was not large — but it would have relieved the pressure of his debts. Isn't it conceivable that it struck Morlock as a form of grim but poetic justice that she be made to repay the money she had lost? There was only one way that she could pay — with her life. The prosecution contends that Morlock exacted this payment.

Now consider the position of the accused. He was an instructor in a small college in a small town. His character, his reputation, were more important to him than would have been the case had he been a mechanic or a farmer. Louise Morlock left his house. She was arrested in a near-by city and only the merciful consideration of the officer who arrested her saved her from being charged with prostitution. He must have lived in fear that it would happen again and that this time it could not be hushed up. There was literally only one way he could be certain that it could not happen again. If she were dead.

We can believe that she made life intolerable for her husband. You have heard what happened when he made a pathetic effort to entertain his best friend in his own home. She shamed him, humiliated him. If this were not enough, she betrayed him with one of his own students.

All these things the defense will repeat to you in rebuttal, and they are true. We do not deny them. But there is another side to the picture. The side that Louise Morlock would reveal if she were alive.

Through the testimony of Thomas Dodson and Atillio Palaggi we have demonstrated that Alvin Morlock had every opportunity to realize the fact that Louise Palaggi was a woman of little education, little refinement. He took the risk of marrying her for reasons that are still his own since he has not seen fit to take the stand. Perhaps he felt that he could shape her to his own desires. Perhaps he was lonely and sought to warm himself at the fire of marriage. Both of these purposes, I remind you, are selfish.

Let us say that his reasons were the most charitable that we can conceive, and the fact will remain that he took a risk and should have been prepared to pay the price should he lose — and we concede that he did lose. It was a bad marriage. But I remind you that it was a bad marriage for Louise as well as for the accused. She had only one recourse, one escape from it. She could drink, pass her days in drunkenness. Alvin Morlock had no recourse save one. He had to get rid of her. You cannot judge if he was justified in doing so. You can only judge whether or not, on the basis of the evidence you have heard, he did or did not kill her. And if he did, was it a murder of passion, an involuntary act on the part of a man insane with fury, or a cold and calculated obliteration of what he considered an evil.

The defense will plead with you that if he is guilty he is guilty only of the former. He did not know, they will tell you, that she would follow him to Abram's Rock on a given day and that therefore he could not have premeditated her death. I submit to you that Morlock planned her death over a period of time and that he waited as patiently as any tiger for the opportunity to spring. The law does not set a time limit on premeditation. A man does not have to plan his crime three months or four or two hours or two minutes in advance of its execution in order for premeditation to exist. The actual purpose of the law governing premeditation is to define intent. Did Morlock intend to kill his wife? I say that he did, and that the moment he waited for arrived on the morning of Sunday, May 20th, when she allowed herself to be tolled to the cliff from which she plunged to her death.

Alvin Morlock did not love his wife. If any love ever existed, he helped destroy it. Yet, when he ran to the filling station to report her fall and to seek help, he pretended to be pitifully broken up. He carried on the pretense with Doctor Sedge and with the medical examiner . . . and I remind you that he was startled when he learned that the medical examiner had been notified. Why startled, if Louise's fall were an accident? And so I say . . .

> *The Commonwealth of Massachusetts vs. Alvin Morlock.*
> *From the summation of Prosecution Attorney Alfred*
> *Gurney.*

After delivering his charge to the jury, Superior Court Justice Dunstan Cameron watched the jurors file from the room in solemn procession. He felt troubled. Before he rose from the bench to recess the court, he called to the bailiff. "Ask Mr. Liebman and Mr. Gurney to come to my chambers," he said.

When Liebman and Gurney arrived Judge Cameron was staring out the high window of his chambers. He turned at their entrance. "Gentlemen," he invited them, "find chairs. I won't take much of your time." He turned to Liebman. "Sam, I don't want you to misunderstand me. I am not criticizing your conduct of the defense, but I don't believe Morlock could have made a worse impression if he had tried. Wouldn't he consent to take the stand?"

Liebman shook his head. "I did my very damnedest to persuade him," he said. "I practically told him it was his neck if he didn't get up there. I guess you noticed his expression — the jury did."

Judge Cameron nodded. "Lack of expression would be a better description. I don't believe he showed the slightest sign of emotion throughout the entire trial."

Liebman shrugged. "I told him, for God's sake to look as if he were sorry about something — anything. Judge, I was appointed to defend Morlock. He's indigent and couldn't afford counsel after the way his wife stripped him. In spite of that, I give you my word that I did everything that I could. I worked harder to try and make a case for him than I have since I was admitted — and you know how long that's been. It's almost impossible to defend a man who won't defend himself."

"I'm sure of that, Sam. You did your best. Still, I'm worried about a reversal if the jury comes in with the verdict I think they'll reach. He made a poor impression."

Liebman shook his head. "Morlock has already told me that he doesn't want to appeal the verdict, whatever it is. I'd like to tell you something else he said. This was after I'd told him that he was just asking for the chair if he didn't listen to my advice. He said, 'If I'm to be executed, I hope the judge will make it as soon as possible.' I've heard that sort of talk before but I always could see the martyr complex behind it. I think Morlock actually means it."

Gurney said, "If they bring in a guilty verdict, appeal is automatic."

Judge Cameron nodded. "That's true," he said, "but the Supreme Court would be prejudiced against him if he didn't actively seek the appeal. Couldn't you have produced a few more witnesses?"

Liebman shook his head. "I wanted to put her brother on the stand," he said. "Morlock wouldn't have it. Actually, he was probably right. If I had used her own brother to attack her character — particularly after the showing the old man made — it would have had a bad effect on the jury. In any case, the prosecution admitted to her poor character. The only defense was to establish Morlock's good character, and he is such a neutral sort of man that even that is difficult. And you, Gurney, made his trip to Providence with Dodson look like the orgy of the century."

Judge Cameron nodded. "I suppose you're right," he said slowly. "Under the circumstances it was almost imperative that Morlock take the stand himself — unless he actually wanted to be found guilty. He was aware of that?"

Liebman nodded. "As I said, I told him that it was his neck if he didn't."

Judge Cameron stood up. "Well, gentlemen, I guess that's all. Thank you for coming."

In the corridor Gurney said to Liebman, "What about lunch?"

"I guess so. Let's go to the Hof-Brau. I could use a drink before I eat. I'll tell the bailiff where we'll be."

When their drinks came Liebman lifted his in a mock salute to Gurney. "You murdered us," he said.

"I don't know," Gurney answered. "If I did, it wasn't your fault. How long do you think, Sam?"

Liebman glanced at his watch. "Two hours," he said. "If it goes three they'll bring in first-degree."

Their food was brought, but neither man ate with any interest. Liebman said, after a lengthy silence, "Your summation was solid, Alfred. What little popguns I had, you spiked."

Gurney shrugged. "Tell me about Morlock," he said. "What was his story about what happened up on that rock?"

Liebman put down his fork and lit a cigarette. "I went to see him the second day after he was arrested," he said. "I told him that I'd been appointed to the case and that I'd looked into it and that the first thing I'd do was ask for bail to be set pending a hearing by the Grand Jury."

Gurney looked interested. "Well?" he asked.

Liebman smiled ruefully. "He told me that he didn't want bail. Then I told him that he should have no secrets from his attorney and asked him what happened up on the rock. He said, 'She fell.'"

"That's all?" Gurney asked.

"That's all. I told him that if he had killed her, his best course was to plead guilty and that, under the circumstances, we might get the charge reduced to manslaughter. His answer?"

Gurney said, "She fell?"

"Correct. And that's all he would say. I pleaded with him to tell me what had happened. I threatened him with a first-degree murder verdict. I even drew him a picture of the chair. He actually took a small, academic interest in that. I tell you, Gurney, I've had clients who were scared numb so that they could only repeat over and over whatever lie they had committed themselves to. And I've had some who couldn't help me because they were in a state of shock. Morlock was neither scared nor in a state of shock. I got the impression sometimes that he was actually sorry for the trouble he was causing me." Liebman pushed his chair back and stood up. "I feel badly about this," he said. "Can you think of anything I didn't do that I could have done?"

Gurney signaled for the check. "I don't think so, Sam."

The courtroom was nearly empty when they returned to it. Only a handful of spectators, grimly determined to be present when the jury came in, clung to their seats. A few court attachés sat listlessly at the front of the room. Liebman thanked Gurney for the lunch and made his way back through the maze of corridors to the detention cells, where Morlock was being held during trial hours. He nodded to the custodian and said softly, "Alvin?"

Morlock sat up. "Hello, Sam," he said.

Liebman said, "I don't want you to worry any more than you can help. Let's face it. They've been out almost two hours already. If they were going to find you not guilty they'd have done it by now. I want you to ask for the appeal if things turn out badly." Liebman argued in vain. After a few minutes he returned to the courtroom. When Gurney saw him, he raised an eyebrow. Liebman returned the gesture with raised shoulders and out-turned palms.

When Liebman had first visited Morlock in his cell two days after his arrest and two months before his trial, Morlock had already decided on the course he would take. He would die — he smiled wryly at the thought that it was quite possible that he *would* die before he would reveal the nature of that last quarrel. On the night of the day that Louise fell to her death, he had known animal panic and great fear that he might be found out. Later the fear became revulsion, shame that he might stand publicly accused of killing her, that before the world he would appear to have risked his life in such a sorry cause. He had killed her because she had trespassed on the most secret recesses of his being, trampling and scuffling with dirty feet, but he could not say this. It would be assumed that he had killed her, if they refused to believe his story of an accident, because she had spent his money, had gambled, had whored. Stewart, the police chief, had indicated when he arrested Morlock that these were the stuff of suspicion. Well, let them. He would not, could not, ask for the pity and the mercy of a jury by telling them what Louise had been any more than he could tell them of her obscene remark about Marianna Cruz. The jury would never be able to understand how he felt about Marianna. He was left no choice but to say that Louise fell, this and nothing more. He said it with the monotonous beat of a metronome and to the great exasperation of Sam Liebman.

In the first days of his confinement, he slept little. He had only to close his eyes, it seemed, and the vision of Marianna Cruz's body hurtling into the green depths of the forest would recur. He had not been there when she actually had fallen and he had never before pictured what it must have been like. The picture had been forced upon him when he saw Louise make the same terrible journey through space; and it returned and returned. He had much time for his regressions and this time he did not have to apologize to himself for making them. In a cell there was little else to do. But there was another difference. He had lost the power to select, to pick and choose from a hundred memories, and the memory that kept returning was one he had avoided for nineteen years. It concerned his betrayal of Marianna.

He had been sixteen, nearly two years older than she, when it happened. She had been his constant companion for four years. If her English had improved, she had changed little otherwise. She remained a shy child with great eyes and an elfin quality that he could recognize even then. If her breasts were beginning to bud, she was unconscious of it. Through long association they could very nearly understand each other without the use of speech. Each school day he waited for her to pass his house. He would walk with her then and so much a habit was this that the schoolboys no longer jeered or made comments when they approached the schoolyard.

It happened that a cycle of teen-age faddism made scholastic ability fashionable. Morlock, who was an excellent student, won several prizes in quick succession and whereas this would have ordinarily gone unnoticed by the student body, the fashion dictated that he be given the same recognition as an outstanding athlete. Morlock, who had never been noticed by ninety per cent of his classmates, who had been invited to not more than two parties in his life, who did not resent being called a stick-in-the-mud, suddenly found himself being lionized. Football and basketball players sought him out, calling him admiringly, "The Professor." He reacted to it in the manner of a ham actor finding himself in a hit show. There was a girl, an early blooming Circe of a girl, in Morlock's class. So pretty a girl that most of Morlock's classmates were in love with her, dreamed pillow-hugging dreams of rescuing her from all manner of terrible situations. Morlock had been content to admire her from a great distance, knowing that she was from another sphere and not reaching to it. When he suddenly became socially acceptable, she sought him out in the corridor.

"Alvin," she said, "we're all going over to Franklin's for hamburgers after school. Why don't you ever come with us?"

She said the words with the graceful condescension of the queen that she was, and Morlock immediately became her subject. Frantically estimating how much hamburgers would come to and if he would be expected to pay for hers — funny he couldn't remember her name now or what she looked like — he said as casually as he could, "I'm not doing anything. Sure — I'd like to."

Fascinated by her, he joined her group of admirers as soon as the last class was finished. When they came to the gate of the schoolyard, Marianna Cruz was waiting for him in the placid certainty that he would walk home with her as he always did. The queen called, "Alvin, your friend is waiting for you. I guess you can't come after all."

They had laughed, then, at him and at drab little Marianna. Morlock, desperate to show his maleness, had said loudly, "Oh, go on home, you little Portagee, and quit hanging around me."

Marianna had turned, her shoulders straight, and walked away. Morlock wanted to run after her and comfort her as he had when the other children had called her that same name on Abram's Rock when she first moved to the neighborhood. But he could not forgo the company of the gold-and-white girl and her court. A day later he came to the defiant conclusion that Marianna was worth ten times as much as any one of them; but at that time, when he hurt her, he did not go to her. And everything else in his life had hinged on his betrayal of Marianna. If he was a second-rate teacher, it was because he had been a second-rate friend to her when she needed him. If his life was a succession of failures, it was because he had failed her when he was sixteen.

That was the unbidden memory that came to Morlock in the cell where he was confined. Marianna never came back to school. He never saw her again. A week later he approached the school to see his classmates gathered in a gossiping little knot inside the gate. One of them said, "Wasn't that awful about the little Portagee girl, Alvin?"

Morlock had been briefly dazed. "What about her?" he asked. "What happened?"

They told him, in fragments and phrases.

"She's dead!"

"She fell off of Abram's Rock."

"Her father went out looking for her when she didn't come home to supper."

"The police were out there. They said she must have slipped."

"My father says it's dangerous up there and they ought to put a fence up or keep kids off it."

Morlock had turned away from them, not ashamed of the tears in his eyes. If he had not hurt her, if he had been a faithful friend, he would have been with her and he wouldn't have let her get too near the edge. Maybe she had fallen on purpose. Maybe it had been an accident. Nobody would ever know, but Alvin Morlock knew this — Marianna would not have died if he had been with her.

They had an elaborate funeral for Marianna. The entire school went and Morlock was pushed and shoved close to the front of the procession. "He was her friend," they whispered busily. "Let him be up front." So they made way for him so that he could be more ashamed.

The fad for scholarship passed and Morlock returned to the obscurity that he was never to leave until he went on trial for his life. Until the time he was arrested for murder he had never once permitted himself to remember the events leading up to Marianna's death. The first time that he did remember it, he combined two memories: the happy time of the pact they had made on Abram's Rock, and the terrible time he had deserted her. The recollection of the manner in which a body twisted and turned as it fell through the air acted as a trigger to his guilty thoughts. He no longer wished to live. He was overwhelmed by remorse that even extended to Louise. After all, he told himself, if he had not married her she would still be alive.

When Sam Liebman visited him and suggested that if he pleaded guilty he might be found guilty only of manslaughter, Morlock had already decided that he would do nothing, say nothing to mitigate his guilt. If he stood trial and was found guilty, he would accept it.

Chapter 16

Sam Liebman sat beside Alfred Gurney, waiting for the jury to return. "Three and a half hours," he said, glancing at the old-fashioned clock on the wall.

Gurney smiled. "You've waited for juries before, Sam," he said. "Stop fretting. Change the subject. How is Morlock taking it?"

"I went back there again a few minutes ago. He was half asleep. You did a job on him — and me."

"I had all the witnesses," Gurney said.

"Sure you did. Where did you get that Stewart?"

"Stewart, the Chief of Police? He's a wonder, isn't he? He had F.B.I. training and it stuck. He'll trip on his own cleverness some day. Still, he made quite a witness — Hold it, Sam."

"What is it?"

"Here they come. They just talked with the bailiff through the door."

A court attendant went scurrying for Judge Cameron while the spectators who had been strolling the grounds, smoking in the corridors, patiently waiting, rustled into the courtroom. When order was called and the jury filed in, a custodian brought Morlock in from the detention cell. He glanced almost blankly at the faces of the jurors. They stared straight ahead, their expressions indicating their awareness of the gravity of their verdict, whatever it was.

When the courtroom was still, Judge Cameron asked, "Ladies and gentlemen of the jury, have you reached a verdict in the case now before you?"

The foreman said, "We have."

"How find you?"

"We find the defendant, Alvin Morlock, guilty of murder in the first degree."

Judge Cameron hesitated, then asked, "Do you have any recommendations?"

"We do not."

Judge Cameron turned to face Morlock. He said quietly, "Alvin

Morlock, you have been found guilty of murder in the first degree by a jury of your peers. Since there has been no recommendation that mercy be shown you, in accordance with the laws of the Commonwealth of Massachusetts I now must pass the sentence of death by electrocution on you. On the 15th day of October, the warden of the penitentiary in which you are confined will see that the terms of this sentence are carried out. And may God have mercy on your soul."

In the two months that Morlock served on death row in Charlestown, he had three visitors. They were Sam Liebman, Thomas Dodson, and Dominick Palaggi. Liebman visited him twice, uneasy with the thought that Morlock was deliberately destroying himself and that he did not deserve to die.

"Alvin," he said, on his last visit, "let me go to the governor and ask for a stay. Man, even if you killed that woman she isn't worth your life. Even a commutation would get you life and you would be a free man in twenty years."

Morlock said, "I appreciate how you feel, Sam. I think that you mean it for me and not as a professional matter. But I don't want to fight it."

Tom Dodson came and sat for half an hour in the visitors' room with Morlock. In that time he did not say half a dozen words. Morlock, at the moment he was sentenced to die, had become entitled, in Dodson's eyes, to some of the respect reserved for the dead. There was an ethereal, a spiritual quality to the atmosphere of death row that frightened and impressed Dodson, and their conversation consisted of Morlock comforting his visitor. When Dodson rose to go, Morlock put his arm around his shoulder. "Don't come back, Tom," he said. "I appreciate your coming and I wish things had been different. You're probably my only friend and I'd like to make it up to you. If it will make it easier for you, I'm not frightened. It's going to be all right." And Dodson left, his eyes streaming.

Last to come and most unexpected was Dominick Palaggi. He came into the visitors' room shyly, and he sat in his straight-backed chair staring at the floor and cracking the knuckles of his big hands while he asked Morlock if he was being treated all right and if the food was all right and was there anything he could get for him. After ten minutes of this he looked squarely at Morlock.

"Louise was no good," he blurted out. "She isn't worth it that you should die if you killed her. I should have killed her myself a long time before she met you."

And Morlock comforted Dominick as he had comforted Dodson.

When Dominick rose to go, he shook hands very formally with Morlock. "Try not to be afraid," he said. "On Federal Hill a lot of us will have masses said for you."

Morlock, as he had told Dodson, was not frightened even when the weeks dwindled to days and the days to hours. He became frightened for the first time when the chaplain came to sit with him for half an hour before his execution — and even then he was more afraid of dying than of death.

When the warden came to read the death warrant and to follow Morlock down the long corridor to the chamber that they referred to only as "the room," Morlock had lost the momentary fear he had known during the chaplain's visit. He shook hands with the three remaining prisoners in death row and accepted their last words. "Don't chicken out, Al."

"Wait for me. I'll be with you in two weeks."

"It's going to be all right. You wait and see." But even as he accepted them and made reply in kind he was moving away from them, caught up in a great wind that swept him out of the chilly corridor of the cell block and back, whirling and spinning, to another time and another place.

He was standing in front of the frame house where he had been a boy and he was waiting for Marianna Cruz; he was telling her that he would walk to school with her and hearing her say, "Then I won't be afraid." Morlock felt the touch of a small hand creeping into his as he walked behind the chaplain and he, in his turn, was not afraid.

"Alvin Morlock, 35, a former teacher at Ludlow College, paid with his life last night for the murder of his wife, Louise. Morlock, who during his trial was icy calm, maintained his composure through his last hours. He showed no sign of fear as he was strapped into the electric chair. Some witnesses, in fact, claimed that they observed a defiant smile on Morlock's face just before the lethal charge was routed through his body."

From the Fall River Bulletin

THE END

THE SNATCH

Harold R. Daniels

Chapter 1

Mollison turned his heavy car from the traffic-burdened main street into the comparative solitude of a backwash of asphalt alley that split two buildings built of old pink brick. Even in the way he drove his car, Lou Morgan thought, Mollison had a flamboyance, a dash. He was not certain that he liked it in Mollison, but he envied Mollison's ability to change his mannerisms as he would have changed a suit. Mollison followed the asphalt between the two walls of brick that shut out the June sunlight until, where still another brick building dammed it, it widened into a long pool of parking space. Here Mollison stopped the car and pointed.

"There," he said. "You couldn't find a more perfect place. In a hundred years they wouldn't look for the kid there." He sat back with the air of having achieved a minor triumph. Morgan glanced unwillingly in the direction of Mollison's gesture. Until now, Mollison's plan had been some thing they just talked about; something they might someday do. They had the place now, and there remained only the time to be set. The plan was taking on a sickening reality.

Mollison had pointed in the direction of a tiny abutment to the main building; a low shed of brick from which sprouted a tremendous chimney, round at the base and tapering at the top like some mighty cannon aimed at the sky.

Mollison talked on. "I've got a key," he said. "I kept it when I was with Decker, Real Estate." He added with a touch of scornful condescension, "I told him he'd never make a dime from the account."

And Decker and Son are worth three quarters of a million dollars, Morgan thought sourly. What was Mollison worth? A hundred dollars? Two hundred maybe?

The two men got out of the car and walked toward the small building at the base of the chimney. Once away from the alley that led into this brick cul-de-sac, they were surrounded by towering pink walls. The old Maynard Mills they were called; a complex of weave sheds and spinning rooms that spread over many acres. The textile machinery was gone, sold for scrap metal long years ago, but the old brick buildings still stood. Too expensive to maintain — too hard to pull down.

There was a scattering of cars in the open court between the buildings. Morgan hesitated. "Won't they notice us going into the building?" he asked.

Mollison waved his hand. "These people? Don't worry about it. Somebody gets hold of a few dollars and starts a business in this old rats' nest because Decker lets them have floor space for nothing. Next month he's broke and somebody else comes in. Don't worry about it," he repeated.

They reached the low building and Mollison unlocked the door and pushed it in. "The old boiler room," he said proudly. "This is the place. It's perfect."

Morgan, glancing about, saw a maze of piping festooning the room. The boiler itself, its great doors open, took up one wall. Against the opposite wall stood an army cot with a filthy blanket for a cover. Against the third wall a pile of coal was heaped. Mollison kicked at a chunk that had rolled from the pile. "They haven't used it in ten years," he said. "Decker put in a little oil-fired boiler for a heating plant in the mill itself. This coal used to be piled up in the yard outside but Decker was afraid some of the poor bastards that live around here would steal it so he had it thrown in here." He paused. "What about it, Lou?"

Morgan hesitated, not wanting to confirm his participation in Mollison's plan. He was afraid of Mollison and of the act that Mollison wanted him to commit, but at the same time he did not want to give this thing up entirely. It had sounded, in earnest discussion on a score of occasions, so simple; so easy. And he wanted the money. He needed the money. He said doubtfully, "I guess it's all right."

Mollison nodded. "It won't be for long, anyway. A day or two and then we'll have the money and it will all be over." He kicked at another lump of coal. It bounced halfway up the pile and a miniature avalanche came tumbling down. Mollison watched it absently and turned to face Morgan.

"You can't change your mind now anyway," he said quietly. "I'm going through with it and you know all about it. Maybe Patsy and me could do it without you — but not if you know about it. You're in it as much as we are."

"I'm in it," Morgan said.

Mollison turned away. "Good," he said. "You ought to be glad to break it off on Anacosta anyway. How long has he had you on the hook?"

Morgan said, "Three years." He did not hate the moneylender,

Anacosta, as bitterly as Mollison did. He could remain impersonal about it; doing what they planned to do, not for revenge, in any sense, but for money — out of his need for money. "I've been thinking about that," he said. "Before they do anything else the police are going to investigate Anacosta's — " he searched for a word and found it — "clients."

Mollison shook his head. "He won't call the police in if we handle things right. But all right, suppose he does? How many suckers do you think Anacosta has? Fifty? A hundred?" Mollison snorted scornfully. "Better than five hundred would be nearer right and most of them — a lot of them, anyway — are businessmen who get caught short." He smiled. "They'd think you were a solid citizen if they came across your name. If they do check up on you what will they find? You'll be at your job. You won't have any open connection with this thing. Patsy will have the kid right here in this room."

Morgan brought up the matter that he had skirted carefully up to this time, not wanting to face it in its brutal reality. "How are you going to let him go?" he asked. "He'll be able to remember the place — and Patsy and you, for that matter."

Mollison lit a cigarette and flicked the burned match toward the coal pile. "You don't know Anacosta," he said.

"He's like all those Dagos. Works the hell out of his own kids but when they have kids of their own — well, he's the kid's grandpa; he'd do anything in the world for him. We'll tell him that if he lets the kid open his mouth after we turn him loose, we'll get the kid, one way or another. Or if he goes to the police after he has him back." Mollison kept his voice casual, dismissing the subject by the very lightness with which he considered it.

Morgan was only partly reassured. "How long will we have to keep him here, do you think?" he asked.

"A day or so," Mollison answered him. "Just until we get the money. That's the weak spot — arranging to get the ransom. That's right where most kidnappings break down. We've got to think of a way that's safe and sure and foolproof." He shrugged. "You've seen the place. Let's get out of here."

The two men left the boiler room, Mollison locking the door behind them, and walked back to the car. When they were headed back toward the downtown section Mollison turned and glanced at Morgan.

"You know," he said, "I never figured out how you got on the hook with Anacosta in the first place. You're not a gambler. I don't know what you make in the bank but you must be good for a pretty good week's pay. What did you do — get caught short taking money out of the till and have to see Anacosta and the mustache boys?"

Morgan asked stupidly, "The mustache boys?"

"The muscle men; Anacosta's collectors," Mollison said impatiently. "You didn't think Anacosta was operating by himself, did you? How much do you owe?"

"Three hundred dollars," Morgan said.

"Did he make you write him some predated checks?"

Morgan, wishing that Mollison would stop his infernal questioning — it was actually none of his business anyway — said, "Yes."

Mollison snickered. "You wouldn't want them to clear at the bank so I suppose you go out to his place and buy them back yourself as they come due. I'll tell you what, Lou — you just miss picking one up for one week. One week, that's all. And you'll find out who the mustache boys are." They were out of the business district now and rolling through a back street lined with great clumsy hulks of mansions. In front of one that had been converted into a rooming house Mollison pulled the car over to the curb. He turned the ignition switch and sat drumming lightly on the steering wheel with the palms of his hands. So calm, Morgan thought. He had to give him that. Mollison had nerve. "What about tonight?" Mollison asked. "You coming out to the club?"

Morgan nodded. "I guess so. What about Patsy — do you think we ought to talk to him tonight?"

Mollison shook his head. "Not yet. Not until we're absolutely ready to move. Patsy won't talk if I tell him not to, but there isn't any point in telling him about it just yet."

Morgan opened the door on his side but he did not immediately get out. "Suppose he doesn't want to go in with us?" he asked.

Mollison laughed in genuine amusement. "Patsy thinks I'm the next thing to God Almighty," he said. "He'll do anything in the world for me. Didn't you ever see the way he looks at me? Like a hound dog. And I'll cook up some story for him. Patsy will believe anything I tell him."

Morgan had had no real doubt that Mollison could enlist Patsy. Poor, half-witted Patsy. A laugh; a real laugh when they got going on him at the club. And yet he had an almost tangible air of viciousness about him. Not everyone could recognize it, Morgan supposed. Maybe just those who saw Patsy through the dark glass of their own self-awareness.

Mollison said again, "I'll see you tonight then?"

Morgan nodded, and Mollison waved casually and drove away. Morgan watched the car disappear around a corner before he turned and walked up the cracked cement path to the house. He moved slowly, not wanting to be alone with the thought that the last bridge had now been crossed. He was committed beyond all turning back to Mollison's conspiracy to kidnap the eight-year-old grandson of Anacosta, the moneylender. A month ago it had been a matter for casual discussion, brought about by the coincidence of the widely publicized kidnapping of a banker's son and the careless opinion — whose? — that Carmen Anacosta could put his hands on more money than even a banker could. Half a dozen men at the bar of Morgan's club had been involved in the discussion, Morgan and Mollison among them. The remaining four men had forgotten the discussion as easily as they had entered it. Not Mollison. On the following evening, Morgan now remembered, he had brought up the subject of kidnapping again, this time for Morgan's sole benefit and again as if casually.

"There hasn't been any word on the Glennon kid," he had said. "They'll never find him." He shook his head in doubtful admiration. "Fifty thousand dollars in small bills. How would you like to have half of fifty thousand dollars, Lou?"

There had been in the very wording of the question the suggestion of a partnership, Morgan now remembered. Half of fifty thousand. Half of an amount of money.

"I could use it," he had admitted. Had it been such a terrible admission? Anybody could use half of fifty thousand dollars. Suppose he had added, "But I don't need it bad enough to get it that way," would Mollison have dropped the whole thing right then? Probably not. Mollison had seen something, some defect in Morgan's character, and he had worked away at it, gnawing like a dog at a bone.

A night or so later he had nodded to Morgan at the bar of the seedy little club that they both belonged to merely because it gave them the privilege of drinking after hours. "Well," he had said, "they got away with the money," making it sound as if he had told Morgan that his favorite baseball team had won a crucial game. . . .

Morgan walked through the first floor hallway to his room and entered it, locking the door behind him. Mollison had been very clever about the whole thing. He had never proposed; he had only suggested. "You know," he had said once, "it wouldn't be hard to kidnap someone if you planned it all out in advance." And again, "I don't see why they make such a big thing of it. It isn't any worse than half a dozen other crimes." And Morgan had agreed — in theory, at least — with this bit and that until Mollison decided it was safe to go further with him. Little by little Mollison had become more specific, pointing out that the Anacosta kid would be a natural, if anyone were to seek a logical victim. And one night he had sat in a booth at the club with Morgan and said, "Lou, I'm in a bad jam. I've got to have some money and I know how to get it — a lot of it. You've got plenty of larceny in you — don't get sore; you've already admitted it lots of times. Between the two of us we can get enough to keep us both happy."

Morgan had not been particularly shocked, now that he thought about it. Only afraid, and Mollison plausibly tried to quiet his fears. "This Anacosta is a moneylender; a thief. He won't go to the police because there are too many things he doesn't want them to know about — or the income tax people either. You ought to know."

Morgan had, by that time, told Mollison of his own involvement with Anacosta. Later, thinking about it, he wondered if Mollison hadn't known about it all along. . . .

So it had started as a casual conversation about a kidnapping, and it had led to this. Here he was, safe in his room. Tomorrow or next week he would be party to a kidnapping. . . .

Once he had agreed, Mollison had kept after him and after him, never letting up for a minute.

"The thing is to have a foolproof way of getting the money. That's half the battle. We've got to work that out, Lou."

And later: "You work in the Drover's National — Anacosta has an account there. I've seen his checks in the car agency office. You see how it will work out, Lou? You'll know right away if he makes a withdrawal to cover the ransom — and you'll know if anyone makes a record of the serial numbers on the bills. If we hit him hard enough and fast enough there won't be time for that — but one way or another, if we know about it in advance, we'll know how to handle the money. How can we miss?"

And Morgan had made his own contribution to the plan. Between checking and savings accounts Anacosta, kept a balance of nearly fifty thousand dollars. When he told Mollison this — privileged information and thus his first criminal participation in the plan — Mollison had scoffed.

"You think that's all? That's just what he pays taxes on. Look, Lou. He's got to have a safe deposit box. That's how the discount boys do business. You watch him when he comes in the bank. Could you make an excuse to go in the vault if he goes there?"

Morgan could and he did, and he had just a brief glimpse of a great deal of money in thick, opulent sheaves. This had pleased Mollison. "All right," he said. "We'll tell him seventy-five thousand dollars."

Morgan threw himself down on the bed. Would he back out now even if he could? Mollison's plan seemed to be foolproof. And he could use half of seventy-five thousand dollars. Ah, God — just once not to be poor. Just once to be free — off the hook with Anacosta and back in a secure position of decent respectability with the bank.

Chapter 2

All of his life Louis Morgan had been poor. Not the unashamed, patched pants poverty of the West Side but genteel poor, which was infinitely worse. If you lived, as the Morgans did, on Argonne Street, you would literally starve before you would accept relief. He had heard his mother say a hundred times that she would do just that. He remembered her now as he lay on his bed and tried to get Mollison and his plan out of his mind. She was a gaunt woman who hugged to her breast the fact that she had married a Morgan. Not the main branch of the family but nevertheless a Morgan. Louis was thereby also a Morgan and subject to all of the obligations of family with none of the advantages. His father had been a common drunkard with no redeeming or endearing characteristics; a little wretch of a man bullied by a world he could never quite cope with. The house on Argonne Street had been an inheritance. Louis's father would have sold it a dozen times over if his wife had let him. It was a monstrous ark of a place; impossible to heat even if there had been money for coal and for insulating the roof. There never was. She made him keep the house and be damned to the cold. It was a symbol to her. An Argonne Street address.

Morgan thought for years after her death that he had inherited her personality, and it was only after his father's death, much later, that he realized with something approaching horror that he "took after" his father almost completely. Such of his mother's character as he could find in himself, he discovered, had been bludgeoned into him by the sheer mass of her will.

More than once she had spent the money that was needed for food to buy him shoes or a new coat. "You're a Morgan," she would say fiercely. "You can't go to school looking like some ragamuffin from the West Side."

When he had a chance to take over a paper route that would bring in a few badly needed dollars each week, she made him refuse it. "You're a Morgan," she said. "You don't have to peddle papers like some immigrant's son." This at a time when they had lived on corn-meal mush for three consecutive days.

He remembered his father having a succession of jobs ranging from night clerk in a hotel to sales clerk in a hardware store. None of the jobs lasted for any long period of time and after a while there was not even the optimistic pretense that they would. The name Morgan — even a minor branch — had a certain value and it led to an occasional decent job for his father; the length of time he held it being determined by the date of his next drunken payday. When Louis was eleven his father was given such a job. He was hired as assistant manager of a travel agency; the thought of his employer being that he might attract other and richer Morgans. He was given access to substantial amounts of cash, and the temptation was far beyond his control. He took what he could put his hands on, abandoning his wife, his son and the house on Argonne Street. He was gone for a week, and at the end of that time he returned, white and shaken. Louis happened to be in the kitchen; he had just come home from school when his father came in at the back door. His mother was also in the kitchen. His father closed the door behind him and asked nervously, "Are they looking for me?"

His mother said furiously, "Of course they are. Get out. Get out. Don't let them arrest you here. Why did you come back anyway?"

His father shrugged his thin shoulders. "I'm broke," he said. "I got drunk, I guess, and somebody rolled me. I'm hungry, Clara."

She hissed at him. "So are we." Her voice rose. "Get out, now. Go on away from here. I don't want you to get caught where people know us." She put both hands on his shoulders and thrust him toward the door. Louis, frightened, began to cry.

Someone had seen his father sneak in at the back door and reported it to the police — or perhaps they were watching the house all along. At the moment that she pushed him toward the door, it opened and two uniformed policemen shouldered their way inside. "All right, Morgan," one of them said, "you're under arrest."

Louis retained a vivid memory of the neighbors out on their front porches, watching as they pushed his father — he seemed so weak and so small beside the two policemen — into a patrol car and drove away, with a screaming of the siren. His mother stayed inside, weeping with humiliation. Louis Morgan continued to cry, and he did not know then whether it was out of pity for his father or out of that same humiliation that agonized his mother.

His mother died when he was just out of high school, and the house went for taxes in that same year. He would have liked to have kept it but he did not fight for it with his mother's passion. He found that he was quite as comfortable in a rooming house.

He had been unpopular in high school and in his years at the Drover's Bank. He had fallen into the face-saving device of reciprocity — if they didn't like him, he didn't like them. He told himself that it was because he was a Morgan. A poor one but a Morgan nevertheless and consequently a little above the average run.

When he had been at the Drover's Bank for five years he received a letter from the warden at the State Penitentiary. His father, it informed him, had died — of natural causes — and did he wish to claim the body?

Morgan had not thought of his father in years. There had been a rather pitiful letter of sympathy when his mother had died, but he had never accepted the overture by answering it. In his room he read the letter informing him of his father's death, and when he had finished it he felt an aching pity for the dead man. Poor old man. Dying alone in a prison without a friend in the world. Out of his remorse, Morgan traced bonds between himself and his father, and it was then that he decided he was not his mother's son at all. He was his father's image. He too was alone and friendless. He too was mediocre and overburdened with living up to a family name that had done nothing for him. And having risked this moment of honest insight, he immediately felt a compulsion to disprove it.

He joined the club where he was later to meet Howard Mollison, not so much because it permitted him to buy liquor after hours but because he could refer, in wash-room conversations with the other employees of the bank, to "my club." The implication was that it was a country club or a downtown fraternal club. Actually it was a seedy little bottle club of no standing.

He began to attend bazaars and balls where socialites mingled with the common people in the name of charity. He scrimped and saved to buy fairly decent clothes, and he took great pleasure in standing on the side lines as if he were merely lending his presence. It was this pattern of behavior that finally got him into trouble, entangled him with Carmen Anacosta, and made him a conspirator with Howard Mollison.

He danced, at one such affair, With a dowager, and when they introduced each other, she repeated, "Morgan? Louis Morgan?"

He said casually, "Yes, I'm with the Drover's Bank."

"I don't know why I haven't met you before, Mr. Morgan. I know some of your family, don't I?"

"I'm sure you do. I don't get out very often myself. The bank, you know."

He let it be known that he had lived on Argonne Street and that he had sold the house. Too big, you know, and the taxes were fantastic. The upshot of the conversation with the dowager was that he was asked to visit her on her estate for the week end.

It was a year — and a group — in which there were more women than men. Morgan, had he been possessed of a little more money or a great deal more charm, could have fitted in with the group he met on that first week end. He did fit in, for a time. He began to go to expensive night clubs with the younger crowd. He went at first with some embarrassment; he had no idea what it might cost him and he was relieved when someone else picked up the check. Someone always seemed to pick up the check,-and he had no idea that the men of the group he was traveling with kept a rough sort of accounting of who paid and when. Morgan never volunteered to pay. There came a night when, after dinners and drinks, one of the men took him aside and asked coldly, "Isn't it about your time to pick up the tab, Morgan?"

He had perhaps ten dollars in his pocket, and the check would amount to something over a hundred. Morgan made some foolish, fumbling excuse. Forgot his billfold. The man said, "I thought so," and turned away.

He had to redeem his standing; had to. There was a theater party scheduled for the next evening. There would be dinner afterward. In his cage at the bank Morgan estimated what the entire affair would cost. Something like three hundred dollars. He had nothing like three hundred dollars and he couldn't arrange a loan in so brief a time.

There was money available. Right in front of him, neatly packaged. The tellers didn't check their money each night with the cashier. They merely locked it in their cash boxes. Morgan took three hundred dollars, reassuring himself that it was only because there was no time to arrange a formal loan.

He paid for the theater tickets and the dinners. He was not flamboyant about it, but there was a slightly hysterical quality about the way he demanded the check, and he was too elaborately casual when he glanced at the check and put money on the waiter's tray. They could tell, he knew later. They could tell. The invitations stopped coming. There was the matter of the three hundred dollars. In the cold light of the next day he became aware of his position. He could not borrow from the loan department of his own bank. The cashier might — just might — want to check his cash box without waiting until Friday. He could hardly go to another bank and give his own bank as a reference. There remained Carmen Anacosta, the moneylender.

He borrowed three hundred dollars from Anacosta. He was to pay back four hundred. To secure the loan he gave the money lender ten forty-dollar checks, predated a week apart. The system was simple and sure. If he failed either to pick up the checks as they came due or to deposit enough money to cover them he became guilty of issuing fraudulent checks and the law would then work for Anacosta. Because of his position in the bank, Morgan preferred to pick up the checks from Anacosta for cash as they became due. After he had paid off the three hundred dollars — plus interest — Morgan was free for a time. Then he borrowed again when he was invited to the Adirondacks by a hostess who had been abroad and who had not received the word that Morgan was — he faced it — a phony. He was never again quite out of debt to Anacosta. . . .

He lay on the bed in the rooming house and convinced himself that Mollison was right. Anacosta was a Dago Shylock. He was fair game for anyone with the nerve to take him. Only, he wished that he could be sure that it was going to be as simple and as harmless as Mollison claimed.

Chapter 3

After dropping Morgan at his rooming house, Mollison turned the car back downtown and stopped in front of a bar. He wanted a drink — needed a drink — badly. Morgan was showing a bad yellow streak and it had taken all his salesman's persuasion to keep him in line when every nerve in his own big body was stretched and raw with strain. He could hate Morgan for demanding persuasion and assurance when he had need of every last power of thought to save himself. So many things to remember, to keep straight, dates and names in a book, each of them a hangman's trap to be tripped by a moment's carelessness. The Anacosta business would have to be taken care of soon.

There were two or three men at the bar when Mollison entered. He put a bill down and said, "Scotch." Then, unable to resist making the gesture, he added, "Give these fellows whatever they're having." They would look his way now and murmur their thanks, nod their approval. They would envy him for a big, breezy, well-dressed man with the money to buy drinks for whomever he wished, and this, to Mollison, was of the greatest importance. If enough people thought you were a somebody, you could almost convince yourself that you were what they thought you were, instead of what you knew you were in the thin hours of the morning. When the bartender brought his change he pointedly did not glance at it. Instead, he looked at his own reflection in the mirror. His face was, like his body, big — but with its hard lines blurring like the sharp edges of an ice cube in a highball and becoming rounder, softer just as the big body was changing. All right — at forty a man had to lose some of his edge of condition. Mollison sipped at his drink, keeping his eyes averted from those of the other men at the bar and simulating a preoccupation with weighty matters to discourage any overtures. Mollison needed their approval and he blossomed under their admiration, but he had learned that their conversation was apt to be either dull or maudlin.

He glanced at the clock behind the bar. Ten minutes past five. Bar clocks were set ten minutes ahead; that made it just five and if he hurried he could get back to the office before Lillian left for the day. She would be looking for him and she would be sullen and sarcastic if he didn't show up. The hell with her. He would stall her as he had a score of times before with some story about a prospect. Right now, with all the things he had on his mind, he couldn't face the thought of seeing Lillian.

He ordered another drink. The other men at the bar, he was aware, had been waiting for this moment. Would he buy another round? Big, well-dressed guy like that, he just might. When the bartender brought his drink he did not this time nod in their direction, and they turned resignedly away. In another mood Mollison might have bought the second round, but the thought of Lillian irritated him, made him perverse. Damn Lillian. Damn her money, too, which she never let a man forget. Never let a man forget that she signed the paychecks either. In a way you could say that she had gotten him into this mess, but who would have figured her to be the way she was? And she liked to whittle away at his confidence too and what was a salesman without confidence?

He had had it once; really had it. Way back in high school — even then he could sell anything, promote anything. Advertisements for the class book. Punch board chances on radios — you name it, he could sell it. Mollison smiled at the recollection. A lot of the people he'd solicited for the class book gave him money and then told him that they'd prefer to remain anonymous. He had kept the bulk of the anonymous donations since there was no way in which he could be checked. The punch boards had had rigged winners or no winners at all.

Mollison ordered another drink and looked again at the clock. Too early to eat and too late to go on back to the office. He started reminiscing again, enjoying it, using it as an excuse to avoid thinking of the Anacosta business.

Those had been good years and there had been better ones to follow. College; two years of it and even as a sophomore he had been a big man. A big man physically, too; looking older than his classmates. There had been a fad for panty raids even then and he had gotten into the room of a sexy looking sorority pledge. The bitch, he thought. She had given him every possible come on and then had hollered rape when they got caught. So that had been the end of college. They called it assault and got her to drop the charges and told him to be on the next train out of town. So what? By that time he had known the score. Enough so that he decided never to work for a living. Not a big, bluff, hearty looking guy like himself. But that sorority bitch. She'd had it coming. Mollison wished he could run into something like that instead of what he had — Lillian.

There was the Army. Two years of it and it hadn't been so bad.

Knowing the score as he did, he had put in for the Quartermaster Corps and assignment to the European Theater and he hadn't missed a bet after he got over there. There was a clique; a loose sort of club in the services. Its members were the men who were out for what they could get and no bones about it. The top echelons were the pilots who had regular runs back to the United Kingdom where pounds were pegged at half and even a third of what they would bring on the continent. The low ranks bullied German housewives into surrendering Leica cameras and Zeiss binoculars for chits presumably authorized by various town majors.

Mollison's own particular racket had been sugar with an occasional melon of penicillin from Medical Corps supplies. Two years of it and Mollison rotated back to the United States and a discharge with close to ten thousand dollars in cash. He had never heard a shot fired in anger, but would become theatrically sullen when asked about his service overseas. "I'd rather not talk about it," he would say, hoping that this would create the impression that he had seen things too grim to remember, which was effective with a certain type of woman. Or again he would loudly explain how he despised men who bragged about their combat records when most of them had never been overseas. Thereafter he would tell some rather colorful and completely fictitious adventures of his own.

The ten thousand dollars lasted only a few months. Mollison spent it in Miami and in Las Vegas, and when it was gone he became a salesman and it made no difference what he sold. Bonds — real estate — it didn't matter. For a big, hearty guy like himself there were always selling jobs. He smiled at another recollection. It was a good thing there were a lot of jobs because he had gone through them fast enough. Drinking and high living but mostly women — young, expensive women.

He ordered another drink. All that money, he thought. Now he was jammed up over a few thousand dollars — really jammed up to the point where this Anacosta thing was the only way he could get enough quick money to square himself. Once he had made thirty thousand dollars in one year. That was real estate — the real estate market right after the war when the Veteran's Administration was approving anything with a coat of paint on it and the banks were standing in line to put up the money.

Mollison sipped at his drink, knowing from experience the way it would take hold, lifting him up and letting him forget about the jam and about Lillian. He chuckled again at the thought of the real estate deal he had had. What a pitch it had been. "Here you are folks. This is what you call solid construction. Take a look at that kitchen, lady. Every modern convenience. Look at all the outlets. (But don't plug in more than one appliance on that number fourteen wire or you'll blow a fuse.) What's that? Plaster walls? Nobody uses plaster any more, mister. You want a damp house? That's what plaster does for you. Dry wall, that's what you want. (Only don't let Junior hit it with his tricycle or he'll go right through it.) That's inlaid linoleum there. You like the pattern? Tell you what — we got another house going up down the street. You buy it and I'll let you have your choice of patterns. (Just don't come early and see the junk wood we're hiding with the linoleum, lady.) Sewer? You want to pay sewer taxes? What's wrong with a septic tank? You can't beat a septic tank. (Just so you don't have an automatic washing machine or like to take a bath every day.) I tell you folks, this is a *house*. Did you notice that every one in the development is different? This is going to be a wonderful community in another year."

Wonder what the houses looked like now, Mollison mused. He hadn't stayed around a year to see if the development really became a wonderful community. There had been some trouble about down-payment money — he had clipped the contractor for a bundle with that dodge — and after that it didn't make sense to hang around. Not when there were other cities and other real estate developments. And when the VA tightened up so you couldn't make a hard sell of a cracker-box house on filled land any more, somebody came along with the aluminum combination-window deal.

"Lady, I'm glad you mentioned that. Some of our competitors say they have genuine self-storing windows. Maybe they have — but they can't sell them at a price to match ours. (These store all right. But wait till you try to un-store the screens next fall.) You don't want to go on heating all outdoors all winter do you? Of course you don't. These windows and doors will pay for themselves in two years time in fuel bills alone. You don't have to pay for them now. Just make a deposit and we'll deliver and install your windows in two weeks."

There wasn't as much money in the windows as there had been in the houses, but there was enough and there was the advantage that sometimes — not often but just once in a while — you bumped into a bored young housewife who acted as if she might like to play games. Easy enough to find out. You made an off-color remark. Not really smutty but enough so that she got the idea. If she took that and laughed you made a pass. If she went for that you were in — and if she changed her mind afterward, that was her tough luck. What could she do? Holler rape and then have to live down the talk?

So aluminum windows for a couple of years until the Better Business Bureau and a lot of government snoopers killed that turkey; and then back to real estate, here in this town. Not new houses, this time. Regular real estate for Decker and Son and strictly no pressuring. And by God he'd showed them that he was a salesman. He'd done as well as anyone else; moved some tough property. Then Decker had accused him of misrepresenting some property — not that he minded misrepresentation, the dried-up old bastard, but in this case it had cost him some money so he fired Mollison. After that, for the first time — in how many years? — it had been a little harder to get a job. He had had to take a job — straight commission, no salary — with a cemetery promoter, working from a telephone in a boiler room filled with other telephones and other bluff, hearty men. "This is Howard Mollison, Mrs. Smith. I represent the Green Lawns Association. You're familiar with the name, I'm sure." Making it fast, keeping the voice low pitched to catch the interest of the housewife on the other end of the wire before she realized that it was a pitch and hung up. Swapping dirty jokes and pictures between times with the other men. Working his tail off while the closers made the real money. He had stood a month of it before he met Lillian Kramer in a downtown cocktail lounge. And hadn't that been something!

Mollison's memory of the meeting with Lillian was acute, sharpened by the abrasiveness of his present hatred for her. She was forty-two years old — she said — on the night that he first saw her, which was over a year ago; a stocky woman with a sallow complexion and brassy yellow hair. She was girdled so tightly that her figure, from the front, was as parallel as a post, and her bust billowed from the pressure. Mollison, looking at her in amused contempt over the rim of his glass, had said to the bartender, "Hey, Jerry — what in hell is that?"

Jerry had glanced in her direction. "That's a quarter of a million dollars," he had said matter-of-factly. "Her name is Kramer. She owns an automobile agency." Seeing Mollison's expression he had cautioned, "If you want to move in there, watch it. She didn't come here to get picked up."

Taking the warning for what it was worth, Mollison moved slowly; he had no particular plan in mind, but Jerry's remark was a challenge. And you never knew what you could do if you got close enough to that kind of money. Rather than try to catch her eye or send a drink to her table or any of the obvious overtures, he had waited until there was a particularly noisy outburst from a group farther down the bar. Then he had turned and caught her eye and managed to get into his own expression a sort of weary resignation to such poor manners; a sort of "isn't it too bad we have to put up with this kind of people" look which automatically established his own status as that of a gentleman. She had responded with half a smile; but he had turned away from her, taking it easy. He didn't actually speak to her until several evenings later.

Once he had eased into the habit of talking with her he found her only a little more difficult to handle than a hundred other women he had known. The fact that she came to the same cocktail lounge night after night showed that she was interested. Knowing that he would probably be there she could have gone somewhere else if she wasn't interested. After a time he suggested that they visit another place he knew of. From there it was only a series of familiar steps. Dinner. A nightcap in her apartment...

Mollison made his discoveries. She did have an automobile agency, left to her by a dead husband; and she ran it with an iron grip and total efficiency. She did have a quarter of a million dollars and she intended to hang on to every cent of it. He discovered later still that she was two women — the executive, wearing expensive dresses and a cold front over the grasping cunning of her French peasant breeding; and a mixture of wanton and harridan when away from her office in the agency. And she never mixed her characters. Mollison, after he was fairly well entrenched as her companion and lover, asked her for a job.

He got it but on a strictly business basis. And up until three weeks ago he hadn't made a nickel from it that he hadn't earned. Three weeks ago.

Mollison finished his drink and ordered another. He had been drinking too much lately, but what could a man do? He had been living in a sick fright for the last three weeks; jumping whenever the telephone rang, the mailman came, another salesman took a contract to the bank. The Anacosta thing had to go through. He could square Lillian if he had enough money. He couldn't just pack up and get out of town the way he used to do. This time they would have him on a felony and he had no doubt whatever that Lillian would swear out a fugitive warrant for him within ten minutes after she found out. And they would find him, sure as God made little apples. If he wanted proof he had only to remember — as if he could forget — that day three weeks ago when the whole thing had started.

He had been on the used-car lot on his regular turn when the grimy little man came up to him and said, "Your name is Mollison, isn't it?"

Big smile — he'd had nothing to worry about then. "Sure, Jack. Somebody tell you to look me up? You've got the right idea. I'll give you as good a deal as I gave them. Now what did you have in mind? I've got a Chevy over here, clean as the day it left the showroom. Three years old and I'll give you a real buy — you got a trade-in?"

The grimy little man smiled and Mollison could see two gold teeth. "No trade-in," he said. "I'm not interested in a car just now. I'm interested in you, Mr. Mollison."

Mollison thought frantically. There was nothing against him in this town; he hadn't a thing to worry about, so he said angrily, "If you don't want to buy a car, Jack, I've got other things to do."

The little man kept smiling. "Just the same, I think you ought to talk to me. You want to talk right here, it's all right with me. I just wanted to give you a break."

The perpetual smile shook Mollison. "What did you want to see me about?" he said.

The grimy man — Mollison had only an impression of griminess; the little man wore a clean shirt and a well-pressed cheap suit — said, "I don't work in this town, Mr. Mollison. I work out of Des Moines. You were in Des Moines once."

Mollison remembered Des Moines as he remembered more than a dozen cities where he had worked. He could not make an immediate connection between the name of the city and anything he might have done there. Phony Canadian stocks? Real estate? He had sold something; probably taken somebody, but for how much and how criminal it was he could not recall. Stalling for time, he said, "I might have been. What about it? Who are you anyway? I don't know you."

The little man scuffed one foot absently against the blacktop of the used-car lot. "My name is Griffin," he said. "Ed Griffin. Thing about me, Mr. Mollison, is I got a camera eye." Mollison could sense a diffident pride in the way Griffin made the comment. Griffin hurried on to explain. "What I mean is, anything I see I can remember. Like if I read a book I can recite it back to you almost word for word. I bet I could make a lot of money if I could get on one of those television quiz games. Anyway, I remember you, Mr. Mollison. From Des Moines, I mean. They got a picture of you at city hall."

Mollison, forcing himself to remember, had it at last. It had been, for him, an off-beat graft; something a little different that he had gotten into three, maybe four years ago. Some newspaper or other had been backing a charity drive. March of Dimes? Easter Seals? He had been hired on a salary basis to do the promotional work. He had done a competent job of it — he had collected something in the neighborhood of eight hundred dollars in a few days but he hadn't turned it in. He had taken a train East instead. Now he said, "You didn't come five hundred miles to find me by accident. Who blew the whistle on me?" His own immediate reaction had been that Lillian had written to Des Moines. Almost immediately he rejected the thought. She didn't know about Des Moines. Maybe she had been nosing around about him, but the trail back to Des Moines was winding and hidden. And why would she have done that? She seemed pretty happy with the situation the way it was.

Griffin looked puzzled. "Nobody blew the whistle on you, Mr. Mollison."

Mollison said wearily, "Knock it off. What are you, anyway? Cop or district attorney?"

"I'm not either, Mr. Mollison. I work for a finance company, chasing dead beats. There are these two brothers, Cahoon, their name is. They owe us fifteen-hundred dollars on two notes. We got word they were here so the company sent me out to see if I could scare them into getting something up. I just happened to see you, Mr. Mollison, but like I said, I got this camera eye. Whenever I go out on a job I always go downtown, last thing before I leave, and look over the wanteds. They got a couple of hundred of them, anybody wants to look at them. When I get where I'm going I walk around town instead of riding in cabs, and I keep my eyes open. I spotted you in a diner yesterday, drinking coffee. Wasn't looking for you but there you were."

Mollison felt relief briefly. "Then you haven't got a warrant. Hell, you can't do anything to me."

Griffin shook his head. "Grand larceny, Mr. Mollison. The morning paper was backing that drive. They'll prosecute, and grand larceny is extraditable."

I could run, Mollison thought. I could move on again. But moving on, starting again — the old drive wasn't there. And he had this good thing going for him with Lillian.

Griffin stared at his shoes. "I don't have to turn you in, Mr. Mollison. I mean, I didn't come out here looking for you. I just happened to see you."

Mollison said bitterly, "That's my tough luck. How much?"

Griffin lifted his eyes as far as Mollison's belt. "I figure a thousand dollars."

"You blackmailing bastard."

Griffin shrugged. "I've been called names before," he said. He lifted his eyes briefly to look directly at Mollison.

Mollison saw naked scorn before Griffin dropped his gaze again. "I can't raise a thousand dollars," he said.

"I'm a blackmailing bastard," Griffin said quietly. "You said so yourself. That's my price. Only, I'll tell you, Mr. Mollison. I don't think I'm quite as bad as you. Stealing money from crippled kids stacks up worse than taking it from a fat thief like you." He straightened his thin shoulders. "If the Des Moines cops ever get you down in the basement at the hall maybe you'll get the idea. You going to pay?"

Mollison nodded his head. He had to swallow several times before he could speak. "All right," he said. "It will take me a little while to raise a; thousand dollars."

Griffin turned away, then paused. "That's all right, Mr. Mollison. I'll come by Friday for the money." He took a step toward the street and paused again, turning to face Mollison. "I make a living tracing dead-beats," he said. "You wouldn't be any trouble at all. Between now and Friday I'll know where you are every minute." He turned again toward the street, and this time he walked on while Mollison stared after him. He had about thirty dollars in his pocket. On Friday he would get his check, good for another hundred dollars or so but he needed that money to keep himself going; buy his meals; pay for the small apartment he kept but seldom used since taking up with Lillian Kramer. At the thought of Lillian he felt a sense of relief. She would lend him the money. If she wanted to be hard-boiled about it he could pay her back in weekly installments out of his pay. Mollison did not think again of running, of getting out of town. For an insignificant little man Griffin had been very convincing. What had he said? "I'll know where you are every minute." Mollison didn't doubt it.

That night he took Lillian to a night club and was very attentive, but he did not bring up the subject of borrowing money. It did not occur to him that she would refuse, but it would do no harm to soften her up. On the following evening he stopped, by prearrangement, at the modernistic ranch house that her husband had built for her. She had just showered when she came to the door, dumpy in a quilted dressing gown, to let him in. She had hairpins in her mouth and she said through them, "Hello, Howie. Come on in while I finish dressing."

He followed her to her bedroom and stood leaning against the door jamb, watching her put her make-up on. Dowdy old bag, he thought. The least she could do was keep out of sight when she wasn't fixed up. He made small talk for a few minutes and then said, as casually as he could, "By the way, Lil, I've got a little matter I've got to clear up and I'm short. Let me have a thousand for a few weeks, will you?"

Without looking up she said matter-of-factly, "No."

Mollison was bewildered, as much by the flatness of the refusal as at the refusal itself. "I really need the money, Lil," he said plaintively. "I was counting on you to lend it to me."

She turned to face him. "You didn't have any right to count on me for anything, Howie. You're good company. We have a lot of fun but you could do better than me and I've been waiting for something like this. I'm not sore at you for trying, but I wouldn't let you borrow a nickel. You're about the worst credit risk I could imagine."

Mollison had raged, cajoled and finally begged, in that order, but he could not move her. Finally she said, "Oh, get out, Howie."

He had left her house, furious, and slammed into his car. There was another car parked a short distance up the street. He convinced himself that Griffin was in the other car, watching his every move, and his fury turned into fear. He had to get the money for Griffin, and in his desperation he had thought of Anacosta, not as a kidnapping victim at that time but as a usurer. . . .

Mollison finished his drink on the memory of the first night he had thought of Anacosta, and started to leave the bar. It was the *if*, the maddening, frustrating *if* that had brought him to this terrible point of no return. *If* Lillian had let him take the money he needed to pay Griffin off. *If* Griffin, the dirty little blackmailer, hadn't happened to see him in the diner. *If* Griffin hadn't happened to have a photographic memory . . . Mollison had convinced himself thoroughly that he was being persecuted by the fates. All the *if*'s. It did not occur to him that he had been lucky, that he had grifted and cheated and lied throughout his adult life and never, until now, been cornered. He walked to the curb and got into his car. It was almost time to meet Morgan at the club. And maybe tonight would be the time to tell Patsy. Anacosta... the Dago bastard. If he had let him take some money this wouldn't have happened. He wouldn't have to be plotting to kidnap the moneylender's grandson. Served him right, the Dago bastard.

Chapter 4

Mollison drove carefully toward the club. He had had perhaps one too many drinks; they were bitter and brassy in his throat and he knew he must smell of whisky. He could not afford to be stopped for a traffic violation now. Just one day away from the auto agency; just half a day to appear in traffic court and the world could blow up in his face. He couldn't get Anacosta off his mind, and he returned again and again to thinking about the moneylender, as a man will touch a sore tooth with his tongue knowing that it will pain him.

The funny-dirty part of it was that he had first thought of Anacosta with a tremendous sensation of relief. That had been on the night he had stormed out of Lillian's house. Anacosta, of course, would lend him the money to pay Griffin off. It would cost him; no doubt it would cost him plenty but he would have paid any price just then to get Griffin off his back. After leaving Lillian's place, Mollison drove to the Italian section of the city where Anacosta lived. Anacosta's house was an ancient three-decker with ornate railings about the wide piazzas that projected from each floor.

Mollison, up on the porch, rang the bell and waited, seeing the hall light flick on.

Anacosta himself came to the door, shuffling in worn carpet slippers. He was a stocky man in his sixties with a great shock of yellowish white hair. He needed a shave; the dirty gray stubble on his jowls was matched in color by the matted hair that showed through the gaps in the heavy underwear that he wore in spite of the spring warmth. He wore an old pair of serge pants with the suspenders loosened and trailing behind him nearly to the floor. He asked suspiciously, "What do you want?"

Mollison said, "I need a small loan for a little while, Mr. Anacosta."

Anacosta stared at him coldly. "Who told you who I am? Why do you think you can borrow money here?"

Mollison felt a murderous rage begin to churn in the pit of his stomach. That he should have to "mister" this old Dago and make explanations to him! With a salesman's easy facility he smiled to conceal the anger, and said, "I work for the Kramer agency, Mr. Anacosta. My name is Mollison. A lot of my customers do business with you." Was he going to keep him standing out here for the whole world to see?

Anacosta thought for a moment and then said, "Come in," his voice surly. He led the way through a musty-smelling hall to a small room that was crowded with old-fashioned furniture. There was a roll-top desk in one corner. Anacosta seated himself at the desk so that his back was to Mollison. "I don't say that I lend money," he said. "I don't say nothing. You tell me how much you want and why you want it and we see."

Mollison said, "A thousand dollars."

Anacosta shook his head. "Fifty or a hundred, maybe I let you have. A thousand? How do I know you? How I know you pay me back?"

Mollison said, "I make a hundred a week and better. I'll pay you back."

Anacosta stood up. "You come back tomorrow," he said. "Maybe we do business. You write out your name on a piece of paper and say where you work, where you live."

Mollison lived through the following day and returned in the evening. Anacosta was sitting in a rocking chair on the front porch, watching a small boy playing on the meager lawn. As Mollison stepped up on the porch Anacosta shook his head. "You don't get no money, Mollison. I look you up. You got no credit, no friends. Nobody knows where you come from. I got nothing for you."

Mollison protested. "You loan money to strangers all the time. Guys come in to buy a car, never had a regular job in their life. I send them here and you give them the money. Why can't you do business with me?"

Anacosta shrugged. "I'll tell you," he said. "You come to my door and you tell me you want a small loan. A thousand dollars, you tell me. A thousand dollars is a small loan? How much money you got, mister big operator? Five bucks in your pocket?" He leaned forward and Mollison could hear him breathing heavily through his nose. "You know what you are? You are a phony. Ten cents I would not lend you." His voice rose. "Get out. Get out, you phony!"

Mollison, caught by a raging frustration, took a step toward the old man. Barely in time he remembered the things he had heard about

Anacosta; about the people who borrowed and didn't pay up. "All right," he muttered. "I'm going."

He returned a day later to plead with the moneylender, to offer him any terms. He was refused again but on that third visit he saw Louis Morgan come furtively from the house and hurry up the street. He knew Morgan slightly; they belonged to the same club and even in his agitation he stored up the knowledge that Morgan had business with Anacosta. Morgan — he worked in a bank, didn't he? It was interesting that he had business with a moneylender.

After his final refusal by Anacosta, Mollison tossed and turned in his bed throughout most of the night, alternating between an almost manic anger at Anacosta and a devouring fear of Griffin. Just when he had decided to pack and run for it and take the chance that Griffin would lose his trail, the idea came to him. It was so beautifully simple, so easy, that he turned it over in his mind for several minutes, looking suspiciously for the gimmick, the catch. He could find none. It had risk, of course, and he would have to be very careful, but it would at least give him a few days of blessed respite — and he could always pay the money back in such a way as to get himself out from under.

He got up early on the following morning and dressed with more than usual care, feeling the need of the confidence that a good appearance gave him. Lillian was in her office when he arrived at the agency. He put his head in at the door and smiled.

"You're not sore about last night are you?" he asked. "I was in a little jam. It's all right now."

She looked up and returned the smile. "Why should I be sore? It didn't cost me anything."

He thought, it will, you bitch, but he said, "Well, I'm sorry anyway. See you tonight?"

She said, "Why not?" and bent her head to some paper work on her desk.

Mollison walked through the showroom and out to the side of the building where the used cars were ranked in a long and gleaming line. He half expected Griffin to approach him but he no longer feared the little man. He was going to get his money for him — today. If he had to wait around for a little while he wouldn't mind.

A mechanic was working his way down the line of cars, warming the motors. (Step in and see how she starts up, mister. Been sitting there a week but I'll bet you she'll start on the first kick.) Mollison waited until he got out of a car and then said, "Eddie, how's about that '54 Hudson in the back row?"

Eddie spat. "That's a real dog, Howie. I told Mrs. Kramer she ought to wholesale it off and take her loss on it. It ain't got no more compression than a flit gun without I rebore it and it ain't worth it. Car's been abused too much."

Mollison shook his head in tacit disapproval of those people who abused cars like the Hudson. "You don't think we can move it then? I mean, even if you hoke it up?"

Eddie rubbed his fingers on a piece of waste before he shook a cigarette out of a crumpled packet. "Not a chance," he said after he had accepted a light from Mollison. "It's two hundred dollars under the Red Book right now but nobody in his right mind would touch it with a ten-foot pole. I tell you, Howie, that there is a real dog. Can't keep the crankcase oil off the plugs."

Mollison said, "Thanks, Eddie. I thought I had a bite but if it's as bad as you say I won't waste my time." He watched the mechanic move slowly down the line. A yellow tag was tied to the windshield wiper of the Hudson. Mollison took a notebook and a pencil from his breast pocket and began copying down the motor number, body number and other details written on the tag. When he had the information he wanted, he strolled, as casually as he could, back to the small office that was set aside for the salesmen. There was a wooden desk equipped with a typewriter in the center of the room. He sat down at the desk and took a long white sheet of paper from the top drawer; this he fed into the platen of the typewriter. The first blank line appeared beneath the title in boldface, *Conditional Sales Contract.*

Mollison had prepared himself carefully once the idea had come to him in the early hours of the morning. The name that he filled in on the first blank line, the place of employment, the wages received, the ostensible down payment — he was careful to choose a figure that represented almost a third of the value of the green Hudson — were fictitious. The address that he supplied for the imaginary buyer of the car was not fictitious. It was the address of his own apartment. When he had finished filling in the blanks in infinite detail — credit references, next of kin, insurance — he had a piece of paper that was very nearly as negotiable as currency. He knew. He had made out hundreds of similar contracts — not with imaginary buyers but otherwise identical to the one he had prepared. The banks never bothered to check up. Why should they? They retained title to the car until the last note was paid and they left it to the auto dealers to protect them by getting enough of a down payment so that the balance was always less than the wholesale price of the car.

When he had finished with the contract Mollison read it through carefully. He had expected to be nervous now that it was done, but he found that he was not. He felt a curious sense of triumph instead. He had felt it when he sold jerry-built houses, inferior aluminum windows, building lots lost in the middle of a swamp. Screw them all. Screw Lillian. He would have to meet the payments when they came due, but in the meantime he would have the use of some of her money, or the bank's. He finished the job by making out in duplicate a blue slip, a transfer of title for the Motor Vehicle Department.

The Kramer Agency did business with three banks. Customer's choice, if he wanted a choice. As an ostensible customer Mollison chose the Industrial National. Half an hour after the bank opened he walked in and confidently approached the mortgage department. To the vice-president who greeted him he said, "Good morning, Paul. Want to okay this? Guy wants the car for his vacation."

Paul smiled. "Sure, Howie. What's the balance?"

"Eleven hundred. He put up five hundred in cash."

"How is the book value on the car? Right up there?" .

"Seventeen hundred."

"Job all right?"

"He's a machinist. Worked in the same place for six years." Mollison handed the time contract and the blue transfer of title to the banker. "Take a look."

Paul took the papers and glanced at them casually. "I guess it's all right, Howie. We haven't had any bad paper from the Kramer agency since I've been here. What do you want me to do — have a check made out for the agency account?"

This was the critical moment; the burning of the bridges. Mollison said indifferently, "Mrs. Kramer is sending me out to the wholesale auction to pick up a few bombers for the high school trade. Better give me cash. We make a private deal sometimes and cash helps the price." Now it was done. If the banker had the slightest suspicion and called the agency; if just this one time he decided to check the place of employment of the fictitious buyer of the green Hudson . . . If, if, if.

Paul said, "Sure', Howie. Wait a minute and I'll make a slip out and you can pick up the cash at the paying teller's cage."

As simply as that it was done. Mollison walked out of the bank with eleven hundred dollars in cash — and saw Griffin waiting for him.

He paid off Griffin — he had no choice — with a thousand dollars of the money. The extra hundred he considered a bonus for his cleverness. That evening it amused him to be entertaining Lillian Kramer with her own money. It was really the bank's money, he supposed, but if anything went wrong the agency would be responsible because, as was customary with salesmen, he had been made an officer of the company in order to approve installment applications.

On the Tuesday following the transaction with the bank, Mollison was due for his normal turn in the used-car department. He preferred selling on the new-car floor; there was more money to be made there, but all of the salesmen had to take their regular turn in used cars. He dawdled over his breakfast and showed up late at the lot. The mechanic, Eddie, was changing a tire on a tired-looking sedan when Mollison sauntered from the office, and paused to watch him.

Eddie looked up. "Hello, Howie," he said. "Light me a cigarette, will you? My hands are all grease."

Mollison lit a cigarette and stuck it in the mechanic's mouth. He made the traditional joke about the tire. "What are you changing it for? It's only flat on one side."

Eddie grinned. "Yeah, but it had to be the bottom side." He stood up and pulled the jack from under the sedan. "See anything different?" he asked.

"About what?" Mollison asked.

"The car lot. See anything missing?"

"I'll bite. What's missing?"

Eddie laughed, his teeth white against his grimy face. "That dog," he said. "The '54 Hudson."

Mollison turned to stare at the rear row of cars. The green Hudson was gone. He started to say, "Oh, hell," but held it back.

Eddie, the moron, kept nodding and grinning. "There's this guy I met," he said, "with a '54 just like it except that the body is shot. Good motor in it, though. He offered five hundred cash for the one on the lot if I'd help him swap motors. I told Mrs. Kramer she ought to take him up on it and she said all right. She gave me twenty bucks for the sale."

Like a dog, Mollison thought. Wagging his tail and waiting to be praised. And all he had done was ruin Mollison. The bank he could deal with. Make the payments on the false account and take his chances. With the green Hudson sold he was in desperate trouble, not with the bank but with the Motor Vehicle Department because a transfer of title on the Hudson had already passed through the bank. When the legitimate buyer put through his own transfer, Mollison was going to be all done. There was the faintest possibility that the clerk who processed the transfer wouldn't catch the duplication of motor and serial numbers. Too faint. How many green '54 Hudsons were bought and sold in a week? Maybe they cross-filed by motor number anyway, in which case the false sale would be as obvious as a bloody nose.

Mollison hurried to the office, making some vague sort of excuse to Eddie. One of the other salesmen was at the desk. Mollison said, "Let me at that a minute, will you, Sam?"

Sam said curiously, "Sure, Howie. What's the rush?" and pulled back.

Mollison riffled through the transfer duplicates in the desk, hoping that the papers hadn't been taken into Lillian Kramer's office. He found the transfer on the Hudson almost at once. He didn't want to arouse Sam's interest any more than necessary, so he memorized the name and address: Joseph P. Hunt, 3211 Spring Street.

Sam was mumbling about the inequity of letting mechanics knock off commissions that salesmen should be getting. Mollison said brusquely, "I got to make a call, Sam. Hold things down, will you?"

The green Hudson was parked in the yard of 3211 Spring Street when Mollison drove up. The hood was raised and a man in a T-shirt and dirty slacks was bent over the motor. Mollison got out of his own car and asked, "Mr. Hunt?"

The man in the T-shirt straightened up. He appeared to be in his middle thirties. There was a smudge of grease on his cheek and his eyes were hidden behind thick glasses. He said, "I'm Hunt."

Mollison had had little time to plan an approach. He had to be careful, he knew, but beyond that he had to get the Hudson back at any cost. "I'm from the Kramer Agency," he said. "I'm sorry this happened, Mr. Hunt, but I already had an order on that car when you bought it. They shouldn't have sold it to you."

Hunt shrugged. "That's tough," he said. "I already bought it as far as I'm concerned. For cash."

Fighting his own scraped nerves, Mollison said genially, "We want to pay you for your time and trouble, Mr. Hunt. You paid five hundred for the car. We'll give you five fifty. You make fifty dollars on the deal and I keep my customer happy."

Hunt said doubtfully, "I was going to take the motor out of it and put my own in. Cost me seven fifty for body work on my own car."

"Make it five seventy-five," Mollison said, not as genially. "No red tape, no nothing. We'll just tear up the transfer on the Hudson and I'll get you your money."

Hunt grinned. "Tear up the transfer? What's the matter — is this iron hot or something?" He paused, and the grin left his face while his expression became shrewd. "What did you say your name was?"

Mollison was becoming increasingly impatient. What did the bastard want? A seventy-five-dollar profit on the deal should be enough. "Mollison," he said. "I told you I'm from the Kramer Agency. Well, what do you say, Mr. Hunt?"

Hunt shook his head. "I'll tell you what I say. I say I think I'll call up the agency and find out what your racket is. You come in here and want to buy this dog for seventy-five dollars more than I paid for it. Then you want me to tear up the transfer on it. I've bought a lot of cars in my life and I never yet heard of a salesman making a deal like that." He turned and started toward the house.

"Wait a minute," Mollison said.

Hunt turned back as if he had been expecting Mollison to call after him. "I got a minute," he said.

Mollison pleaded in desperation. "I've got to have that car," knowing as he did so that he was laying himself wide open, putting himself completely at Hunt's disposal.

Hunt nodded. "It's for sale," he said. "I figure it's worth a thousand dollars. That's without I call the agency."

Mollison said, "I'll get the money," knowing that the only way he could raise it would be to repeat the time contract swindle he had used to get the money for Griffin.

He forged another contract that morning, going to a different bank but using the same methods and the same lies. He stored the Hudson — useless to him — in a rented garage. On the following day Eddie, the Kramer mechanic, approached him on the lot.

"Hello, Howie," he greeted him. "Say — I hear you bought back that green Hudson."

Mollison lied halfheartedly. "I meant to tell you I sort of promised that car to a customer."

Eddie nodded. "Sure," he said. "Say, Howie, I'm a little short this week. Could you let me take fifty for a few days?"

Mollison loaned him the money, knowing that he would never get it back and that from now on there would be other loans. He raged inwardly at the crookedness of Hunt and Eddie, and never saw the irony in the situation.

On that same day the story of the kidnapping of the Glennon boy broke in the Eastern newspapers. Mollison heard it and ordered a drink at the club bar; it was the subject of all the conversation there and up until that moment it was interesting only as a news item about a monstrous crime. He was full of his own troubles; the fear that Lillian would catch up with him at any minute or that Eddie would squeal or that Griffin would come back for more money had him in a constant sweat. Someone mentioned that Anacosta, the moneylender, had more ready cash than any banker; the words were spoken half in jest. At that moment Louis Morgan ordered a drink from the bartender and Mollison remembered that he had seen Morgan at Anacosta's house.

And also at that moment Patsy Galuk, the handyman at the club, brought in a mop and pail to clean up a puddle of spilled liquor. Mollison put them all together: the kidnapping; Louis Morgan — who worked in Anacosta's bank; Anacosta himself and the fact that he had a grandson — he had seen the kid, hadn't he?; the availability of the loyal Patsy Galuk; all his troubles. And out of it all was born his plan.

Now, three weeks later, he had Louis Morgan in his pocket as an accomplice, he had found a hide-out, he had completed almost all of the detail work. Entering the club, he looked around, hoping that Morgan was already here. Maybe tonight they would tell Patsy after all. In any event he would have to be brought into the plan sooner or later. Patsy was going to be indispensable as a watchdog over the kid when they took him to the boiler room. Something more. Mollison had a part for Patsy in the plan that Morgan didn't know about and wouldn't know about until it was too late for him to back out. The thought brushed the corner of his mind that Patsy might even be made the fall guy. He sniggered as he thought of the lie he had devised to tell Patsy. "There are these Dagos that owed me some money, Patsy," he would tell him. Calling them Dagos was a good touch since it implied that he and Patsy belonged to a better, superior group themselves. "One of them is separated from his wife. He has a kid. What we're going to do is get the kid and hide him away until he pays me what he owes me. If he doesn't pay, I'm going to turn the kid over to its mother and he'll never get him back."

Patsy, out of his fanatic loyalty and need to belong with *somebody,* would believe it. Patsy would be the watchdog. And — although he couldn't tell Morgan about this yet — Mollison thought that Patsy might also be used as an executioner, or at least an undertaker. Because he had no intention of letting the boy go free when they had the money.

Chapter 5

There are small villages with white church steeples and green lawns, scrupulously neat, and these are New England. There are noisy, incredibly busy cities sitting astride the major highways, each with its approaches lined with gasoline stations and roadside restaurants and these too are New England. But not its bone and its cell structure. Neither the bigger cities nor the villages could have produced a Patsy Galuk. Sea captains and mortgage-foreclosing squires and horse traders built the villages, and their day had been past for a century and New England did not die with their passing. And the really big cities are barely staving off oblivion by fostering natural-gas lines and insurance companies, naval air stations and machine-tool factories, so that although they are a part of New England they are not its essence. That essence lies between the cities and the villages. — in the mill towns. Howard Mollison could have been born in any one of a hundred cities. Louis Morgan could have been reared in Waukegan or Cedar Rapids or Seattle. Patsy Galuk could only have been produced by a mill town.

A New England mill town can only be found on a river. It was built there perhaps a hundred or a hundred and fifty years ago; located there so that the river could carry away its waste. You will know it, if you look, by its rows and rows of identical houses. And you will know it when you see the particular mill for which the particular town was named. The mill will be made of pink brick and it will be enormous, sprawling over literally acres of ground. It will be three stories high and it will have a saw-toothed roof, built that way to let light in. The mill will be very nearly empty; the looms gone, the dye vats sold for zinc, the warpers and cards for scrap metal. There is no more money to be made in textiles; not in Fall River or Lawrence, nor in Pawtucket or Lynn. Here and there a few feet of floor space are taken up by a plastic molder or a shoe shop or a mill outlet but, for the most part, the mills stand idle. If you drove toward such a mill from the west toward evening you would see the glass of the saw-toothed roof catch fire from the reflected light of the sun so that the whole valley in which the mill stood seemed to be filled with wine — or blood. Go soon, if you would see it, because the mills are vanishing. One burns to the ground every so often — they make a spectacular blaze because the wooden floors have been drying out for . . . how many years?

The Galuks are not vanishing. Galuk's great-grandfather came from Poland to work in the mills at four dollars a week. There was a block of company houses where the Poles were given quarters. There was a block for the British — they ran the looms — and one for the Germans, who did the bleaching and dyeing. The Poles were laborers. Other mills brought in French Canadians and Alsatians; and Irish — the lace and linen mills — and Portuguese.

The Germans mistrusted the British. The British, who were, after all, craftsmen, despised the Germans and were contemptuous of the Poles. The Poles, in frustration, hated both the Germans and the British. To show this hate they built and patronized a Polish store and attended only Polish dances. (The Germans and the British and the French and the Irish likewise banded together.) The Poles married only Poles just as the British married only British and the Germans only German. After a generation or two the mills stopped importing workers — wages were up to six dollars a week by then — and there were, suddenly, no new Poles, no new Germans and no new British families. The Poles began marrying cousins as did the other groups. After a few more generations there were small sections in each town where each family was interrelated, and in some cases the blood was unhealthy. By the time that Patsy Galuk was born — in 1922—the percentage of imbeciles and cretins per thousand births was alarmingly high. Not that Galuk was really an imbecile or even a moron. Muddily, thickly, he could think. You could call it thinking, just barely.

Patsy worked as a handyman-court jester in the club to which Howard Mollison and Louis Morgan belonged. He had a stocky frame by birth; by his way of life it had become padded with soft and pallid fat. His face was quite wide — wider, it appeared, than it was long, so that he had a squashed down look. His head was large and his brownish hair usually long and unkempt; his lips were thick and rubbery. When he opened his mouth, which was often, he showed no teeth at all in his upper jaw between his two canines while the teeth in his lower jaw were broken and blackened. The club kept Patsy because he worked for almost no money and because he was amusing to a certain percentage of the membership. Patsy was a buff and a butt. Butt for anyone's practical joke and buff for whatever struck his fancy. When an electrician was called in to replace some faulty wiring, Patsy was told to help. For days thereafter he paraded about the club with all manner of pliers and screw drivers sticking from his belt. He would look wisely at every light fixture, every electrical outlet. He was, in his own mind, an electrician. The members would tell him of some fictitious electrical problem and Patsy would listen, set his jaw grimly and squint his eyes — and offer to come over and fix it someday. A week later he helped a painter, and he traded the screw drivers and pliers for a hip pocket full of brushes and scrapers and a giveaway white cap with a cardboard bill. So easily he changed his trade: But he had two loyalties that never changed, and these were to the police and to Howard Mollison.

Somewhere he had found a police badge. It was long obsolete but it was made of nickel and it held a high polish. Some member had convinced him that possession of the badge conferred authority, and it became Galuk's obsession to direct traffic whenever sirens wailed near the club. Whenever a siren was heard, someone would call, "Patsy! Where is Patsy? Get him out there before the whole street gets snarled up!" Others would join in. "Hurry up, Pat. Don't forget your badge."

Patsy would hurry grimly to the street where he would impartially stop all traffic as long as he could hear the sirens. Then he would come back into the club with an air of weary resignation. "The bastards," he would mutter. "Some of them wise bastards are looking for a ticket."

And they would congratulate him on a job well done.

He was not always funny. Once a new club manager fired him. Galuk refused to believe that he could be fired and he stood in the lounge of the club screaming the foulest obscenities at the manager for half an hour. Patsy was a formidable fighter; the manager was afraid to try to put him out and he finally called the police. Even then Patsy put up a violent struggle. For the next week he waited outside the of the club to waylay the members individually and beg to be taken back. Out of pity, or because they missed him in some perverse way, enough of them were persuaded so that he was taken back, apparently penitent.

Louis Morgan had watched many of Galuk's antics but he had

never found them amusing. Patsy would laugh with the members — at himself, more often than not — and he had a very loud, harsh laugh. Morgan, watching him one evening, realized that there was something wrong with Galuk's laughter. After a time he decided that it was because there was no humor in it at all. It seemed the laughter of an idiot; pure sound effect signifying nothing. Galuk frightened Morgan.

Galuk idolized Howard Mollison, partly because he was big and well dressed and good looking; everything that Patsy was not. He had additional cause for worship. Mollison, tongue in cheek, treated him as a friend and an equal. He would come into the club and put his arm across Galuk's shoulder. "What d'you say, Patsy, everything going all right?"

"Sure," Patsy would answer him, enraptured at the companionship. "Sure, Howie."

Mollison would nod. "That's good. You keep an eye on things, Patsy. We can trust you." He would wink at the other members. "You getting your share, Patsy?"

Patsy would flatten his thick lips in a secretive grin. "I do all right."

Mollison would nod again, his expression serious. "I'll bet you do."

The audience would laugh while Patsy, misunderstanding, would nod his head. "Sure, Howie." He would glance darkly at the other members. "Wise bastards around here. I bet I get more than they get."

Mollison was certain that Patsy would do anything for him and that he would keep his mouth shut if he were told to do so. Patsy had a childish reverence for secrets and promises.

On the evening of the day in which they had visited the mill and inspected the boiler room, Morgan and Mollison sat in the club and discussed Patsy.

"I've been thinking about it," Morgan said, "and I can't see why we have to bring Patsy into it. You said yourself that nobody goes near that end of the mill. When we get the boy, why couldn't we just tie him up and leave him?"

Mollison had his own reasons for wanting Patsy to be a party to the kidnapping. He couldn't tell all of these reasons to Morgan, who had already shown himself to be pretty chicken, so he lied.

"It will be safer to have Patsy watching him," Mollison said. "I've got to show myself around; you'll have your end of things to take care of. We'd have to sweat it out wondering if he was getting loose if we left him alone. It's damn hard to tie somebody up so they can't get loose if you give them enough time — even a kid. And besides, there are the rats." The thought of the rats was sheer inspiration.

"The rats?"

Mollison nodded. "That old mill is full of them. Some of them as big as cats. We couldn't leave the kid tied up in there all by himself."

Morgan said, "I guess you're right." He almost felt a little better about Mollison. Too hard; too cruel. A little too quick and easy about how they'd return the boy after they got the money. But at least he was showing some concern for the boy now. "Yes, I suppose we do need Patsy," he agreed.

Mollison smiled. "The best part of it is that he won't know what's going on. I've figured out a story to tell him that will cover it. He'll believe anything I tell him." And, hoping Morgan would do the same, Mollison quickly told him the story he'd concocted for Patsy Galuk.

Chapter 6

A day later Mollison said, "We've gone over it a hundred times, Lou. Getting the kid will be easy — right?"

Morgan said doubtfully, "I guess so."

Mollison became a little impatient. It showed in the rising inflection of his voice and in the quick little pushing motion he made with his hand. "He walks home from school every afternoon. Goddammit, I've watched him, I know what I'm talking about. I'll take a car from the lot and stick on a set of plates somebody left on a turn-in a couple months ago. After I drop him off at the old mill I'll put the car back on the lot and take the plates off and throw them away. If somebody does get the license number and they trace it as far as the agency we'll just say we don't know anything about it. People are always leaving plates on cars when they sell them." His expression became faintly injured. "I'm taking all the chances, Lou. All you have to do is drive Patsy out there to watch the kid."

The two men were sitting in the back room of the club; a place seldom used except for occasional poker games. Mollison had a whisky and water in front of him; Morgan, a bottle of ale. Morgan asked, "Have you told Patsy yet?"

Mollison shook his head. "Not yet, I've been waiting until we could think out some way of getting the money — some way that would be foolproof. There's got to be a way, Lou. But I can't wait much longer." He held the thin edge of his palm against the front of his neck. "I'm in a bind right up to here."

Morgan picked at the wet label of the ale bottle with his fingernail. What he had to say now he didn't want to say. It was his idea, his original contribution; and he would not be able to put it off on Mollison once said. He said deliberately, "I think I know a way it can be done."

Mollison leaned forward, breathing audibly through his nose, "Well, for God's sake," he said, "how?"

"After we — after you have the boy," Morgan said, "we're going to call Anacosta. You'd better do the talking. Anacosta just might recognize my voice."

Mollison frowned. "We already agreed on that," he said. "I'll call him and tell him that we have the boy and that we want seventy-five thousand dollars in cash if he wants him back. So what then? How does he get the money to us?"

Morgan drew his hand away from the bottle, aware that it betrayed his nervousness. "If he goes to the police, we'll know," he said. "The first thing they will want us to do is record the serial numbers of the bills at the bank and if that happens, I've got to know about it. Any of us at the bank will know about it."

Mollison swallowed some of his drink. "All right, Lou," he said. "All right. We know that. And I already told you that he won't go to the police. He can't afford to. He's still got the mustache boys."

Morgan nodded. "I know," he said. "So we just can't give him a chance to get organized." He glanced at Mollison, and for the first time in the three weeks since Mollison had outlined his plan Morgan, felt a glow of superiority. He, Morgan, was taking charge; planning things that Mollison, for all his big talk, was incompetent to plan. He leaned back in his chair. "Why don't we get the boy in the morning?" he asked.

Mollison, puzzled, said, "I don't see where that makes any difference."

"It makes a big difference. If we get" — Morgan could not bring himself to use the word kidnap — "the boy in the afternoon, the way you planned, Anacosta will have all night to think things out. He can arrange to have men following him every step he takes regardless of whether he calls in the police. If we take him in the morning and call Anacosta right away, make him go to the bank for the money immediately, what chance will he have to arrange a trap?"

Mollison slapped the table top with his open palm. "No chance," he said. "No chance."

Morgan nodded. "That's what I mean. If you call him at, say, ten o'clock, and he gets to the bank within a few minutes after you call, we could feel pretty certain that he hadn't had the chance to get help. The problem will be to convince him that we have the boy and that we mean business. The kind of business Anacosta is in, I imagine he's been threatened before. That's another thing. The boy is his grandson. Won't he think that it should be up to the boy's father to handle the negotiations?"

Mollison laughed shortly. "Anacosta's son — the kid's father — doesn't have a nickel. The old man gave them the house they live in, the car they drive and the clothes on their backs. He worships the grandson. Don't worry, Lou — he'll pay."

"You mean, he'll pay if he thinks we have the boy," Morgan corrected. "How can we convince him?" He was seeing the affair now as an academic problem; a matter of strategy and logistics.

Mollison said thoughtfully, "It will have to be good. I might get him to a telephone and have him call the old man. That would be pretty risky. I'd have to handle the kid and try to call at the same time. If he put up a struggle it would attract attention and that would be it. Don't forget, it will be broad daylight."

Morgan said quietly, "The stadium."

"The stadium?" Mollison repeated in puzzlement.

"The municipal stadium. There's one of those glassed-in telephone booths at the end of the parking lot. I guess they put it there for people who want to call cabs. Nobody could get within a hundred yards of it without you knowing it. Couldn't you take him there and let him talk to his grandfather?"

Mollison said, "That's it. That's it, Lou. I can drive up and take him into the booth with me. If he makes a fuss, who's to know it? It won't take more than a couple of minutes."

Morgan, feeling the intoxication of command, smiled faintly. "It will be worth a dozen ransom notes," he said.

"But that doesn't get us the money," Mollison hedged. "What happens after the old man leaves the bank with the money? What do I tell him to do?"

Morgan poured the remainder of his bottle of ale into his glass, but he did not immediately drink it. After a moment he said, "We'll do it like this." And he began to explain to Mollison just how they would get delivery of the money. . . .

Chapter 7

From his parked car Mollison could see the boy coming down the street, walking aimlessly, a painted lunch box in one hand and a schoolbook in the other. Mollison had watched him half a dozen times and he had always come alone. There had been the bare chance that he would pick up a companion on this morning but he hadn't. The boy was eight years old and his name was Carmen — named for his grandfather as an investment, Mollison supposed. He was walking toward Mollison's car with a small boy's disregard of time — or pure enjoyment of it. Mollison glanced at his watch. Fifteen minutes before nine and so far right on schedule. Morgan should, by this time, have left Patsy at the mill.

Now the boy was almost abreast of the car; a fat kid with a pasty white face. Too much spaghetti and ravioli. Fat little Dago kid. Mollison got out of the car and walked around to the back, pretending to put something in the trunk and turning when the boy was exactly opposite. Try it the easy way first. "Hey, there," he said in mock surprise. "Aren't you Carmen Anacosta's grandson?"

The boy stopped. Almost daily he was warned against talking to strangers or taking candy from them or riding with them but this was a big, well-dressed man; not like the scary ones on TV — and he knew Grandpa Anacosta. "Yes sir," he said, running the words together.

Mollison smiled. "I thought so," he said. "Your grandpa is a good friend of mine." He turned and started toward the driver's side and then paused. "Hop in," he said as if it were an afterthought. "I'll drop you off at the school. It's right on my way." As he spoke Mollison opened the door on the passenger side and held it wide. There was no one in sight toward the rear of the car; if the kid didn't get in and he had to grab him, the door would partially screen him from anyone coming from the other direction. One way or another the kid was getting in the car and once in he wasn't going to get out. Mollison had gone to the used-car lot early to pick up the particular car he was using. He had carefully removed, the window and door handles from the inside on the passenger side and he had mounted a discarded set of license plates.

The boy hesitated and then said, "Thanks, mister," and got in. Mollison slammed the door after him and went around to the driver's side.

So far so good. The whole thing hadn't taken over a minute or so, and the first of the four major risks that he and Morgan had decided were the minimum they would encounter was successfully passed. They had no control over the second risk. Mollison was to call Anacosta at eleven o'clock. Not five minutes before and not five minutes after. When the kid didn't show up at school would the teacher call his parents? As far as he and Morgan had been able to find out, it wasn't routine for the teacher to check — Mollison had found this out by slyly bringing up the subject of juvenile delinquency and hooky playing at the club bar. Morgan hadn't thought of that. That had been his own idea.

Mollison headed the car downtown for only a short distance before he turned off into a side street. The boy said immediately, "The school isn't this way, mister."

Mollison said, "This is a short cut," and drove a little faster. When the boy protested he told him to shut his mouth, his raw nerves overcoming his judgment.

The boy was more angry than frightened. In his home he was seldom even scolded. Sometimes his father or his mother in quick Latin anger would slap him, but they were always abject immediately afterward. They had never, in his life, told him to shut up. He said quite loudly, "You let me out or I'll tell the police on you."

Mollison kept his head straight ahead. The boy could think of no greater threat than to call the cops as he beat frantically against the glass with the palms of his hands. Mollison, still not looking around, slapped him hard against the side of his head so that he sprawled half on the seat, half on the floor of the car. He began to cry helplessly.

Mollison glanced again at his watch. Not quite nine. He drove toward the Maynard Mill, but instead of parking where he and Lou Morgan had parked when he had first shown Morgan the mill, he drove the length of the parking lot and pulled the borrowed car in tight against the low boiler room annex. To the boy he said, "Stay where you are," and got out of the car. He pushed the door of the boiler room open. Patsy Galuk came to the door to meet him, a grimly important expression on his face.

"Lou brought me," he said. "Lou brought me out here. I was ready this morning when he came after me. What you want me to do now, Howie?"

Mollison waved him back. Moving swiftly he opened the car door and dragged the boy from the car into the boiler room, clamping one hand over the small face so that the boy had no chance to cry out. Once inside the door, Mollison shoved him forward so that he had to take little tripping steps to keep his balance. He slammed against the far wall of the room and turned like an animal at bay to face his tormentors. "You dirty stinkers," he said. "My father will fix you."

Patsy moved forward to stand facing the boy, his hands on his hips, his expression deliberately ugly. "Dago bastard," he said ferociously. "Little Dago bastard."

Mollison pushed him back. "Let him be, Patsy, as long as he doesn't give you any trouble." To the boy he said, "Get up on that cot and sit there and don't make a sound. If you so much as move do you know what this man will do to you?"

The boy could make no sound. He shook his head. His face was grimy where he had knuckled his eyes, and tears of fright made tunnels in the dirt.

"He'll cut you up in pieces," Mollison said. He turned to face Patsy. "I'll be back in an hour and a half. Don't make any noise. Don't let him make any noise and don't even put your head out the door. All right?"

Patsy, without taking his eyes from the boy, said, "Sure, Howie. Don't you worry about this Dago bastard making any noise." He had taken up a position facing the boy, with his arms akimbo.

Mollison turned toward the door and hesitated. "Patsy," he said, "I think I'll lock you in. That way there won't be any chance of anyone sneaking around."

Patsy, who had not moved, said, "Sure, Howie."

Mollison left, locking the door behind him. Leaving the boy with Patsy was another risk; Morgan had wanted to leave him bound and gagged. Mollison, thinking ahead, had won the argument.

He drove to the Kramer Agency with deliberate care, not wanting a traffic summons at this stage. He left the car a block from the used-car lot to avoid the risk of having Eddie, the mechanic, or one of the salesmen notice that he didn't have the conventional dealer's plates on the car.

He usually avoided Eddie, who was becoming openly demanding these days. On this day he sought him out deliberately, wanting to be noticed. He was aware now that he was slightly elated, almost as if he had had several drinks. The plan was going smoothly. He was keyed up but not at all frightened.

"Eddie," he said, "I've got that blue Ford out. The battery was down.

I had to leave it for a quick charge." That explained the absence of the car.

Eddie said — he seemed sincere enough — "I'm sorry as hell, Howie. I'll stick another one in it when you bring it in."

So much for Eddie. Mollison moved around talking to Lillian, kidding with the other salesmen. When it was ten-thirty he mentioned casually that he had a call to make. He then eased out of the lot, walked to the car in which he had picked up Anacosta's grandson, and drove to the mill.

Patsy Galuk was still standing in the same spot when Mollison again opened the door of the boiler room. He glanced around to see who it was, but he immediately turned back to face the boy with the same animal stare. "He ain't moved, Howie," he said. "I didn't let him make any noise either."

Mollison said, "That's great, Patsy. You did a good job. I'm going to take him with me now to call his old man about the money he owes me. You're going to wait right here, right?"

Patsy nodded grimly. "Right here, Howie."

Mollison took the boy's arm. "You come with me," he said.

The boy came almost eagerly. This man had hit him and hurt him when he had pounded on the window of the car, but he was not as frightening as the man he called Patsy. Mollison pushed in beside him and drove out of the mill yard.

The municipal stadium was located on a patch of reclaimed swamp land two miles more or less from the downtown area. One city administration had built the stadium proper; a subsequent group had had to make the best of paving the approaches to the place. There were acres of black-top parking area. Mollison, looking about him as he drove in, could see two cars wheeling in aimless circles. Student drivers, learning to drive where there was small risk of accident — no hazard, since neither of the cars were close to the minaret of the telephone booth which Morgan had described. He parked the blue Ford as close to the booth as he could get and pulled at the boy's arm. "Come on," he said. "We're going to call your grandfather."

The boy had stopped his sniveling. Mollison opened the door to the booth and shoved him in, pushing in after him himself and turning so that the boy was trapped between his knees. He had memorized the telephone number of the boy's grandfather and he had a coin already in his hand when he entered the booth. He reached up and dialed expertly.

Twice he heard the distant buzz of the completed circuit before he heard the click of a receiver being lifted and a heavy voice with a marked accent saying, "Yes? What is it?"

He had talked to Anacosta very briefly a few times after the night that Griffin had first approached him and demanded money. There was only the remotest possibility that Anacosta might remember his voice, but why take unnecessary chances? Mollison affected a false baritone as he countered Anacosta's question with one of his own. "Is this Anacosta?" he asked.

"This is Anacosta. Who is this? What do you want?" The expression was thickly arrogant.

He would not be arrogant much longer, Mollison thought. Before he could answer, the boy, recognizing Anacosta's voice, cried, "Gran'pa! Gran'pa — a man has got me — "

Mollison, before he could realize that the outburst was favorable to his plan, acted in sudden and angry reflex, cuffing the boy on the back of his head as hard as he could in the cramped space. The boy's mouth was driven against the hard mouthpiece of the telephone, breaking one of his teeth and bringing blood and saliva in a pink gush. The boy cried out in pain and shock, and Mollison clamped his forearm across his face, muffling the sound. He could hear Anacosta, as frantic as the boy, calling, "Carmen! Carmen!"

Mollison, still holding his forearm against the boy's face, said, "Shut up and listen." He waited for a moment. Anacosta stopped calling the boy's name and only the sound of his heavy breathing pulsed in the receiver. Let him sweat. Let him know that this wasn't some poor devil wanting to borrow a few bucks. Mollison said, "You heard the boy."

Anacosta said, "I heard. Look you. I give you what you want but don't you hurt him any more. Please don't hurt him any more. I find you and I cut your heart out if you hurt him."

"You won't cut anybody's heart out. Say it."

Anacosta's voice was inexpressibly weary. "All right. I won't cut anybody's heart out. What do you want so I get him back?"

"Seventy-five thousand dollars. In cash. This morning." When Anacosta did not immediately answer, Mollison had an idea. He released the pressure against the boy's face just enough so that his crying became audible, then tightened his grip again. "Did you hear me?" he demanded.

"I heard you. All right. I'll get you the money. What do you want me to do?"

This was easy. The old man had folded up just the way he had told Morgan he would. Mollison said, almost contemptuously, "Listen, then. You leave the house right now and go down and get the money out of the bank. Don't take your car, walk. Get it any way they give it to you but get it.

"Take a paper bag, a brown paper bag, with you. The biggest one you've got in the house. You put the money in the bag. Go out of the bank and walk down Elm Street to the Greyhound bus station. There are some pay lockers in the west entrance. The numbers start with two hundred. You put a dime in the slot of the first empty locker you come to after two hundred; it doesn't matter what number it is." Mollison paused. Time to give the old Shylock another dose. He released his pressure on the boy's face, but he had stopped crying. Mollison said, "Say hello to your grandfather, kid." When the boy, too frightened to speak, said nothing, Mollison slapped him lightly across the face. "Say hello," he ordered again.

The boy managed to say, "Gran'pa — " but he could get no further words out and subsided into spasmodic weeping.

The weeping was as good as words anyway. Mollison let Anacosta listen for a few seconds before he continued. "Put the money in the locker and take the key with you. Leave the terminal by the south entrance and walk across Pleasant Street to the common in front of the railroad station. You know where I mean?"

Anacosta said, "I know. I know. Let me talk to the boy again for a minute. Please."

Mollison said, "Later," feeling a sensation of power at having made Anacosta crawl. "You'd better keep listening," he continued. "There's a drinking fountain on the common. There is only one so you can't make any mistake. You stop and get a drink of water. Listen, Anacosta — there's a pedal on that fountain. You step on it to make the water come. Put the key under the pedal and move on — and don't look back."

"I won't look," Anacosta promised eagerly. "I don't want the money, mister. You can have it — just so you don't hurt the boy. I give it to you. You will let him go when you get the money?"

"If you don't try to trap us we will. We're watching your house right now. We'll watch you when you leave and all the rest of the time. If you so much as talk to anyone, you're cutting the kid's throat. Do you understand that?"

"I understand."

Mollison brought his wrist up with difficulty and glanced at his watch. Eleven-eight. So far the timing was accurate almost to the second. He said, "Get your hat and coat and leave right now — and remember that we'll be watching you."

"Let me say one word to the boy," Anacosta pleaded.

Mollison released his grip slightly. "Go ahead," he said. "Make it fast."

Anacosta said, "Carmen?"

The boy gasped, "I'm here, Gran'pa."

Anacosta hurried his words. "You do what the man says, now. You do whatever he says and everything will be all right. You hear what I said?"

Mollison interrupted. "He heard you. Now move." He hung up the receiver and waited a moment before he put another coin in and dialed Anacosta's number again. That was another of the risks they had accepted. If the number was busy it would mean that Anacosta was calling for help; the police or the mustache boys. It was not busy. He heard Anacosta's voice anxiously saying, "Yes? Yes? I am just leaving." Mollison set the receiver down gently; not on its hook but on the small shelf that the telephone company provided beneath the instrument. They had tried this, he and Morgan. Anacosta's line was now out of action. If Anacosta tried to call out he would get only a busy signal. After three minutes the operator would put a howler on the pay station booth, but there would be no one to hear it. After a time she would call the service department and a road man would come out to check the telephone, but in the meantime Anacosta's line was useless to him. Mollison left the booth and got into the car, pushing the boy ahead of him.

The biggest risk of all was Anacosta himself. They had no one watching him. Mollison had to make the call, Patsy had to serve as warden in the boiler room, and Morgan had to be at the bank. They could only wait, and see if the combination of Mollison's threats and the near-frantic devotion of the old man to his grandson were an effective enough combination to keep him from running up to the first policeman he saw or stopping at the first drugstore with a pay station in it. Mollison felt the first light film of perspiration on his forehead and the palms of his hands, but he was not aware of being afraid, except in one sense: he was afraid that something might happen to prevent him from getting his share of the money, now that they were so close to it. He drove back to the boiler room and left the boy. He paused long enough to replace the door and window handles on the car and then drove downtown and parked as near to the bus station as he could. He did not enter the terminal. Instead he bought a newspaper and found a vacant bench a hundred feet from the drinking fountain on the common that fronted the railroad station. He settled down to wait.

Chapter 8

At approximately the time that Howard Mollison waited for the Anacosta boy to come by on his way to school, Louis Morgan was admitted to the Drover's National Bank through a side door by a uniformed watchman who gave him the greeting appropriate to a teller with ten years' seniority. Whereas Mollison waited for their victim more in a perverted form of excitement than in fear, Morgan, this early, was close to panic. Only the force of routine had gotten him through the morning so far. You arose and you washed; you brushed your teeth and dressed and shaved and then took a downtown bus, getting off and stopping at a coffee shop for toast and coffee. You did these things, after so many years, out of habit; and if these things were the same it almost seemed as if everything else were the same too. Except that it wasn't. At this moment, if Mollison had carried out his part of the plan, he was an accessory to a kidnapping. Even while he walked into the vault and took out the locked cash box that he had checked in the previous day, he was a party to the most heinous crime of them all.

He was aware that his hands were trembling as he took the box from the vault and hurried quickly to his own cage, where he pretended to be busy sorting the money that it contained; this occupied his hands and had the further effect of discouraging conversation by the other tellers.

The doors opened, and there was a quick little clot of early customers. This too was routine; a cherished routine, it seemed now, not dull and pointless as before. People came in and handed you chits and you gave them money. Or you gave them chits and they gave you money. It had seemed futile to the point of absurdity but Morgan would have made almost any sacrifice to have nothing else to look forward to for the rest of his life. Mollison must have the boy by now.

Had he been seen? Had someone called the police that a man was abducting a child? Had they caught him already — and had he confessed and involved Morgan? Morgan's hands trembled and the woman who was making a savings deposit at his window looked at him intently.

"You look white as a sheet," she said. "Are you all right?"

Good God, he couldn't afford to have people notice him. He had never before appreciated that it could be a blessing not to be noticed, to be obscure, neuter . . . He said lamely, "I have quite a headache." He even managed a smile that felt as artificial as it was. "I saw a technicolor movie last night. It always seems to bother my eyes the following day."

The woman glanced at the pass book. "I've heard people say that," she said agreeably. "Still, you ought to see your eye man."

She turned away. So much for her — but she had noticed his pallor and she was a stranger. It followed that the people in the bank would also notice it. When there was a lull in the morning's activity, Morgan left his own cubicle and walked into the adjacent one. The teller turned to meet him.

Morgan said, "You've got the early lunch period, haven't you, Vega?"

Vega nodded. "I go off at eleven-thirty. Why? You want me to bring you in something?"

Morgan shook his head, hating to ask a favor of the other teller. The bank personnel thought he was a snob, that he considered himself something better than they were; and he was aware of the way they felt. He had no alternative. He had to be free at eleven-thirty and he had to explain the pallor that he could not possibly hide, so that if they talked about the kidnapping in the washroom on the next day or the next, no one would think it strange that Louis Morgan had been very upset when Anacosta came to the bank to pick up the ransom money. He said, "I'm supposed to go out at one. Would you mind trading with me — if you haven't any special plans, I mean." He added quickly, wanting to establish the good-fellow relationship that the other bank employees seemed to value, "I've got a block-buster of a head — went to a stag dinner last night. I thought if I got some coffee and some fresh air I might live."

Vega smiled sympathetically, thinking that perhaps Morgan wasn't quite such a stuffed shirt after all. "Sure, Lou," he said. "You look pretty rocky."

Morgan thanked him and hurried back to his own cage; he had arranged to be off at eleven-thirty without having to go to the assistant manager and plead a headache.

He glanced at the lobby clock. Ten-thirty. Mollison was to call Anacosta at eleven — at exactly eleven. The call would take six or seven minutes — perhaps as much as ten. It would take Anacosta — allowing for his age — anywhere from twelve to fifteen minutes to walk to the Drover's Bank — so that he should walk in the door between twenty minutes and half past eleven. If he did not, Morgan would know why. It would mean that he was calling the police — and how soon after that would they be coming for him? He had an almost pathological fear of the police. Not because they represented punishment but because of the humiliation they could subject him to — as they had once before when he was eleven years old, when they had come to arrest his father.

Morgan glanced at the clock and was astonished to see that it was ten minutes past eleven. He had been lost in a dangerous reverie which had, however, almost gotten him through the terrible waiting time. There were only some twenty minutes left now until Anacosta would come walking in the door to get the money for himself and Mollison. Or until the police would come. Mollison had claimed that he could tie up Anacosta's telephone so that he couldn't call out. He was supposed to have convinced the old man that he was being watched so that he wouldn't stop off at a drugstore or a gas station and use a public telephone to tip off the police — but had he been that convincing?

Customers came to his wicket, and he waited on them with numb efficiency while he planned his actions when Anacosta came in. Should he wait on him himself or pass him along to Vega? He could work it either way by merely speeding or delaying the customers at his own wicket so that the line in front of it would be short or long. He decided that he could not face Anacosta directly himself. If he worked it so that he would go to Vega's cage, he could still see everything that went on. Safer that way. He began to slow down his own paper work so that a line formed almost immediately.

Twenty minutes past eleven. Twenty-five. Unbelievably Morgan now felt almost calm, but it was a fatalistic calm. Either Anacosta or the police were going to come in the door. Nothing he could do about it. He slowed his line down a shade, wanting to have enough people waiting in front of his wicket to justify delaying the lunch period he had traded with Vega until, one way or another, it was over. At eleven-thirty, Anacosta walked in — alone. Morgan watched him cross the lobby, walking with the erratic shuffle of an old man trying to hurry. The old man's face was gray, his eyes staring. Morgan had seen him a hundred times; at his home when he went there weekly to redeem his predated checks and, occasionally, in the bank when Anacosta came there on business. He seemed to have aged, to have lost the usual brutal, surly confidence. Morgan momentarily felt pity for him until he remembered that he was, after all, a usurer and worse, according to Mollison.

It could still be a trap. Maybe the police were following. Maybe they had picked up Mollison and were looking for reactions; maybe that's why they were having the old man pick up the money as if nothing had happened. But would he look so stricken? He could not affect the shocked expression on his face, Morgan decided. Still he could not face the man. He bent over a sheaf of deposit slips, watching Anacosta covertly. He was walking toward the enclosure that held the safety deposit boxes, pausing only to identify himself to the guard before he passed from Morgan's sight.

Morgan felt a nervous elation. It was working. It was working. He jumped, startled, at the sound of a voice calling him. It was Vega in the next cage.

"Lou," he called. "Hey, Lou — you want to send those people over to my cage while you go and get that coffee?"

Morgan glanced up. "No thanks," he said. "I can finish with these two." He pulled the triangular block of wood with the word *Closed* on it over in front of his cage and smiled at the two men who were still in line. "I'll take care of you gentlemen before I go," he said, amazed that the smile had come easily.

There was a nicety of timing needed now. He wanted time for Anacosta to reappear from the safety deposit vault, and yet he wanted to be on his way to the door at that exact moment so that he would not appear to be following the old man. There was another factor involved — would he be going to one of the tellers to make a withdrawal now, or could it be possible that he had seventy-five thousand dollars in the safety deposit box? Mollison had thought that he probably kept that much in nonrecorded funds, and Morgan remembered the size of the sheaves of bills that he had seen on the day he had followed him into the vault. It was possible. If it were in hundreds that would mean that there would be only seven hundred and fifty bills; a huge sheaf but one that could easily be concealed in a paper bag.

Morgan finished with the two men, walked back to the employees' lockers for his hat, and returned to the lobby, dawdling as much as he dared without being conspicuous. Anacosta had not appeared by the time he had stalled as much as he could, and he walked out the door with a nod for the guard.

Anacosta would be walking down Elm — if he were actually going to follow Mollison's instructions. Morgan walked half a block down Elm and stopped at a newsstand-lunchroom that had four stools posted in front of a marble counter gritty with spilled sugar where it was not gummy with slopped milk. Out of natural fastidiousness he usually avoided the place — Vega claimed that the coffee was the best — but this was no usual day and the lunchroom was a perfect observation post. He would have liked a cup of coffee but decided against it. It might be served too hot to drink, and if Anacosta went by he would have to leave it and that might stick in the counterman's memory.

"A glass of milk," he said. He put a dime on the counter, buying with it the right to get up and leave whenever he wished without having to fool with a check. He had half finished the milk when Anacosta walked by. He had to force himself to wait while he finished the milk and let the old man get a half block ahead. He was carrying a large paper bag.

All he could do now was follow Anacosta to the bus terminal; he could not follow him inside — the risk would be too great — but he could watch from across the street and see how long he remained inside. If he didn't come out in five minutes, they could assume that he was contacting the police. In all their planning, he and Mollison had never really decided what they would do if he delayed longer than the allotted five minutes. Pick up the key, perhaps, and hire some kid to go get the bag from the locker? If they had had another confederate now, he could have watched Anacosta during the two most dangerous gaps — when he left his house to walk to the bank, although he was supposed to think that he was being watched, which should have the same effect, and in the bus terminal. Morgan, watching from across the street, saw Anacosta emerge from the terminal and cross Pleasant Street. He no longer had the bag with him.

They were so close now. A few minutes to wait to be sure that the old man didn't look back or change his mind, and then he would be picking up the key and going back to the terminal for the paper bag full of money. Seventy-five thousand dollars. Half of that was thirty-seven thousand,-five hundred. Morgan wondered what Mollison was going to do with his share. He was in some sort of a jam; no doubt about that. As for his own share, Morgan was first going to pay off Anacosta. He thought it almost hysterically amusing. Anacosta's own money. How would he do it? Change the money into small bills — twos and fives — and pay off the two hundred dollars all at once? No. No, damn it. The worst thing you could do was show money after a kidnapping. No, he would go on paying him off a few dollars each week. Mollison claimed that Anacosta wouldn't go to the police, but Morgan was sure that the minute he had the boy back safe he would get the FBI, the police and the Army and Navy if he could work it.

It was time. Morgan crossed the street, taking the same route that Anacosta had taken. The old man was not in sight. Mollison was sitting on a bench in front of the common reading a newspaper. As Morgan approached, he lowered the newspaper and nodded faintly. Without making any sign of recognition, Morgan walked deliberately to the drinking fountain and bent over as if to tie his shoelace. The key was in the little niche behind the foot pedal; flat and brass and gleaming. Morgan picked it up, then bent to take a drink of water. He could not swallow it even though his throat was dry. Suddenly he was afraid again. So far, barring the apprehension of Mollison by the police, he had been fairly safe — almost an innocent bystander. He had not talked to Anacosta — he had never even seen the boy. Now he was to pick up the money, and he approached it with the same fear with which he would have approached a live bomb. He had argued about this phase of the plan with Mollison, wanting Mollison to take the key and get the money.

"The hell with that," Mollison had said. "You want me to do everything; snatch the kid and arrange for the ransom and pick it up, too. What are you supposed to do to earn your half? Let's face it, Lou. You could go into a bus station and nobody would see you if they were looking right at you. You look as if you might even live there. I couldn't do that. I'd stand out. People could remember me."

Morgan had admitted there was a certain amount of truth in Mollison's argument. Now he walked back toward the station. Look at the key and get the number so you won't have to search around when you get into the terminal, he told himself. Two hundred and six.

All right. You know where the two hundred series lockers are. Walk toward them. There was a crowd in the terminal. People waiting for buses, waiting for friends. Waiting for him? He couldn't turn around and walk out now. If some of the waiting people were the police, that would be as suspicious as going to the locker. He moved toward the green cabinets, feeling a warm trickle of perspiration slide from his armpit and down the length of his ribs. Two hundred and two — two hundred and four. Two hundred and six. It was the bottom tier. He bent and fumbled with the key with numb fingers. It hung and then slid into place. The tumblers fell into line and the door swung open. The paper sack was there. He picked it up, aware of a fleeting surprise that it was so heavy. Don't hang around and get your face remembered. He walked out into the stream of pedestrian traffic on Elm Street and headed downtown, feeling that his face was burning. After two blocks a car pulled up beside him. He was afraid to look around until he heard Mollison's heavy Voice.

"Get in," he said. "Is it there?"

He had not dared to look in the bag. He hurried around the front of Mollison's car and slid into the seat. Only when Mollison had let in the clutch and sent them rolling away did he uncurl the top of the bag and look in to see the solid looking edge of a sheaf — it looked like the edge of a mail order catalogue — of bills. Hundreds and hundreds of them. Morgan had the double standard common to bank employees and pari-mutuel clerks. Money, during business hours, was a commodity, something to be handled and distributed and counted but not of any obvious value. Money only took on meaning outside of the bank or the pay window at the track. This money, this common brown paper bag full of money, had meaning. It was his — his and Mollison's.

Chapter 9

They would both keep their jobs — for a time, at least — even if there were no furor in the newspapers about the kidnapping. Maybe Anacosta would go to the police and maybe not; but if he did go it might be kept out of the papers, for a time, anyway, and they would never be able to be quite sure that an investigation wasn't being conducted. They had decided that much when they first planned the kidnapping.

Mollison asked, "Do you want to eat? This is your lunch hour, isn't it?"

Morgan shook his head. He could not even remember what it felt like to be hungry. "No," he said. "You can drive around for a little while and then drop me off at the bank."

Mollison nodded. "Just as if nothing had happened. You've got to remember that, Lou. We both do. Remember what I said — it's the ones who go crazy with the money that get caught. How much did you say Anacosta had you on the hook for?"

"Two hundred dollars."

"Well, don't do anything foolish like paying him off right away."

Morgan wished that Mollison would stop treating him like a child. The exhilaration that had come from actual contact with the money had faded swiftly; now there was only the dull lethargy that came from sustaining a high emotional key for too long a time.

Mollison suddenly laughed aloud and slapped Morgan's thigh. "What are we worrying about?" he demanded. "We made it, Lou."

"We made it," Morgan agreed. "What about the boy? When are we going to let him go?"

Mollison fumbled for a cigarette. "There isn't any rush," he said. "You don't expect to turn him loose in broad daylight, do you?"

"No, I guess not. Couldn't you just leave the door unlocked and let him get out by himself? We didn't figure this end of it out the way we should have."

Mollison said impatiently, "There isn't anything to figure about it. Let me worry about it, Lou. We can't do anything until after dark anyway. He's safe with Patsy. Now what about the money? Do you want to hold onto it until tonight?"

He was trying to show how much he trusted him, Morgan thought. Offering to let him hold the money when he knew damn well he couldn't carry it back to the bank with him. A cheap, show-off gesture. "No," he said. "You keep it. I'll come up to your place tonight after work. You'd better drop me off at the bank now. I don't want to be late." He was annoyed with Mollison and himself. They had planned for every possible circumstance in the actual kidnapping, but they hadn't taken the time to figure how to clean up the mess they had made, how to return the boy. And now that he thought about it, Mollison had been evasive all along whenever they had discussed what they would do once they had the money. He didn't like it.

The bank was almost empty when Morgan re-entered the lobby.

Vega smiled and shoved the *Closed* sign in front of his own wicket. "How's the head?" he asked slyly.

Morgan frowned. "A little better," he said. Vega was acting normally. Anacosta had been able to get all of the ransom money from the safety deposit box without going to Vega to make a withdrawal; Morgan was sure of this because of the short lapse of time between his own departure for lunch and Anacosta's reappearance as he passed the lunchroom down the street. He was doubly sure now. If Anacosta had made a major withdrawal from his account, Vega would be gossiping about it as he locked his cash box and prepared to leave. Vega seemed, like the rest of the bank personnel, to like to talk about other people's money — probably because he didn't have any of his own, Morgan thought dourly. He opened his cash box, and had a sudden thought. What assurance did he have that Mollison wouldn't take all the money and leave town? He would be safe enough, God knew. What could Morgan do — swear out a warrant? Hire detectives? By the end of the day the thought was a constant torment, and he had convinced himself that when he got to the apartment Mollison would be gone. There was one glimmering of relief in the thought. If Mollison had gone, perhaps it was because he had already turned the boy loose and was afraid that he might be identified.

Mollison's apartment was a tiny two-room affair in a brick cliff on the west side of town. Morgan hurried up the hall and pushed the bell beside the living-room door. As if he had been waiting with his hand on the knob, Mollison opened the door. He had a drink in his hand. "Come in, Lou, and quit worrying. The money is here."

He led the way into the apartment. A table radio blared from one corner of the room. Mollison gestured toward it. "I just listened to the five-thirty news. Not a thing about it. Not a damn thing. What would you like to drink?"

Morgan sat down. "Whisky and water," he said.

Mollison left the room and returned after a moment. He had a highball glass in one hand and a large-sized manila envelope in the other. The envelope bulged, so that the flap gaped like a mouth. Mollison bounced it in his hand, nearly dropping it. "Thirty-seven thousand five hundred. Do you want to count it?"

Morgan shook his head, thinking, did the damned fool have to act so coy.

"What about Patsy?" he asked.

Mollison tossed the envelope to Morgan. It was surprisingly heavy, and he clutched it between his knees to keep it from falling to the floor. "What would Patsy do with money?" he asked. "If he showed up at the club with more than ten dollars they'd want to know where he got it. I'll give him a few bucks and he'll be just as happy."

"I suppose you're right," Morgan agreed. "What about the club — won't they be wondering where he is?"

"Who's to wonder? I'll say I gave him a chance to earn a few bucks washing cars over at the lot. I'm going over in a little while and bring him a couple of sandwiches to hold him until dark. How about coming along with me?"

"All right," Morgan said. He hesitated. "We'll have to bring something for the boy to eat too. I don't want to get out of the car, though. There's no need of him seeing me." He had a curious compulsion to see the boy even though it was dangerous to take the chance of being seen by him.

Mollison's voice had a cynical edge. "Sure," he said. "Play it safe, Lou. When you stop and think about it you've been pretty safe all along."

Morgan said angrily, "That's the way we planned it, Mollison. You did your share and I did mine. And if it comes to it, we're equally guilty."

Mollison stood up. "All right — all right. Let's get on over there. Do you want to leave that here?"

"I'll take it with me. After we leave there you can drop me off near my place. I want to pick up my own car."

They drove toward the old Maynard Mill almost in silence. A tension had sprung up between them; Morgan could feel it growing like some monstrous black cloud, but he could think of nothing to say that would dispel it. They stopped at a diner, and Mollison waited while Morgan got out and bought hamburgers and coffee and milk.

There were only two cars in the parking area behind the mill. Neither of them was within a hundred yards of the boiler room. Mollison pulled in beside the low building and got out.

"You can't see through the windows," he said. "He's probably lying on the cot. Stand beside the door and you may be able to see him." He fumbled with a key in the lock.

Morgan got out of the car. "You've got Patsy locked in?" he asked, incredulous.

Mollison half turned, one hand still on the doorknob. "I told him it was for his own protection," he said. "Did you want him wandering around the mill? — Don't be stupid, Lou — and let me handle Patsy my own way." He swung the door open. Morgan dodged to one side, but Patsy came halfway out the door and saw him.

"Hello, Howie," he said. Less eagerly he added, "Hello, Lou. Did you get the money?"

Not knowing the fairy tale that Mollison had told to explain holding the child, Morgan asked in shocked fear, "What money? What are you talking about?"

Patsy said disgustedly, "The money them Dago bastards owe Howie."

Mollison held out the paper sack of sandwiches. "Here's some sandwiches for you and the kid, Patsy. We got the money."

Patsy nodded his head in righteous approval. "Good thing they paid you, them bastards," he said. "Damn good thing."

Mollison moved toward the door. "Did you have any trouble with the kid?" he asked.

Patsy backed into the room to make way for Mollison. "I didn't have no trouble," he said proudly. He glanced toward Morgan to see if he was coming in. When Morgan did not move toward the door he continued, "You want me to stay here some more, Howie?"

"For a little while. I'll be back bye and bye. You eat your sandwiches and give some to the kid if he wants any."

Morgan moved toward the side of the door. Looking in at a long angle he could just make out a huddled form on the cot. The face was hidden as if the boy were sleeping, face down. Until he actually saw the boy he had considered him a chattel; something impersonal that he and Mollison had taken in order to extract money, and not as a someone that would feel pain and hurt and misery. He hurried back to the car, unable to cope with the helpless sympathy he felt for the boy. There was a bright side. Pretty soon it would be dark. They could drop him somewhere he knew and he could find his way home.

Mollison came out to the car after a few minutes. He got in, glancing at his watch as he slid behind the wheel. "Almost seven," he said. "It will be dark by eight." He nosed the car out of the parking area and into the heavy stream of traffic on the boulevard before he spoke again. "Look, Lou. There isn't any need for you to come back when I turn the kid loose. If you were with me he'd have to see you when he got in the car and there isn't any real need for you to take the risk. I'll come back and pick him up and dump him off downtown some place. Right after dark."

Morgan's immediate sensation was relief. He had no desire to see again the living evidence of what he and Mollison had done. And Mollison was right; there was no need for him to take the chance that the boy might some day see him again. He agreed quickly before Mollison might change his mind, but he could not convince himself that he fully believed Mollison, nor that he could wash his hands of the boy now and make them clean. Mollison became expansive. "The kid might go into the bank with his grandfather some day. If he saw you tonight he might recognize you. There's no chance that he'll see me. Anacosta doesn't buy used cars, and if he did he wouldn't be apt to bring the kid with him."

Mollison had let Morgan out at the garage that he rented near his rooming house. It was a one-stall compartment in a line of similar compartments, and only a chicken-wire partition separated it from the neighboring stalls. Though Morgan had missed tools and petty items from his dashboard compartment on other occasions — he suspected that the owner of the garages had his own key and padded his rentals by pilfering — he had little choice of hiding places. He didn't dare take the money to his room and leave it, knowing, as he did, that his landlady made periodic shakedowns of her roomers' belongings.

The floor of the garage was hard-packed cinders. He opened the trunk of his cheap sedan and took out a screw driver and the round iron extension handle of a jack. When he was certain that there was no one else in the building, he began to hack a hole in the floor. If he pulled the car as far ahead as possible, the hole would be underneath it. There was a plastic-covered pillow in the front seat. He ripped the plastic along one seam and pulled out the foam rubber insert. He took fifty dollars from the envelope that Mollison had given him. The remainder he wrapped in the plastic and buried in the hole which he then covered up as neatly as he could. It was not a good hiding place but it would do. In the next day or so he would find a better one.

His hands were grimy from the work and he fretted about them as he put the tools away. He did this, he knew, to distract himself, to keep from thinking about the boy, thinking about Mollison. But he could not maintain the deception because he *was* thinking about Mollison. Mollison saying, "I'll turn the kid loose. There isn't any need for you to come with me, Lou." Or, "I've got some sandwiches for Patsy." Not for the boy.

Morgan, dropping pretense, faced reality. The boy had been with

Patsy and Mollison — Mollison, for God's sake, had even used names. Lou. Patsy. And Patsy had called him Howie. Would Mollison let the boy go to tell the police that three men named Lou and Howie and Patsy had kidnapped him and kept him in a room with a big furnace in it? Mollison had said it himself — "You could walk in the bus station and nobody would know you were there, Lou. I stand out. People remember me." And they did remember him. Even an eight-year-old boy would remember him and be able to describe him with some accuracy. He remembered Mollison assuring him that they would so frighten Anacosta that he would somehow keep the boy quiet when he had him back. And Morgan had believed him because he wanted to believe him.

But now, standing in the garage, Morgan let the blind scales drop from his eyes and faced the truth as he had not dared to face it before. Mollison did not intend to let the boy live. He had never, from that first conversation in the club, intended to let him go after the money was paid. Morgan could not let it happen. Embezzler he was, and hypocrite. Phony, and kidnaper. Not a murderer. Morgan tried frantically to remember the scene an hour ago; to remember if the little form on the filthy cot had moved during the time he watched — or had he been looking at a corpse. Morgan faced reality and could not bear it. He made one inarticulate sound, half cry, half groan, and got into the car, remembering just in time that he had closed the garage doors before he started digging his cache. He got out and opened them and jumped into the driver's seat again, scraping his shin raw against the bottom of the door and not even feeling it. On the way back to the mill he tried to convince himself that the boy *had* moved and that he would be in time to stop Mollison from what he knew Mollison planned.

After he let Morgan off, Mollison stopped at a bar and had three, drinks, one after the other in rapid succession. He needed them. What he was going to do now was not going to be easy. It had to be done, though. It just had to be done in spite of the bull he had fed Morgan about letting the kid go as soon as it was dark and safe. He was waiting for the secrecy of the night all right, but it wasn't so he could take the kid downtown. What a soft, pansy type that Morgan was. If he had told him in the beginning that they would have to get rid of the kid he would have backed out. What a damn fool, too, to think that they could let him go. He ordered still another drink. He could feel no slightest effect from the ones he had had. Morgan was a pansy, all right. It was unfair that he should get half the money for what he had done. What *had* he done? Found out how much money Anacosta had. And he had picked it up at the bus terminal, but what risk had there been in that? Practically none, and the way they had pulled it off proved it.

He debated having another drink and decided against it. But he stopped at a liquor store a block from the bar and bought a fifth of whisky. Later he would need it. He was sure of that. Getting back into his car he drove slowly toward the mill.

Patsy was still on guard when Mollison unlocked the door to the boiler room. He was sitting on a broken crate, with the residue of the sandwiches he had eaten strewn around him. The little carton of milk that Morgan had bought for the kid stood on the floor, unopened. Patsy wiped his mouth and said, "He didn't want to eat, Howie, so I ate his sandwich. That was all right, wasn't it?"

Mollison glanced at the cot. The boy had turned on his back now. He lay perfectly still, staring at Mollison. Mollison looked away and said absently, "That's all right, Patsy." He walked across the room, past the great iron maw of the boiler, looking at the gauges and valves. An old destroyer boiler, bought cheap after the First World War. Somewhere along the twisted road of his life he had picked up a little knowledge of steam equipment. Not that he needed much here. The water level cut off; the relief valve — none of those things cut in until you had a few pounds' pressure. There was a chain hanging from the stack itself behind the boiler. That's all you needed. Open it a crack and the damper leading to the firebox would lift and you had a draft. Open it more than a crack and the draft would suck the hat off your head from across the room. There was the broken crate that Patsy was sitting on, and there were some short lengths of two-by-four shoring in back of the building. With those you could start a coal fire — and there was plenty of coal because old man Decker had locked it in here to keep the poor bastards that lived near the mill from stealing it. Mollison could feel the whisky now. It felt as if it had lodged in his throat and was burning a hole there.

"Patsy," he said, "you remember what I told you? About those Dagos that owed me money?"

Patsy shook his head vehemently to show just how well he remembered. "Sure, Howie. Them Dago bastards owed you some money for a long time and they wouldn't pay you."

"That's right, Patsy. They didn't exactly pay me back yet but they're coming here tonight to get the kid and to give me the money they owe me. Remember what I told you? One of them left his wife and took the kid with him?"

Patsy nodded violently. "Sure. And if they don't pay you back you'll turn the kid over to his mother and they'll never get him back. I know that, Howie. Cripes sakes, you told me that." His expression was injured. "You told me lots of times."

Mollison said apologetically, "Well, look, Patsy — they don't want anyone to know about it. They don't want anyone here except me when they come to bring the money. You know how it is, don't you?"

Patsy had looked forward all day to riding back to the club in the car with Mollison; driving up to the curb and getting out, the two of them, laughing and talking the way the members did. He asked wistfully, "You mean you want me to go?" He brightened. "I could wait for you somewheres and we could go back to the club in your car."

Mollison pretended to think for a moment. Then he said, "I've got a better idea, Patsy. You go on out and get a cup of coffee or a beer or something. Take your time about it and come back in an hour. Don't come back before that because they might still be here." He took out a bill and handed it to Patsy.

Patsy brightened up. "Sure," he said. "And then we can drive to the club in your car, right, Howie?"

Mollison repeated, "Sure."

Standing in the doorway, Mollison watched Patsy shamble off into the thickening darkness. He debated getting the fifth of whisky from the car and decided that he would. There were a few minutes yet until full dark and he could use another drink. He opened the door on the driver's side and reached in, not turning his head away from the door to the boiler room in case the kid should make a bolt. In a way it would be easier if he did because now — since he didn't try to get away — he had to go in there and stand over him and do what he had to do. And what had to be done after that was going to be worse. Back in the boiler room, he tilted the bottle to his lips and drank three or four times. It burned and it gagged him and it still did not make it any easier to think about the next hour's work. The boiler room was completely dark now; he could literally not see his hand in front of his face. There was a naked electric light bulb hanging in front of the water gauge on the boiler. The current was probably turned off in this end of the building but it was worth a try. He lit a match. The flare seemed garish in contrast to the darkness of the room. He strained to reach the pull chain on the light socket and pulled it. Too much light. He hastily turned it off again while he groped for one of the blankets on the cot. At his touch the boy made a frightened, animal sound and squeezed himself against the wall. Ignoring him, Mollison stretched the blanket across the windows. They were already opaque with dirt and whitewash, but it didn't hurt to be sure that light didn't get through a crack somewhere. When he was finished he turned on the light again and inspected the job he had done in the dark. It would do. He sat down on the crate that Patsy had occupied earlier and looked at the boy. He was still squeezed up against the wall. All right then. Get it over. He stood up and took a step toward the cot, and decided that he would have another drink first.... This was what he had been afraid of all along; that he wouldn't have the nerve to go through with it when the time came. Find the nerve, then. Find it in the bottle of whisky. Find it in the thought of what would happen if he didn't kill the kid and they were found out. Find it in the picture of what the cops would do if they caught them. There were those pictures in the paper whenever the police caught a kidnaper. They always looked as if they'd been run over by a truck. Cops did that. Down in the basement rooms of their police stations. Cops — and everyone else — hated kidnapers so there couldn't be any question of turning the kid loose. What was he, anyway? Just a Dago kid. But knowing all along that he might lose his nerve, he had included Patsy in his plan. Crazy Patsy who would do anything Mr. Mollison told him. He knew he couldn't make himself do the boiler part of it. What was it he would tell him? "Look, Patsy — something happened to the kid. He must have smothered in his blankets. Patsy, we've got to get rid of his body. Patsy — " And then he would tell him something to explain. That the Dagos had come and paid him the money? No. Better to say that they just hadn't showed up. Patsy would forget after a while probably. He forgot most things. And Lou Morgan; he was going to be sore about it but what could he do? Morgan had half the money, and none of the dirty work. Mollison took another drink from the bottle. Now, no more stalling.

There was the sound of a motor, of tires grating against tar. There was the sound of a door slamming and pounding of feet and the hammer of fists at the door. Mollison actually felt the blood drain from his face. The police? Or was it Anacosta and his mob, which was much worse. Who had told? Morgan. It had to be Morgan, damn him and his yellow streak. He looked around. There was no way out. There was a door but it led into the mill, not to the outside. While he tried to think, to pull himself together, he heard his name called. "Mollison," the voice said. "Let me in. It's me, Lou."

For a moment relief weakened Mollison's knees so that he stumbled as he went to the door. He opened it and Morgan pushed in. Mollison, still reacting from panic, said, "You son of a bitch. What are you doing here?"

Chapter 10

All the way across town, from the garage where he had hidden his share of the ransom to the old Maynard Mill, Morgan tried to think of what he would do, what he would say, when he confronted Mollison. He drove more recklessly than he had driven in all his life, driving the car as he tried to drive his brain, desperate to be there in time. He felt as if he had been drugged, half conscious during the time they had planned the crime, and was only now waking up. It had been there to see all the time. Mollison had intended to kill the boy right along — and was that why he had dragged Patsy into it? Patsy. He would be there too — not that it mattered. If it became a matter of violence he was no match for Mollison alone, let alone Patsy, and he knew it. When he slammed the car to a stop in front of the mill and battered his hands against the door, Morgan had no idea how he could stop Mollison — if Mollison hadn't already killed the Anacosta child.

When Mollison opened the door and demanded to know what Morgan was doing there, Morgan felt a violence of his own rising to match Mollison's, but he controlled it. "Close the door," he said sharply. The thing to do now was to take the initiative. "Where's Patsy?"

Mollison said, "He's gone out. He'll be back. Lou, for God's sake, you know how risky it is for us to be coming and going here."

Morgan had hurried over to the cot where the boy lay face down. He pulled the dirty blanket back. He could not see the boy's face but he could feel the small body shudder at his touch. He was alive. There was that much to be thankful for. He was thinking more clearly now than he could ever remember thinking. He took in the bottle of whisky that Mollison had put down, judged Mollison's own condition from the amount that was gone from the bottle. If he could get Mollison a little drunker it might help. He said, "I wanted to see if you'd let him go yet. I've been thinking about it, Howie. Maybe it wouldn't be safe to let him go just yet." Time to be careful now. Be sly about it. He walked over and picked up the bottle. "I could use a drink," he said. He pretended to drink deeply but actually he merely tasted the whisky before he passed the bottle to Mollison. "Have one?" he asked.

Mollison took a large drink. His eyes were just the slightest touch bloodshot; his speech just the slightest bit slurred. "I thought you were pretty damn anxious to let him go as soon as it got dark," he said. "What made you change your mind?"

Morgan tried to use the logic that would appeal to Mollison. "I've got the money," he said. "I've got it and I like it and I don't want to take any chance on anything happening that will keep me from spending it. Even if — " He hesitated, giving Mollison an opening.

Mollison said, "Even if what?" He thought for a moment and said, "You came right in. You came right in where he could get a good look at you."

Morgan nodded. "You see what I mean?"

Mollison asked stupidly, "What?"

"I mean, it doesn't make any difference whether he sees me or not, Howie. I don't think we can afford to let him go. Not now. Maybe not ever."

Mollison stared at him intently for a long moment. Then he began to laugh softly. "I'll be a son of a bitch," he said. "The money really opened your eyes, didn't it?"

Morgan pretended a nervous impatience that he did not actually feel. His nerves were cold, frozen, as he drove his thinking. Convince Mollison that he had changed his mind and wanted now to kill the boy. Convince Mollison and buy time with that conviction. Time? Time to think. Morgan's conscience drove him far enough to make him try to prevent the murder of the boy, but beyond that he had as yet no plan. But get the time.

"Let me have another drink," he said. He drank again from the bottle and passed it back to Mollison, hoping that he would also drink out of habit, or reflex. Mollison did, deeply again. Morgan said defensively, "You must have thought about it too or you would have let him go by now."

"I'm way ahead of you," Mollison said. His expression was sly. "You don't think I ever really meant to let him go, do you? Use your head, Lou. Half an hour after we let him go the cops would have our names and addresses. Let's face it. If I hadn't told you we'd let him go you'd have been too chicken to go through with it, wouldn't you? You're yellow, Lou. At least you were until you got your hands on that money."

Mollison was beginning to feel the whisky more strongly now. He was becoming patronizing, arrogant. The drunken superiority of a big man over a littler man. Morgan said, "That doesn't matter now. What do you plan to do with him? And take it easy on that whisky." The nagging remark about the whisky was a calculated goad. Mollison responded by taking another drink.

"I can handle it," he said in surly defiance. His eyes narrowed. "You want to know what I plan to do with him? Why me? You're the brain. What would you do?"

Morgan, afraid that he had pushed the bigger man too far, tried to appease him. "All right, Howie," he said. "Don't get sore. I just thought that you must have something worked out, that's all."

Mollison said secretively, "Sure I have." Abruptly his mood changed. "You're all right, Lou," he announced. "Just don't tell me what to do." He continued with a touch of smugness, "You know what this building is, don't you?"

Morgan nodded. "A boiler room, you said."

"Sure. A boiler room." Mollison jerked his head toward the maw of the boiler. "That's the boiler. Know what would happen if we had a fire in there — what we could put in there? There wouldn't be nothing left." His voice was thickening. He added in maudlin confidence, "I don't think I could do it, Lou. I could do the other part, but sticking him in there afterward . . ." He shook his head. "That's one reason I got Patsy. He'll do it if I tell him. I can scare him into it. Tell him the cops will get us if he don't. Or the Dagos." He outlined for Morgan the story he had made up for Patsy to explain holding the boy.

Morgan was sickened as Mollison told him his plan for the disposal of the body. He took a small drink from the bottle — it was nearly empty now — and passed it to Mollison. "That was pretty clever thinking," he praised Mollison, overcoming his revulsion.

Mollison said expansively, "I had another idea about Patsy," he said. "Everybody knows he's a screwball. If they ever started getting close, Anacosta or the cops, I mean, we could frame the whole thing on Patsy some way. I got a couple of ideas, but they need a lot of work."

Morgan drove his mind back to something from his boyhood; when it was fall, when the first cold nights frosted the lawn with silvery hour, when there was a little coal in the basement of the house on Argonne Street. He said anxiously, "It's a great idea, Howie, but it's too risky. About the boiler, I mean."

Mollison demanded arrogantly, "What's wrong with it?"

"It's like a furnace in a house," Morgan said. "A coal furnace, I mean. The dust and stuff that settles on the bricks on the inside of the chimney goes up like a bomb the first time you start a fire in the winter. Sparks fly all over the place. A chimney that's stood for years without a fire in it like this one will look like a blowtorch when it's lit. Somebody will be sure to see it and report ft." He applied the spur again. "You'll have to do it some other way." Morgan felt as if a part of him were separated from his body and was watching the way he was handling Mollison — watching with a surprised admiration. A touch of the spur, a slackening of the rein, thinking in the same groove as a half-drunken brute. But it was dangerous. Dangerous. And Patsy might come along at any moment.

Mollison was turning sullen again — as Morgan had anticipated. "Oh sure," he grumbled. "I'll have to do it some other way. You make it easy for yourself, don't you, Lou. You've got your share of the money and now you want me to take care of everything."

It came to Morgan that he had not thought of the money, the money that had once seemed so important, since he buried it under the garage floor. The money, the kidnapping, all that had happened in the last few weeks seemed unreal, as unreal as it was to be sitting in an abandoned boiler room talking about the murder of a child. Unreal. Unbelievable. Good God, how could he have done it? How could he have conspired with this drunken animal just for money?

Morgan glanced in the direction of the cot and wondered if the boy was awake, listening to them talk about what they were going to do to him. He must be nearly out of his mind with terror by this time. He waited impatiently, almost frantically, for Mollison's slow brain to follow the channel he had dug for it with his every remark, his every attitude since coming into the boiler room.

Mollison reached for the bottle again, his motions fumbling and misdirected as the whisky took a firmer hold. Morgan, watching him intently, could tell the precise instant when the pattern of Mollison's thinking fell into its predicted design. It was as if a switch had been thrown. The bloodshot eyes narrowed in drunken cunning. The reaching hand became still. The heavy head aimed at him like a gun.

"Well — you," Mollison said. "You do it."

Morgan felt his nerves relax. He had made Mollison suggest it. The danger now would be in pushing it. Mollison had the wary suspicion of a drunk. Protest a little. "Not me, Howie," Morgan said. "You said yourself that you'd do it. You're the one that planned it." Close now. Close to the time when he would let Mollison make him take the boy out of this place.

Mollison felt relief of his own through the blur of alcohol. He had never wanted to kill the boy, to make himself do it. It was just something that had to be done. Hell with it Let Morgan do it. He had done his share. "You said my plan wasn't any good," he jeered. "That lets me off the hook. Now you think of something. I'm out of it."

Morgan said slowly, almost as if he were thinking out loud, "It would have to be somewhere else since we can't use the boiler."

Mollison at once became suspicious. "Why not right here? There has to be another way to get rid of him afterward." He jerked his head toward the door that led to the main part of the mill. "We could hide him in there if we wanted to."

Morgan shook his head. "That wouldn't be very smart, Howie. Someday he would be found. Then the police would want to know why this place was used and they'd start asking who had keys. They'd go to Decker right away. Do you think that Decker would forget that you worked there once?"

Mollison shook his head. He reached for the bottle and put it down again when he found that he had emptied it. "I need a drink," he said. His voice was almost petulant. "All right. If it isn't here, where will it be? It's your baby now."

Morgan considered protesting further and decided against it as being risky and pointless. "I know a place," he said. "It's about ten miles from here; an old farm with a caved-in well in the back yard. I could dig it out a little and put him there. They'd never find him, and if they did they couldn't connect him up with either of us."

Mollison grinned. "I want to see you do it, Lou. What are you going to do — strangle him?" He pointed toward a corner of the room. "There's a piece of two by four there you could use for a club."

For a moment Morgan was frightened, thinking that Mollison was baiting him; that he had known that he didn't intend to kill the boy. Then he realized that Mollison's desire to see him kill the boy was an expression of the man's cruelty. He must know, must sense that it would be torment for Morgan to do it. "You said it was my problem," Morgan said. "I'm not going to do it here." He sought for a quick lie.

"Killing him is bad enough. I'm not going to drive around with a body in the car. I'll do it when I get there."

Mollison seemed to sober momentarily. "Lou," he said, "you can't make any mistakes. You can't turn yellow again."

Morgan, who had moved toward the cot, laughed shortly. "What did you think I was going to do?" he asked. "Turn him loose?"

"I guess not. You know what I mean, Lou — and don't get sore. You just made your mind up after you got your share of the money. To get rid of him, I mean. You know it's got to be done, that's all."

"I know it. You don't have to tell me. Do you want to come along while I do it?" Morgan took a calculated risk in the sarcastic question, hoping that he had judged Mollison's condition accurately.

Mollison seemed to have dropped again into a semi-drunken daze. "It's all right," he said, waving his hand limply. "Go ahead and take him. It's your neck as much as mine if you don't go through with it."

Morgan picked the boy up in his arms. The small body tensed. He was awake, then. He made no sound. "What are you going to do?" Morgan asked.

"I'll wait here for Patsy," Mollison answered. "Are you going to come to the club after you've done it?"

"I don't know. I doubt it."

Mollison shrugged. "Suit yourself," he said.

Only after he had put the boy in the back seat of his two-door car did the reaction from the strain of the last fifteen minutes hit Morgan. When it did it doubled him over the steering wheel and he had to fight his way erect to start the car. He headed out of town. He had a little time to think now. Just a little because he had the boy in the back seat to consider. Until this moment his every resource in thought and action had been consumed in getting the boy out of the boiler room. He had no idea what he was going to do with him now. Except that he couldn't turn him loose because to turn him loose was to die and Morgan was not prepared to die.

He drove out of town cautiously. There was no sound, no movement from the boy in the back seat. When the stretches of dark road between diners and filling stations and drive-ins began to get longer and to occur more frequently, he glanced at his watch and saw that it was almost ten o'clock. He reached and turned on the radio and fiddled with the tuning knob until he located a local station broadcasting a news program; when he had it tuned in he listened impatiently while the commentator waded through a mass of detail concerning politics, labor scandals and baseball scores. Nothing at all about a kidnapping. Mollison was probably right. Anacosta had not gone to the police. Unless he had gone and they were sitting on it. They did that sometimes.

He was becoming gradually aware of the magnitude of the problem he had on his hands now that he had the boy safely away from Mollison and Patsy. Turn him loose to go home? Impossible. Not when he knew names and faces. Morgan shuddered. Supposing he turned him loose and he did go home and tell his grandfather. He might not go to the police. He might take matters into his own hands and that was something more to be feared than the police. No, he couldn't let him go. But what, for God's sake, could he do with him? He toyed with some bizarre notions and rejected them as fast as he conceived them. Put him on a freight train and then go home and get out of town. Morgan admitted to himself that he hardly knew where the freight yards were, let alone how to find an empty car and open the door. Or rent a room in some near-by city and fill the boy with narcotics; just enough to keep him unconscious while he, Morgan, went back to his place and got his share of the ransom money and fled. Fled where? And what did he know about narcotics, where did you get them, how did you use them? The very fact that the solutions he arrived at were so completely ridiculous impressed Morgan with the impossibility of the situation he was in. He was startled when the boy called to him from the back seat. He could not make out the words and he reached down and snapped off the radio and said, "What?"

The boy said, "I want to go home. I want my father and mother."

Morgan felt an unreasonable rage at the boy, the cause of his trouble of the moment. "Shut up," he said. "Shut up and lie down on the seat." He turned to see if the boy was following his order. He was. He subsided back on the seat in the mute apathy of fear gone beyond fear.

Morgan had a sudden thought. If he were kind to the boy, if he brought him back to Anacosta and admitted his part in the kidnapping but pointed out the extenuating fact that he had saved the boy's life, maybe they wouldn't kill him. He could tell them about Mollison and where to find him and depend on their mercy. Then he remembered that Anacosta was reputed to have no mercy and, believing this, he rejected the thought and was left with no idea at all. A little tag end of pity was aroused in him by the memory of the boy's white face and terrified obedience to his command, and he half turned to glance at him again. "Look," he began, "I'm not going to kill you, if that's what you're afraid of. I won't kill you if you do exactly as I tell you." More to himself than to the boy he said, "I don't know what I am going to do with you but I don't want to kill you."

The boy in the back did not answer, and Morgan turned his eyes front again and glanced at the instrument panel. The old car burned almost as much oil as gasoline, and he continually watched the oil pressure gauge out of long habit. The pressure was at twenty, high enough for the weary old motor, but he saw with a sickening sense of disaster that the fuel gauge needle was already against the stop below the empty mark. He looked ahead to see if he could find the glow in the night sky that would mean a filling station, and for a moment he was relieved when he saw not only the glow but the station itself a half mile ahead. The relief died with the realization that he would have to drive in with the means of his own destruction in the back seat. He regretted now that he had told the boy that he was not going to kill him. If the boy was not afraid that he would be killed he would cry out, would try to break away from the car, would try to get the gas station attendant to notice him. Yet he had to get gas. Morgan slowed almost to a stop and spoke to the boy again.

"Listen to me," he said, trying to make his voice sound full of deadly purpose, "I'm going to stop in a minute to get gas. I want you to lie down on the floor and not make a sound." He thought about that and changed his mind. A boy asleep on the seat he could explain. A boy lying on the floor of the car, if the attendant happened to see him, could not be easily explained and would be remembered. "No," he said. "You stay right on the seat where you are and put the blanket over you and pretend you're asleep. Do you understand me?"

The boy mumbled something — Morgan could not quite make out the words — but he took them for assent.

"If you don't," Morgan added, "I'll kill you. Or I'll take you back to the other men and let them do it." He turned in the seat and glanced again at the boy. He had not moved, apparently, since the last time Morgan had looked at him. He lay on his side, his fists doubled and tight against his chest.

He was almost abreast of the filling station. Morgan turned in and stopped beside the glistening red pumps. He waited for the attendant with a sort of fatalistic calm. If the boy screamed or attracted attention now, it was the end.

The attendant approached the car in a careless saunter, whistling softly between his teeth. He walked toward the front of the car, not passing the back. Good, for the moment, but when he pumped the gas into the tank he could hardly help looking into the rear seat. Morgan leaned out and said, "Ten gallons, please."

"Sure, mister. Regular or high test?"

"Regular."

The attendant said, "Regular. Right," and moved to the rear of the car. Morgan heard him fumble with the gas tank cover and then the humming of the pump. He turned his head and watched the boy and saw the boy staring back at him. He did not move. Morgan said between his teeth, "Close your eyes and make believe you're asleep," and the stare was gone.

An hour or a day and he heard the clatter of the hose being put back into its rack; heard the footsteps of the attendant; heard him say, "Ten right. Check your oil and water?"

Morgan handed money to the man. "No thanks," he said. He had a few cents change coming. "That's all right," he said, and started the motor. The man hadn't seen the boy. Or, if he had seen him, he had thought nothing of it. And why should he?

He began to drive aimlessly back toward the city, trying again to solve the problem of the boy, but this time armed with a new weapon. The boy was so frightened that he would do what he was told. Knowing that, perhaps he could find a way.

Chapter 11

Morgan drove aimlessly for another hour. He was afraid to stay on the road much longer; the suspicion attached to a man driving an old car with a boy in the back seat would increase in geometric progression with the lateness of the hour. He listened to another news broadcast, and again there was no mention of a missing or kidnapped child. The boy in the back seat was, by this time, asleep or pretending to be.

He needed a plan, but it could wait. More immediately he needed a place to take the boy, and it came to him with startling clarity that he knew of such a place. It had to be isolated. It had to be such a place that his coming and going could either be concealed or would attract no attention. It had to be a place where the boy, if he made noise or tried to make some sort of signal to passers-by, would not be seen. It must be fairly close because he had to leave the boy and go to the club to meet Mollison. It had to be the old Maynard Mill. It had all the qualifications — hadn't it been hand-picked by Mollison? He started toward the mill, trying to think of what he would need. A flashlight. A heavy screw driver to pry open the door of the boiler room if Mollison had been sober enough to remember to lock it when he left. Some cord or heavy twine. A blanket. He had a blanket in the back seat, and the flattened end of the lug wrench in the back of the car would do for a screw driver or pry bar. He had a flashlight in the dashboard. It needed batteries but that was no great problem since he was no longer afraid to stop at a service station. He did stop at the first station he came to and he bought another five gallons of gas to camouflage the purchase of the batteries. There was twine in the car; he remembered out of a corner of his mind having seen it a hundred times, and he was finally able to focus that memory and recollect that it was the heavy draw string used in the cheap seat covers of the car.

He was convinced by this time that he could hide the boy in the mill until he could think of a way out of the dreadful predicament he found himself in. It was big enough; Lord, there must be acres of it. There must be rooms or old offices or supply closets; some sort of place. There was the door leading into the main building from the boiler room for access. Locked or not, he could manage to get it open; must manage to get it open. Something that Mollison had said bothered him, kept returning to irritate him because he could not quite remember what it was. Then it came to him. Rats. Mollison had said that the building was infested with them. Rats? In an old textile mill? Another of Mollison's lies, made up to justify bringing Patsy Galuk into the plan. What would the rats find to eat? Well, he couldn't do everything for the boy. He would have to take the chance that Mollison had been lying.

There were no lights at all burning in the occupied section of the mill when Morgan drove, as quietly as he could, through the parking lot and up to the now familiar spot beside the boiler room. The gigantic old building loomed against the faintly reflected nimbus of the city's lights like a mighty cliff of brick and mortar, staring at him from a thousand blind eyes. He eased the car door open, not wanting to waken the boy, and got out. He thought of something and he got back in and drove close to the side of the building so that the door could not be opened on the passenger side. He got out again and closed the door on his own side. Now the boy could not get out without having to pass him. He felt for the knob of the boiler-room door. It turned with the pressure of his hand, and the door swung free. Something jangled in the lock. The keys. Mollison had been drunk enough to forget them. He masked the flashlight that he had taken from the dashboard compartment with his free hand and pressed the switch with the other. The keys were caught up on a piece of fine chain that was riveted to a block of wood. There were more than a dozen of them. Morgan stuck them in his pocket and went back to the car. He leaned in awkwardly over the folding seat and shook the boy. He awoke immediately with a small cry.

Morgan said, "Come on with me and for God's sake, don't make any noise."

The boy said sleepily, "Are we home?" doubtless remembering some late family expedition, and then he must have suddenly remembered what had happened and began to whimper. "I don't want to go in there," he said. "You're going to hurt me."

Morgan said in an urgent whisper, "I'm not going to hurt you. Listen to me. Those other men want to hurt you. They want to kill you, do you understand? I'm trying to help you but you've got to do just what I tell you. Now come on."

The boy crawled into the front seat and clambered to the ground, nearly falling. Morgan clutched at him with one hand and reached into the back seat for the blanket with the other. He half led, half pulled the boy into the boiler room. He then pulled the door closed and turned on the flashlight long enough to find the string that turned on the bulb that hung from the ceiling. The boy stood perfectly still, blinking in the harsh light. Morgan said, "I've got to go out to the car and get something. You sit on the cot there and wait for me. Listen, boy — do you understand that I'm trying to help you?"

The boy nodded, staring at him, but he did not speak.

"You've got to realize it," Morgan insisted. "You've got to help me, help me or they'll get you." He added ruefully, "And me too."

The boy spoke. "I'll mind," he said. "If you won't hurt me."

Morgan said, "Then sit on the cot and wait. I won't be long."

He went out, closing the door swiftly against the betraying light within, and went to the car again. The feeble batteries in the flashlight gave only a hint of light. He unscrewed the base and shook the old batteries out onto the ground and replaced them with the ones he had bought at the filling station. When he pressed the switch the light came on with a blinding glare. He hastily switched the light off. He thought for a moment and then bent and picked up the useless batteries and hurled them far into the darkness. There must be no indication that he had returned to this place.

He moved as swiftly as he could. If Mollison sobered enough to remember that he had left the keys he might come after them — he certainly would come after them, knowing the danger of leaving them in sight. If Anacosta went to the police, any single event out of the ordinary presented a risk and Mollison, sober, would realize it. Morgan opened the door of the car and found the bow at the end of the drawstring. He ripped at it. It came free in his hand, and he pulled the full length of the string from the seat cover like a night crawler from its hole when he had been a small boy.

He did not open the back to get the lug wrench. The door to the boiler room was open. As for the door to the main building, one of Mollison's keys would probably fit it.

When he slipped into the boiler room again, the boy was sitting on the edge of the cot just as he had left him.

Morgan went directly to the small door that led into the main part of the mill. It was not locked but it was stuck to its frame with the warpage of long disuse. He had to tug at it with the most of his strength before it grated open, and when it did it released a heavy smell of old machine oil and cotton lint, of dry-wooden flooring and ancient dust. He flashed the light ahead of him, and it was swallowed by the cavernous depths of the vast room. Hastily he turned the light toward the floor so that no passer-by might catch its gleam through the windows. He backed into the boiler room and said to the boy, "Come on. We've got to find a place for you to hide." It did not strike him as ironic that he was allying himself with the very person against whom he had committed the most criminal of acts.

The boy got up. He seemed to be sleep walking. Morgan stood aside to let the boy precede him into the mill. He hung back at the impact of the vast emptiness, and Morgan urged him on. Morgan was becoming increasingly afraid that Mollison might return for the keys, and his impatience with the boy increased with this fear. And yet he felt a great sense of pity for the youngster; when they had passed into the blackness of the main room he took the boy's hand and felt it clutch his own. Together they moved forward, following the yellow glow of the flashlight. The floor was pitted with jagged holes, the wounds left by the removal of the looms that had once stood here, rank on rank upon rank, and the boy stumbled several times. Once

Morgan could not hold him up and he fell on his hands and knees, but he did not cry out, although he limped heavily thereafter.

Morgan was searching for an office, a storeroom or any other separate space where he could leave the boy, but there seemed to be none. After a time they came to a stairway opening off the great room and, thinking that perhaps the offices had been in the upper part of the building, Morgan started to climb the stairs, helping the boy as much as he could. At the head of the stairs he found a door. It was locked and he took out Mollison's keys and stabbed at the lock with one key after another until he found one that fitted. He opened the door and flashed the light inside and saw that there were two rooms, with a door, standing open now, between them. The first room had apparently been a reception room. It had no windows. Morgan said, "Wait here," to the boy and stepped into the front room. He glanced around it hastily but his haste was not the result of any fear that the boy would try to escape. It would be almost impossible even for a grown man to find his way down the stairs and through the big loom room in the evil-smelling darkness. He shut the door leading to the front office and locked it with the key that still transfixed the lock plate. The key he fit into his pocket before he turned to look around the reception room. There was a second door in the room. Morgan opened it and saw what had been a washroom. There was a toilet bowl without a cover, the tank drunkenly awry on its base. There was a wash bowl, and he opened one of its taps, not really believing that there would be water in the rusty pipes. There was none. The pipes must long since have frozen and thawed, frozen and thawed so that they were hopelessly split.

Morgan remembered the rats and directed the light around the baseboard. There was no opening large enough even for a mouse, except in one corner where a floor board had been ripped up. There was a crooked legged table in the center of the room. He turned it over so that it covered the hole in the floor. The boy followed him with his eyes. Morgan had done all he could now, he felt. He put the light on the floor and called to the boy, "Come over here."

The boy came over, still staring at Morgan, and Morgan wondered if perhaps the boy had not been driven insane by fear. He said, "Look — I've got to leave you alone here."

The boy began to cry immediately. "I don't want to stay here," he said. "I want to go home. . . . My knee hurts me and I want to go home."

Morgan glanced at the boy's leg. The trousers were ripped at the knee from the fall, and the edges of the cloth were dark with blood. He said, "Let me look at it," and pushed the trouser leg up while he shone the light on the wound. It was a bad scrape, nothing more. Morgan said, "It will be all right," and cursed himself for having shown his compassion for the boy. It would have been better to keep him terrorized. Mollison would have known that. Too late now for that. The boy had already detected the softness in him.

"You'll be all right here," he said. "There isn't anything here that can hurt you. I'll go back down and get you the blanket from the car and later I'll come back and bring you something to eat. Those other men are kidnapers. You know what kidnapers are?"

The boy had stopped crying. "Sure I know," he said. "And you're one of them. I heard you talking with them."

Morgan said, "All right. Then you know what I was supposed to do, don't you? I was supposed to kill you. If they know you're here, they'll do it themselves. Listen — it's just for a day or two until I can work out a way to get you home. I'm trying to help you. Do you believe me?"

The boy said doubtfully, "I guess so. You don't sound like the other men. But do I have to stay here? I'm scared."

Morgan said, "There isn't any other way. You remember now — if you make any noise or try to get out of here, the only ones that will hear you will be the men that want to kill you, You lie down on the floor now and go to sleep."

The boy obediently lay down and stared up at Morgan with wide eyes. "Will you leave the light with me?" he asked.

Morgan said, "I can't," and started for the door. At once the boy was on his feet, running to Morgan, clutching him around the legs. "I'm too scared," he cried. "I'm too scared."

With a viciousness born of his own panic, Morgan pushed the boy away. "Damn it," he said, "you stay there like I fold you." He closed the door behind him and locked it, trying not to listen to the muffled sounds of wild sobbing in the locked room. He started down the stairs. When he was halfway down he stopped to listen. The sounds that the boy was making did not reach even this far. He hurried back through the empty reaches of the big room and out into the boiler room, where he picked up the blanket he had taken from the car and forgotten to take with him into the mill. He glanced at the cot where there was still another blanket and wished that he could take it, but decided not to. Mollison, if and when he returned for his keys, might miss it and wonder why it had been taken. He could take no smallest chance with Mollison now.

He hurried back through the mill and up the stairs again. He could not hear the boy crying. When he opened the door and shone the light inside he was sitting in the farthest corner of the room, his legs drawn up, hugging his knees. Morgan said, "Here's the blanket," and started to close the door again. Something held him. After a moment he said, "Oh, for God's sake, here," and rolled the flashlight toward the boy. He locked the door again and started to feel his way dangerously down the stairs and back to the boiler room.

The light from the boiler room made a feeble glow that penetrated weakly into the big room, so that when he had covered half of its length he could see enough to move with some speed. He glanced around the boiler room to see if he had left any trace that would give his return away; he saw nothing and started for the door leading to the clear night. Halfway to the door he paused to look at the bunch of keys that Mollison had left. There were, as he had hoped, duplicates to the boiler-room door and the door leading into the main part of the mill. There was even a duplicate key to the door of the room in which he had locked the boy. He twisted this key and one of the boiler-room keys from the chain that held them and put them into his pocket. His last action before turning out the bulb was to glance at his watch. It was nearly midnight. Mollison had asked him if he planned to meet him later at the club and he had been vague in his answer, but Morgan was certain that Mollison, when the liquor died out in him, would feel a driving need to see him, and to hear that he had killed the boy. He would go to the club.

Chapter 12

After Lou Morgan left the boiler room, taking the Anacosta boy with him, Mollison waited impatiently for Patsy Galuk to return. Morgan had given him a bad scare when he had driven up and slammed on his brakes outside the boiler room, but it had worked out all right. Morgan was going to take care of the kid and now he wouldn't have to make up another story for Patsy. He would merely tell him that the Dagos had come and taken the boy and that would be an end to it. Then they would go out to the club. Soon. Mollison ached for Patsy to come back. He wanted another drink; he knew that when the liquor wore off he would have to think, and right now he didn't want to think unless it was about the money that he had hidden in his dingy little apartment. Too much thinking; that had been his trouble these last weeks. About Lillian and about the pyramiding danger from the car notes he had falsified. Now he could fix all that; get square again. He reached for the bottle again and swore when he remembered that it was empty. He was oppressed by the boiler room. He turned out the light and went out to wait in the car.

Patsy came ten minutes after Morgan left with the boy. He came up to the car stealthily when Mollison called to him — now why did the crazy bastard do that — and whispered, "Did they come yet, Howie?"

They? The Dagos. "Yes, Patsy," Mollison said. "They took the kid."

"Did they pay up?" Patsy asked.

"Sure they did." Mollison felt a lift in his mood. What was to worry? In fifteen minutes he would be sitting in the club with a big drink in front of him. "Come on," he said. "Let's get out of here."

He reached for the ignition switch and started the motor, forgetting the keys dangling in the lock of the boiler-room door.

Patsy sat up straight beside him as Mollison drove expertly through the after-movie traffic out to the club, proud to be in the same car with him, practically an equal with Mollison. Patsy hoped that some of the club members would be lounging near the door; that they would see him get out of the car and see Mollison come around from the driver's side; that they would watch him enviously as he walked into the club side by side with Mollison. Only, he wished that the big man would talk with him, joke with him the way he did in the club.

Patsy made his voice grim, ominous. "A good thing those bastards paid you back," he said. Anxious to please Mollison, he added, "You'd have fixed them good if they didn't, Howie. And I watched the kid good too, didn't I?"

Mollison was startled and then angry. "Patsy, I told you it was a secret about the kid. Something you weren't supposed to talk about or you'll get me in trouble. You want to get me in trouble?"

Patsy said penitently, "Hell no, Howie. You know I wouldn't do that. Only I thought, just you and me — "

Mollison turned to face him for a moment as he paused at a traffic light. "Not even between you and me." The terrible danger of any loose talk from Patsy penetrated his drunken haze. "What are you going to tell them about this afternoon and tonight? What did I tell you to tell them if they asked?"

Patsy answered dutifully, "I'll tell them I washed cars for you at the garage," he said. "And I went to a movie tonight and you picked me up on the way back to the club. Isn't that right, Howie?" he asked anxiously.

Mollison, relieved, said, "That's right, Patsy. Don't forget it." He had earlier rehearsed Patsy in his lines. They were good lines. Patsy often did earn a few dollars washing cars at the lot and he was a fanatic about movies. After a few days Patsy's feeble brain would forget the truth and come to believe the story he had parroted. Mollison reached in his pocket and took out a few bills. He handed them to Patsy.

There were only a few members at the bar when Mollison and Patsy walked into the club. Mollison had temporarily sobered when it had become necessary to warn Patsy to keep his mouth closed, but he had had to fight to keep his thinking straight. He was ready to surrender to the blurred drunkenness that his brain cried out for. He said, "See you, Patsy," and answered the too-loud, insincere welcomes of the other men. He bought a round and a round was bought for him in return. He joked and listened to jokes but he never once completely rid himself of the nagging thought of Lou Morgan and the boy. Had Morgan done what he was supposed to do — or had he been caught doing it? It had been foolish to turn the kid over to Morgan, hadn't it? Was Morgan so yellow that he couldn't make himself do it? After several more drinks, the non-reality did come to him so that he forgot Morgan for the moment, but he paid a price. He began to feel sick. There was a small table near the bar with several chairs placed around it, and he walked unsteadily over and sat down. Immediately he had a new problem to face. Patsy Galuk came from the back room, washed and hair combed, and sat down across the table from him. Patsy had two highballs in his hands. He put them on the table and said, "Here you are, Howie. Have one on me."

This was something new and dangerous. Patsy had a peculiar sort of liberty to talk and act pretty freely at the club. He was tolerated as a sort of mascot by the members but never as an equal. He might sit at a table with a member, but it was always with a defensive attitude of "I'm as good as you are. I can sit here if I want to." When he sat down with Mollison there was no such pushy belligerence. He sat down as an equal, as a friend, as the sharer of a secret. His bringing the drinks was a symbol of his self-awarded status. Patsy was never allowed to buy drinks. He never, as far as Mollison knew, had ever drunk anything heavier than beer, usually donated by the members.

Mollison was immediately aware that the men at the bar were staring curiously at him and at Patsy, and he flogged his weary brain for a solution. Carry it off as a gag. They expected gags of Mollison, didn't they? And they knew, the way Patsy sucked around him. He reached out for the drink that Patsy had brought him and lifted it in a mock salute. Ironically he had to imitate a drunken slur in his voice. "Thanks, partner," he said. He winked at the men at the bar in such a manner that Patsy could not see. "Patsy and me are partners," he explained. "We're going to open up a — " He explained in obscene detail what he and Patsy were going to open up, and the men at the bar laughed dutifully. Just Howie Mollison piffling some gag on crazy Patsy. Looked kind of funny there for a minute. But that's all it was. Just a gag.

When the men at the bar had laughed and turned away, Mollison finished the drink almost in a single swallow. He smiled at Patsy and put a bill on the table. "Get us another one, Patsy," he said, trying to re-establish the dog-master relationship. Had to be careful, though. Damn careful. He knew that with only the slightest provocation Patsy could turn against him with an idiot's frenzy.

Mollison sat across from Patsy for half an hour, keeping up the pretense while his head ached and his stomach churned. Finally the club steward called Patsy to do some chore, and Mollison was alone. He had, by this time, reached a peculiar state of drunkenness. His system was saturated; his bloodstream could absorb no more alcohol. He could become no drunker and so he became less drunk, more perceptive; and with every moment his awareness of the danger of his situation became clearer. By this time he intensely regretted letting Lou Morgan take the Anacosta kid. He was yellow — my God, he was yellow. Yellow enough to panic after he killed the kid, so that he would leave the body wherever he killed him without taking time to conceal it or to cover traces that could lead back. Tire tracks, maybe. Or something with fingerprints on it — bank workers were always fingerprinted weren't they? Or a jack handle or some other tool from his car that they could trace. Something. His own idea, the boiler, had been better. What had Morgan said? It would make a lot of sparks? What did Morgan know about boilers? If only he didn't have to think. But he did. There was the business of the forged car notes. He had to get them all paid off — there were four of them now — and in such a way as not to attract attention. But he was tired of thinking, tired of worrying. He got up from the table and walked to the bar despite the headache and the sick rolling of his stomach. Talk and laugh with the boys at the bar so that you couldn't think, couldn't worry yourself crazy. And sweat out Morgan. . . .

Morgan came into the club an hour after Mollison returned to the bar. When Mollison looked up and saw him coming in alone — no police, no mustache boys with him — he felt a relief so great that he had to hold on to the bar. He called loudly, across the babble of conversation, "What's new, Lou?" He had to stay in character as the hail-fellow of the club to justify his leaving the group he was with to join Morgan.

Morgan had come directly to the bar, taking a position a few feet away from the nearest patron. Mollison, approaching him, came up on the far side so that their comparative isolation was preserved. He called loudly, "Bring us a couple of Scotches, Gene," to the bartender, keeping up the smokescreen of joviality. "We'll be in a booth." When they were out of earshot of the bar, he demanded, "Did you do it? Is everything taken care of?"

Morgan hesitated before answering. He had to imagine the attitude of a man who had just murdered a child. Dejected? Numb with horror? Stupid with fright? He had to be convincing. Numb, then.

"I did it," he said, and decided to let a little hysteria creep into his inflection — or did it creep in involuntarily? He wasn't quite sure. "I did it," he repeated. "I told you I'd do it, didn't I? I did it."

The bartender brought their drinks and left them alone. Mollison said, "Drink this. You need it," and pushed a glass toward Morgan. When Morgan had finished the drink he pushed the second one toward him. He now felt a morbid interest in Morgan's crime. "How did you do it?" he asked.

Morgan pretended to shudder. "I choked him. It was terrible, Howie." He reached for the second drink and finished half of it.

Mollison thumped Morgan's thin shoulders. "You did fine," he said. "I was afraid you wouldn't have the guts." He was feeling some of the old exuberance now. "You did fine, Lou."

Morgan searched for detail, wanting to convince Mollison here and now, while he was drunk and consequently less critical, against the time which must certainly come when he would have doubts. "He fell asleep in the car," he said. "I stopped at the place I told you about and went in the back seat after him. He woke up just when I reached for him." He added thinly, "It took a long time, Howie. Longer than you'd think." He finished the remainder of the drink and signaled for more.

"Was there anything on the late news about it?"

Mollison said, "I didn't hear anything. I told you Anacosta wouldn't blow the whistle. Not for a while, anyway."

"I hope you're right."

Mollison said, "Sure I'm right." He hesitated briefly and then asked, "What did you do with him then?"

The drinks came and this time Mollison kept one for himself.

Morgan sipped at his more slowly, wanting to keep his head clear. Mollison was lucky. He only had to worry about Anacosta and the police. He, Morgan, had to contend with the police and Anacosta and Mollison. "I told you about the well," he said. "I shoved him down in it and then I shoveled dirt in to cover him up. Nobody will ever find him." In the same breath he could have bitten his tongue off. *Shoveled dirt in.* With what shovel? Did he carry a shovel in the car? Did he find one lying around out there in the dark? He would say that it was a figure of speech, that he had actually used an old board or something. He waited for Mollison to seize on the slip, but Mollison overlooked it. Overlooked it now, while he was drunk. He would think of it later, Morgan was sure. Just as he would think of the keys that he had left in the boiler-room door. He wanted to remind Mollison of the keys in some way so that he would go and get them or, perhaps, ask Morgan to recover them. As long as the keys remained where Mollison had forgotten them, Morgan could never return to the mill with any confidence that Mollison would not show up unexpectedly to get the keys. Morgan could think of no way in which he could explain his presence at the mill if Mollison found him there, and yet he would have to return again and again until he had thought of a way to release the boy without risk to himself. He would, have to bring food and water and the reassurance that he was not abandoned. As casually as he could, Morgan asked, "Did you turn out the light when you locked up? Somebody might wonder if they saw a light burning."

Mollison nodded. "It wouldn't make any difference anyway," he said. "I covered the window up." He paused and seemed to be thinking while he felt in the pocket of his jacket with one hand, working his clumsy fingers like a mouse in a sack. "Damn it all," he said. "I left the keys in the door."

Morgan wanted to volunteer to get them but he decided that it would be too out of character. As a presumed murderer with the blood fresh on his hands, volunteering to go back to the mill would be the last thing he'd do.

Mollison said, "I'll have to go get them in the morning. It'd be too risky to drive in there now. There might be a prowl car nosing around."

Morgan moved back from the table. "You'd better do it early," he said. "I'm going to have one more drink and go home." He did not really want the drink. It was part of the character he was creating.

Mollison said, "I'm going to stay a little while longer." When Morgan left the club, Mollison had returned to the bar. He had a drink in his hand but he seemed to be more interested in studying the glass than in drinking its contents. Morgan met Patsy Galuk in the entryway; Patsy was carrying a paper bag showing the hard outlines of coffee containers. Patsy said, "Hello, Lou," and seemed to want to stop and talk. Morgan nodded and brushed past him and out of the door.

Chapter 13

After leaving Mollison at the club, Morgan drove his car into its rented garage. He left the headlights on while he got out to open the doors. As far as he could see, under the strong light, the money hole that he had carefully covered had not been disturbed. He locked the garage and went to his room, certain that he would not be able to sleep. Oddly he did sleep, almost at once, so that it was like a surrender. He awoke after an hour or so to go to the bathroom, and when he returned to his bed he tried to stay awake to plan a way out of the impossible situation he had created for himself.

He lay back with his arms folded under his head, listening to the quiet little sounds of an old house at rest, wondering if there were mysterious noises in the old mill and, if there were, would they frighten the Anacosta boy more than he was already frightened — or was that possible? He eased his conscience slightly by remembering that he had, after all, left the flashlight so that the boy wasn't in total darkness. Far off a bell struck twice, the sound rolling sweetly through the night quiet. Two o'clock. Friday already. It would be a busy day at the bank and he didn't know whether to be glad or sorry. The time would pass more swiftly — but at the same time he would find it less convenient to get away long enough to visit the boy in the mill. And that he had to do. He had to bring him something to eat in the morning — as soon as he could be sure that Mollison had been there, picked up the keys, and left.

He forced himself to think about the two binding limits of his dilemma. He could not kill the boy himself, nor could he let Mollison do it and deny, to himself, the responsibility for the murder. He could not sacrifice himself for the boy by risking the certain capture that his release would entail. *Certain capture if he was where he could be captured.* He began to work out a cautious timetable. Friday. No chance today. There were some few things that he had to do before he could leave. Monday was the day for the tellers' audit at the bank. He had to be there for that. Not that he was short, but to be absent would point suspicion at him at once. Call up and make some excuse maybe? Nobody excused themselves from an audit. And if Anacosta went to the police over the week end, wouldn't the police as a matter of routine come to the bank from which he had taken the money — and wouldn't Morgan's absence be grounds for quick suspicion? Farfetched? Not when his own life was in the scales. So, not Monday. But he could ask for three days beginning Wednesday. The audit would be over, and he had the time coming to him. Then — take the money and get on a plane for New York. From there a fast train to Chicago. From Chicago he could telephone the police and tell them to look in the mill for the boy. And, immediately, another plane. New Orleans or the West Coast. They would get to the boy and he would tell them that three men named Lou and Patsy and Howie had kidnapped him. They would work it out from the names, but by that time he would have a clear start. What did Mollison say? "You could walk through a waiting room and nobody would even see you, Lou." All right. Change a name and put on new style glasses. Get a job as a bookkeeper or something. Something where they didn't take fingerprints.

Morgan fell asleep on the plan. He thought about it anxiously when he awoke in the daylight. So often the things you planned at night looked differently in the morning. He could find no flaw except one that occurred when he was brushing his teeth. What about his Social Security number? He couldn't use his own. The government claimed that the files of Social Security numbers were inviolate, but Morgan didn't believe it. Could they be faked? He would have to find out before he tried for a job on the West Coast or in New Orleans. Meantime, he wouldn't starve. Not on Anacosta's money.

While he was dressing, he heard the insistent beeping of an automobile horn in the street outside. In irritation he raised the shade and drew the curtain aside to look out. Howard Mollison stood on the sidewalk gazing up at the house. Even as Morgan watched, he bent to lean in and push the horn button again. Morgan opened the window and waved and pointed to indicate that he would be right down. He then turned away from the window and finished dressing in full panic, trying to speculate through his fright what Mollison might have learned, how he had found out that the boy was alive.

Mollison had left the club a few minutes after Morgan. He was not anxious to be alone; he would have preferred to stay at the bar for another hour or two but Patsy Galuk approached him, all too obviously eager to demonstrate how friendly he was with Mollison, and Mollison had neither will nor wit to continue the pretense that it was an elaborate joke he was playing on Patsy. He went home and to bed but, unlike Louis Morgan, he could not fall asleep at once. His head ached abominably from the tension that had twisted him, strained at him, throughout the day. He lay in the dark and tried to anticipate anything that might go wrong now and trip him. He would have to be careful about redeeming the forged notes, but even if he made a mistake he could buy his way out. Lillian Kramer, the iron woman, would want money more than revenge. She would let him pay the notes off and get out of town, if anything went wrong — but only if the kidnapping was still a secret. Otherwise there would be a connection between the payment of a heavy ransom and the fact that he had money to pay off notes with. He would deal with it. He could handle it. But what about Lou Morgan and Patsy Galuk? Patsy, hanging around on a man's back forever. And did the guys at the club believe it was a gag or did they wonder why suddenly Patsy was acting like he owned Mollison? *Lou Morgan.* Yellow as butter; if there were ever any pressure on him, he'd open up like a baked potato. So yellow that it was hard to believe, sober, that he had really agreed to murder the kid. Hard to believe — but what else? If he hadn't, the police would have all three of them down in some basement right this minute. So he hadn't let the kid go and if he hadn't let him go, he must have killed him and thrown the body in the old well the way he said he had, and shoveled the dirt in to cover him up. Mollison, his fat body perspiring in the lumpy bed, felt a need to see the place where Morgan had hidden the body; a need to be sure. He got up as soon as it was full daylight, with his head aching and the inside of his mouth tasting foul. When he bent to tie his shoes he felt as if his skull were splitting across the temples. He drove toward Morgan's place, stopping at a diner for a cup of coffee which he could not finish.

Morgan's most frightening thought as he hurried down the stairs to meet Mollison, was that Anacosta had gone to the police and that, in some way, they had made a connection and were already in pursuit. Hardly less frightening was the thought that Mollison had in some manner discovered that he had not killed the boy.

As he came up to Mollison, he said, "What's wrong? What's the matter?" Even as he asked the question he was aware of a strange feeling about Mollison. He did not like the man. In retrospect he was certain that he never had liked him. Yet he had a bond with Mollison; no matter what happened, or where they went, for the rest of his life the bond would exist. Something more than mutual dependence. In a way he would be closer to the fat man than anyone else could ever quite be and the same, of course, applied to Mollison. Strange wedding.

Mollison stepped away from the car. His face was a sick white, almost the color of lard. "Nothing's wrong," he said. "I just wanted to check with you about last night. Look, Lou — you're sure that you — did what you said you did? You're sure that you covered up afterward? I mean, everything went just the way we planned it so far. The only thing we've got to worry about is if somebody finds the kid."

Morgan pretended an irritated indignation. "I told you last night," he said. "I don't want to go to the electric chair any more than you do. I didn't leave a trace."

Mollison persisted. "Don't get sore, Lou," he said defensively. "Don't forget, it was dark. You might have overlooked something or left something behind. It isn't that I don't trust you but I'd like to go out there with you and check. All right?"

Morgan thought, he doesn't believe I killed the boy. He doesn't believe it. He said to Mollison in an imitation of controlled fury, "You must be out of your mind. You want to go out to that old abandoned house and prowl around in broad daylight? What do you want to do — commit suicide?"

"I guess you're right," Mollison said. His attitude was something close to humble.

Morgan pressed him, sensing that Mollison responded to bluster. "Talking about covering up, what about those keys? Did you get them yet?"

Mollison shook his head. "Not yet. I didn't feel so good this morning. Not like driving out there so early."

"You'd better get them now," Morgan said contemptuously.

Mollison nodded. "I guess you're right," he agreed. He moved toward the car and paused. "You're not sore, are you?"

"I'm not sore," Morgan said, "but don't ever call me yellow again. You'd better have a drink or something to straighten yourself out. You can't go to work looking like that."

Mollison got in the car and started it. Morgan watched him drive away with a faint sensation of pride. He had driven Mollison, pushed him, taken the offensive. So far it had worked. So far. He started for the garage and his own car.

Mollison drove toward the old mill, barely conscious of the early morning traffic. He felt a great wonder that he had so underestimated Lou Morgan, and with the wonder a great relief. He no longer thought that Morgan lacked the courage to murder or that he would be so frightened by the act that he would lose his head and fail to conceal all evidence of the crime. There was iron in Morgan. If he had known that, he thought, if he had known that he wouldn't have had to recruit Patsy Galuk for the kidnapping. They could have worked it out between the two of them. Patsy — there was another worry. He had to discourage the damned idiot without provoking him. Maybe Lou could think of something. Mollison allowed himself the luxury of thinking about the money for a few moments. There had been no time for thinking of the money since Anacosta had left it in the locker. Something else Morgan had said — what was it — you can't go to work looking like that? Mollison stopped at a dingy bar room and had two fast drinks. He felt better immediately and lingered for another before he drove on out to the mill. The keys were still hanging on the door. He put them in his pocket and got back into the car.

Morgan drove toward the mill after Mollison had disappeared in the traffic, but he took a street that paralleled the one Mollison was traveling. He tuned in on an early morning news broadcast; when he made a stop at an early opening neighborhood grocery store, the newscast was not complete and he sat in the car and listened while the announcer finished the national news and ran through the local round up. There was no mention of a kidnapping. In the store he bought two quarts of milk, a loaf of bread and some cold cuts of meat.

As an afterthought he bought a package of paper cups. Maybe it would have been better to buy sandwiches at a diner. Still, if he couldn't get out to the mill again until after dark, the milk and the cold meat would make a lunch for the boy. And the milk would substitute for water. Maybe later he could pick up a Thermos picnic jug and fill it with cold water. And a toothbrush and maybe some clean clothes for the boy. Let's see — Friday until Wednesday. Six days, nearly. Seven, actually, because he wouldn't call the police about the boy until he was in Chicago.

He spent twenty minutes in a diner over two cups of coffee, killing time until he could be certain that Mollison had been to the mill and left. Only then did he drive up to the boiler room and let himself in with the duplicate key he had stolen from Mollison's bunch. He glanced around as he hurried through the room. One blanket was still hung over the window. Mollison should have taken it down. He would have liked to take it down himself — it would look a little odd from the outside — but he decided against it out of fear that Mollison might at some time, for some reason, come back and notice that it had been moved. Better leave it alone.

Even by daylight the mill was dark. Years of dirt and soot had collected on the windows, so that what light came in was watered and weak. Morgan hurried toward the stairway. It was almost eight o'clock and he had to be at the bank at nine. Hurrying, he stumbled over something that tipped over with a metallic clatter, which made him wince and look down. He had knocked over a box of card spindles; long, wicked-looking skewers of steel, rusted, now, that rolled under his feet. There were dozens and dozens of boxes of the spindles and he must have been lucky, he decided, to have passed through here last night in the pitch dark without knocking some of them over.

He fumbled noisily with the lock on the door of the room in which the boy was imprisoned, not wanting to startle him too much when he opened it. Dark as the mill had been, this room, having no windows, was darker yet, so that he had to blink and wait for his pupils to dilate before he could see the boy, even though he left the door open. While he waited he called, "Are you awake? I brought you something to eat."

The boy, as he could now see, was huddled in the corner where he had left him, the filthy blanket drawn about him. The flashlight, the batteries long since burned out, lay beside him. As Morgan watched, the boy sat up slowly, clutching the blanket around him. "My leg hurts," he whimpered. "My leg hurts. I want to go home."

Morgan said, "Pretty soon now. Here. Drink some milk."

Morgan filled one of the paper cups and handed it to the boy. He drank thirstily, but when Morgan offered to make him a meat sandwich he refused it.

"I'll leave it here," Morgan said. He bent to look at the boy's knee. It looked, in the half light, worse than it had the night before when the boy had fallen. The edges of the scraped skin were puckered and stiff with dried blood, and the area around the wound seemed to be somewhat swollen. Morgan wished that he had brought water so that he could bathe the cut. He wondered if it would help to wash it with some of the milk but decided not to. Weren't there bacteria in milk? He said sympathetically, "I know it hurts. When I come back I'll bring some stuff to put on it that will make it better."

The boy had lain down again after finishing the cup of milk. As Morgan spoke he struggled up again. "Can't you stay with me?" he asked. "I'm scared by myself."

Morgan patted his shoulder awkwardly. "I'll come back pretty soon," he said. "And as soon as I can I'll fix it to send you home. You've got, to remember to be quiet though. You know what I told you about those other men."

When he left the room, the boy was still sitting up, watching him out of wide and frightened eyes. Taking it pretty well, Morgan thought, for a little boy. He fixed in his mind the list of things he must remember to bring with him when he returned. Something for the boy's knee. It struck him as mildly sardonic that he should be worrying about the boy's knee when his own neck was at stake. But he did worry about it as he drove to the bank.

Chapter 14

Mollison had made false notes in four names in three different banks and he felt a great need to clear them up. It was possible that he could send in the monthly payments on each note as they became due, but that was risky. On three of the notes he had used his own address. On the fourth, since it was with a bank already holding a note with his apartment address, he had used the address of his club. The receipt from the bank would be mailed there. He had carefully kept the duplicate copies of the transfer papers for the cars on which the money was theoretically loaned. That fourth note — what was the name he had used? Swanson? The club manager would get the letter from the bank. He had to think of some lie to tell the manager to explain the letter and to assure the man that it should be delivered to him, Mollison. Another lie. He was sick to death of lying, sick of the need to keep track of the lies he told so that they wouldn't boomerang on him. He owed eleven hundred dollars to the Industrial National — plus interest — for the note on the green Hudson that he had forged to raise money to pay off the little blackmailer Griffin.

On his way to the Kramer Agency and the day's work he stopped off at his apartment. For lack of a better hiding place he had put his share of the ransom money in a sealed glass jar, and this he had placed in the toilet tank. He took twelve hundred and fifty dollars in fifties from the jar and replaced it in its hiding place. From his desk he took the contract presumably made out by the man who had borrowed the money on the Hudson. Half an hour later, with the money and the contract in his pocket, he walked into the Industrial National and spoke to the same vice-president with whom he had originally negotiated the note.

Mollison said, "Hello, Paul. How's business?" Not too eager. Not too anxious. Be smooth.

Paul said, "So, so. What can I do for you, Howie?"

Mollison said casually, "Guy bought a car from us a couple of weeks ago. Name was Swanson." No, damn it, *no!* Swanson was the one whose receipts would be sent to the club. That first time, on the Hudson — what was the name? Right there on the contract in his pocket but he couldn't pull it out and look at it, not with the vice-president looking at him curiously. He tried desperately to remember the name. Carr? Carter? *Carling.* "I was thinking about another account," he continued. "It wasn't Swanson it was Carling. Peter Carling."

Paul showed interest. "One of our accounts? What's the matter? Did you find out he misrepresented his salary or something like that?"

Mollison laughed shortly. "Nothing like that. He's a machinist. Nice guy. He came in yesterday to have us check the transmission on the car he bought. He just got a big check from the company he works for — seems he made some suggestion to save labor. He wanted to pay off the car to save the interest. I told him I'd be down near the bank today and I'd drop in and take care of it."

Paul immediately lost interest. "Well, sure, Howie," he said. "Any one of the credit department clerks will take care of it for you." He turned to stroll across the bank lobby. Mollison went to a credit window and paid off the Carling note. He walked out of the bank feeling some relief but also a sour bitterness. He had borrowed eleven hundred on the car originally. Griffin had gotten the major share of that. Now he had paid back almost twelve hundred dollars to the bank and he had paid a thousand dollars to the man — what was his name — Hunt? — who had legitimately bought the green Hudson off the lot. And fifty dollars loaned to Eddie, the mechanic. To show for it, he had the green Hudson, useless to him, and he even had to pay garage rent to keep it out of sight. And he still had to pay off three more notes on cars that were sitting on Lillian Kramer's used-car line. That Swanson thing had been a near miss. He couldn't afford to fumble his lines like that. He decided that he would pay off the Swanson note on the following Monday.

He also decided, on the way out to the agency, to stop for another drink. And wasn't he drinking too much lately? Maybe. After he had the notes all paid off and he didn't have to worry so damn much he would cut down. He parked his car near a dingy tap room and went in. The place seemed familiar; after a time it came to him that he had been in here before. When was it? A couple, maybe three weeks ago, when he had first taken Lou Morgan out to show him the boiler room where they would hold the Anacosta kid. He had stopped in here on his way back from leaving Morgan off, wanting a drink because of the strain of trying to keep Morgan's nerve up. What a joke that was. Morgan had more nerve than he had. Sometimes those quiet little guys were like that, he guessed. He ordered a Scotch and drank it and then ordered another one, not wanting to leave and go out to the agency. Lillian. He didn't want to look at her. Now that he had Anacosta's money maybe he wouldn't have to. Maybe he could line something up that wasn't so old and that didn't have to strap itself in with girdles. No rush, though. Just knowing that he could do it made it easier to think of going on with Lillian.

The bartender had a small radio playing on the shelf behind the bar. Mollison was barely aware that it was turned on; hardly conscious of the inane chatter of an early morning disc jockey. He heard the words, "And now the news," and out of reflex he gave the radio part of his attention; just enough so that he would be aware of any item that he wanted to hear.

The announcer said, "Word of the kidnapping of a local child has just been received. The child, son of Mr. and Mrs. Louis Anacosta of

Grave Street in this city, is eight-year-old Carmen Anacosta. First reports indicate that the child was kidnapped en route to school yesterday morning and that a ransom was apparently paid by the child's grandfather, Carmen Anacosta, who is well known in local real estate and financial circles. The kidnapping was made known when the boy's mother appealed to the police shortly after nine o'clock this morning. For further details keep tuned to this station."

Mollison's first reaction to the broadcast was a thick anger. Anacosta hadn't been able to keep the boy's mother from blowing the whistle. All right, then. All right. He'd had his warning. Mollison remembered tardily that the boy was already dead and then rationalized that the old man hadn't known that; never would know it and he'd have to live with the fact that if he had stopped the kid's mother from going to the police, maybe the boy would still be alive. He ordered another drink. By the time it came the second reaction had set in. The police. And with the police the FBI. Mollison chewed at his lip, remembering the stories he had seen on television about the FBI and the things they could do. That time in New York. What had they done — looked at the handwriting on a million license applications or something like that? But even the FBI had to have something to go on and there was nothing. No handwriting. No letters. The boy had been picked up in a nondescript car with license plates that were untraceable even if someone, by some miracle, had noticed them. And Morgan had hidden the body where it would never be found. Where was the weak spot? Patsy Galuk wouldn't connect the kid they had held in the boiler room with the kidnapping. That was the trouble with Patsy — he couldn't connect things. But he was loyal to Mollison.

Mollison finished his drink and hesitated. After a minute he walked over to the wall telephone and dialed the number of the Kramer Agency. When a girl in the office answered, he said, "This is Howie Mollison, Betty. Look, tell Lillian I probably won't be in today, will you? Tell her I got a couple of, prospects I want to see across the city." He hung up and walked back to the bar. He would have one more here and then he would take a ride out to the club. He had too much on his mind to hold his end up at the agency right now.

It was from Vega, the teller in the neighboring cage, that Lou Morgan first learned that the Anacosta boy's mother had gone to the police. Before he heard it from Vega he was aware of an increase in the tempo of behind-the-wicket gossip, but his preoccupation with his own crisis prevented him from making any inquiry. Vega finally came to his cage and borrowed several packets of hundred-dollar bills. While he signed a receipt for them he asked, "Did you hear about it? My God, he was in here getting the money yesterday."

Morgan almost immediately realized what Vega was referring to — what else could it be? He was not greatly surprised. He had never had Mollison's faith that the kidnapping would be kept from the police. He *was* surprised by his own reaction. He had so much confidence in his own plan for escaping the city with the boy unharmed that he was not even greatly frightened by the thought of the police and the FBI. He asked Vega querulously, "Hear about what?" wanting to get as much detail as he could from Vega's gossiping.

Vega said excitedly, "The kidnapping. Somebody kidnapped old Anacosta's grandson and collected almost a hundred thousand dollars ransom. He was in here yesterday, Lou. You saw him."

Morgan said, "I guess I did at that. Just before lunch, wasn't it?" To have denied seeing Anacosta might have been dangerous. Since he was admitting having seen him he might as well put a little frosting on the cake.

Vega became ponderously grave. "That's right. It's a terrible thing, Lou. A terrible thing."

Morgan nodded. "Have they got any idea who did it?"

Vega shook his head. "The police say they think it was an out of town gang. They'd say that anyway just to have something to tell the reporters. He got the money from his safety deposit box — he must have because he didn't make any withdrawals from any of his accounts." He added maliciously, "The internal revenue will want to know why he had that kind of money in a safe deposit box, I'll bet."

Morgan said dryly, "I'll bet."

After Vega had bustled back to his own cage, Morgan fell into the automatic motions of a Friday at the Drover's. He made entries, handed out and received money, and cashed checks without having to think about it. He used most of his faculties to polish his plan. He debated going to the vice-president in charge of personnel and asking for the three days, starting on the following Wednesday, that he would need to implement the plan. He decided against it. The FBI and the police, if they were as clever as he had heard they were, would be visiting the bank soon. If they started asking questions about personnel, he didn't want it fresh in the vice-president's mind that Louis Morgan had just asked for some time off. Monday would be time enough. And in the back of his mind remained a persistent, fretful concern for the boy who was right now lying in a dark room in the deserted Maynard Mill. He wished that he had been able to bring him some water. And maybe some medicine for his scraped knee.

Patsy Galuk heard about the kidnapping while he was cleaning out the beer cooler behind the bar at the club. It was close to noon and there were several men at the bar at the time. He had his arms in the slimy water up to his elbows and he was going about the job with a great splashing as if to call attention to the fact that Patsy Galuk was cleaning the beer cooler. He did everything with that same unbalanced flamboyance. If he was cleaning out the basement of the club, he got dirtier than necessary and then made a point of letting the members see him. If he was merely mopping the floor, he paddled in the soapy water, wetting his shoes and the cuffs of his pants. He worked, when he worked, like a motor without a governor. He had an intense interest in any conversation of which he was not a part although, more frequently than otherwise, he could only understand a small part of what was being said. He heard one man say, "Anything new on the kidnapping?"

Another member asked, "What kidnapping? I haven't seen a paper yet this morning."

"Some Dago kid. What was his name, Jerry?"

"Anacosta. Old Carmen Anacosta's grandson."

"Yeah, that was it. They kidnapped him yesterday morning. The old man paid them off."

"How much did they get?"

"I've heard everything from a hundred grand to half a million."

"Did they return the kid?"

"Hell, no. They're not going to either. You take it from me, he's dead right now."

"Yeah, I guess. Tough. A hundred grand or better you say?"

"That's what I heard on the radio. You know, that's a funny thing. Remember a few weeks ago they kidnapped that kid in New York — what was his name? Glennon? That was it — Glennon. Well, right after that we were talking about it right here at this very bar and we got to talking about how much money Anacosta had. You were here, weren't you, Jerry? Sure you were. And Howie Mollison. Mollison was the one that did most of the talking. And Al was here and I think Lou Morgan. We were only just talking about it, like I said, and damn if someone didn't figure it out the same way we did."

They began a discussion of the baseness of kidnapers, each pointing out in more gruesome detail what should be done with them when they were caught. Patsy Galuk lifted his dripping arms from the beer cooler, disregarding the water that trickled into his sleeves, disregarding the conversation. His expression became fixed, wooden, as he walked from behind the bar and shambled into the little room where brooms and mops were kept. He was trying, deliberately trying, to think. What was it the man had said? A Dago kid was kidnapped? A Dago kid. A Dago kid. What else had he said? Howie Mollison and Lou Morgan had talked about kidnapping the Anacosta kid weeks ago. For one of the few times in his life, Patsy reasoned; knew the emotional satisfaction of putting two facts together so that they made still another fact. It was a Dago kid they had held in the boiler room, wasn't it? That was a fact. Mollison had talked about how much money Anacosta — a Dago — had. That was a fact. The third fact — Mollison and Morgan had kidnapped the Anacosta kid.

Patsy walked the floor and wrung his big hands as conviction grew within him. Kidnapers were terrible men; everybody said that. They should be tortured and hung, especially the ones that kidnapped little kids. But what could he do, what could he do, knowing that Mollison and Morgan were kidnapers? Mollison — he thought primarily of Mollison rather than of Morgan — Mollison was his friend. He had another thought. If he told On Mollison and they caught him, somebody else would take the credit. Into his mind crept a small picture. Patsy Galuk, rescuing the Anacosta kid from the boiler room and triumphantly bringing him home to his parents while people clapped him on the back and said what a hero he was. Then he remembered that the kid hadn't been there when he and Mollison left the place the last time. What had Mollison said? The Dagos came and got him? What a liar that Mollison was. Liar, liar, liar. Liar kidnaper. Patsy began to grow furious with Mollison. But, oh, how nice it would be if he *could* find the kid and rescue him. Nobody could take the credit from him if he did that. Nobody. Oh, Mollison was a liar. Maybe he had lied when he had said that the Dagos had come and got the boy. Maybe he had double lied and nobody had come to take him at all. If they hadn't, then he was still in the boiler room. Simple. Patsy would go and rescue him. Only where was the boiler room? Some, big factory, like, and it was across town. He knew that much. And it had a big chimney on it. He could take a cross-town bus and then he could look for the place until he found it.

He came out of the storeroom and sought out the steward. "I got to go out for a while," he said importantly. "I got to check up on something."

The steward grunted and turned away, and Patsy started for the door. He was a step away when Howard Mollison walked in. Both men pulled back; Mollison because he didn't want to become involved with Patsy at the moment and Patsy because he was not sure how he should act. He could call the cops right now, if he wanted, but they might just laugh at him like the times when members sent him in to fix traffic tickets; and then what would Mollison do to him? And if he called the cops, even if they did arrest Mollison and find the kid, they would take all the credit. Patsy put on what he thought was an innocent expression and sidled past Mollison.

"Hello, Howie," he said. "I was just going out."

Mollison was at first relieved, but the naked transparency of Patsy's forced, and furtive, manner struck him almost immediately. The fact that Patsy didn't stop to talk was, in itself, unheard of. He said with a joviality that was false as Patsy's innocence, "What's the rush, Patsy? I thought you and I were partners. Come out to the bar and I'll buy you a beer." He wanted no part of Patsy but he had to test him.

Patsy edged toward the door. Mollison watched him almost break into a run when he reached the street, and felt a thread of fear tug at his raw nerves. He sought out the manager and bought him a drink, trying not to worry about Patsy until he had cleared up the matter that had brought him to the club this early.

After they had finished the drinks and ordered another round, Mollison said, "By the way, Fred, I've got a little deal cooking you can help me out on."

The manager, sensing a possible touch, displayed no great enthusiasm. Mollison continued, "I'm on salary and commission with the Kramer Agency, you know. I had a chance a little while back to sell a couple of late models for another outfit. I've got a little graft going if you can help me out."

The manager, realizing that it was not a touch after all, nodded. "Well sure, Howie," he said. "Anything at all."

Mollison continued. "It isn't much," he said. "Just some papers that will be sent to me here at the club. I can't use my own name or the agency will find out about it. These papers will be addressed to Mr. Swanson. Hold them for me, will you, Fred?"

"Sure, Howie. How about a drink on the club?"

Mollison shook his head. "Not right now, Fred." He hesitated. "I was going to get Patsy to put in a couple of hours washing cars this afternoon. Did you send him out somewhere?"

The manager looked bored. "I didn't. He came to me a little while ago and said he had some important business to check up on. I don't know what he was talking about."

Mollison said, "Thanks, Fred. See you," and hurried to the door. The thought of Patsy with important business to look after was terrifying. He had badly overestimated Patsy's devotion. He felt an irrational anger. It was as if a pet dog had suddenly turned on him. A most dangerous dog. He felt an enormous relief when he saw Patsy two blocks away, standing at a bus stop. Mollison's first impulse was to drive alongside and invite Patsy into the car. He decided against it. If Patsy had guessed that he had been made a party to a kidnapping he might become violently angry — and Patsy, with his crude strength, could be a terrible opponent. It would be better to wait and see where he headed. At the last moment he could always take the chance of accosting Patsy. Mollison got into his car and idled the motor, waiting, like Patsy, for the bus. When it came, it was a cross-town bus. That fact had significance. If it were a downtown bus, Patsy might be going directly to police headquarters — or to the FBI office in the Post Office. A cross-town bus? Across town was the old Maynard Mill, of course, but what would Patsy want there? Patsy got on the bus with a grotesque swaying of his backside. Mollison eased the car after the bus, staying close as it made its ponderous way through the noon traffic.

Patsy got off five blocks away from the Maynard Mills, and Mollison immediately pulled his car in to the curb. He watched curiously as Patsy looked about him, with his head tipped back as if he were looking for something well above street level. What was he looking for, the crazy bastard? Like a dog that has found the scent, Patsy suddenly lowered his eyes and began to walk purposefully ahead. He turned right at the first cross street; a cross street that would take him directly to the mill.

Chapter 15

Patsy Galuk walked in his rolling shamble down the side street toward the Maynard Mill. He had had no great difficulty in finding the place; he had known it was across town and a bar — the bar to which Mollison had sent him for a beer on the previous night — identified the general locale. The sight of the chimney pinpointed the mill. He made these decisions through the thick and muddy morass of his thinking. His mind worked as a Maine pond is said to work in springtime, sending up fragments of ancient debris. Images of the public notice he would receive when he rescued the Anacosta child came bubbling upward like clear globules of air. He had convinced himself, more by the power of his wishing than by any logic, that Mollison had lied when he said that the Dagos had come and gotten the boy. He would find the boy in the boiler room and he would take him out and bring him to his parents. It did not occur to Patsy that he had no idea of where the boy lived.

Mollison, in growing panic, started the car again and followed Patsy. He was no longer in any doubt about the idiot's destination — he was puzzled only about the motivation. What did he want to go there for, for God's sake? Unless he thought that the boy was there. Mollison was certain by this time that Patsy knew of the kidnapping and that he had guessed that the child he had guarded was the victim. His purpose, then, was to release the boy. It must be. And after that to accuse him, Mollison, for whatever glory it would bring him. But the boy wasn't there. Lou Morgan had killed him and hidden the body, so there was nothing for Patsy to find. Mollison decided he could not let Patsy go prowling around the boiler room. He himself could drive up in his car and stop and nothing would be thought of it. If anyone noticed him they would think he was an owner's representative or an insurance inspector or the like. With the whole city alerted to a kidnapping, Patsy, with his apish appearance — he could serve as a model for a depraved kidnaper — would certainly draw attention to the boiler room. And to himself. He would be picked up on sight, just for his looks. Worse than that, he was a police buff. He would probably go to the police voluntarily. *I know who kidnapped the Anacosta kid.*

If Mollison could talk to him for just a minute he was certain that he could get him into the car. *If* he could have that minute without any frenzied denunciation in the middle of the street that would bring the police. What then, with Patsy in the car? Mollison faced the problem and made his decision without evasion. Patsy would have to die and Howard Mollison would have to kill him. Not tomorrow or an hour later or some other time but now.

He fed gas to the car and drove up beside Patsy, who by now was directly opposite the driveway leading into the mill yard. Because everything depended on the show he put on, Mollison called jovially, "Hey, Patsy, what are you doing in this part of town? Get in and I'll give you a lift wherever you're going."

Patsy held back, not out of fear. Mollison was the kidnaper. Mollison was the liar. He was the one to be afraid. He held back because he wanted no delay between now and the glory he'd have as soon as he rescued the Anacosta kid. He said evasively, "I'm just taking a walk, Howie. I don't want to ride. You go along."

Mollison said plaintively, "I thought we were buddies, Patsy. Are you sore or something?"

It was the best approach he could have used. Nobody had ever cared if Patsy were sore or not, and he responded in spite of his anxiety to be rid of Mollison. "I ain't sore, Howie," he said. A terrible doubt came to Patsy. Supposing Howie wasn't a kidnaper? Suppose he hadn't been lying — he didn't act like a kidnaper right now. Then he would have lost his best friend. His only friend. The only one who ever took the trouble to ask if he was sore. "I ain't sore," he repeated. All right. He would get in the car with Howie and then get away from him after he'd ridden with him a little way to show that he really wasn't sore. He could always come back to get the kid — if he was there. He opened the door and got in, still suspicious of Mollison but protecting himself if it turned out that he was wrong.

Mollison drove in toward the boiler room. "I just thought I'd come back and check up to see if I locked the door," he said.

Patsy twisted his hands nervously. He must have been wrong about Howie. But he had been so sure. He had wanted so much to be the one who brought the Anacosta kid home. If he could see inside the boiler room, now. If he could think of something to tell Howie why he had to look inside, then he could see if the kid was there.

Mollison made it easy for him. He said, as he pulled up beside the boiler room and stopped the car, "I think I left a little whisky in the bottle I had in there, Patsy. Let's go inside and see if we can squeeze out a drink." If he had not had so much on his mind now, he would have taken time for some self-congratulation on the way he had handled Patsy. He wondered briefly if he had convinced Patsy enough; if he could convince himself enough when Patsy saw that the room was empty that it would not be necessary to kill him. No. Patsy obviously had had the idea in his head and he would never quite lose it. Sooner or later he would say something; remember something, talk too much.

Mollison unlocked the door of the boiler room and stood aside as Patsy eagerly brushed by him, blinking his small eyes in the dim light and glancing from side to side. The room was obviously empty. Mollison bent and picked up the whisky bottle he had emptied the night before. "Too bad," he said. "It's empty. Well, I guess we might as well get out of here, Patsy. We can stop somewhere and get a drink."

Patsy was baffled. He sensed that Mollison knew of his suspicions but for some reason he wasn't going to hold it against him that he had thought — what he had thought. Or maybe he had tricked him in some way. He said, "Sure, Howie," and started past Mollison.

Mollison had picked up the whisky bottle but he hadn't put it down. As Patsy stepped past him, he brought it crashing down on the back of his skull. The bottle made a sodden chunk, like a maul driving a stake, and Patsy lurched to his knees. Strangely, the bottle did not break. Patsy half turned to face Mollison as he struggled to get to his feet. The blood welled up in a frightening tide to mat his coarse hair. He said, "Howie — Howie — " and Mollison, in panic, swung the bottle again, sideways so that it thudded against Patsy's temple. This time he went full length on his belly. Unbelievably, he struggled again to get his feet under him. He did not speak but made a gasping, choking sound in his throat. Mollison threw the bottle aside. He had to fight the urge to run away from this monster who would not die. Beside the furnace, there was an iron bar used to break up clinkers in the cheap, soft coal. Mollison picked it up and swung it, again and again in revulsion and terror. Patsy no longer moved. Mollison sat down on the edge of the cot and put his head in his hands while great drops of sweat formed on his forehead and trickled down his cheeks. His legs were trembling; he could not rise again until they steadied. He looked once, and once again, at the body of Patsy sprawled on the dirty cement floor. Each time he looked away hastily, knowing that he would shortly have to do more than look. He could not leave Patsy lying there, although he thought briefly about doing just that. Some day — in a week or a month or two — an agency man would be showing a client the mill. That's all that would be needed. Patsy would be identified and connected with the club and from the club to Mollison. Mollison shivered. He wondered if Lou Morgan had felt like this after he killed the Anacosta kid. *Lou Morgan, of course.* There was the answer to his problem. If Morgan had hidden one body where it could never be found, he could hide another. But should he tell Morgan? How was the law on that? Morgan was a party to the kidnapping — he had murdered the kid. Now Patsy was dead, and that was a product of the kidnapping; so wasn't Morgan guilty of Patsy's murder too? Mollison tittered. Morgan was going to be surprised to learn what he had become a party to. What would he do — call him up and say, "Lou, I've got another one for you?" He sat on the cot, in near hysteria, for another five minutes; a fat man rapidly falling apart. Then he pulled himself together enough to make some sort of plan. He would call Morgan at the bank and tell him that he had to see him — in the boiler room would be as good a place as any. And after dark so that they could take the body away from this place and get rid of it.

After a day or so, when Patsy didn't show up, the club manager might or might not report to the police that he was missing. Nobody else would care enough to bother. There was the slight danger that the police might possibly connect Patsy's disappearance — if it was reported—with the kidnapping, but so what? They might guess at a connection; but they could do nothing with it, could they? Nothing.

Mollison got up finally, and dragged the sprawled body toward the coal pile. The heavy, dead weight seemed to resist his tugging out of some malevolent obstinacy, but he managed. Now the body was out of the way but that was not enough. He mopped his streaming forehead and glanced about the room. No shovel, although you would expect to find a shovel in a boiler room, wouldn't you? Stolen by some resentful boilerman when the mill closed down probably. There was a wide board in the pile of wood he had gathered earlier when he had planned to start a fire in the boiler. Mollison picked it up and began to sweep coal from the pile until he had nearly covered Patsy's body, covered it enough so that it no longer accused him. Then he scraped some of the fine, powdery coal from the edges of the heap and scuffed it across the heavier blood splotches in the center of the room, smearing them and darkening them so that they became less obviously what they were. When he was finished he left the boiler room, locking the door behind him and emerging into the shock of bright daylight. He could see himself now, streaked and smeared with coal dust and sweat. On the cuffs of his trousers were some dark specks that must be blood, although he could not remember that it had spattered enough to reach him. He had to clean up somewhere before he did anything else. He got into the car and drove away, stopping at the first filling station he came to. Without waiting for the attendant to come up he hurried toward the side of the building where a sign said *Men,* calling over his shoulder, "Fill her up."

He washed his face and hands vigorously, then took a paper towel, soaked it in water after he had wadded it into a ball, and dabbed at the spots on his trouser cuffs. The paper came away with a pinkish tinge, but the spots darkened with the water and he could only hope that they would disappear when the cloth dried. He thought carefully about what he was doing in order to avoid thinking about Patsy and what he had done to him. Not that he felt remorse. What was Patsy? A moron. Of no use to anyone. Now there was only one person who could betray him and that was Morgan — but Morgan was so hopelessly involved himself that he could never go to the police. Mollison began to feel quite a bit better about the whole thing. It had worked out, hadn't it? Now that he knew how much nerve Morgan had — and hadn't he been tough this morning? What was it he had said? "You must be out of your mind? Don't ever call me yellow again." Morgan was one of those cold, icy ones, all right. Nothing to worry about from Morgan. All they had to do now was hide Patsy's body and be careful about how they spent the ransom money — for a while, anyway — and everything was going to be all right.

Mollison walked back into the sunlight and paid the attendant, giving him a tip out of his growing sense of safety. All he had to do now was call Morgan at the bank. And have a couple of drinks as a reward for the way he had handled Patsy.

He parked in front of a bar and went in, wondering pleasantly whether he should have a drink before or after he called Lou. Before — why not? He had earned it. With the drink in hand, he looked about him while he sipped it. A nice bar. Nice looking bunch of guys playing pitch down at the angle of the bar where the bartender could play and still tend to the drinks. He moved toward them, taking his drink with him. He felt none of his habitual superiority. He wanted the sense of being like these men, like any man who had not committed murder. He nodded to one of the players and the man nodded back. Pleasantly. Nice guys. "Let's have a round here," he said.

This time they all smiled and nodded. One or more of them said, " — luck, Mac." Mollison didn't want them to think he was a big shot because he had bought a round of drinks. He wanted them to think that he was a nice guy, too.

The telephone call. He had to call Morgan. He said, "Excuse me," and walked over to the telephone booth that stood beside the front door. There was a directory hanging from a chain and he looked up the number of the Drover's Bank and dialed it.

"I'd like to talk with Mr. Morgan," he said, when he had a connection. "Mr. Louis Morgan. He's a teller."

The voice on the other end was cool and feminine and the expression managed to convey the impression that it was not bank policy for employees to receive telephone calls on bank time. Not employees of Morgan's level. The voice said, "One moment, please." There was a pause and it came back again, faintly gratified. "Mr. Morgan is at lunch," it said. Bank policy had been vindicated. "Is there any message?"

Mollison said, "No. No thanks. It wasn't important," and hung up. He felt better after the call. There was no hurry. They couldn't do anything about Patsy until after dark anyway, and there had seemed something so pleasantly normal in the message that Morgan was out to lunch.

He drifted back to the card game and the bartender said, "Why don't you sit in, Mac? I've got some cleaning up to do in back."

Mollison said, "I'd like to," and pulled out a chair. He felt something of the nervously guilty elation of a working man stealing time in a bar when he should be working or going home with the paycheck. He said, "My name is Mollison. Call me Howie."

The other players introduced themselves. Shack. George — Mollison's partner — and Red. Mollison acknowledged the introductions and ordered another round of drinks. Red stopped him and bought the round himself, and Mollison felt himself going out to these men. Needing the companionship of men as a bulwark against his awareness of Patsy lying dead in the coal pile, he stripped himself of the conceit and the sham with which he had faced the world for almost all his years. He exposed himself, for the first time in twenty-five years, without any pretense at all; wanting only acceptance on their own terms. He even regretted that he was better dressed than these men. After twenty-five years the relief from the burden of hypocrisy and bluster was almost too great. He felt light, naked, as if he had stripped off great layers of fat. In all those years he had doubted Howard Mollison's ability to make a living, even to survive as Howard Mollison. He had been X different men to make a living at X different jobs. Now he played cards and he drank and he bought when it was his turn; all this with no lies, no reserve, no, ego. He loved these men and he could have wept that he had not discovered years ago the elation of being just himself.

Red: "What do you do for a living, Howie?"

Mollison: "I sell cars. New ones, used ones. The Kramer Agency on Elmwood Avenue." No implication that he was a vice-president in the company and could arrange a hell of a break on a deal. No cryptic suggestion that he was something more than a used-car salesman ...

Shack: "I never saw you around here before, Howie. Where do you live?"

Mollison: "I live in a dump on the other side of town." No claim to anything else. No insinuation that he lived in a first-rate apartment and was just slumming. No lie. No mention of his club as if it were some exclusive fraternity for rich men only. No lie. No bluff.

The afternoon wore on with all four men becoming a little drunk. Mollison won a few dollars and lost a few and couldn't have cared less. Several times he thought of calling Lou Morgan again but each time he put it off. It was much easier to play cards and drink and pretend that nothing had happened. He procrastinated to avoid the devilish reality that he had kidnapped a child and murdered a man and that he could never really walk with men again. What the hell — he was walking with men, wasn't he? These men, Red and Shack and George, actually liked him. So what he had done didn't show. It couldn't show. When — and it happened less often through the afternoon — he thought of Patsy lying in the coal pile and remembered that he had to get Lou to help him get rid of the body, a sick gray despair closed in around him. Whisky dissipated the gray cloud like a breeze whipping away morning mist. He had to do something about that. Drinking too much, lately. Do it tomorrow. But ah, God — if he were only a plain working man like these others. The kind he had sold the swampy lots and the cheap aluminum windows and the crackerbox houses to. If he were only not a kidnaper, not a murderer, but just a mark working in a factory.

Red said, throwing down his hand, "It's almost seven o'clock. We've killed the afternoon — let's go get something to eat. How about you, Howie?"

Mollison thought once more of Patsy and decided that it could do no harm to wait a while. No telling where he could reach Lou Morgan now, anyway. "Sure," he said.

They got up from the table in a noisy group and went out the door. On the street a uniformed policeman waited. He said, not unkindly, "Hello, Shack. You, George, and Red. The lieutenant wants to talk to you down at the precinct."

Shack said impatiently, "Oh for God's sake, what's he want now?"

The policeman shrugged. "The heat's on about a kidnapping. He probably just wants to talk to you boys. Probably won't hold you too long. He's having all the ex-cons brought in, not just you guys."

Mollison fought back the impulse to sidle away from the group and run, fast and far. But that would be the worst thing he could do.

The policeman glanced at him curiously. "What's your name, Mac?"

Mollison wondered if he should give a false name. It was just possible that Anacosta had given the police a list of names of men he had turned down on loan requests and who might have kidnapped his grandson out of revenge. Would he remember Mollison? Yet, if he gave a false name, the policeman might ask for identification. The risk was too great. "Mollison," he said. "Howard Mollison. I don't know these men. I just happened to get into a card game with them."

The policeman frowned. "Mollison," he said. "Mollison. You got a record, Mollison — like your buddies here?"

If he'd had the nerve left, Mollison would have assumed a righteous indignation; but he merely said, "No."

The policeman turned to Shack. "What about it, Shack? You know this Mollison?"

Shack shook his head. "Like he said, he just got into a card game with us. Look, Eddie — we didn't eat yet. How about you let us stop at the diner before we see the lieutenant?"

"I guess so." The policeman turned back to Mollison. "You can go, Mollison."

Mollison turned away and then half turned back. He said tentatively, "I'll see you fellows sometime."

Not one of them answered him.

Mollison, knowing what he had yet to do, could not do it. Instead he picked up a bottle of whisky and drove to his apartment. He took off his shoes and lay down in the dark, fully dressed, weak and sick. When the bottle was half finished he fell asleep.

Chapter 16

Louis Morgan left the bank at five. He had been increasingly aware of concern for the Anacosta boy; and this irritated him. He was doing all he could, wasn't he? He had actually saved the boy's life, hadn't he? In spite of the irritation, he decided not to wait until dark to return to the mill. There was little more risk in going there by daylight than at night, he told himself.

He picked up his car at a parking lot and started toward the outskirts of the city. In less than an hour he made four separate stops. The first was at an auto supply store, where he bought a gallon size Thermos jug and half a dozen flashlight batteries. He had paid for them and was on his way out of the store when he saw a display of foam rubber automobile pillows. He turned back and bought one, telling the clerk a foolish and unnecessary little lie about wanting to sit up higher in the driver's seat of his car.

He found a small dry goods and notions store for his second stop. He bought towels and soap, a tooth brush and paste and a small basin. He glanced at some boy's underclothing on a counter and wanted to buy some, but this he could not make himself do. Too risky, with everybody in the city conscious that a small boy had been kidnapped.

His third stop was at a neighborhood grocery store, where he bought more cold meats, a bottle of milk and a loaf of bread. He added several cans of tomato and pineapple juice. While he was paying his bill at the cash register he picked up several bars of candy from a display counter.

He stopped, for the last time, at a drugstore and took the Thermos jug inside with him. Stopping at the soda fountain he asked to have it filled with water. "I just bought it," he explained. "I want to see how long it keeps stuff cold."

While the clerk was filling it, he wandered to the back of the store and bought gauze bandages and iodine and adhesive tape. If the boy's knee was really infected, iodine might not be enough.

"I'd like to get some penicillin," he told the clerk.

The clerk stared at him. "You mean straight penicillin? You can't buy it without a doctor's prescription. You're not supposed to inject it yourself either."

He couldn't of course, get a prescription. "The iodine will do," he said. He hoped it really would do.

When he left the drugstore he turned on the car radio for the six o'clock news broadcast. The kidnapping was the lead story on the news program. It consisted of one fact — the kidnapped boy was still missing and no further word had been received from the kidnapers — the rest of the commentary was police conjectures and promises. Morgan drove into the now-familiar spot behind the boiler room as the news program ended. He turned off the radio and got out of the car with the Thermos jug dragging at one arm and the remaining packages encircled by the other. He had to put them down outside while he unlocked the door and then again on the inside while he relocked the door. When he picked them up again they were heavy and awkward so he clasped both hands around them like a pregnant woman holding her stomach to climb a flight of stairs. He could just see over the packages; he couldn't look down at all, and therefore didn't notice the blood smears that Mollison had tried to cover with coal dust after he dragged Patsy's body across the floor. He had to put the packages down again to drag open the door leading into the main section of the mill, and he swore petulantly. When he did pass through into the main room, he stumbled over a box of the card spindles and nearly fell. Somehow he blamed the Anacosta boy for this; he was making him go to a great deal of trouble. Angry at the boy, angry with himself, he finally reached the landing and the door leading to the room where the boy was a prisoner.

He could see fairly well by the light from the landing door, once he had opened it; enough to make out the huddled form of the boy, apparently asleep, in the same corner of the room where he had left him. Morgan felt a brief flicker of dismay when there was no stirring under the dirty blanket. If he were dead? Impossible. Nothing could hurt him here. He said too loudly in the quiet of the dingy room, "I'm back. I've brought you some stuff."

There was movement under the blanket at the sound of his voice, and Morgan felt some relief as he put down the clumsy packages, and fumbled for the burned-out flashlight. He unscrewed the base, shook the dead batteries into his hand and inserted new ones. The boy, who had sat up, seemed to recoil from the sudden light, blinking his eyes like an animal caught in the glare of headlights. He asked, "Are you going to take me home now?"

Morgan said, "Not yet." He felt the distaste of a literate man at the use of the word, "kid," so he repeated, feeling an old sense of bondage with the boy merely from the use of his name, "Not yet, Carmen. Pretty soon now."

He had expected the boy to wail, to cry, to beg. Instead he sank back on his blanket rather listlessly, as if he had known and been resigned to the answer in advance. "My knee hurts worse," was his only complaint.

Morgan puttered with his packages. "We'll fix it," he promised.

He glanced about for the package of paper cups he had brought in the morning. They were where he had left them. The cold meat and the remainder of the milk were untouched. "I'll get you something to eat," he said, "then we'll fix your knee. What about a sandwich?"

The boy said indifferently, "I don't feel like one. I want a drink."

"Sure," Morgan said, almost jovially. "Sure. What will it be — milk? Water? How about some tomato juice or some pineapple juice?" He listed the supplies as if proud of their profusion, feeling almost happy that he could offer some relief to this miserable child.

The boy said, "Pineapple juice, I guess."

Morgan reached for the can and remembered that he had not brought an opener. He was tempted to tell the boy to drink milk but almost immediately he remembered the boxes of steel card spindles that were stacked on the floor below. They looked like stilettos. They were sharp; they would most certainly puncture the thin shell of the tin can of fruit juice. "I'll be right back," he promised, and hurried down the stairs to get a spindle.

Back in the room again, he made two small punctures in the can and handed it to the boy. He drank half of it, and Morgan said, "Now let me make you a sandwich."

"I'm not hungry," the boy repeated.

It would be better if the boy would eat. Nothing at all since morning? Weren't boys supposed to be always hungry? Uneasily Morgan said, "You ought to have something." An idea came to him. "I'll tell you what, I've got some water and soap here. You let me get it ready for you and you wash up and brush your teeth and it will make you feel better. Then we'll look at your knee." A clean-up would have made him feel better if he were dirty and miserable — why not the boy?

The boy sat up. "I've got to go to the bathroom," he said.

Morgan said, "Sure. I'll help you. It's right over there."

"I had to go once today already but I couldn't see when I got there," the boy said. "I only made water though. I had to do it on the floor."

"That's all right," Morgan reassured him. He helped the boy to his feet and led him toward the filthy bathroom that opened off the room. He held the light for the boy and then helped him back toward the blanket when he was through, noticing now that the boy was limping badly. He splashed water from the Thermos jug into the basin and helped the boy wash, delaying as long as he could his examination of the scraped knee. When he did finally roll the boy's trouser leg back to look at the knee he was shocked to see that it was swollen almost half again its normal thickness. A heavy scab had formed over the injury but there was a hard and granular red margin about the scab. What germs were there in this ancient mill? What filth, what bacteria, what microbe had gotten into the wound? Morgan imagined for a moment that there was an evil odor to the wound. He said in a falsely cheerful voice, "It will be all right. You'll see." He fumbled out the bottle of iodine and tried to paint it on the wound with the glass stylus that was attached to the rubber cork. It kept scraping against the scab, letting the yellow-brown iodine trickle uselessly down the healthy skin surrounding the injury. Morgan finally wet a tiny corner of the towel directly from the bottle and swabbed the wound with it. The boy did not flinch — and wasn't that a bad sign? Wasn't iodine supposed to sting? Maybe they had fixed it somehow so it wouldn't, he told himself. He wrapped gauze around the knee and pulled the trouser leg down again. "There," he told the boy. "That didn't hurt, did it?"

"I guess not."

The boy still did not want to eat. Looking at him Morgan could see a certain grayish pallor in his face. The boy's forehead was dry and warm to the touch. It was only natural, wasn't it, that he would have a little fever — with a knee like that and the shock of being taken away and hidden in this little room, half scared to death?

Morgan gathered up the bread and the meat and the milk that he had brought in the morning, leaving only the fresh food. The room smelled bad enough without adding the odor of spoiled food. He said, "I've got to go now, Carmen. I'll be back in the morning and pretty soon it will be safe to take you home."

The boy stirred. "Will you leave the flashlight again?" he asked, with the first sign of interest he had shown.

"Sure I will," Morgan promised, and was immediately caught up by a new idea. There was a light in the boiler room, wasn't there? Then there must be current in some of the lines in the old mill — maybe in this very room. He shone the light toward the door land saw the expected switch. Swinging the light in a vertical angle he saw a dusty fixture overhead. He stared toward the switch and hesitated. Would a light be seen from outside? No. There were no windows in this room. He had checked that before he used the flashlight on the night he had brought the boy here. The door to the inner room was locked and tight. What little light might escape under the door would never find its way into the night. He flicked the switch with his forefinger. There was the customary click but the room remained dark. He felt a bitter disappointment. And then he remembered a metal fusebox set into the wall on the landing; something he had half seen, half noted. He went out to the landing and pulled the cover on the box. There were half a dozen circuit-breaker switches in the box, neatly labeled, *Hall, Outer Office, Inner Office,* and so on. Inner office? Would that be the room where the boy was — or would that be the outer office? He glanced again at the switches and saw that they were neatly ranked in the position marked *Off.* Hurrying back into the room he searched for and found the key to the adjoining office. He opened the door and made sure that the light switch was off, masking the flashlight with his cupped hand because this office had windows. He closed the door but did not lock it and went back to the landing. He threw the switch marked *Outer Office* and immediately there was the warm glow of light streaming out onto the landing. Morgan hurried back to the closed door of what he had proved to be the inner office. He glanced inside just to be certain that no light had come on, and then he closed and locked the door again. He felt a tremendous exultation. He had provided light. Faraday and Edison and a forgotten electrician had helped Lou Morgan to mitigate his sins.

When he had made his way back to his car, locking all the doors of his passage, he felt suddenly drained, unable to summon the will to get away from the place. That poor scared kid up there alone in the old factory, waiting for Morgan to set him free. And for what, for what, had Morgan done this to him? For the ransom? For money to cover his thefts from the bank and free him of Anacosta? For money that would let him pretend to a social and economic position that were beyond him? Money was not enough, would never be enough, just as Argonne Street, by itself hadn't been enough. You were something or you were nothing. Or you were a kidnaper. And if you were a kidnaper, you couldn't atone enough. Still, he was doing the best he could to save the boy, wasn't he? If Mollison had had his way, the boy would be dead by this time. He started up the car and drove toward his rooming house. On the way he stopped and threw out the stale food he had taken from the mill. Friday. There would be five more days of this.

At three o'clock in the morning, Patsy Galuk came to sit on the foot of Howard Mollison's bed and gibber at him. Mollison awoke with a soundless gasping scream, and Patsy vanished. Mollison had been sleeping fitfully; now he woke fully to find his clothing soaked with sweat. He could smell on his own body, the odor of fear. He sat up, his mouth open and working as he sought for breath. The thought of the bottle that stood on the bedside table was immediately reassuring, as though a promise of salvation. He reached for it and drank greedily, scarcely tasting the liquor. After a time he closed his eyes, but he opened them again immediately. In his half-conscious state he was afraid that Patsy might come back again to sit on the foot of the bed. He waited for his head to clear, for the alcohol to take hold and give him back his reason.

There had been a recurrent dream since he had thrown himself on the bed hours earlier. He had been walking in a strange place, holding his hands before him to protect his face against something. Vines? Spider webs? Something. And those hands had swollen to monstrous size; had become great, pulpy balls of flesh with sausage fingers. Alternately they had shrunk, dwindling to nothing at all while he screamed and wept. And Patsy Galuk had been in the dream, so that Mollison had awakened to see him sitting on the foot of the bed, and he had looked to see if the grotesque head were really beaten into a red paste. Somehow it hadn't been, although he remembered how Patsy had looked when he had hidden him in the coal pile. Patsy had looked almost as normal — and as real — as ever.

Several minutes passed before Mollison was able to distinguish between what he had seen and what he had dreamed and to come to the sheepish conclusion that he had been through a nightmare. He glanced at the clock on the bureau. Three o'clock. Ten minutes past three, exactly. He measured the whisky remaining in the bottle. There were four hours stretching in front of him before he could get up and go down into the daylight. Four hours. He would have to ration the liquor carefully, try to reach a stage that would leave him alert enough to keep Patsy away but would not betray him into full sleep where the nightmare could get at him.

He tried to think what he would do now. They — he and Morgan — would have to get rid of Patsy's body as soon as possible. Tomorrow — today, really, at the latest. He gave up thinking, content to leave it to the mind and iron nerve of Lou Morgan. He would tell Lou first thing in the morning and let him plan what they should do. He had done his share. He had silenced Patsy, hadn't he?

Mollison never questioned in his own mind his abrupt change in attitude toward Lou Morgan. He had, before the kidnapping, considered him prissy, almost effeminate. He'd had doubts about Morgan's courage in carrying out his assignment in the crime. Now, because Morgan had volunteered to kill the Anacosta kid and hide his body — because Morgan had coldly and scornfully warned Mollison to brace up — Mollison had surrendered his leadership. He had surrendered it willingly, gladly. It was easy to let go, to let Morgan be responsible for whatever thinking had to be done. It did not occur to him that in so doing he was also trying to give Morgan the responsibility for the crime itself. Because Mollison, to this hour, had felt not the slightest remorse for what had been done. And if he wished Morgan to have the responsibility for the kidnapping and the murder, he told himself, it was only because of his sensible desire to escape a terrible punishment if they were caught.

Shortly after seven o'clock — it was now Saturday—-Mollison got up from the bed. He could no longer endure the knowledge of Patsy Galuk buried in a coal pile with his head battered in. He had to share it.

He drove through the empty streets toward the rooming house where Morgan stayed. The front door was unlocked; he walked in to a hall that held half a dozen urns filled with Boston ferns and elephant plants. There was a wide staircase, and he climbed it to another hall, this one running the width of the building. He could almost guess which door led to Lou Morgan's room, having seen Morgan leaning out the window when he had come here earlier — Lord, was it only yesterday? He called softly, "Morgan, hey — Lou."

Morgan was already awake and half dressed. He opened his door and saw Mollison standing in the hall, and his first sensation was one of shock. Mollison's face was a yellowish-white, with the bristles of his beard showing as black specks, almost like the pinfeathers on a plucked chicken.

His hair was uncombed and his clothes rumpled. He looked fifteen years older than the dapper salesman who used to chatter with

Morgan at the club. Morgan said, "Good God, what are you doing here? Come in before somebody sees you."

Mollison walked into the room and sat on the edge of the bed. Morgan shut the door and turned to face him, aware that he could actually smell Mollison, who gave off an odor of alcohol and perspiration. Morgan remembered the way Mollison had responded to his earlier bullying. He made his expression coldly scornful. "You look like a wino from skid row," he said bitingly. "You need a bath."

Mollison said humbly, "I know, Lou. I had a hell of a night." He didn't mind that Morgan was sneering at him, contemptuous of him. He accepted this as further evidence of Morgan's cold nerve, Morgan's taking charge. "Lou," he continued, "Patsy's dead." It sounded better that way, better than "I killed Patsy."

Morgan had been putting on a clean shirt. He stopped with his arms halfway through the sleeves and demanded, "What did you say?"

Mollison repeated, "Patsy's dead. I had to kill him."

When Morgan said nothing for a moment Mollison rushed on. "I had to stop him," he said. "I went out to the club yesterday noon and he knew all about it, Lou. I could tell just from the way he looked at me. Cripes, you could read his face like a book."

Morgan had been briefly stunned. Now he began to realize that, whatever Mollison had done, the police didn't know about it yet or Mollison wouldn't be sitting here explaining. He said, "Go on."

"I didn't think he'd figure it out," Mollison said. "You know the fairy tale I told him about some guys owing me money, to explain about us having the kid. Anyway, right after I got there he sneaked out of the club. I followed him and he headed right for the mill."

Morgan began to button his shirt slowly. "And you killed him for that?"

Mollison's voice took on a whining note. "I told you, Lou, he knew all about it." He went on, a little resentfully, "I never thought Patsy would turn against me even if he did know. He knew and he was going right to the mill to see if the kid was still there. He probably wanted to be a big hero. I got him in the car and took him to the mill, told him I wanted to go back and check to see if everything was locked up."

Morgan felt a real pity for Patsy. But then he reminded himself that he had been going to betray Patsy and Mollison to the police on Wednesday, anyway — telling them where the boy was equaled betrayal. And once the boy talked . . .

Mollison went on. "Don't forget, Lou," he said, "you're in this as much as me."

"Don't be an ass," Morgan told him. "It isn't a question of who did it. Where did you kill him? In the boiler room?"

"Yes."

"How did you do it?"

"I hit him on the head with a bottle." Mollison shuddered. "He wouldn't stay down, Lou. He kept trying to get up and I thought he'd kill me. I took an iron bar from the furnace and I kept hitting him."

"Did you leave him there?"

"I couldn't move him by myself. I dragged him over and pushed coal down on top of him. Nobody can see him unless they know he's there and look for him. Can't we take him and put him in the same place as the kid?"

Morgan said scathingly, "You're not very bright, Howie. Suppose they found the two bodies together, how long do you think it would take for them to trace Patsy back to the club?" He had to be convincing. Mollison had already asked to see the place where he'd said he'd buried the boy's body. A persistent evasion might make him suspicious again if no valid reason went with it. "And if they traced him back to the club, it wouldn't take them five minutes more to start thinking about you. Everybody would tell them that Patsy always hung around you. We'll get rid of him somewhere else. Have you been out to the club since then?"

Mollison shook his head.

"Why did you wait until now to tell me about this?"

"I tried to call you, Lou. I called the bank but you were out to lunch. So I had a drink to try and settle my nerves and then I guess I had quite a few."

"I guess you did. You're a foul sight right now. You can't go to work looking like that. Did you show up at all yesterday?"

"No, but I called in to say I wouldn't be there."

"You'd better show up today. Not like that. You'll have to go home and take a shower and clean up. You've got to get hold of yourself. If you start walking around looking like a tramp, people will start wondering about you. We can't afford to have people wondering about you."

"I know, Lou. I'll go home and clean up. It was just that I kept thinking about Patsy and I had to tell you about it." He felt better. Lou had taken command and everything would be all right now.

Morgan, fighting for time to think, said, "You haven't been out to the club since Patsy left there, so you'd better show up there, too. I'll go myself about noon. Try to get there a little after that. And listen — when you get there look around the place and ask, 'Where's Patsy?' Don't wait for somebody to ask you. You ask first. You'd better get moving now. You should get to the agency on time — and try not to attract any attention."

After Mollison left, Morgan went to the window and watched him emerge from the door and walk to his car, foreshortened from this angle. Morgan, looking down into the sunny street, felt something of the same sense of isolation from humanity that had driven Mollison into the saloon after he had killed Patsy. Turning from the window he picked up his car keys. He wanted to go quickly to the boy in the mill. He had been shocked by Mollison's report of murder, but he was a party to that murder — and to an even more loathsome crime. He supposed Patsy would be missed for a while at the club but he doubted if there would be a serious attempt made to locate him. The greatest danger in Patsy's death was in its effect on Mollison, who was obviously cracking up. He would have to help him pull himself together for just a few days longer and then it wouldn't matter. As for Patsy's body, it could stay where it was, in the mill. He would have to work something out to tell Mollison — tell him that he'd taken care of the body himself, for some reason or other — and then he would drag it back into the main part of the mill in case Mollison wanted to see for himself that Patsy had been taken care of. Sometime between now and noon he would think of something to tell Mollison.

Chapter 17

Mollison walked into the auto agency office only a few minutes late. On the way in he had met Eddie, the mechanic who had guessed at his manipulation of the green Hudson, and Eddie had said nothing, just grinned at him. Grinned strangely, Mollison thought. As if he knew something. Mollison walked past the girl at the file desk and said, "Hello, Betty. Can I sell you a good used car?" He tried hard to affect the old confidence and swagger, but he missed the mark and he knew it.

Betty looked at him doubtfully. "Lillian wants to see you," she said. "She tried to get you yesterday after you called."

"Didn't you give her my message?" Mollison asked.

"I told her," Betty said. "It was after that that she tried to reach you. She's sore about something."

There had been a time when Mollison would have said — and meant — "She can go to hell." Now he felt only a sick worry. The bank. It must have been the bank. Somebody had caught up with the winding trail of paper transactions he had made. He asked anxiously, "What's it about, Betty? You got any idea?" He wanted to ask her if Lillian Kramer had had a call from the bank before she started looking for him, but he couldn't bring himself to do it.

Betty shook her head. "I don't know, Howie," she told him.

"Is she in?"

"Not yet."

"I'll be out on the lot," he told her. "Call me on the PA speaker when she comes in."

Lillian Kramer came half an hour later. When Mollison heard Betty paging him on the PA system, he excused himself from a customer with a muttered, "I'll be back," and hurried into the office, wanting to get it over with. He had no strength in him, no spirit. Nothing to fight with, to lie with, to hedge or bluff with.

Lillian was seated at her desk in her private office. She looked up as he came in and said, "You, Howie. Sit down. I'll be with you in a minute." After the minute — Mollison spent it trying to light a cigarette that he didn't want — she looked up again. "I think you've been stealing money from me, Howie. The banks are closed today so I can't do much about it. I'm going to find out Monday morning — unless you want to tell me about it now."

Mollison started to protest and she interrupted him. "Don't waste my time lying, Howie. I had a call from the bank at two o'clock yesterday afternoon. They said that they had some of our paper on a man named Swanson and that the residence and place of employment he gave are phony. I looked at our sales records. We don't have any Swansons. The address this Swanson gave is a private club. They know you there, Howie. I called. So don't lie. Just let me know how much you've gotten into me for. After that I don't want to hear anything. I don't want to know anything. Just tell me how much and how soon you're going to get the money back to me."

Ah well, Mollison thought, there had always been the chance that the bank would check. Now that he was caught he accepted it fatalistically enough. Because there was no other way out, he began to tell her about the phony sales. When he was half finished Lillian reached for the telephone. Mollison said, "Wait, Lil."

"Don't call me Lil, you crooked bastard."

How he hated her, the fat, self-satisfied bitch, sitting there with his very life in her hands, but he crawled. "Wait, Mrs. Kramer," he pleaded. "You're not calling the police, are you?"

"Why not? You stole my money. I've got to make good at the bank."

"If you do that," he said, "they'll tie up whatever money I've got. Look — I can pay you back now." He tried to regain a little of his dignity. "I only borrowed the money for a little while, Lil — Mrs. Kramer. I made a deal and I got it back. I can give you every cent of it. I can pay up every note and you'll still have the cars. You haven't got anything to lose."

She showed the interest that he had expected when he mentioned paying the money back. "How soon can you pay it back?" she demanded. "I won't go for any salary deduction pitch."

He said hastily, "Today. Today, Mrs. Kramer. I'll have it for you in an hour. It comes to just over five thousand. If you pay the notes off with it right away you'll save almost six hundred dollars in interest over the face value of the notes."

"Where are you going to get that kind of money in cash on a Saturday?"

He was aware of the desperate risk in admitting possession of so much when the whole city knew that a ransom had been paid within the last two days, but he had no choice. Money — immediately available — was all that was going to keep her from putting him in jail. His mind flickered to a sudden thought. Suppose he let her put him in jail; let her charge him with embezzlement. Would they look for a kidnaper in the city jail? He rejected the thought with regret. He knew that he could not stand to be locked away, with no knowledge of what Morgan might be doing or how the police were progressing. Not without losing his mind. He reached for a lie. "I only used a little of the money I got from the bank," he said. "I thought I was going to need more than I did. I've still got most of what I got from them. The rest I made on a little deal." He could only hope that she would not press him for details about the deal. His brain was incapable of making any further effort.

She stood up. "I'll go with you," she said.

"That's all right That's all right, Mrs. Kramer," he assured her. "I don't blame you." He hesitated. "After you get the money, are you going to prosecute me?"

She looked at him coldly. "I don't know what I ever saw in you, Howie," she said. "I'll hold off until Monday. If it turns out that you don't owe more than you've told me about, I *might* let it drop. Or I might not."

An hour later she stood on the sidewalk in front of Mollison's apartment house. She had accompanied him to the door of his rooms; she even checked to see that there was no fire escape before she agreed to wait in the hall while he got the money.

"I'll take the car," she said. "If you use a Kramer car again it will be because you bought it. And don't forget to come in Monday morning while we go over your crooked paper."

He said, "Yes, Mrs. Kramer."

"And don't try to leave town. If you do I'll have a fugitive warrant sworn out so fast it will make your nose bleed."

She drove off noisily. Mollison watched her go, and while he watched he shivered with inarticulate rage. He felt as though she had emasculated him, outraged him. He would have given a great share of the remaining ransom money to drive his fist into her face, over and over again. . . .

Louis Morgan left his rooming house a half hour after Mollison. He walked to the garage and backed his car out, and it was only after he had gotten out and closed and locked the door that it occurred to him that he had not even bothered to look and see that the hiding place where he had placed his share of Anacosta's money had not been disturbed. He drove toward the Maynard Mill through the bright morning, stopping only for a cup of coffee for himself and a cup of tea in a paper carton for the boy. He had a vague recollection of his mother serving tea instead of coffee to him on cold mornings, and of her explanation that coffee was somehow bad for children's nerves. Not that this was a cold morning, but a hot drink might just make the boy feel better. As an afterthought, he ordered two fried egg sandwiches to be wrapped to go. The thought of fried egg sandwiches at this hour of the day was nauseous, but eggs were symbolic of a good breakfast and there was no other way he could carry them.

He drove into the alley and across the paved parking strip to the boiler room. Getting out of the car, he remembered the clumsy routine of last night; the putting down and picking up of his packages while he struggled with the doors. He would, he decided, leave the paper bag full of food in the car while he unlocked the outer door and pushed back the inside one. He was halfway to the door when he heard the sputter of wheels and the dying sound of a switched-off engine. Key in hand, he turned. A black sedan with a white police shield painted on its side had nosed in behind his own car, effectively blocking it. A uniformed policeman got out of the car and walked ponderously toward him.

Morgan's immediate thought was that Mollison had finally cracked up — certainly he had been on the edge of it when he left Morgan's house — and had been picked up. No, there hadn't been time for that. Or Patsy — oh, God, Patsy was twenty feet away on the floor of the boiler room. But they couldn't have found him or this policeman wouldn't be walking toward him now with his hand nowhere near his gun. He could do nothing now except be grateful that he had left the food container in the car.

The policeman glanced from side to side as he came up. Sizing up the car, the registration plates, and Lou Morgan. He asked mildly, "Have you got business around here, mister?" If his suit had been rumpled, the shirt dirty, the face unshaved, the manner would have been vastly different, Morgan supposed. Now he had to act unruffled, businesslike; had to conform to his own appearance.

Morgan said firmly, "I certainly have, officer." He volunteered no further information. He hoped that he had already disarmed the policeman some by his dress and manner. Policemen had to be careful, he supposed, when it came to dealing with the neat and the clean. Now let him make the next move, reveal what his purpose was, what he knew or guessed.

The policeman said — uneasily? — "I was talking with the night boss in the little plastic shop over there." He gestured toward the bulk of the mill where the little fly-by-night concerns rented space. "He said he'd seen cars stopping up this way. Thought they might be stripping the piping out of the mill."

Morgan frowned. "Piping?"

"They do that," the policeman explained. "Go into these old mills and take the piping right out. Lot of it is lead. They sell it to the junk dealers." His tone indicated that he knew very well that a man of Morgan's appearance would not be stealing scrap metal, but he did not move on. His attitude indicated that he would wait as patiently as necessary for Morgan's explanation.

Morgan said, "Oh yes. I've heard of that happening. Well, that's not what I'm doing here." Small joke. Small joke while he thought.

"I'm with the Drummond Company," he lied boldly. "You've heard of them. Industrial Architects. Our offices are out of town, in the state capital. We're making a survey to see how much it would cost to modernize this old ark." There was no Drummond Company and Morgan decided to flavor the lie with a little half truth. "The agency that handles the building has been having trouble trying to get rid of it."

The policeman nodded affably. "I hear that Decker was trying to unload," he said. He gave no sign that he intended to leave, and Morgan knew that the next move was up to him. He could not just stand here, talking to the policeman. What had Mollison said? "I pushed coal down on top of him." Morgan had to move — and he could only hope that Mollison had pushed enough coal; that he had sufficiently covered Patsy Galuk's body so that it would escape a casual glance.

He fumbled with the key in the lock of the door, making it obvious that he *had* a key for whatever substance it would lend to his story of surveying the mill. The policeman waited patiently. When Morgan swung the door open he followed him in, glancing about with some interest. Morgan stared at the coal pile; he could not help himself. It seemed prosaic enough. No outstretched hand. No outline suggesting a human figure. Oh God. There was a black shoe sticking out of the bottom of the pile. He walked toward the pile, partially cutting off the policeman's vision.

"Dirty old place," the policeman said. He gazed at the window where Mollison had hung the blanket. "Wonder what that's there for?"

Morgan saw the empty whisky bottle that Mollison had flung aside after clubbing Patsy with it. "I imagine the night fireman used to have some parties in here," he said.

"There's one of his bottles on the floor." God — was that a trace of blood on the bottle? Would the cop notice it?

The policeman nodded. "That's probably it," he agreed. "Or maybe some of the winos from over on the avenue have been getting in and using the place for a flop." He turned toward the door. "I hope Decker decides to modernize the place and get some tenants in here. This end of the city has been dead for too long as it is. Well — I'll see you."

Morgan nodded his head — he could not bring himself to try and speak — and the policeman left. Morgan heard the growl of the starter and the crunching of the wheels as the police car backed and turned. When he was sure that the cruiser was gone, he went to his own car and got the packages containing the sandwiches and tea. He had been lucky, unbelievably lucky. Apparently the policeman had never connected the kidnapping with the presence of strangers in the mill. If he had, if he had even remotely considered that there might be a connection, he would not have been satisfied with a mere glance at the boiler room. He hadn't even asked Morgan's name. He'd had the preconceived idea that someone might be stealing pipe from the mill. Since Morgan was obviously not a vandal or a thief, he had been satisfied. If the policeman had had the slightest bit of imagination — but he hadn't. Morgan had no guarantee that the next one would be as dull.

He locked the door behind him and made his way along the now familiar route to the room where the boy was imprisoned. The light was still burning and he left it on while he hurried toward the boy. He was asleep. His breathing was shallow and very fast and his forehead, when Morgan touched it, felt very warm. He awoke at Morgan's touch but he did not try to sit up; instead he lay quite still, staring up at Morgan.

Morgan said, "I brought you some eggs and some tea."

The boy answered listlessly, "I don't want any. I don't feel like eating."

Looking at him Morgan could see his lips were cracked — and dry. "How about some juice?" he asked. "There's still some tomato juice left." The boy had not asked, this time, when he was going to be taken home, and this worried Morgan as much as the boy's obvious fever. He couldn't just give up. It was only until Wednesday. Morgan reached for the Thermos jug. There was still water in it. He wet the end of the towel he had brought earlier and bathed the boy's forehead. "How about drinking some of that juice now?" he repeated.

The boy said disinterestedly, "All right."

Morgan searched around for the card spindle he had used to puncture the pineapple juice can. He jabbed two holes in the tomato juice can and held it to the boy's lips. He drank several swallows and then pushed it away. "I don't want any more," he said.

Morgan watched helplessly as the boy's eyes closed again and he drifted into an apparent light sleep. He told himself that that was best, that sleep was the great healer; but he made a poor argument of it. He felt an odd mixture of deep pity for the boy and an angry frustration that he had had to add to Morgan's problems by becoming sick. After a moment he pushed the blanket away and, as gently as he could, shoved the boy's trouser leg up. The flesh around the bandaged knee was swollen hard and tight and the reddened area around the wound had spread upward and downward. He pulled the trouser leg down again and said softly, "Carmen?"

The boy made no answer. Morgan said, "I'll leave the tea and sandwiches. And I'll come back to see you this afternoon. All right? Do you want me to bring you anything?" Morgan asked hopefully.

The boy did not open his eyes. "Some comic books, I guess," he said.

Morgan said, "I'll bring you a whole lot of them."

The boy was sleeping when Morgan left the room and locked the door behind him. He made his way back through the mill toward the boiler room, getting away from the boy but not getting away from reality. The boy needed medical care and he needed it soon. Without it he might not survive until Wednesday. Morgan paused to consider this. All of his planning had been based on keeping the boy upstairs until he himself could leave the city without arousing interest. The teller's audit was to be held on Monday and he had not considered leaving before then. He asked himself why and decided that it was habit. His books and cash were in immaculate order. What if he left now — this afternoon — and called the police from — say — New York? By the time they talked to the boy and learned that men named Patsy and Lou and Howie had kidnapped him and went on from there to find out who Patsy and Howie and Lou were, he could be on a train for still another city. He had been concerned with the reaction of the people at the bank. But sooner or later, whether or not he waited until Wednesday, they would learn that Morgan was a kidnaper and a party to a murder. He wondered if he had been making excuses to himself to avoid tearing up whatever roots held him to this place. No matter. He would go this afternoon.

He stopped in the boiler room and looked at the coal pile. After a brief consideration he walked toward it with coal dust gritting under his feet. He found a board and scraped more coal down from the pile so that Patsy's foot was covered. Then he left.

The change in his plans meant he would have to move quickly. There were clothes at the cleaners and laundry to be picked up. He thought about this and then mocked his own frugality. The clothes could not be worth over fifty dollars or so. He had, under the floor of the garage, almost forty thousand dollars of Anacosta's money. What else? The car? He would leave it in a garage somewhere and take an airline limousine to the airport. It came to him that there was no one to say good-by to, nothing in this city that he loved or would miss. So easy it was to leave. So quick.

He stopped at a drugstore and went in to call the airport. There was a flight to New York leaving at two in the afternoon and, yes, he could have a reservation. The name, please?

Morgan hesitated while he considered using a false name. It wouldn't make much difference, he decided. Once the word went out to look for Louis Morgan — age such and such, height, weight — a false name would only delay the police briefly. And if it were detected now, it could endanger his escape before he even started. He gave his correct name.

Actually, now that he had only three hours left to make his farewell to a city where he had spent his entire life, he had time to spare. There would be time to pick up the dry cleaning, if he wanted. Time to pack — and there was something to do. Buy a decent suitcase. He had never owned a real leather bag. He would stop at a luggage store and get one. Then he would get his money from under the garage floor and go home to pack. Suddenly he was very anxious to be gone. He got back into his old car and drove toward the better shopping district.

Chapter 18

Mollison went back to his apartment after Lillian Kramer drove away. He paced the floor, thumping one big meaty fist into the open palm of his other hand in futile rage. He was completely humiliated. Somewhere, he remembered, he had lost his control over Louis Morgan. Since then he had become the whipping boy for everybody. Lillian Kramer, damn her. And Patsy, who had started out to betray him. Well, he had taken care of Patsy and some day, if things worked out, he would take care of Lillian Kramer. And Lou Morgan. Oh, Morgan was all right. He had disposed of the kid and he had been cool enough when he had learned of Patsy's murder. Except that he was acting a little too snotty.

Well, all right, then. He had had to pay Lillian off. He had come out of it pretty well after all. He still had more than thirty thousand dollars left. And he had been fired before. From better jobs than the one with Lillian, by God — and he wouldn't have to pay any more blackmail to that little rat of a mechanic, Eddie. All in all, forgetting the lousy way Lillian had treated him, it hadn't turned out so bad. He decided that he would drift over to the club and have a drink. He was out on the street before he remembered that Lillian Kramer had taken the car away. Swearing violently, he walked a few blocks to a bus stop.

He got to the club at eleven o'clock. It was noisy with the Saturday morning crowd and just hearing the greetings and the laughter, the bustle and confusion of the group at the bar, made him feel better. What had Morgan said? Ask for Patsy. Don't wait for them to ask you. He said hello to half a dozen men on his way to the bar. Fred, the manager, was filling in and Mollison said, "Hello, Fred. Let me have a Scotch and water." He paused just long enough to put a puzzled look on his face and continued, "Where's Patsy?"

Fred splashed water into a highball glass and pushed it toward Mollison. "I don't know," he said angrily. "He didn't show up last night either. The crazy bastard is never around when you need him."

Mollison said in a soothing voice, "Take it easy, Fred. Have one with me. Patsy probably got shacked up with something and decided to make a week end of it."

Fred mixed a drink for himself and held it up in brief salutation. "I suppose so," he agreed. "Or maybe he took a fit and got run over by a car or something."

"What do you mean, 'took a fit'?" Mollison asked. He had heard many things about Patsy — never that he was subject to fits.

Fred shrugged. "He's epileptic or something. Four or five years ago he threw one in a five and dime store downtown. I always said if he threw one in here I'd run him off the place." He started to move toward a more congested section of the bar. "Thanks for the drink, Howie," he said.

Mollison nodded. This new bit of information about Patsy could be important. He would be sure to remember to tell Lou Morgan about it. Maybe they could make something of it. Dump Patsy somewhere and let it look as if he got hit by a car or something. The fact that Patsy was an epileptic would make it seem logical that it could happen to him.

He had several more drinks, refused as many invitations to sit in on a gin rummy game. He wanted to see Morgan and he found himself, by noon, watching the clock over the bar. When the hands diverged to indicate half past twelve and Morgan had not appeared, he called to Fred.

"I've got to take a little ride," he said. "I've got a real bomber off the car lot. How's for letting me take your car for an hour or so?"

Fred said, "Sure, Howie," and tossed him the keys.

Morgan paid forty dollars for a pigskin bag and bought a few other items of comparable quality. But he did not particularly enjoy the purchases. The clerk who waited on him gave him the impression that he was fully aware that Morgan was not used to — probably didn't deserve — such fine things. He drove by his garage and took out the money that he had hidden there before he parked in front of the rooming house and went in to pack his clothes. He took his time — he had more than he needed of that — but even so, when he had folded the last necktie, when he had cleaned his personal toilet articles from the bathroom, it was only a few minutes after twelve-thirty. He had given some thought to Howard Mollison. He had agreed to meet him at the club about noon. Since he had decided to leave town immediately, there was no point in seeing Mollison. If he was going to crack up — and if he got drinking with the bunch at the club he probably would — let him. An hour after Morgan's plane landed in New York he intended to call the police and tell them where the Anacosta boy was. After that it wouldn't make much difference whether Mollison fell apart or not. They would be after him in a matter of hours, or maybe less.

He picked up the good pigskin bag and his older, cheaper one and glanced about the room. There was nothing of importance left. A newspaper. A pair of shoes that weren't worth packing. That was about it. He still had more than an hour to kill, and had a sudden impulse to see the Anacosta boy again. He couldn't help him — but he could tell him that he would be taken to his mother and father very soon now, and that would certainly make him feel better. What was it he had wanted? Comic books? He would stop and get a stack of them.

Mollison was a block away from Morgan's rooming house when he saw Morgan walk down the front walk to his car and put two suitcases in the back seat. He had halted at a stop sign, and for a moment, as he watched Morgan, he was too shocked to react. And then a violent, unthinking anger took hold of him. Morgan the cold, Morgan the iron-nerved, Morgan who had contemptuously told Mollison to straighten himself out, was running out. Mollison stabbed at the gas pedal intending to run Morgan off the road, to stop him any way he could. He was unfamiliar with the borrowed car. The carburetor was flooded with gasoline it could not vaporize, and the motor stalled. Mollison foolishly ground at the starter and pumped gas at the same time. The motor bucked and would not start. When he recovered enough of his composure to let the motor rest for a few moments, Morgan's car was far down the street. When Mollison did get the motor started, Morgan's car was no longer in sight. He followed in the direction Morgan had gone, knowing that Morgan might have turned off at any of a dozen intersections but unwilling to give up the chase while there was the slightest chance he might find him.

After the first violence of his anger had receded, he began to think of what he might do if he caught Morgan. If he had not stalled the car he would have intercepted him near the rooming house and, in his fury, he would have beaten Morgan, half killed him. Now he knew that to have done so would probably have been to expose and destroy them both. What he had to do now — if he caught up with Morgan — was to threaten him; make him help with Patsy's body. He had a weapon — Morgan had been the one who had actually killed the boy. No matter what the law said about both of them being guilty, Morgan had murdered the kid. Driving more evenly, Mollison thumped his fist against the wheel. What had Morgan said — act normal? Show up at your job? Don't call attention to yourself? So now the great Morgan was running away, leaving him to take the rap.

He saw Morgan's car again just before he reached the most heavily congested downtown area. The car was parked at a drugstore, and Morgan was not in sight. Mollison looked for a parking place. There was none. He pulled to his right and started to double park but immediately the cars behind him began to pile up. Some of the drivers honked their horns in outrage and a beat cop started a tentative step toward Mollison's car. He slipped it into gear again and pulled ahead. He was lucky. Four blocks farther on he found space to park. He shut off the motor and started to get out of the car, intending to walk back toward the drugstore. What would he do then? Walk with Morgan to his car; not let him get out of his reach. At that instant he saw Morgan, carrying a package of some sort, come out of the drugstore and walk quickly toward his own car. Mollison got back into the driver's seat. Morgan was almost sure to come this way; the intervening streets were hardly more than alleys. Maybe it would be better this way. He could intercept Morgan where there weren't so many people around. Then, if he had to use force, he might be able to do it without witnesses.

He let Morgan's car and several more go by before he slid the borrowed car out into the traffic. Morgan probably wouldn't recognize Fred's car, but it wouldn't hurt to be careful.

He followed steadily, curious at first about Morgan's route. This was not the way to any of the major highways leading out of the city. This was the way to — no. What would Morgan want to be going there for? After a time he had to believe it. Morgan was heading for the Maynard Mill.

When Morgan drove into the parking area behind the mill, Mollison stopped his car for a few moments. Morgan could not get away. There was no other way out of the place, and so he could give him time to get out of the car and give himself time to speculate on why Morgan had come back to this place. To see if Patsy's body was still there, perhaps? But why would he want to do that? How did he expect to get into the boiler room — unless he had a key — and hadn't it seemed to him that there weren't as many keys on the bunch that time he had gone back to get them? Mollison started the car again and drove around to the boiler room, stopping with a vicious stab at the brake just inches short of Morgan's car. Morgan was standing at the door with a key in one hand, a package in the other; he turned quickly as Mollison stopped and got out of the car. "Mollison!" He said it as if he didn't believe what he was seeing.

Mollison walked toward him, noticing that Morgan's face had gone a sick white. Scared blind. He had reason to be. He said, "Hello, Lou." Not angrily. Just fencing right now. There was time — plenty of time.

Morgan, not knowing how much Mollison knew or had guessed, said, "I wanted to see if everything was all right. I mean about Patsy. We've got to get him out of there, Howie."

Mollison said, "I know. Where did you get the key, Lou?"

Morgan could think of no quick lie. He was actually sick now with physical fear. He was no match for Mollison, fat and clumsy as Mollison was.

"Get inside, you bastard," Mollison said and crowded behind Morgan, pushing against him. When they were inside he said, "Turn on the light." As Morgan reached for the light Mollison slapped his face. "Tell me about the key, Lou," he said. "Tell me about the suitcases you've got in the car." He slapped Morgan again, and Morgan went to his knees with tears of pain coming to his eyes.

"Cut it out, Howie," Morgan said, knowing that he had lost any control over the bigger man. Mollison wasn't going to cut it out.

Mollison felt his manhood returning to him. Lillian had made him crawl. Eddie the mechanic had squeezed him for money — and the little man, Griffin. And this miserable wreck had sneered at him, told him what he should do. Now look at him. On his knees, crying like a baby or the neighborhood sissy when the local bully belts him one and knocks his bag of groceries out of his hand. The package — Morgan had dropped it when he went to his knees. Now he was trying to pick it up. Mollison kicked it out of his hand. It tore open and a rainbow of bright pictures cascaded out of it. Comic books. Comic books, for God's sake. Comic books?

"You bastard," Mollison said. "Where have you got him, Lou?" He glanced around the room. "Not here. Where is he, Lou?" He moved toward Morgan, his mouth working.

Morgan scrambled to his feet. There was a piece of board on the floor. He snatched it up and swung it at Mollison's face, hitting him on the forehead. The skin split and a red mask of blood formed immediately, blinding Mollison.

Morgan started for the door but Mollison backed toward it, blocking it so that Morgan could only run into the main section of the mill. He slammed the door behind him, hoping to gain a little time if it stuck; it did. He was halfway down the vast room when he heard Mollison roaring after him. "I'll get you. I'm going to kill you, Lou!"

He raced toward the stairs leading to the room where the boy was. Behind him he heard Mollison, bellowing like something out of a nightmare. He fumbled with the key and got the door open just as Mollison reached the stairs. He was just able to get inside and lock the door again before Mollison hurled himself against it so that it shuddered on its hinges. He leaned against it, feeling the vibration as Mollison pounded on it with his fists. Mollison was berserk, shouting incoherent threats. In the corner on his blanket, the Anacosta boy stirred but did not sit up. He lay with his eyes open, watching Morgan.

The door was strong. Apparently it would stand up against Mollison's fists for a time. Morgan tried to think, to clear his head. He could not reason with Mollison — that was obvious. There was no way out of the room except the door leading, to the stairs — and Mollison waited there. Quiet, now. Planning? Plotting? Morgan thought that he could hear the bigger man's harsh breathing. There was the door to the inner office, of course, but it offered no means of escape.

From outside the door Mollison called, almost gently, "Lou? Lou, listen — you've got to let me in there. We can figure a way out. Lou? Lou?"

Morgan would sooner have let a tiger in the room. He made no answer and Mollison began to shout again, working himself into a frenzy that lasted for almost a minute. Then he was quiet again. Listening intently Morgan heard his footsteps receding down the stairs. He was crazy if he thought that would tempt him into coming out. After a few moments he heard the footsteps again and Mollison's voice. "All *right* then, damn you," he said through the door. "I gave you your chance."

There was a wide crack at the jamb of the warped door.

As Morgan watched, the thin edge of a sliver of steel probed through the crack. A screw driver? Some tool from the car? Morgan rushed toward the door; but even as he made the move, Mollison put his weight against the other end of the wedge and the door sprung far enough away for the lock to clear its socket. Mollison flung the door open and stood framed there, the blood blackening on his face.

He stepped into the room and stared toward the boy on the blanket. "I'm going to kill him, Lou," he said softly. "I'm going to kill him just the way we planned. You'll have the pleasure of watching. Then I'm going to kill you." He closed the door behind him and locked it.

Morgan backed toward the boy, shielding him. Mollison lashed out at him with his heavy fist. The blow caught Morgan on the bridge of the nose and he felt something break while a shockingly intense pain blinded him. He went down, grabbing at Mollison's legs. Mollison kicked at his face and walked past him.

Morgan, lying on the floor, rolled to his side and tried to get up. He ignored the pain, forgot his terror. He could not let Mollison kill the boy. The steel spindle that he had used to open the fruit juice cans was within reach. It was pointed at both ends so that it made an awkward stabbing instrument. He wadded a handkerchief In his palm and picked up the ugly piece of metal and crawled to where Mollison, his back turned, knelt beside the boy. He got to his knees and thrust the spindle as hard as he could into Mollison's wide back. It was surprisingly difficult to puncture the flesh deeply. The pointed steel cut through the web of his own thumb, but he hardly felt it. Mollison screamed in pain and tried to turn around, and Morgan withdrew the spindle and struck again with all of his strength. This time the steel went in very deep. Mollison shuddered and coughed and pitched forward over, the boy's body. Morgan got to his feet and shoved

Mollison's body aside. The boy's eyes were closed, and Morgan, in swift panic bent over him. No, he was breathing. Probably fainted from shock and fright — but he was burning with fever.

He felt nauseated now. Patsy lying dead under the coal pile downstairs. Mollison — probably dead — lying here. Nauseated and bone-deep weary. But he was free now. He could go downstairs and get one of his bags and take some clean clothes from it. There was a little water left in the Thermos jug. He could wash most of the blood from his broken face and he could get in the car and go out to the airport. He could, except that he was too tired, and suddenly there seemed no point in running.

The boy would describe him, probably would even remember his name. And even if he didn't, they'd begin to connect him with Mollison — from the club, from remembered bits of conversation at the bar. They'd find both he and Mollison owed money. And his sudden disappearance from town — who ever heard of good old, steady Lou Morgan suddenly taking off on a trip? Where would he go. Why? They'd put it all together and they'd come after him. So why bother? Why run from the inevitable? Why run from something that he had coming to him — that was really what it was all about, wasn't it? Lou Morgan — he had to smile at his own dramatics — was going to have to pay. And suddenly he felt almost relieved. Because suddenly, for one of the few times in his life, he also felt like a man. . . .

Morgan bent down and picked up the limp body of the Anacosta boy who stirred and mumbled but did not awaken fully. Down the stairs and out to the car. Mollison's borrowed car because his strength was melting from him and he couldn't be bothered backing it out of the way so that he could use his own car.

Drive through the streets, catching a glimpse of a startled expression here and again when people saw his bloody face. Seeing the familiar buildings but seeing them somehow through the eyes of a stranger.

The familiar buildings. The post office. After a while, the hospital. He drove following the pointed arrows that said *Emergency Room,* because this was certainly an emergency. The pain was building up again, making things blur. He parked the car helter-skelter, blocking the driveway and paying no attention when someone shouted, "Hey!" at him. He picked the boy up again and walked into the smell of disinfectants. There was a nurse at a desk and he ignored her, strode on into a room where there was an operating table with a white sheet on it and a young-looking intern who came toward him saying, "Who clobbered you?" even as he took the boy from him and put him on the table.

Morgan said, "I'm all right. I think the boy has an infection."

And then there were nurses and other doctors. They were grouped around the boy, and they were washing Morgan's face, and he tried to wave them away from him because if they knew what he had done they wouldn't want to help him. So he told them. After a little while there were policemen in the room in addition to the doctors and the nurses but the doctors kept on doing painful things to his nose and his punctured hand.

Before they took him away he asked the young intern, "Is he going to be all right?"

One of the policemen said, "What do you care, you son of a bitch?"

The intern said, "Take it easy. And we'll finish fixing him up before you take him out." To Morgan he said, "He's got a strep infection, maybe from that cut on his knee, and he's got a high fever to go with it. He's in rough shape from neglect and shock. He'll probably be all right, though."

Morgan said, "Thank you." He waited patiently for the doctors to finish with him so that he could tell the police about Patsy Galuk and Howard Mollison. And then maybe he could begin to tell Lou Morgan about himself.

THE END

www.ingramcontent.com/pod-product-compliance
Lightning Source LLC
LaVergne TN
LVHW021803060526
838201LV00058B/3218